To Julie — the love of my life.

Thank you for always supporting me
and being a part of my adventures.

VECTOR

TRADECRAFT: PHASE ZERO

Michael Shusko

The views expressed in this work are those of the author and do not necessarily reflect the official policy or position of the Department of the Navy, Department of Defense, nor the US Government. This is a work of fiction. Any resemblance to persons living or dead is purely coincidental.

ISBN-13: 978-1-53726-175-1
ISBN-10: 1-53726-175-4

Copyediting by Debra Manette
Proofreading by James Fraleigh
Interior book design and typesetting by John Reinhardt Book Design
Cover design by Ty Nowicki

1

HOW COULD *I have been so stupid?* Jawad Khattib thought as he stumbled through the empty parking lot toward the emergency room entrance. It was not the first mistake he had made recently, he realized as he wiped the sweat off his brow. Just a few short days ago his face was plump and full of color. Yet the reflection in the bathroom mirror before he left his apartment was unrecognizable. That chilling image jolted him into fleeing his small Beacon Hill apartment in the middle of the cool Boston night. That, and the blood that had just appeared in his vomit like a death knell. As bad as he felt, he had known it would be faster to walk the few blocks rather than wait for an ambulance. Perhaps the fresh air would make him feel better.

The onslaught started twenty-four hours earlier with minor pain in his abdomen. A flu had been going around his workplace, and some of his coworkers were sick. He thought nothing of it. Besides, he had always had a sensitive stomach, and the food in this country sometimes made the upset worse. He thought he would just ride it out and the symptoms would be gone in a day or so. But they had only worsened. This afternoon he began throwing up violently, and large, ugly bruises erupted across his body. A crippling, debilitating pain had spread steadily, followed by a fever that prompted him to finally seek help at this late hour.

The fever was now scorching his sensitive skin. During the slow and painful trek to his destination, he finally came to the realization that he was to blame for his malady. Was this the goal of his work? Was he the first unknowing, unwilling victim of his own creation? He wasn't sure if the shudders he was experiencing were due to the physiologic changes occurring in his frail body or the thought of what he had unleashed on the world. Either way, he knew his condition was dire.

In the distance, he saw the red sign. He knew he was close, even if he could not make out the shapes of the large white letters. Fortunately, at this hour there was little traffic, or he probably would have been killed crossing the street on his wobbly legs. A quick end was all he could ask for, he thought. That would be much better than the suffering that racked his body. A suffering, he knew, that was only the beginning, if his research was accurate.

The automatic glass doors opened as the bright lights blinded him. The noises emanating from the sterile facility only amplified the jackhammer going off in his head. This place was his only chance. A chance he knew was a long shot at best.

"Please help me," he said in a strained, weak voice as he leaned heavily on the reception counter.

The middle-age triage nurse at the Massachusetts General Hospital Emergency Room was familiar with this plea. But the man's gaunt look and hollow eyes propelled her up out of her seat and around the counter.

"Bob!" she shouted over her shoulder. "Get out here with a gurney! STAT!"

This was my work. But it wasn't supposed to be like this. Or was it?

"I'm dying" were the last words spoken by Jawad Khattib as he collapsed on the cold tile floor of the waiting room.

2

T-BONE JAMES pulled around the corner into the alley alongside the café. Lee didn't understand his partner's excessive caution, but he would, as always, defer to T-Bone's investigative experience. Covering the rear exit was smart, even if this was supposed to be a routine stop. The third of the day, as a matter of fact. But that was okay with Lee. After last month's disaster, he hoped he never had to draw his weapon again.

Leaving T-Bone in the black Mustang, Lee Jansen got out and circled around to the front of the building. The sign was generic enough: *Arabian Café*. Surely no terrorists would be hiding *there*. Even from the sidewalk he could see that the café was empty. *Odd*, he thought, glancing at his watch. Downtown Alexandria, Virginia, midmorning. The café should be hopping—the last of the breakfast crowd finishing up their meals as a busy waitstaff cleared tables quick as they could in

VECTOR | TRADECRAFT: PHASE ZERO

preparation for the lunch rush. It should look like all the other shops in the neighborhood.

Down the street, Lee heard the unmistakable sound of a vehicle gunning its engine. He looked up just in time to see an Uzi pointed at him through the passenger window of a speeding truck.

He hit the deck hard as bullets whizzed by his head, slamming into the brick wall next to the café's entrance. Lee rolled several times in a crisp military evasion and rose to his knees as he drew his Glock to return fire. But the truck had already moved into the flow of traffic. It was too dangerous to engage in a firefight on the noontime streets of Alexandria, Virginia. At least he noted the DC license plate: DF5 949.

T-Bone circled out from the alley and screeched to a halt next to Lee.

"Get in," T-Bone commanded through the open window.

"What the hell was that?" Lee replied as he squeezed his two-hundred-pound frame into the passenger seat.

T-Bone, calm as always with a big grin on his face, sped away and navigated the Mustang through the busy streets. "Well, partner, looks like we're in for an old-fashioned car chase."

Tyrone James, "T-Bone" to his friends, was a former Secret Service agent who had become a task force commander for the National Operations Center at the Department of Homeland Security. He was clearly enjoying the turn of events as he swerved the Mustang through traffic. "Looks like they didn't want you sampling their hummus this morning," he said with a raised eyebrow.

The two agents had been sent to the Arabian Café to investigate the suspicious computer activity of a Yemeni on the DHS Terrorist Watch List. Over the past several weeks, the National Cyber Security Center had picked up an increase in computer chatter between Abdullah al-Harbi from his hideout some-where in the northern Pakistan mountains and someone named bin Talal at an IP address that bounced around numerous loca-tions in the DC metro area. At the two other locations they had checked this morning, hacked wireless routers had been used to broadcast messages to Yemen. Lee had fully expected this stop to be the same. Until the bullets started flying.

Al-Harbi, a senior leader in al-Qaeda, had orchestrated the kidnapping of an American English language teacher from the Yemeni International Linguistic Center in Sana'a several months back. Gruesome video of the teacher's beheading went viral and put al-Harbi on the map as a major al-Qaeda player. The National Operations Center director wanted to find out who in the DC area had been having conversations with the terrorist leader regarding a "new weapon" al-Harbi's group was planning to use on American soil.

"Call in the plate," T-Bone instructed as he floored the car. "There's an outdoor market full of people up ahead on King Street, and we're headed right for them. We gotta stop that truck. See if the NOC can get some patrol cars to block the road before they get there and all hell breaks loose."

"Got it," Lee replied, dialing the NOC watch officer. As the car sped through the street, Lee identified himself and reported: "We're tailing a black Ford-250 pickup with tinted windows, DC plates Delta Foxtrot five niner four niner. At least three suspects are in the truck. They are armed and dangerous. Heading north on Royal. Block routes to King Street. Copy?"

"Roger, copy. Wait one," came the reply.

"Wait one? What the hell is he talking about?" snapped T-Bone. "Does he think we're out getting doughnuts or something? This will all be over in *one*. Tell that fool we need assistance *now*!"

"Negative," Lee replied to the NOC as he watched the gap between the Mustang and the pickup narrow. "I repeat, we are in a high-speed pursuit of armed suspects. Shots fired. Headed toward King Street market. Need intercept now!"

"Copied all," the agent on the other end of the line replied. "Do not engage suspects. Repeat, do not engage suspects."

"Man, hang up the damn phone. Idiots," T-Bone exclaimed. "We gotta end this before anyone gets hurt. Hold on." T-Bone stomped on the accelerator. The Mustang roared forward and smashed into the back of the F-250, causing little damage but sending a clear signal to the driver that their lead had evaporated. T-Bone looked for an opening to the left, but there was heavy oncoming traffic. To the right, a row of parked cars blocked their path.

"There's a bus stop coming up on the right. Shouldn't be any street parking in front of it. If there's no bus there, I'll shoot pass them on the right and cut them off."

"T, don't be crazy! There's no way you'll be able to pull alongside them that fast, let alone pass them. Even if you could, that truck will run over this little car."

"Maybe so, but it'll slow 'em down and give more time for the cavalry to get to King Street. Besides, have a little faith in ole Betsy here. She's got horses under the engine. Look up at the curb. Is it clear?"

Lee craned his neck to the right to see around the pickup truck. The entire curb ahead of them was clear, thanks to the bus stop and a loading zone just beyond it. He braced for impact.

"Okay, hit it."

T-Bone whipped to the right of the pickup and gunned the engine. They pulled even with and then ahead of the truck— just as space to complete the maneuver evaporated.

Lee caught a glimpse of the truck's front seat passenger as they passed. Under different circumstances, the surprised look on the man's olive-skinned, bearded face would have made him laugh.

The Mustang drew clear of the truck, and as T-Bone was about to swing left to cut them off, Lee shouted "T, look out!"

A Cadillac Escalade had pulled out into the Wolfe Street intersection ahead of them, directly in their path.

T-Bone stomped on the brakes. The pickup shot past them and T-Bone swerved back onto the road, but the right rear of the Mustang clipped the Caddie's front end.

"T, be careful, man!"

"My bad! Just a little dent. Don't worry, DHS will take care of that," joked T-Bone as he continued to close in. But his demeanor changed suddenly as he watched the rear window of the pickup truck slide to the left and the barrel of a shotgun emerge.

"Get down!" T-Bone screamed.

Lee looked up just in time to see smoke fuming from the shotgun's double barrels. Buckshot pelted the windshield. Lee was slammed against the door as his partner swerved hard right to avoid the barrage. The Mustang's front tire hit the curb at full speed and sent them airborne. The passenger side of the car hit a light post, spinning the car and flipping it onto its left side. Sparks flew as the Mustang slid down the street and came to a screeching halt against a parked Chevy Tahoe.

Dazed, Lee slowly opened his eyes. He felt blood running down and into his ear from a cut on his forehead. He turned to look down at his partner, lying crumpled in his seat. Blood covered T-Bone's mangled face.

Tyrone James had taken the brunt of the buckshot that had shattered the windshield.

Instinctively, Lee reached down to check T-Bone's carotid artery. Nothing. His worst fears were confirmed.

His partner was dead.

Anger overtook his sadness as he thought about T-Bone. Peering through the empty space where the windshield used to be, Lee noticed a crowd of people gathering. The men responsible for the death of his partner would not be among them. They had done their job.

The terrorists had disappeared.

3

BOSTON CHILDREN'S HOSPITAL was located within a few blocks of some of the most prestigious medical institutions in the world. Brigham and Women's Hospital, Dana-Farber Cancer Institute, Beth Israel Deaconess Medical Center, and Harvard Medical School were all a stone's throw away, as was Emma's office at the Harvard T.H. Chan School of Public Health.

Dr. Emma Hess, board certified in internal medicine as well as occupational and environmental medicine with fellowship training in toxicology, was in high demand at each of those prestigious institutions. It was late morning in the pediatric ICU and Emma was finishing rounding on her last patient consult. She stood at the nurses' station and reviewed the lab results on three-year-old Alisha Washington.

"Have you been able to wean down any of the vent settings?" Emma asked Paul Holder, a young pediatric intensivist, outside Alisha's room. When Alisha presented in the emergency room yesterday, she had to be intubated to help keep her blood oxygenation at a safe level.

"No. She still has a lot of fluid in her lungs and didn't put out much urine overnight. Not sure how she'll do off the vent. Unfortunately, her kidneys took a hit."

As Emma brushed her blond hair to one side, she realized how tired she was. She had been consulted on Alisha's case yesterday and had spent all afternoon and most of the evening researching the possible causes of the girl's condition. She was no closer, however, to figuring out what had poisoned the youngster. Alisha's grandmother had brought her to the emergency room with severe breathing difficulties yesterday morning. The ER staff suspected some type of poisoning, but her cluster of symptoms didn't fit most of the more common toxins that she could have come into contact with. The girl's toxicology screen was negative for everything the ER staff could think of that would cause her pulmonary system to collapse so quickly. Alisha had to be intubated right away because severe pulmonary edema compromised her breathing. After she was admitted to the ICU last night, her liver and kidneys began to fail. Fortunately, the ICU team had been able to stabilize her, but she was still in critical condition. That, coupled with her only other clinical sign—a deep red rash on her left wrist—left the doctors baffled. Hence, Dr. Holder had called Emma, Harvard's leading expert on toxicology and environmental exposures.

This sequence of events flashed through Emma's mind as she reviewed the chart. Alisha's labs were holding steady...for now. Emma took a deep breath and ran her fingers through her hair. Sitting beside the bed was an elderly black woman with one hand on a Bible, the other stroking her unconscious granddaughter's hair. The police had put Sheila Collins through the wringer the night before. Emma walked around the bed and sat beside the weary woman.

"How was your night, Mrs. Collins?"

"I told you yesterday," she said softly, taking off her glasses, "call me Sheila. Please. You're the only one around here who doesn't believe my no-good ex–son-in-law that I tried to kill this child."

Boston PD had spent the better part of the evening interrogating Sheila, then searching the apartment she shared with her granddaughter in Roxbury. Emma had noticed the accusing looks Sheila received from the police and even some of the hospital staff. Judgment had already been passed. Emma had to figure out what had happened to Alisha before any more victims showed up at the hospital. Or the morgue.

"Try not to worry. We'll get through this," Emma replied, squeezing the woman's hand. She was first and foremost a scientist, basing her conclusions on facts. But Emma had feelings, too, and she couldn't believe that a woman this worried could poison her granddaughter.

"You're an angel," Sheila said.

Emma noticed a few framed pictures on the bedside table. She picked up a portrait of Sheila with a woman in her mid-twenties holding a baby.

"That's my baby Tonya on the day Alisha was born. She died a few months ago, supposedly after a fall."

"Supposedly?" asked Emma.

"Her husband used to beat her. I know he threw her down them steps. She didn't *trip* like Lionel claims," Sheila scoffed.

"Lionel is Alisha's father?"

"Yes. I got temporary custody of Alisha because of Lionel's long arrest record. I keep trying to get the police to look into Tonya's death. I think accusing me of hurting Alisha now is his way of getting me to stop pushing the police. He's no good, Doctor. That man's just plain evil."

Emma picked up another picture. It looked like a print from a digital camera, complete with a date stamp on the corner.

Three days ago. Sheila was holding Alisha tightly, and they both looked so happy sitting on a park bench together.

"He's been in trouble with the law and mixed up with drugs way before he met my baby. Poor Tonya couldn't see it, though. She fell for his charming smile and big muscles. I tried to tell her, but she wouldn't listen. He left Tonya and poor Alisha the day she was born. Just walked right out on the two of them. Can you believe it, Doctor? How can someone leave such a beautiful angel?" Tears filled her eyes as she looked down at Alisha, lying helpless in the ICU bed.

"What did the police tell you, Sheila?" Emma asked. Sergeant Ricucci from Boston PD had said they were going to search Sheila's apartment. Although he had told Emma last evening that Sheila wasn't necessarily a suspect, they had to conduct a thorough investigation. If poisoning was involved, however, and if the evidence did not definitively point to an unintentional overdose, Sheila Collins would have a difficult time legally keeping custody of her granddaughter.

"They said Lionel said I tried to poison Alisha. The big sergeant that you saw questioning me last night, he told me Lionel lodged a complaint against me, telling them I would rather kill Alisha than give her to him. Can you believe it? But I know what he wants her for. With a baby living under his roof, he'll be eligible for more public assistance. All that man wants is more money. You think he'll spend any of it on Alisha?" she asked.

While Sheila was talking, Emma became engrossed in the picture of Sheila with Alisha. "Is this date correct? Did you just take this picture?"

"Yes. I just took it on Sunday. We were flying kites in the park. Look at my baby, Doctor. Look how healthy and strong she was."

"What's this bracelet she's wearing?" Emma asked, pointing at Alisha's left wrist.

"Why, that's a good luck charm. My niece sent it to Alisha for her birthday a few weeks ago. In Haiti, where my niece lives, it's supposed to ward off evil. Although it didn't seem to keep Lionel away," she said pointedly. "I don't believe in all that voodoo stuff, but Alisha was fretting about eczema on her hand and wrist. I thought the bracelet would cover it so she didn't have to look at her rash."

"She has eczema on her left wrist? Right where this bracelet is in this picture?"

"Yes. Why?"

Emma's questioning had moved beyond idle chitchat. "Are these beads bright red, with a black spot?"

"Why, yes. Alisha loves it. She says it reminds her of ladybugs."

Emma jerked back in her chair, and the metal legs squealed against the floor. "Sheila, I need this bracelet. Where is it?"

"Home. They took her bracelet off in the ER last night and gave it back to me along with her clothes. I sent them home with my sister when she went to feed my cat last night. Why, Doctor? Does it mean something?"

"It might. Did Alisha ever chew on it or swallow any of the beads?"

The grandmother started to frown. "She did like to chew on the bracelet. I'd fuss at her all day. But she never swallowed any of them, so I thought it was all right."

That confirmed Emma's hunch. "Sheila, I think Alisha has abrin intoxication."

"What's that?"

"Jequirity beans contains abrin, a strong toxin. They're very dangerous, but many cultures, including some in the Caribbean, make jewelry from the beans because of their bright colors." Emma knew from her training in toxicology that jewelers got sick just by threading a needle through the beans and then accidentally sticking themselves. If Alisha had been chewing on them, she might have broken the hard shell and ingested or inhaled some abrin That could cause the pulmonary edema that she was experiencing. And if the beads were damaged by her biting on them, and the bracelet came in contact with her skin, especially skin that was cracked from eczema, the abrin could be easily absorbed. "Listen, I'll be right back."

Emma left the room to track down the pediatric intensivist.

"What is it, Emma?"

"Paul, look at this," she said, handing him the photo. "It's *Abrus precatorius.*" She saw the blank look on his face and realized that outside of toxicologists, few people in the American medical community would know about the hazards of the jequirity plant. She herself would never have made the connection without seeing the picture. "Jequirity beans. Run a urine test on her. Tell the pathologist you're looking for L-abrine. It's a biomarker for abrin."

"Will the pathologist even know what that is?"

"In most hospitals, probably not. But Boston Children's is not like most hospitals. He'll know or know where to look it up. Hurry."

The pediatric intensivist left to order the nurse to get the urine sample from Alisha.

"Will my baby be all right?" Sheila asked, standing in the hall and looking hopeful.

"I think so, Sheila. They gave her activated charcoal in the ER. That takes care of most ingestions, but we're more worried about inhalation and maybe some skin exposure here. She should stabilize on the ventilator. We'll know more in a few days. In the meantime, I'll let Sergeant Ricucci know we believe we've found the source of the *accidental* poisoning."

Emma headed off to the emergency room to see if Ricucci was still in the hospital. Boston PD assigned an officer to provide security, liaison, and investigative duties for any potentially criminal cases that presented. Hopefully, Ricucci was still on duty.

She allowed herself a small pat on the back. Alisha would recover with aggressive therapy in the ICU. Abrin intoxication could be lethal, but chances of survival increased dramatically with prompt, supportive care in a specialty hospital. And after Emma spoke with the sergeant, Sheila Collins should no longer be a suspect.

As she turned the corner near the doctors' work station, her pager went off. She looked at the number, sat down in one of the station chairs, and called her boss from her cell.

"Good morning, Doctor," Rick Caruthers answered. Caruthers was the director of occupational and environmental health at Harvard and Emma's immediate supervisor. He was responsible for assigning cases of suspected environmental or occupational hazard exposures like Alisha's to the doctors in the department. Once assigned, the physician would review the case, determine the environmental exposure, and advise any treatment or corrective action if required.

"Rick, I think I found it," Emma replied. "Alisha's intoxication. It was from a bracelet made from jequirity beans. The test results confirming it should be back in a matter of hours."

"Really?" he said. Although Caruthers was not a physician, he had a Ph.D. and was an accomplished researcher in environmental health. "Not too common in these parts. How's she doing?"

"Stable, but not out of the woods yet. At least we can work with the ICU team to predict her clinical course now that we know the source of her intoxication. And clear her grandmother of any wrongdoing."

"Great work, Emma." The tenor of his voice changed, as though he were shifting subjects. "I saw your car in the parking garage here, but you weren't in your office. I knew you had to be making rounds. Tell me, do you ever sleep?"

"I know, Rick. Now that we've diagnosed what happened to Alisha, I'll take some time off, I promise." Caruthers was always trying to get Emma to take better care of herself. She worked long hours because she had patients to care for, a full teaching load at both Harvard Medical School and the Harvard T.H. Chan School of Public Health, plus a number of ongoing research projects. She actually thrived on her hectic schedule, even though it left her little time for a social life. Apparently, even professional women in their mid-thirties needed to have a social life. Or so Caruthers had told her on more than one occasion.

"Actually, this was one time I wasn't going to tell you to slow down. I've got another case for you and it's a high priority." His voice thickened a bit, as though he were nervous. "I just got a call from the Feds. They want us to look into the death of a researcher at Mass. General last night. Sounds interesting."

The federal government hardly ever asked them to look into someone's death. She began jotting down some quick notes as he relayed the facts about the death of a molecular biologist named Jawad Khattib.

"The ICU team at the General thinks it was radiation poisoning leading to sepsis," her boss explained.

"Sure, that could do it. High-dose radiation exposure severely damages the immune system. With nothing to fight it off, gut bacteria leaks into the bloodstream and causes sepsis," Emma said.

"Well, get this, Homeland Security wants our input. They think he was working on a dirty bomb," explained Caruthers. "I guess they're worried because he was an Arab researcher. Sounds far-fetched to me, but I don't have all the intelligence reports they do."

That bit of information further captivated her attention. After the Boston Marathon bombing, officials had been more sensitive to any incident even remotely linked to terrorism. Although she didn't like the racial profiling part, a bomb mixed with radioactive material would threaten the entire Boston metropolitan area. But, first things first, she cautioned herself.

"I wonder if Khattib used X-rays or radiation therapy in his research," she said.

"Don't know. That's for you to find out," Caruthers answered. "And do it quick. The government's sending one of their folks up from DC to help you out. He's some sort of radiation weapons expert or something. Should be here tomorrow."

"Tomorrow? I have a full clinic and lecture schedule today and tomorrow, and I'm still helping the ICU team here with Alisha's care. I won't have much for him then," Emma replied.

"Just do what you can. I'm sure the ICU team is more than capable of taking care of Alisha. I think the Feds are being paranoid, anyway. Just get them off my back, okay? I'll get someone to cover some of your classes," Caruthers told her before hanging up.

Emma sat back and contemplated her new case. There were a number of ways a researcher could be exposed to enough radiation to cause harm, if that was even what caused Khattib's death. Maybe he *was* working on a radioactive device. She was no expert on terrorism and was curious whether working on a homemade radioactive device would cause enough cellular damage to lead to death.

She groaned at the prospect of working with a bomb-sniffing federal agent. Would he even understand the first thing about toxicology? Was this just a witch hunt? The U.S. government might have its suspicions about Khattib, but he was, even in death, now her patient. She would be objective and endeavor to pursue the truth wherever it led—and she'd be damned if any federal agent was going to get in her way.

4

THE ARCHITECT paced the Oriental rug. The ancient kings of Persepolis and their rows of solemn soldiers seemed to watch as he walked over their hundred-year-old silk-woven faces. The man was tall and lanky with a drawn face and ink-black eyes. Standing silently in the background was a bespectacled, skinny young man with a shiny mop of disheveled black hair.

The old man stopped in front of a large window to contemplate the news he had received. He could not believe that the project—indeed, the *mission* of the Order—was now at risk because of a researcher's carelessness. Even the soothing view of his beloved mountains through the glass could not soften the blow. It was time for damage control.

"How could this have happened? Did we not have safeguards in place?"

He could see his young assistant steeling himself against this assault. "Sir, Khattib was hand-picked. He was a brilliant scientist and a highly skilled researcher. What happened to him could have happened to anyone."

"Apparently not skilled enough," snapped the old man. "And if my memory serves me, it was you who brought Khattib to us. You said he would provide us with the breakthrough we needed for this most important work."

The assistant hung his head. They both knew it was true. He had scoured the graduate and postdoctoral programs at the most prestigious universities in the Northeast to find the right researcher. Plus, Khattib was an Arab. That was an added bonus.

"It is only a setback. His research is intact, and he had progressed further than expected. Even Khattib could not have known how close he had come to achieving our goals."

"That does not help us if the project is discovered prematurely because of his mistake," the Architect chided. "I'm told the hospital alerted the authorities about his death. There will be an investigation. What then?"

"They will find nothing," the assistant replied firmly. "His blood will be clean. They will find no trace of the weapon."

"And what about the circumstances? I am told the manner of Khattib's death has already raised questions," countered the Architect.

The assistant had no answer. Khattib had died a grisly death. To make matters worse, he had sought out help at one of the best hospitals in the country, if not the world. Yes, there would surely be an investigation.

"We must ensure this does not get out of hand," the Architect continued. "Shut down this arm of the project and focus all of our efforts in our lab here, where we can better control the research." By "shut down" he meant silence any leaks. "Pull in all samples from the different labs. Then proceed with refining the delivery system here, in house. Work around the clock. The vector still needs to be perfected, but apparently the weapon itself works well. Jawad Khattib can attest to that from the afterlife. I have taken preliminary steps to keep the authorities off our trail."

"How?"

"I have been assured the investigation will go nowhere. For added security, however, I have asked for one of our own to ensure no one gets too close to us. He is skilled at cleaning up messes like this one in Boston and will take care of anyone investigating this matter. The time is not yet right for the world to know our work. But it will be soon."

"Of course," said the assistant, fidgeting nervously.

The Architect could tell the young man was anxious to leave the office. He turned back to the picture window, and the assistant took that as his cue to leave. But before he made it to the safety of the door across the darkened room, his mentor spoke again.

"This project is bigger than you and me. It is the last hope for the survival of our people and our way of life. Nothing can get in the way of its success. Do you understand what I am saying? *Nothing and no one.*"

Those chilling words were enough to drive the warning home. The Order would not accept any more mistakes. Not from anyone.

5

HELLO, DR. HESS. Looks like you're busy as usual," the security guard said.

Emma had rushed into the library between classes and was fumbling for her Harvard ID. The guard knew her well and waved her through. Like many Harvard physicians who needed to stay up to date with the most current medical research, Dr. Hess was a frequent visitor to the Countway Library of Medicine. The largest academic medical library in the world, it included rare artifacts and historic medical documents as well as the most recent literature on medical advances.

"Thanks, Roy," Emma replied, smiling at the kindly old man. She entered the elevator and pressed the button to the third floor. As she walked through the Warren Anatomical Museum on the top floor, Emma passed the fragmented skull of Phineas Gage and his infamous railroad tamping iron, along with other odd medical artifacts.

Emma found her favorite table overlooking the lower levels, pulled out her laptop, and went to work. After a quick search, she identified the articles she needed and scribbled down the volume numbers. It only took ten minutes to locate the journals. Years of walking these sacred stacks made Emma's search routine.

As she walked down the long corridor back to her table, she saw a large, bald man standing behind her chair, peering down at her computer. Without looking up at her, as if he felt her presence, he turned and walked away. Emma only caught a glimpse of the man's face. He was dressed in black slacks and a sports coat. But his upright carriage, his clipped way of walking, made her cringe. She paused until the man disappeared around the corner.

Once he had, Emma took hold of herself. She was letting her imagination get the best of her. Everything at the table appeared to be exactly as she left it.

She sat down and looked around to ensure no one was watching her. Once satisfied she was being overly cautious, she continued her work, poring through the journal articles. The anxiety left her as she drifted away into a world of science, the world in which she felt most at ease.

Emma grew up surrounded by medicine in a small, quiet town on Boston's South Shore. Her father was a family physician and her mother the only pharmacist. Like most teenagers, Emma longed for life in the big city and left for New York after high school to study at Columbia University. As she matured into womanhood, she found herself longing for her family and Boston roots. After graduating top of her class from Harvard Medical School, she stayed to complete her residency in internal medicine.

It turned out that seeing a new patient every fifteen minutes in her internal medicine clinic left her unfulfilled. Wanting to do more, Emma returned to Harvard for a master's in public health and a second residency in occupational and environmental medicine. Specializing in toxicology, she was able to find her niche at the Harvard T.H. Chan School of Public Health, rooting out dangerous toxins and environmental hazards in the greater Boston area.

After solving a few high-profile cases, Emma became a minor celebrity. She had made the headlines in New England newspapers a few years back after uncovering chemical pollutants in a reservoir serving rural Massachusetts communities. Emma was able to associate the contaminated drinking water with liver failure in three local children and force the local government to take action.

She was not used to all the attention she received, both from the medical community and from eligible bachelors after her face was plastered in the newspapers. Emma used her newfound fame to push for better environmental regulations, earning her even higher praise.

Elevated to full professor at her alma mater, she began instructing student doctors in the fine art of toxicology while she continued investigating complicated occupational and environmental exposure cases. Although she had evaluated many cases, this was her first foray into the murky world of terrorism and weapons of mass destruction.

But she welcomed the challenge. After all, hadn't she dedicated her life to the pursuit of public health? It wasn't that she didn't want to have a "normal" life. A husband. Maybe a couple of kids. She had even been engaged a few years back. Her fiancé, however, couldn't understand her passion for her craft and dedication to her patients. It seemed the time and energy Emma devoted to her cases was more than he could accept, and the wedding was called off.

She closed a third journal, disappointed that there wasn't more research on dirty bombs. The last journal she'd collected, however, held some promise. She thumbed through the thick journal and found the article written by a noted radiologist at the Walter Reed National Military Medical Center in Bethesda. The abstract described the presentation of radiation sickness after exposure to a dirty bomb. She knew that while ten grays of absorbed radiation was universally fatal, even doses as low as half a gray could cause symptoms. What she did not have a firm grasp of, however, was how radiation could be used in weapons.

If Khattib had been involved in some kind of radiologic weapon development, she needed to know how much exposure he could have gotten while working on the device. Certainly the government would have more questions as to how Khattib developed radiation sickness, but Emma's primary concern at the moment was for the healthcare workers who may have been exposed to radiation while treating him, not to mention anyone in the neighborhood of his lab.

Emma, continuing to read, discovered how various unstable radioactive isotopes could be combined with conventional explosives to make radiological dispersion devices, or "dirty bombs," as they were widely known. Although usually not very lethal, dirty bombs had become sought-after weapons by terrorist groups because their explosion causes widespread panic and exhausts medical resources due to the need to treat and decontaminate a staggering amount of victims. There were countless potential sources of unstable isotopes to make these weapons in mines and storage depots worldwide, since they were commonly used in many professions, such as medicine and geology.

Fortunately, very few terror attacks using dirty bombs had been carried out, and most of the information in the article was speculative. She closed the journal and leaned back in her chair. She had no idea how much radiation a dirty bomb could release. It could be almost any amount. But if Khattib had fallen ill and died from radiologic exposure, others were definitely at risk.

Worse still, Emma realized that if the source of the radiation was still out there, emitting radioactive particles and energy, the greater Boston metropolitan area was also at risk. More radiation sickness patients, and more deaths, loomed unless the source was found.

She glanced at her watch. It was 12:15 p.m. and she still had a full clinic schedule this afternoon. It was going to be another long day. On her way out, she noticed the guard reading the *Boston Globe*.

"Roy, can I see that paper for a minute?"

"Sure thing," he answered, handing her the paper. "Patriots lost, though."

Emma didn't hear the comment as she focused on the headlines. She found nothing about Khattib and his mysterious death at Mass. General.

Not completely surprising, she thought as she handed the paper back to the guard. The Department of Homeland Security must have gone to great pains to keep the story quiet in order to avoid a panic, which suggested that DHS was genuinely concerned that Khattib was a terrorist. One terrorist attack was too much for any city to bear, and Boston had already been hit hard.

She would have a lot of questions for the federal investigator tomorrow. Emma was confident in her abilities as a physician and scientist but was not prepared for the dangerous world of terrorism. And maybe Khattib wasn't working alone.

"Roy, did you see a large, bald man come in here? Black slacks and jacket?"

"No, ma'am. No one like that came through here this morning. Is something wrong?"

That was odd. Everyone entering the library had to pass the guard and swipe their Harvard ID. Who was the man she saw at her table, and why did she get that strange feeling when she saw him? Perhaps she was just jumpy thinking about terrorists running around Boston planting dirty bombs.

"Everything's fine, Roy. Thanks."

Emma exited the library and walked through the courtyard to the adjacent building where her office was located. Reaching the entrance to her building, she felt the strange sensation that she was being watched. She turned around and there the man was again, standing across the courtyard near the library. His piercing eyes bored into her. She turned and hurried into the Harvard T.H. Chan School of Public Health. After showing her ID to the guard inside, she looked out the window toward the library. The man was gone.

6

HELL, NO!" Lee shouted at his boss. "I'm staying here and finding out who did this."

Lee was sitting in the back of the ambulance as he spoke with DHS Director of Counterintelligence Jay Kowalski, who stood outside. The paramedics were concerned about a head injury, and Lee had acquiesced to an examination only after Kowalski intervened.

"I understand, Lee. And I promise you, we'll find out who was responsible for Tyrone's death. But I need you to go up to Boston on this assignment. They don't have anyone with the military EOD experience you have. If this researcher was making a dirty bomb like the CIA thinks, the folks up in Boston will need your help finding it."

"Why do they think this guy was a terrorist, anyway?" Lee asked. The last thing he wanted to do was spend a week in Boston chasing his tail while T-Bone's killers were on the loose.

"Don't know, but the brass wants it checked out. That's why I need you to go up there and see if there's a terrorist connection. Commonwealth Fusion Center's running down leads on sleeper cells in the area, but they're already short staffed."

Lee also knew what Kowalski wasn't telling him. The director had seen the murderous look on Lee's face before, and he was sending Lee out of DC before there was more bloodshed.

"Listen, I'm fine," he protested. "I know they sent you down here because they think I'm a loose cannon and I'm going to go on a shooting spree. I'm not, okay? All that's over."

Seeing Kowalski's doubt, Lee leaned back against the inside of the ambulance and closed his eyes. He wasn't sure if even he believed his own words.

Kowalski put his hand on the agent's shoulder. "Listen, Lee. You've been through a lot over the past year. First Gina. Then the boy. Now T-Bone. I've known you a long time. Trust me, you need this. Besides, this is coming from higher up. They've already decided you're the man for the job."

Lee shook his head. Bureaucrats. They sit in their offices and move people around like chess pieces. They don't know the street. They don't know how to find T-Bone's killer.

A young man walked up to Kowalski. "Sir, we're taking the two workers in the café in for questioning."

"Good. You handle it, Erik," Kowalski told the man, much to his surprise. "Find out who did this."

"Don't you think you need someone with a little more experience on this case?" Lee sat up, protesting. "No offense, kid, but you're just a boot."

Erik Kaiser was fresh out of college. A master of linguistics, he had been recruited while he was still at Georgetown. Although new to DHS, he had jumped into his job in Counterintelligence Programs and had released a number of insightful reports. This was his first real field case, though.

"Give him a chance, Lee," Kowalski interjected before Kaiser could defend himself. "He was no greener than you were when you first reported to my unit in Baghdad. Besides, I'll be working closely with him on this one. Don't worry, we'll get to the bottom of it."

A paramedic stepped past Kowalski. "I've got to do a neuro exam on him now," he said, closing the door as he stepped into the ambulance. Lee's blood pressure was rising with each outburst, and he was already uncooperative.

"Jansen's a good man," Kowalski told Kaiser as they walked away. "I recruited him into the DHS a few years after he got his degree. We first met in Baghdad in the early part of the war. I was a company commander and he was with an EOD team assigned to me for support. He's one brave SOB and is a whiz at weapons, but he's a bit of a hothead. After he got back to the States, he got married. It was good for Lee. His wife had a calming effect on him. But she came down with cancer and passed the summer before last. Ever since he's had a sort of death wish. You heard what happened when Lee was on the gangbanger's case not long ago. After that mess, Agent James took him under his wing. Jansen did somewhat better after that. I'm worried that he'd go off the reservation if he stayed around here now that James is gone."

"Yes, sir. I understand," Kaiser replied. Although this was his first case, he had been part of the backup team in Lincoln Heights that had helped clean up after Lee took down a house full of gang members virtually single-handed. Including shooting and killing an unarmed teenager. "I appreciate you trusting me with this investigation. I won't let you down."

"I know," Kowalski replied. "Let me know what you find out after questioning those two suspects. I'd be interested in what they have to say."

"What about Jansen? Should I keep him in the loop?"

"No, he's got enough on his mind. Report directly to me and let me know if you need anything," Kowalski replied as he walked away.

"Will do, sir." Kaiser stood on King Street, surveying what was once Agent James's car. Kaiser had only been on this job for a few months, and already he was assigned a major case involving international terrorism and a dead federal agent. He had the unsettling feeling that he would need all the help he could get.

"Hey, Kaiser," Lee called from the back of the ambulance, the door now open.

The young agent turned around and approached Lee. "How are you feeling?" he asked.

"I'm fine. Listen, keep me up to date on what's happening with this investigation, you hear me?"

Kaiser thought about what Kowalski had told him. "Jansen, I got it. I can handle this."

"Okay, maybe you can. I shouldn't have jumped to conclusions about your experience." Lee paused to let that sink in. "But T-Bone was my partner. And a friend. He was there for me when I needed him. He saved my career. Hell, he probably saved my life."

"I know. I'll find out who's responsible," Kaiser said.

"Yeah, well, that may be tougher than you think. They knew we were coming. How else were they ready for us, waiting in their truck with weapons drawn? I was a sitting duck out there."

Kaiser reflected on Lee's words. "You're not suggesting..."

"I'm not suggesting anything. All I know is T-Bone's dead and someone tipped those bastards off that we were coming. Obviously it wasn't me, so that makes me your only friend right now. I may have to go to Boston tonight, but I can still help you. Maybe if we put our heads together, we can find out who did this."

Kaiser wasn't sure if disobeying an order from his director so early in his career was wise. But he also didn't want to end up dead like Agent James.

"Okay, but you have to tread lightly, Jansen. You know your reputation. It'll only make keeping you in the loop more difficult if you ruffle feathers in Boston. If we're going to do this, let's keep it between us and let me lead the investigation down here. I'll call you and let you know what I find out, and we can talk through some ideas. Okay?"

"Agreed," Lee said. "And Kaiser—watch your back. Someone wanted a bloody gunfight out here today. That's why they sent me. They think I'm trigger happy after Lincoln Heights. We need to find out who and why before another agent gets set up."

7

R ICINUS COMMUNIS, otherwise known as the cas-
tor-oil-plant, has many beneficial uses throughout
the world," Emma said to the packed lecture hall. She
had decided to change the subject of the talk from
lead exposure to ricin because of Alisha's case. It was her morning lecture, and she was anxious to finish so she could get over
to Massachusetts General to meet with the physician who took
care of Jawad Khattib.

"Its oil has been burned in lamps for millennia to produce
light, and the plant itself is used to decorate homes. Various
parts of the plant were used in ancient rituals, in jewelry, and
even in cosmetics to prevent dry skin. In the modern era, castor
oil is well known for its medicinal purposes, from its current
use as a laxative or as an additive to antifungals and anti-inflammatories to new research into its cancer-fighting properties,"
she continued, trying to hold her audience's attention. "Some

researchers in the petroleum industry are even looking at castor oil to produce biodiesel."

"But," she emphasized, using her pointer to highlight the castor seeds pictured on the slide on the large screen behind her, "make no mistake about it. What you see before you is also one of the most lethal toxins known to man. The LD50 for ricin, a protein derived from the castor seed, is as little as 22 micrograms per kilogram," she said, emphasizing how small the lethal dose of ricin was. "That's about the size of just one grain of salt."

She paused to let this fact sink in and to gauge the students' reactions. "It is common knowledge in the medical community, even among most new students like yourselves, that ricin is a dangerous toxin. However, the sheer magnitude of its lethality is a sobering reality that we must not forget.

"Back in 1978, a Bulgarian dissident by the name of Georgi Markov was murdered in London," she continued as the picture of a middle-age man with salt-and-pepper hair flashed on the screen. "Traces of ricin were found in his body. It was later determined that he had been injected with a tiny pellet contaminated with ricin. Do you know how? An umbrella was modified to shoot the toxin into Markov's leg. He was injected on a street corner by a KGB assassin and was dead a few days later."

All eyes were on Emma now. Any vestige of boredom had been wiped from the faces of the two hundred medical students as they processed the implications of her story. A few were intrigued to learn how medicine could be used as a weapon; some abhorred the use; and all feared it.

"So, learn ricin well, students. Any questions?"

One student in the front row raised a hand. "That was an isolated case, Dr. Hess. I mean, ricin is not something that will show up frequently in the ER. We can't possibly learn every rare exposure and pathogen and be expected to put weapons of mass destruction at the top of the differential diagnosis every time a patient presents with bizarre symptoms."

Emma removed her reading glasses and put both hands on the podium. This was going to be her most important lesson to these young doctors, one she had learned by solving difficult cases that others could not. It was a lesson not taught in books. "Actually, that *is* the expectation," she answered, trying to strike a chord, "if you want to save your patient's life. Let me ask you something. What happens when you mix bleach with vinegar or another home product like a drain or toilet bowl cleaner?"

The student shrugged his shoulders. "A mess, probably," he said to some chuckles from his fellow students.

Emma nodded. This student was going to have a tough year ahead of him. "Actually, something a bit more ominous. Bleach and vinegar are everyday household items people use to clean their kitchens and bathrooms. In fact, some people even mix the two. But they'll only do that one time. You see, bleach is sodium hypochlorite. Mixing it with any acid can cause the release of chlorine gas, which, as you know, is toxic. As a matter of fact, the more potent the acid, the more poisonous the gas released. It will choke, burn, and kill in a matter of seconds if the mixture of acid and chlorine is strong enough. So, you see, these dangers are not limited to some far-off battlefield or terrorist arsenal. These hazardous compounds exist in every home, office, and lab across the U.S. of A. Mark my words, you *will* see it again. Even if it's just on my test at the end of the course," she said with a smile. "That's about all I have on toxicology today. We'll pick up again next week. Thank you as always for your attention."

The young doctors-to-be erupted in a flurry of activity as they put away their tablets and laptops, grabbed their backpacks, and chatted with friends. Emma darted down the aisle and out of the lecture hall before she could be stopped for questions. Today she had no time, though answering postlecture questions from eager students was usually one of her favorite parts of teaching.

She made her way onto the grassy quad surrounded by buildings of arguably most prestigious medical school in the country.

"Dr. Hess?" called a voice behind her.

Emma turned her head slightly and replied over her shoulder, "I'm sorry, I'm in a hurry. Can you come by my office during my office hours?"

"Dr. Hess, I'm Agent Lee Jansen from Counterterrorism at the Department of Homeland Security," he announced. "We need to talk."

Emma turned to face him. "Excuse me?"

Lee held up his DHS ID and badge for her to see. "I was sent up here to look into the death of Jawad Khattib."

The man in front of her was handsome and rugged, despite his bandaged forehead. He was a big man with strong cheekbones, a chiseled chin, and tousled brown hair. He was definitely younger than she expected when Rick Caruthers told her someone from DHS would be coming. She had pictured more of an analyst type, with a conservative, government-issued charcoal gray suit, a plain white shirt, and heavy prescription eyeglasses. The agent standing before her was almost a foot taller than her five foot six. For a moment his deep blue eyes mesmerized her, and she found herself stumbling for words.

"Yes, yes," she said, shaking it off. "I'm sorry. Yes, I *was* expecting someone from the DHS."

Emma reached for her cell phone, to cover her embarrassment. She gave it a cursory glance and put the phone back into her bag as she said, "So you think Khattib was involved with a terrorist group?"

Lee looked around, obviously feeling uncomfortable talking about a potentially sensitive case in the middle of a college campus. "Is there somewhere we can talk?"

"Well, actually, I'm on my way to Mass. General now to get more information on Khattib's hospital admission."

"Great, how about I join you? I called Boston PD and had them seal off Khattib's apartment and lab. I was going to go there first, but any information I can get about the cause of death would be very helpful."

Emma didn't generally like outside interference in her investigatory work, but she knew from the tone of his voice that he wasn't really asking. Agent Jansen was coming with her whether she liked it or not.

"Sure," she agreed. "I'll meet you in the ER waiting room in fifteen minutes."

He held up his large hands and answered with a smile, "Actually, I don't know my way around Boston all that well. Could I just ride with you?"

"Come on," she agreed, though she was not too happy about having a passenger.

The two walked down Longwood Avenue toward the parking garage. The leaves on the small trees around Tugo Circle had already begun to change color, and the streets were filled with students and medical professionals from the nearby hospitals and colleges. The pair turned into the parking garage just as an autumn breeze swirled fallen leaves at their feet.

"I actually don't have much information other than the preliminary autopsy report conducted yesterday," Emma said. "Because your office raised concerns about the possibility of terrorism, the mayor had the medical examiner perform a rush autopsy late yesterday afternoon after the body was transferred to the morgue. As you can imagine, the ME wasn't very happy about it, and it wasn't easy getting a preliminary report from him. I'm going to the General to speak with the doctors who took care of Mr. Khattib before he died to see if I can get any more details."

"Who's the general?"

Emma smiled. "It's not a who, it's a what. Massachusetts General Hospital. MGH. The General. All the same thing."

"Oh. I guess it is a good thing I'm riding with you, then," Lee admitted as they reached her red Camry.

Emma smiled, and she felt his eyes on her as she fastened her seat belt, then checked her mirrors before backing out.

"So, what did the autopsy say?" Lee asked as Emma gunned the car out into traffic.

"Well, the official cause of death was sepsis," she explained. "The intense systemic inflammatory response, usually caused by an organism, was complicated by a weakened immune system."

"Radiation would cause his immune system to be weakened," Lee replied.

"Yes, my boss told me that you were an expert on weapons of mass destruction," Emma said. She whipped the car around the corner of Longwood Avenue, and pedestrians scurried out of the way. "Radiation could be one explanation. That's what you government boys think, anyway."

"You don't think so?"

"Maybe," she allowed. "I just don't have enough data to form an objective opinion. Based on the lab results and physician notes I pulled up from his hospital admission and autopsy, radiation exposure is certainly a possibility. But there could be many other causes as well. There's no way to know for sure until I have more information."

Emma pressed down hard on the accelerator to speed through a traffic signal that had just turned yellow.

"So tell me, Agent Jansen, why do *you* think Khattib was a terrorist?" she asked. "At least, that's what your office seems to believe, according to the person who contacted my boss yesterday."

"Call me Lee," he said. "I don't really know if Khattib was a terrorist or not. He died suspiciously, possibly from radiation poisoning. He was a biomedical researcher and, yes, he was an Arab. I know that sounds like racial profiling, but we have a responsibility to the American people to check these things out. You have to admit, the average person doesn't get exposed to enough radiation to kill them."

"True, but Khattib was not an average person. He was a biomedical researcher. And I pulled up his medical history. His last radiation health physical was just a few months ago—it was clean."

"So he did work with radiation—otherwise he wouldn't have been on a medical surveillance program for radiation exposure," Lee replied.

"It wouldn't be uncommon for a biomedical researcher to have been exposed to medical radiation in some capacity, depending on the projects he was working on. If Khattib used radiotherapy in the research of cancer treatment, radiographic imaging, or interventional radiology, he could very well have been exposed to large amounts of radiation. In fact, most cases of radiation sickness today are from overexposure to medical diagnostics and treatments."

"Do you have any details on his research?" asked Lee.

"No, not yet. Apparently, he worked for a commercial lab, not a university."

"I know," Lee answered. "His file said he worked for a lab called Cambridge Institute for Genetic Research."

"So you have a *file* on him," she asked. "What else does it say?"

"Actually, we don't know much about Khattib, which is why I'm here."

Emma was beginning to see that Lee was a straight shooter, and she appreciated that.

"Believe me, if there was any hard evidence that he was a terrorist, Boston would be crawling with an army of DHS and FBI agents. Considering the circumstances surrounding his death and the Marathon bombing several years ago, you can see why the government has some concerns." Lee drummed his fingers on the dashboard. "My boss wants me to check things out and let him know if DHS needs to send in the cavalry. But it'll probably turn out to be a false alarm."

"Fair enough," allowed Emma. "Hopefully, we can get to the bottom of what killed him. Just know that there are a plethora of other possibilities for his death. It isn't always as easy as looking at a medical file and spitting out an answer."

"Got it. What about the body?"

"It's at the morgue. An autopsy was conducted by the chief medical examiner here in Boston. A scan of the body revealed no radiation on his skin, even though the physical process that killed him closely resembled radiation poisoning, per the coroner." Emma puzzled over that as she drove. "It *is* odd that the Geiger counter didn't pick anything up. Chronic, low-level radiation exposure could have cumulative adverse effects on the body and not be picked up by detectors, but what happened to Khattib was quick and intense. This wasn't a slow death."

"True, but he could have ingested or inhaled radioactive particles," Lee argued. "External detection devices have a more difficult time picking up those signals."

"Agreed," she conceded cautiously, impressed by the DHS agent's knowledge of the pathophysiology of radiation exposure. "All I'm saying is this doesn't fit the classic picture of radiation poisoning. We have to consider other possible causes as well."

"Such as?"

"Well, infection for one," she informed him. "Cultures and all the tissue studies are still pending. We won't have all of the results for a few days."

Lee's nod confirmed to Emma that this was familiar territory for him. "Okay, so who are we going to see in the meantime?"

"Dr. Manny Ortiz. He was the resident in the emergency room who took care of Khattib. I spoke to Ortiz's boss after I got off the phone with the coroner, and he said Ortiz had some concerns about the case as well," she said. "He didn't give me any details on the phone, though. He said that Khattib was already close to death when he presented to the ER. He stumbled in late the night before last and coded in the waiting room. It took the resuscitation team fifteen minutes to get a heartbeat. However, Khattib never regained consciousness. The exam in the ER revealed extensive bruising all over his body."

"Like he was beaten up or injured in an accident?"

"No. There was no trauma to the skin. He was bleeding from the inside," Emma replied, glancing over at Lee. "Most of his major organs were leaking out. Liver, spleen, kidneys. All had virtually shut down. That's why he didn't regain consciousness. He stroked out in his brain from all of his blood oozing out."

"Radiation poisoning could certainly cause that," Lee said, recalling pictures of Chernobyl he had studied to understand the effects of intense radiation on the human body. Lee grabbed onto the armrest while Emma sharply veered onto Storrow Drive.

Emma hardly noticed. She was starting to enjoy talking out the case with this knowledgeable DHS officer. "You're right, which is why the ICU team listed radiation sickness on their differential. When someone presents to the hospital as sick as Khattib was, you put everything plus the kitchen sink on the list of differential diagnoses. But I'm not convinced yet."

"Why? You don't think radiation was the cause of death?"

"It could be, but as I said, we have to think about other variables. Exposure to a large external dose of radiation would have left burns, but there weren't any physical signs of radiation burns or, as I said, any damage to his skin. Chronic low-level exposure or even internal exposure is also possible, so I'm not ruling out your dirty bomb theory.

"But I'm not satisfied with just that explanation. Let's see what Dr. Ortiz thinks. Then we can head over to the coroner's office. Dr. Adams has a top-notch microbiologist working there. Hopefully, she's analyzed the blood and tissue samples by now, and she can shed some light onto what was happening to Khattib on a cellular level."

LEE SAT BACK IN HIS SEAT and absorbed the information about the case. He'd been sent to assess if radiation exposure and terrorism were involved, or not. But Emma was right, he needed to keep an open mind. He looked out the window and noticed that the already gray sky had grown darker as thick clouds rolled in overhead. The crew shells on the Charles River were all heading back to shore, hoping to beat the storm.

Rain began pelting the windshield. Could this day get any worse? He was stuck in Boston on a cold, rainy day, wasting his time looking into the mysterious death of an Arab researcher that no one knew anything about, who may or may not have died from radiation poisoning that may or may not be related to terrorist activity. At least he had Emma to keep him focused.

His phone rang. "Agent Jansen," he answered.

"Jansen," boomed a voice on the other end. "This is Undersecretary Roland Waters from the Commonwealth Fusion Center. We were expecting you a couple of hours ago."

Lee could tell from the voice of the governor-appointed undersecretary that he was annoyed. Kowalski had told him that the governor of Massachusetts had requested DHS involvement. It was always politically touchy when DHS agents were sent to the state Fusion Centers to assist with a case.

"I'm sorry. I thought I would catch up with Dr. Hess to go over the medical reports and lost track of time," Lee answered. He had to tread lightly. He would most certainly be needing Waters's help in this investigation.

"Okay. But the governor's breathing down my neck on this one. When will you be here so I can brief you on the case?"

"Understood. I'll be there shortly."

Lee took a deep breath and hung up. He knew he should have headed to the Fusion Center upon arrival, but Rick Caruthers had said that the best time to catch Dr. Hess was after her class. She was a moving target after that.

"Problem?"

"No. No problem. How soon will we be at Mass. General?"

"About ten minutes," Emma replied.

"Listen," he said. "Can we make a quick stop before we go to the hospital? I have to check in with the local DHS office. They may have some more info for us." And he'd be able to make nice with the undersecretary for making him wait.

Emma rerouted the trip to the DHS office. As the brownstone buildings flashed by, Lee thought about his dealings with his peers. The most significant people in his life—Gina, by far the most important, but also T-Bone—had stressed the need for him to control his temper. With the help of T-Bone, Lee had managed to salvage his career and pull himself out of the downward spiral after his wife's death. Now that he no longer had the benefit of his partner's guidance, Lee worried he might veer toward the self-destructive path that had led to the fatal shooting in Lincoln Heights.

8

THE REGIONAL HEAD of Department of Homeland Security coordination had an office in downtown Boston. It was an essential part of the joint state–federal Commonwealth Fusion Center formed to integrate all information about regional threats. Lee reported in at the front desk and was shown in to Waters's office.

"Good morning, Undersecretary Waters," Lee said to the older man seated behind a desk. "I'm Agent Lee Jansen. This is Dr. Emma Hess from Harvard."

Waters removed his reading glasses and looked up at Lee and Emma. Emma immediately sensed the tension as the undersecretary spoke.

"Roland Waters, Doctor Hess," he said, shaking her hand, then Lee's. "The governor asked for your involvement to bring federal resources into this investigation. We're knee deep prepping for the president's visit next month and, as you can imagine, need to know what Khattib was up as soon as possible. At this point, we're not quite sure yet what we're dealing with and we're trying to keep it quiet until we know for sure."

"Makes sense," replied Lee. "What do you have so far?"

The undersecretary let out a sigh and picked up a large brown envelope from his desk. He looked over to Emma. "You may want to wait outside, Doctor. We'll be discussing classified information."

"Undersecretary, Dr. Hess has been asked to assist us in looking into Khattib's death. She's part of the case and we'll need her help," Lee said.

"I do have a top-secret clearance," Emma added. Once clearance is given, although access to classified material is restricted when one is not actively working on a case, it is good for five years. "I've done some toxicology work for the local FBI office, and they ran a security investigation on me a few years back. So I'm cleared."

Waters hesitated for a moment. Lee could tell he wasn't convinced. But he handed the envelope to Lee and said, "We don't have much. Driver's license, academic record, and so forth. Khattib was an Egyptian Arab. Came here to study over ten years ago. Got his undergrad in biology and doctorate in microbiology. Been working in Boston ever since. I pulled a copy of his Egyptian passport and visa from INS. Your office in DC also forwarded me a classified email from the CIA asking us to look into any relationship between Khattib and terrorism or weapons of mass destruction."

"Did they say why?" Lee asked, pulling papers out of the envelope and studying them. "Was he on a watch list?"

"Don't know. Those are your people," Waters added, running his hand through his thinning hair. "I have enough to worry about with the president's visit, now this. I need you to find out what's going on. If there is a possibility of a dirty bomb, I'll devote all of my efforts to flush it out. As you might imagine, after the Tsarnaev brothers and Usaamah Rahim and his plot to decapitate one of our officers here, we don't know what or who is coming out of the woodwork next. Maybe this scientist was part of a plot, maybe he was a lone wolf, or maybe he just died of something related to his work. But Boston's been on edge ever since the Marathon bombings and with good reason."

"All right. We were on our way to the hospital to talk to the staff that took care of Khattib when you called," explained Lee.

"Once I get a look at all the medical reports, I hope to have a better idea of what killed Khattib," Emma said.

"I need more than hope, Dr. Hess. I've assured the mayor and the governor that nothing's going to happen on my watch. But I also don't want to create panic or to waste resources on a wild goose chase. Here," Waters added, handing Emma a sheet of paper. "This is the final coroner's report."

"Wow," Emma exclaimed. "That was fast. I only received the preliminary report."

"Like I said, the mayor wants answers."

"This suggests that radiation exposure killed Khattib," Emma said as she skimmed.

"Right. Now I have a dead Arab scientist, killed by radiation. CIA sends me a one-liner to look out for dirty bombs but doesn't tell me why or give me any other info, no matter who I ask. So, you see my concern?"

"Sure. We'll get you some answers, Undersecretary," replied Lee.

"Good. Just do it fast, but quietly. And one last thing, Jansen," Waters said. "I heard about Lincoln Heights."

Emma could feel Lee tense up beside her and saw his jaw muscles flex.

"Let's try to keep that weapon holstered, understood? I can't turn on the evening news without seeing some kind of confrontation between civilians and law enforcement. That's the last thing we need."

Lee felt his anger rise at the implication but tamped it down. It was a skill Gina had taught him. One of many tools that his wife imparted after his tour of duty in Iraq. It was no secret at the DHS that, after Gina's death, Lee had turned to alcohol to ease his grief. After the Lincoln Heights shooting, the news ran stories about Lee's PTSD. One paper even suggested that his alcohol abuse had affected his judgment. Although the DHS internal investigation cleared him of wrongdoing, the damage was done. He had become known as an alcoholic hothead with an itchy trigger finger. Waters seemed to believe the stories.

"Will that be all, Undersecretary?" Lee responded tersely.

The two men stared at each other for a long moment as Emma watched.

"Just report back to me as soon as you find something. Khattib's wallet and keys are in the envelope," Waters stated. "They arrived from the hospital a few hours ago. And, Agent Jansen, I'm sorry about your partner."

Lee nodded and walked out of the office.

"We'll call you when we find something," Emma replied.

"Please do," Waters replied, handing her his card.

Curious about the story behind Waters's concerns, Emma nodded, took the card, and left. Lee was standing next to her car when she reached the parking lot.

"Lee, what was all that about? If we're going to work together on this, I kind of need to know."

Lee looked at Emma. He wasn't one to open up to strangers, but he felt oddly comfortable with her. She reminded him of Gina. It wasn't her looks. Gina was petite, with long, straight brown hair and large, dark eyes. Emma's tall, athletic frame contrasted with Gina's, as did her green eyes framed by shoulder-length blond hair. It was the look in those eyes, Lee decided, that reminded him of Gina: warm, caring, intelligent.

"Last month, I was helping serve warrants on a suspect at an MS-13 house in Lincoln Heights."

"What's MS-13?"

"It's one of the worst gangs in DC. They're some bad hombres. I had a lead that they were helping a Middle East terrorist cell smuggle weapons into the country. I went there to see what I could find. It went bad real quick. Tyrone James, my partner, and I found dozens of them holed up in there, and someone started shooting at us. A teenage gangbanger came out of a side door and opened up at me and Tyrone. I found out at the hearing that he was only sixteen. The shooter ran around the back of the house and T-Bone—that was Tyrone's nickname—and I went after him." Lee paused. It was difficult for him to continue.

"The kid kept shooting at us throughout our pursuit. When we turned the corner of the house, we saw him running toward a shed in the backyard. I yelled at him to stop. He turned and raised his arms like he was going to shoot. And I shot him first."

"Okay. Sounds like self-defense," Emma told him. "It must be difficult to kill a man. But it was either him or you."

"When T-Bone and I approached the kid, he was already dead. The bullet struck him in the heart. He had no weapon in his hand. We found it on the ground near the house. From what the forensics guys said, it must have jammed and he dropped it right before we turned the corner."

"You had no way of knowing that, Lee."

"Yeah, well, that's what the investigation concluded. T-Bone testified that the kid was shooting at us before he took off behind the building. He thought the kid was still armed as well. In the end, I was cleared, but the incident got a lot of media play. I don't appreciate the innuendo in Waters's lecture back there," Lee said, motioning his head toward the building behind them.

"I wouldn't worry about Waters too much," Emma said. "I see his kind in academia all the time. They feel insecure when someone from outside their sphere of control tries to help them. His problem isn't you, it's his own insecurities."

Lee appreciated the support. He also liked the fact that she instantly took his side. "Maybe so, but he can either be a big help in this investigation or an obstacle. We'll see which one it is."

"We have our own leads to investigate. Come on, let's hear what Dr. Ortiz has to say," Emma replied, pulling out her car keys.

9

D AMN IT, pull that tourniquet tighter before this lady bleeds to death," Manny Ortiz grumbled. He was in no mood to play nursemaid to the timid psychiatry intern who was assigned to the emergency room when a trauma patient presented in shock. Manny had grabbed any doctor he could find to help him keep the patient from bleeding to death in his ER.

"Like this," he said in a calmer tone as he adjusted the tourniquet, realizing the poor intern had no clue. The three victims from a car accident on the Northern Expressway had rolled into the busy Mass. General emergency room fifteen minutes earlier. Short-staffed, Manny needed all the help he could muster.

"Get the trauma surgeon on the horn. Tell him we're sending up some business, so prep the OR STAT," he ordered. His bloodied hands maintained pressure on the older woman's femoral artery as the psychiatry intern stood wide-eyed beside him.

"DePena!" he called out to the experienced ER nurse, Millie DePena. "Get me a surgical kit. I need to clamp off this artery before she bleeds all over my new sneakers."

In moments like these he felt like he was back in Afghanistan with the 75th, patching up severely wounded Rangers as they poured in from battle against the Taliban.

"You'd better wait for the surgical team to get here. You're only a resident," the nurse replied as she brought the kit.

"She'll be dead by then. Just give me the damned kit!"

Manny felt the woman's pulse weaken under his fingers as her blood volume dropped dangerously low. Blood filled the wound cavity, and his hands were covered to his wrist in the sticky goo already coagulating on his latex gloves. He knew he only had one chance as he thrust the hemostats blindly into the dark pool. Guided by his fingers' tight grip on the barely palpable artery, he maneuvered the hemostats under his index finger and clamped the bleeding artery. The suddenly bounding pulse reassured him that he got the correct vessel.

"Now get some volume in her before her brain and kidneys shut down. O neg, and get her typed and crossed before the next trauma rolls in," Manny ordered. "Let's go, break time is over, people."

Nurse DePena gave the resident a disapproving look but started inserting a second IV into the patient. Manny blew her a kiss. He was in rare form tonight. As much as it pained him to see his patients on the brink, he couldn't help but relish the adrenaline rush.

Bob Curtis stood up from the nurses' station and called out to Manny.

"Dr. Ortiz, I have Dr. LaBlanc on the line from trauma. He says he's in the middle of giving a lecture and asked if you ran the case by your attending yet to see if an OR was needed ASAP or if it could wait."

"Pompous ass," Manny muttered under his breath. He pulled off the bloodied gloves and hurried over to the nurses' station. He took the phone from Bob.

"Dr. LaBlanc, this is Dr. Ortiz. We have three critical patients down here in the ER. I just clamped off a femoral bleeder on one. Dr. Levine is with the other two, who are in equally bad shape. So, no, I really haven't had time to run it by him, as you suggest. But here's a suggestion for you: Get me a damned operating room for my patient ASAP before she bleeds to death, or I promise that *you'll* be the next patient for the trauma team," he said sternly before slamming the phone down.

"I didn't hear a thing, Manny," Curtis said as the doctor turned and walked away.

Manny returned to his patient. Her blood pressure was still low at 85 over 50, but it was much improved from the 60 over palp when she rolled in. Two IVs were inserted with one unit running whole blood, and the other pushing lactated Ringer's solution. He checked her wounds again; it seemed that his temporary fix would keep her arteries from leaking. For the time being, at least.

"How's she doing?" his attending asked as he returned from caring for the other two trauma patients.

"Better. I got the femoral artery clamped off, no other major bleeders. Secondary survey reveals no other life-threatening injuries. How about the two from the other vehicle?"

"Boy's okay, but the driver didn't make it. Massive head injury. The boy dropped a lung and I had to put in a couple of chest tubes, but he'll make it."

"Dr. Ortiz?" Curtis called out again. Both doctors looked up.

"Dr. LaBlanc just called back. He has two operating rooms on standby, ready for your patients when you are," he announced with a wink.

"Thanks," Manny answered. "By the way, you're probably going to hear from Dr. LaBlanc later," he told his attending, who also happened to be the head of the ER department. Manny instinctively ran his fingers through his thick, dark hair.

"Manny, what did you do this time?" Levine queried, knowing his resident's penchant for ruffling feathers.

"Let's just say I needed to coax Dr. LaBlanc a little to get operating time for our patients. He's probably not too happy with me right now."

Dr. Levine shook his head. He was going to have to bail Manny out of trouble yet again. "You know, I can only do so much. One of these days you're going to mess with the wrong attending, and even I won't be able to save your butt."

Manny Ortiz was, by far, the best emergency medicine resident Seth Levine had ever seen. His experience on the battlefield had honed his medical and trauma skills, and he was head and shoulders above his peers. He was a fierce advocate for his patients, but he spoke his mind a little too freely.

Manny grinned. "You tell them to bring it. I'm sure the medical board *and* the newspapers would love to hear why the good Dr. LaBlanc wanted to delay operating on emergent patients until he finished his precious lecture."

Levine let out a sigh. "Do we have anyone else?"

"Not sure, I was pretty tied up with the MVA. Bob, what do we have?" Manny called out as he furrowed his thick eyebrows and rubbed his stubbled chin.

"Nothing much. A few fours and fives," the nurse answered after looking at the patient board, referring to the categories for nonurgent patients.

"I got it covered here, Dr. Levine," replied Manny.

"Okay. I'll get your trauma and the boy up to the OR. *Try* to stay out of trouble down here in the meantime. While I'm up there, I'll talk with LaBlanc and see if I can keep him from filing a complaint. *Again.*"

"Complaint? For what? All I did was ask for some OR time."

"I'll be back in fifteen," Levine replied, shaking his head and not looking forward to the exchange he was about to have upstairs.

"Okay, my most favorite nurse in the whole world, what's next?" Manny asked Nurse DePena.

Millie DePena was a middle-age, first-generation Filipino nurse who ran her shift with an iron fist. All the young nurses under her charge feared the four-foot-ten, plump woman who never cracked a smile. From day one, she'd clashed with Manny's unorthodox manner. He knew she wasn't a big fan of his, but she did respect his patient advocacy. He figured that was why she tolerated his sarcasm.

"Sore throat in bed three and laceration in six," she replied.

"All right, then, let's get to work," he said, making his way to bed six.

"Dr. Ortiz?" Curtis called again from the nurses' station. Manny looked up to see the worried-looking nurse standing next to a man in a tie and sport coat and an attractive woman dressed in conservative business attire.

Wow, Manny though. *That was fast.* Maybe he finally went too far with his threat to Dr. LaBlanc. The suits from hospital administration were already down there. And, most likely, they'd ask for his resignation from the residency program.

Oh well, I can always return to the military. Manny made his way up to greet them and take his punishment.

"Dr. Ortiz, I'm Dr. Emma Hess from Harvard School of Public Health. This is Agent Jansen from the Department of Homeland Security. We need to speak with you."

Although relieved to hear that his visitors were not from hospital administration, Manny knew that a visit from a Fed and a Public Health doc at the same time was never good. *Someone,* he thought, *was worried about an epidemic or natural disaster or something more ominous.* He wasn't aware of any worrying trends of infectious disease cases in the ER lately. Likewise, there was nothing concerning in the weather forecast. That suggested another possibility: terrorism.

And *that* suggested that unusual patient the other night: Jawad Khattib.

10

D R. ORTIZ," Emma began.

"Please, call me Manny."

"Okay, Manny," Emma said. "You treated a patient the other night. Middle Eastern man in his twenties. Coded at the front desk."

"Hard to forget that one. He was in rough shape. Tough to revive him. Little good it did, though. He died later in the ICU."

"Manny," Lee interrupted. "Can we talk somewhere private?"

"Yeah, no problem," Manny said, turning his attention to the nurses' station. "Bob, Dr. Levine should be back any minute now. The interns are working fast track. Have them take over beds three and six. And keep Nurse DePena away from the interns. I don't want her messing with them. I'm the only one allowed to abuse the interns. Call me if you need me. I'll be in the break room."

"Sure thing, Manny. We got it," Curtis replied.

The three walked the twenty feet to the break room. After Manny shooed away the psychiatry intern who was trying to pour herself a cup of coffee with badly shaking hands, they were alone.

"So, you think there's some connection to terrorism?" Manny asked.

Lee and Emma exchanged glances. They were surprised to hear his first impression.

"What makes you say that?" Lee asked. It was a cop's reply, designed to draw a witness out.

"Well, you're from DHS, she's from HSPH. The patient was a biomedical researcher who died a bizarre, gruesome death. Toss in the obligatory racial profiling, and it doesn't take a neurosurgeon to figure it out. Which is good, because I'm no neurosurgeon."

"Not very politically correct, are you?" Emma asked with a smile.

"No time in my business to be politically correct. People die if I don't do my job quickly. I don't have time for politics or all that touchy-feely crap."

"What exactly did he say when he came in?" asked Lee.

"He asked for help. Said he was dying. Why would he say that unless he knew it to be a fact, like he knew what was going on inside of him?"

"That's a stretch. I'm sure people come into the ER all the time and say they're dying, regardless of the medical issue or the severity of their illness or injury," Lee replied.

"Sure they do. But this man obviously knew something. He was right, wasn't he? Dead by sunup."

"How did he present?" prodded Emma.

"Well, he never regained consciousness after his code. Sats were low, PaO_2 was in the toilet. LFTs were up, platelets and albumin down."

Lee knew the signs of radiation poisoning. Radiation exposure damages a body's DNA but also induces free radical formation, changing ordinary water molecules in the body into unstable molecules that then cause cellular damage. While undergoing advanced ordnance training at the Navy's Energetics Manufacturing Technology Center in Indian Head, Maryland, Lee had studied the biological effects of radiation on living tissue. Liver function tests would be abnormal, indicating massive damage to that vital organ. The liver would cease to form any cells or proteins, such as albumin and platelets. The resulting cellular breakdown throughout the body would release fluid, overwhelming the circulatory system and overloading the lungs and other organs and tissue.

"Sounds like radiation sickness to me," Lee said, putting it all together.

"Could be," Emma chimed in. "What do you think, Manny?"

"He didn't hemorrhage from a hematologic problem, that's for sure. Initial coags were fine. He was neutropenic and septic, in DIC at the very least. Disseminated intravascular coagulation," Manny explained to Lee, "is when the body's clotting system goes haywire and messes up the vascular system. These patients bleed out pretty quickly."

"I know," Lee replied. "It can lead to multiple organ failure, shutting down the lungs, kidneys, and liver. I was an EOD tech in the Marines."

"Impressive. I was a Ranger in a prior life myself," Manny said. "We're going to get along just fine. Anyway, the ICU found that his ANC was down. That, combined with the Fed's input that Khattib may have been a terrorist, led the ICU team to suspect, among other things, radiation poisoning."

"ANC? I'm not familiar with that one," Lee confessed.

This time Emma explained. "The ANC is the absolute neutrophil count. It's a component of the immune system in the blood, and it's usually low when there has been radiation exposure."

"ARDS and renal failure would support that," Manny added, reciting other complications from radiation exposure, including acute respiratory distress syndrome from the fluid overload in the lungs and the shutdown of Khattib's kidneys from DIC.

"Wait. What do you mean, input from the Feds?" asked Lee, wondering who else was involved in his investigation.

"Hospitals have a requirement to report certain types of cases that present to the ER or clinics to the Department of Public Health. This one certainly met the criteria, especially because he was a researcher and the cause of death so uncommon. After we called them about Khattib, the ICU team received a call from your boys at Homeland suggesting they focus on radiation as the main cause of his symptoms."

"Do you know who made that call?" Lee asked.

"Don't know. That's way above my pay grade. I'm just a lowly resident. Besides, I was busy stabilizing your boy."

Maybe Waters made the call, Lee thought. The undersecretary had already told them he received information from the CIA that strongly indicated Khattib was a suspected terrorist. That would certainly have prompted a call to the hospital to make them aware of the possible threat.

"But?" Emma asked, detecting doubt in the resident's tone when he mentioned radiation. "You don't think radiation was the cause?"

"Sure. Maybe. But either Khattib got hit with a massive amount of radiation in a very short time, or he had chronic radiation exposure with symptoms that had been building over the past weeks or so."

"Why aren't these two possibilities plausible to you?" Emma asked.

"If he was hit with enough external rads to cause that much damage acutely, enough to kill him," Lee added, using the term measuring the absorbed dose of radiation, "he would also have been covered with severe burns at the site of exposure."

"Bingo," Manny answered, touching his nose. "Nada. No burns anywhere."

"Okay, how about chronic, accumulated low-level exposure?" asked Emma.

"That's possible. But he would have had *some* symptoms well before he presented to the ER, especially if he was exposed to enough long-term radiation to cause this much damage. I'm sure he was a smart guy. Ph.D. researcher, right? Why wouldn't he have gotten some medical help before symptoms from chronic exposure got this bad? I mean, if he was working on a dirty bomb or something, he would know the risks of radiation exposure. He's a scientist. He would have seen the early warning signs. I doubt he would have waited to seek medical care until he was at death's door, then stumble into the ER at midnight. Besides, he was scanned in the ICU. No radiation detected. Whatever killed him did it quickly. Hours. A day, tops. And it was something he didn't expect. Maybe it started off with common symptoms that mimicked something benign like a cold."

"That's quite insightful," Emma said. "But you're forgetting another possibility."

"Internal exposure," Lee said. "You wouldn't be able to find internal radiation with your standard detection devices."

"You got me there," Manny said. "It's possible. But so are other things. But what do I know? I'm just a dumb ER resident."

"I doubt that," replied Emma. "So, let's explore the other possible causes of his symptoms. What else do we know?"

"He was in full-blown SIRS," Manny said. "But nothing on cultures yet."

Lee was puzzled by the negative results on the bacterial cultures. Some bacteria, usually from the gastrointestinal tract, should be growing in Khattib's blood if he had systemic inflammatory response syndrome, an intense immune response to help fight an overwhelming infection. Bacteria present in a person's blood or urine could lead to organ failure, especially in the liver and kidneys. In radiation exposure, the cells in the gut are destroyed, and the normal bacteria that live in the intestines leak into the bloodstream, causing SIRS. This is the usual cause of death in a person subjected to high amounts of radiation.

"Shouldn't *E. coli* or some other bacteria from his GI tract be growing in his blood?" asked Lee. "If that wasn't the cause of his SIRS, then what killed him?"

"Oh, make no mistake about it," Manny stated. "SIRS killed Khattib. The immune response I saw in him was like nothing I'd ever seen before. Not sure why we haven't seen any bacteria grow in his blood, urine, or cerebrospinal fluid cultures yet, but let's give it a few more days."

"Any other medical conditions that could have caused such an intense immune or SIRS-like response?" asked Emma.

"No underlying medical condition based on what little we had on his medical history," replied Manny. "He had a pre-employment physical done about a year ago. It was in our system. His medical history was benign. Exam and labs were fine back then. Other than his physical, he hadn't been to a doctor throughout his time as a grad student or while working in his research. No meds either. Nothing that would suggest cancer, autoimmune disease, or immunodeficiencies. No signs of pulmonary embolism or trauma on exam or any studies we did."

"What about a toxin?" Emma asked.

"Negative. We ran a drug panel and full tox screen. He was squeaky clean."

"His exam?"

"Severe bruising all over his body. No burns or lesions on his skin, like I mentioned. Internal bleeding. Liver and kidneys shut down. He was unresponsive. Basically, he was a mess. Now,

I may be just a kid from Jersey, but if radiation did all that, even if it was internal exposure, it must have been a whopper of a dose."

Based on Manny's description of what he saw in the ER, Lee was starting to doubt the radiation poisoning theory. He could see from Emma's expression that she had further questions as well.

"I'll tell you, Doc," Manny said to Emma. "I had a lot of radiation exposure medical training and triage drills while I was in the Army, and this just doesn't look like that to me. But I've never taken care of a true radiation sickness case, so maybe I'm not the one to ask. It would obviously be helpful to know what type of research he was doing."

"We're going to stop by his apartment and look for any evidence there. If he was up to anything suspicious, most likely the material would be there instead of at his work. But we'll go to his lab next," Lee answered.

"Thanks, Manny. You've been a huge help," Emma told him.

"Sure, any time," the resident said. "Listen, don't rule out a bioterrorist component. Maybe an organism or toxin that we just can't detect. His case doesn't fit anything in the textbooks. I try to keep an open mind in these bizarre cases, but I know that if it smells fishy, it's usually because it's a fish. You know what I mean?"

"Not really, no." Emma smiled at his expression. "But we'll keep an open mind."

"Just don't rule anything out. Give me a call later and I'll see if any of the cultures are back. Interesting case."

"Will do. Thanks," Lee answered.

The three exchanged handshakes and business cards.

"Now it's time for me to get back to the not-so-interesting cases," Manny said as he left the break room.

"Does bioterrorism seem plausible to you?" Lee asked his new partner as they walked out of the ER. "I know a lot about biological weapons, and I've not seen any that can't be detected."

"I guess it's possible, as is radiation exposure. Right now I can't rule out radiation sickness or a few other possible causes for Khattib's symptoms. This could just be a case of sepsis from a normal organism that we haven't detected or that hasn't yet grown out on cultures. I deal in absolutes and I'm not willing to make the terrorist connection yet, just because he was an Arab or because someone at DHS or CIA or whoever tells us to," Emma replied.

Lee realized she was staring into his eyes, almost like she was lost in them. He was pretty sure that he was not what she had expected when she was told a DHS agent would be helping her on the case. That made two of them: She was so much more than he had expected as well.

Lee finally broke eye contact. He needed to stay focused.

"Well, like I said," Emma continued as she and Lee crossed the street on the way to her car, "I need evidence before reaching any conclusions. But I'll make you a deal. I won't rule out terrorism just yet, including radiation or a biological agent, if you'll entertain the possibility of natural causes."

"Believe me, nothing would make me happier than to learn that Khattib wasn't a terrorist. But if there's even the slightest possibility that he left a dirty bomb behind, I need to know it and need to know it fast."

In his mind, Lee sorted what he'd learned so far. The medical evidence as to cause of death was inconclusive. Both the CIA and his own DHS were concerned enough about terrorism to pull him off T-Bone's case, even though Lee had found nothing suspicious in Khattib's file. In fact, the file he'd received back in DC was thin. Either the government was holding out on him, or they were just grasping at straws.

Either way, this case was bizarre. Emma's enthusiasm for the investigation was clear and encouraging. Lee couldn't remember the last time he felt this same level of excitement for his job, or for anything.

"Is there anybody else we need to speak to before I go to Khattib's apartment?" he asked.

"Coroner's office. Before you potentially expose yourself to any pathogen or radiation, we should probably get as much information about the cause of death as possible."

"I was afraid you were going to say that," replied Lee. "All right, let's go see what the coroner has to say."

11

AS LEE AND EMMA TALKED about Khattib's strange death on the drive to the coroner's office, Lee was struck by the intelligence of the woman sitting behind the wheel. He struggled to recall what he had learned during his explosive ordnance disposal training as well as his experience with weapons of mass destruction just to keep up with her. And even then, he frequently was lost when her medical explanations overwhelmed what he had learned as an undergraduate biology major at UCLA after he left the Marines.

His phone rang, interrupting Emma's explanation of the absolute neutrophil count.

"Agent Jansen," he said.

"Hi, Agent Jansen. This is Erik Kaiser. I got something for you."

"Talk to me."

"The two suspects we got from the café, a Daif and Sanabel Ajeel, were clean. But their brother is Wahab Ajeel."

"Never heard of him."

"The three are Libyan nationals, recently came here from Tripoli. Listen to this. The café, listed in Wahab's name, was paid for in cash. Not sure who's bankrolling him. It doesn't appear that the café was making any money, but Wahab still had a pretty impressive bank account. Six figures."

Lee had heard of this sort of arrangement before. Terrorist organizations often set up fronts for their operatives or sleepers in the States. "Sounds like Wahab had a gig on the side. Any affiliations?"

"None that we could tell so far," Kaiser allowed. "But Wahab is long gone to parts unknown. I suspect he was the shooter. The truck was registered to him. Why else would he have disappeared?"

The memory of T-Bone's bloody corpse inside the car flashed in Lee's mind. "Is there an APB out on Wahab?"

"Yep," Kaiser replied, sounding a little miffed. "We also got a warrant for their house. I'll be searching it later today."

"Okay, good. Hey, do me a favor. Ask your suspects if they know a Jawad Khattib. He's Egyptian. That's kilo-hotel-alpha-tango-tango-india-bravo." Emma looked over at Lee at the mention of Khattib's name.

"They're not very talkative right now, but maybe after a few more hours in the tank we'll get more out of them," Kaiser replied.

"Thanks for keeping me up to date, Erik. Keep up the good work. And, remember, tell as few people as possible what you're up to and keep an eye on your rearview mirror. I can't shake the feeling that the shooter was tipped off we were coming."

"Will do. Stay out of trouble up there and I'll call you later."

"Thanks, man," Lee said, and hung up.

"News about Khattib?" Emma asked.

"No," Lee answered. "I was sent up here because my partner was killed in a shoot-out yesterday. I think the brass wanted me out of the area so I didn't go shooting up DC looking for his killer."

"I'm sure they sent you up here because you're an expert in explosives and weapons of mass destruction." Emma turned slightly in his direction. "Even most physicians don't know as much as you do about the physiologic effects of radiation exposure, from what I've heard so far."

Lee didn't quite agree with her generous assessment of his capabilities. Maybe once he had been good. But that was a long time ago. He also wasn't sure how much help he'd be on this case. None of the evidence suggested Khattib had anything to do with explosives, let alone WMDs. Besides, Lee was usually called in for his weapons expertise *after* a weapon was found, not before the existence of a weapon was even confirmed. He was in uncharted waters on this case.

"Where's this coroner's office?" asked Lee, noticing that Emma had slowed down to the posted speed limit for the first time in several miles.

"Right here," she said, pulling into the parking lot near the main campus of the Boston Medical Center. "Office of the Chief Medical Examiner for the Commonwealth of Massachusetts."

The face of the structure resembled a typical Boston three-story brick office building. However, as they walked to the front door, Lee noticed the length of the building stretched deep into the parking lot. Upon entering, they were ushered into the well-appointed offices of Dr. William Adams.

"I'd say that foul play is absolutely possible," the medical examiner said after the obligatory introductions. Surrounding the accomplished forensic pathologist were pictures of himself with the famous sons and daughters of Boston. Framed diplomas and certificates from prestigious universities and organizations papered the walls. "I've been at this for many years, and this is a curious case."

Dr. Adams took off his reading glasses. His thinning white hair, perfectly styled, sat atop a striking face with surprisingly few wrinkles. Lee couldn't help but notice that the coroner took good care of himself. From the dates on the diplomas, Lee figured that the man was in his late sixties, although he looked no more than fifty.

"I've reviewed the notes from Khattib's hospital admission. Your autopsy shows a similar picture with what was seen clinically," Emma said. "But I'm still not clear as to the rapid onset of his SIRS."

"It's difficult to explain his lab results and complete organ failure from anything but extreme radiation exposure and a very small number of other possibilities," Adams stated. "In this clinical picture, complete with a low neutrophil count in an otherwise healthy young man, I concluded that radiation poisoning led to catastrophic sepsis and death."

The low neutrophil count, Lee recalled, would certainly be a sign that Khattib's immune system was compromised. But he wasn't sure why Adams would focus only on radiation poisoning. He could think of other causes, and he wasn't even a physician.

"Why would you focus only on radiation poisoning?" he asked. "Sure, radiation exposure at a high enough dose can cause a hit to the immune system, but so could other conditions."

"Quite right, Agent Jansen," replied Adams. "But Mr. Khattib had none of those other conditions. No cancer, no immunodeficiencies. Simply put, radiation exposure obliterated his immune system and destroyed the cells that lined his gastrointestinal tract. The LPS toxin from the *E. coli* and *Klebsiella* bacteria that was released from his bowels overwhelmed his body and, without an intact immune system to fight it, ultimately led to his demise."

"Lipoprotein saccharide, or LPS, is an endotoxin found on the surface of many bacteria, even those that live symbiotically within our bodies," Emma explained to Lee. "But if LPS is released into the bloodstream, the body recognizes it as harmful, and an immense immune defensive response is triggered. In healthy individuals, an intact immune system with functioning neutrophils blunts the effects of LPS and prevents the body from going into full-blown SIRS, which is the last-ditch effort to clear the bacteria."

"Make no mistake about it, Agent Jansen," Adams stated firmly. "Khattib died from radiation poisoning. His neutrophils containing the vital LPS blocking enzyme called BPI were totally wiped out. In a healthy young man with an otherwise normal immune system, this happens only in extreme radiation exposure. Although cultures of the bacteria that would have been released from his radiation-damaged intestines are still pending, they will be positive. Trust me. Besides, his entire clinical picture, including the symptoms he exhibited while being admitted in the hospital, supports my conclusions. All of the data points to an excessive dose of radiation as the cause of Khattib's death." Adams sat back in his chair and steepled his fingers.

"Yes, but there was no trace of radiation or burns on the body," Lee replied.

"Internal deposition," Adams answered, referring to ingestion of radiation.

"Certainly possible," Emma affirmed, "but what about his urine?"

Lee wasn't sure where Emma was going with this, and the coroner looked perplexed for a moment.

"Was there any evidence of biomarkers to radiation exposure? Deaminated purines? Pyrimidines? Anything?" Emma asked.

"Very good, Doctor. You know your radiation medicine," Adams replied with a smile. "But there was no urine available at the time of autopsy. He had a Foley catheter in the ICU, so his bladder was empty. Also, I didn't feel the need to test my conclusions any further. As I stated, the clinical picture, along with the laboratory findings, was enough to substantiate acute radiation sickness as the cause of death."

"I'm just surprised there was nothing on the initial labs to suggest a bacterial infection," Emma said. "Not even a trace of *E. coli* or *Klebsiella*. No gut bacteria at all. Nothing that would have leaked from his damaged GI tract to directly cause his SIRS."

"We'll see when the final cultures are back in a few days. Don't worry, Doctor. You'll have your intestinal bacteria found in his blood as further proof of radiation poisoning. But remember to evaluate *all* of the data at your disposal," the old coroner advised as he checked his watch and rolled his chair back from his desk.

"What do you mean?"

"There are nonmedical facts that need to be considered. Mr. Khattib was an Arab, after all."

"I need something stronger than that, Doctor," Emma replied.

"You asked me for my opinion," Adams answered stiffly. "And now you have it."

"What about the body?" Lee asked. "Can we see it?"

"I'm afraid I can't let you examine the body without my presence, and, unfortunately, I have a pressing meeting at the State House that I cannot miss. But I'll see what I can arrange tomorrow."

"Can I at least see what pathology results you do have?" Emma asked.

Lee could see from that Emma was disappointed she could not examine the body. He was also certain that Adams was offended by her request. After all, he was a well-respected pathologist and probably didn't appreciate a physician from the ivory tower second-guessing his conclusions.

Adams let out a sigh as he rose from his mahogany desk. "Of course. Everything is only preliminary, mind you. Our medical examiners' office is quite backlogged, and we haven't yet certified all the results. Some are still pending, like the cultures from the hospital. I'll take you to the lab on my way out."

Together they walked down a short corridor to a set of double doors.

A petite Asian woman in her late twenties was sitting alone at a research bench.

"Sue," called the coroner as they entered the lab.

Startled by the interruption, Sue jumped, sending a book next to her microscope sailing to the floor. The woman adjusted her glasses as she reached down to pick the book up.

"This is Sue Chen, my star microbiologist and resident klutz," Adams said with a smile.

"He-hello," Chen replied, brushing her hair away from her face and crossing the room to meet them.

"Sue, this is Dr. Hess and Agent Jansen. They're investigating Khattib's death. Please give them every courtesy and assistance. I have to run to a meeting now. I'm already late, I'm afraid."

"Of course, Dr. Adams," the microbiologist answered.

"If there's anything else you need," Adams said, extending his hand, "don't hesitate to contact me."

"Thank you, Doctor. You've been very helpful," Emma replied.

Adams turned to leave the lab, but stopped and turned to face them. "There is one last thing I want to be sure we're all clear about," he said. "In light of recent events, my final report will indicate that Dr. Khattib died under suspicious circumstances."

"I understand," Emma said.

Adams nodded and left the lab.

Lee could see that Emma was not satisfied with the coroner's opinion about the cause of death—perhaps because they echoed his own doubts.

"What can I show you?" Chen asked.

"I'd like to see the pathology slides, if you don't mind," Emma said. "Anything interesting?"

"I'll say. I was just looking at his hepatocytes. Fascinating."

The microbiologist gestured for Emma and Lee to follow and hurried across the room to look at the cells from Khattib's liver fixed on a slide.

"She's got a lot of energy, doesn't she?" Lee whispered to Emma.

"Just don't stand too close to her or you may end up like the book," Emma replied under her breath. "Whatcha got?" she asked.

"Well, the liver cells are pretty much like what I saw in the kidney cells. Completely lysed. I mean, they are *gone*. Cell walls totally obliterated. That's why his liver enzymes were so high. After the cells ruptured, all the contents, including enzymes, just dumped into the blood."

"But any clue into what caused the rupture?"

The microbiologist frowned. "That's what's so bizarre. No. Nothing. No pathogens, no toxins. Although I did find a lot of inflammatory cells, which certainly would have caused the cellular damage, but no indication of what caused the inflammation. No signs of infection or anything that would have triggered such a pronounced immunologic response. I have no idea what his body was reacting to so severely."

"No LPS? No bacteria or toxins? Nothing?"

"Nope. Just his own inflammatory cells going crazy, destroying everything in their path."

"But how?" Lee asked. "Even if his immune system took a hit, from radiation or something else, we should see *something* in his blood to cause the SIRS."

"I didn't see any signs of gram-negatives or any other bacteria usually associated with SIRS or radiation sickness. But we'll have to wait for the cultures to be sure about that."

"How about his neutrophils?" asked Emma.

"There were a lot of immature cells and, like I said, the count was low," Chen answered. "But otherwise, they were fine."

"So the cells weren't dense at all? Morphology was normal?" Emma pressed, inquiring about the shape and form of the immune cells.

Brilliant, Lee thought. In radiation sickness, the neutrophil count was low because the production mechanism in the bone marrow had been irradiated and damaged. This would lead to malformed and misshaped neutrophils that didn't work properly. He was glad he had Emma to ask the right questions.

"Nope. They looked okay," Chen informed her. "Basically normal."

Emma shook her head. "What about the GI tract? Any damage in his gut?"

"Some inflammation, but not much," Chen told her. "Enterocytes were basically intact."

"That's odd," Lee replied. "In radiation poisoning, his intestines would have taken an early hit."

"Right," Emma said. "But there was no gut damage. No bacteria or LPS detected so far. Normal-shape neutrophils. Sounds to me like radiation is dropping down on the list."

"But the final cultures aren't back yet," Chen cautioned. "I can't see all viruses and bacteria on my slides. I need the culture results to know if there were any microbial causes of his SIRS. Remember, SIRS has to be initiated by something. The resulting out-of-control inflammatory response was what killed him. I can tell you at least that much. I just don't know what started it all."

"Sue, do me a favor," Emma said. "Can you run a phagocytosis assay and do some chemotaxis experiments on his neutrophils?"

"Sure. But why?"

"Radiation exposure decreases neutrophil function and ability to attack bacteria," Emma explained. "I want to see if Khattib's neutrophils were functioning normally or not. I know the shape was normal, and that leads us away from radiation, but I want to be sure. If his neutrophils had both normal shape *and* normal function, then we can rule out radiation."

Emma turned to Lee. "Okay, he died from SIRS. That much we know. But we don't know what triggered the SIRS. We'll see what Sue finds out with the neutrophil function tests. If the SIRS was not due to radiation, then infection is still high up on the differential diagnosis. But we'll have to wait a few more days on the cultures to be sure. Tomorrow when we see the body, I can check for the presence of internal radioisotopes that are sometimes present in severe radiation exposure."

"Wouldn't Adams have checked for that?" Lee asked.

"I doubt he has a gamma camera. We have one at the Harvard Medical School that I can pick up tomorrow morning before we return. Besides, Dr. Adams seems certain enough with his conclusions that he doesn't need to run additional confirmatory tests, even in light of a lack of data in his own lab to support that diagnosis. I'm just not as convinced as Dr. Adams that Khattib's death was from radiation exposure. I need to see some other objective evidence."

"In the meantime, I'll start doing what I was brought here to do," Lee answered. "Until you get your results that point away from radiation, since Adams's report stated that radiation exposure *was* the cause of death, I need to at least find out if there's any evidence to support terrorist activity or not. Khattib's clinical research may have involved only routine medical radiation exposure, but he could have been working on something more sinister."

"Okay. But I'm coming with you," Emma said. "This is my investigation as well, and I might be able to help connect the dots between Khattib's research and his death, at least from a medical perspective."

Lee considered whether this was a wise idea. He wasn't sure what dark alleys his investigation might take him down, and as a federal investigator and former Marine, he had learned to hope for the best but expect the worst. But Emma had brought him this far, and he might still need her expertise.

"Okay, but there might be some times when I have to go it alone."

"I can handle myself just fine, Agent Jansen," Emma said with a smile.

"Can I come too?" Chen asked excitedly.

"No, Sue. I need you to run those tests and keep going through the samples. There must be something there," Emma replied. "*Something* triggered the inflammatory response that killed Khattib. Maybe it was radiation or maybe it was an infection. Maybe it was something else that we haven't yet identified. But what I do know is that we need to find out what it was before we have another corpse on our hands."

12

THE ARCHITECT TOOK his responsibilities seriously. The Order entrusted him to run this project discreetly but also accomplish the mission quickly. His reputation for ruthlessness and tenacity drove the decision to assign him this critical project.

Yes, he assured himself, he *was* a fanatic. He was protecting his way of life, a future for his people. His was a daunting, history-altering task, and one he would absolutely not allow to fail. Only a fanatic could succeed in this endeavor.

Many, of course, did not see things as he did. The minds of the masses, sheep that aimlessly wandered the planet, were clouded by propaganda and lies that they were spoon-fed by the dangerous and irresponsible media. But he knew the truth, for he was knee deep in the war.

His drive through the mountains was quiet, almost serene. It was not always so, of course. The weather at this altitude could be brutal. The area was renowned for its majestic beauty yet feared for the violent storms that often swept the high, treeless peaks. It was sanctuary for the Architect. It gave him privacy in which he could contemplate the direction and vision of the Order.

"The lab in Boston is shut down and steps are being taken to ensure all samples are brought to our lab," his assistant informed him.

The Architect regarded the young man sitting next to him. Remarkably, this entire project had been his assistant's idea. And it was a good one. All members of the Order agreed to pursue the research. Such consensus among the diverse members was a rare feat indeed. But the threat from abroad was real and growing. A weapon needed to be developed to preserve their way of life from the intruders, so he had thrown his support and leadership behind the project.

The Architect had agreed with his assistant's recommendation to conduct the bulk of the research in New England and the Mid-Atlantic region of the United States where medical infrastructure and research labs were plentiful. It would be easy, his assistant had assured him, to contract out small parcels of the research to labs in an effort to maintain secrecy.

Since no one lab, save the Architect's own, of course, knew the ultimate goal of their work, the chance of discovery was minimal. The collective results, however, would be assembled in the Architect's own facility deep in the mountains where the more sensitive research was close to completion. Here, under his direct supervision, the finished weapon would come together.

Jawad Khattib had turned out to be a brilliant scientist. His recruitment had pushed the project to new heights. His work was so exemplary that he was given larger, more complex tasks that other researchers were unable to handle. That decision, in retrospect, might have been a grave mistake. Because of Khattib's gruesome and unexplained death, the Order's master plan was suddenly at risk of being discovered, even as the project was so close to completion.

"I want our research facility here to redouble its efforts to purify the delivery system," the Architect said. "I want an operational prototype in my hands in one week. We're running out of time."

The words "one week" made the assistant blink.

"But that's impossible, sir," the man squeaked. "True, Khattib's results helped advance the development of the targeting mechanism, and his death confirmed the lethality of the weapon itself, but not of the vector. His research has opened up new doors, but we haven't had the breakthrough we need to formulate a functional delivery vector to complete the weapon. Remember, although Khattib's targeting protein was successful, it was the failure of the vector delivery system that led to his death."

Despite the apparent scolding from his assistant, the Architect flashed a rare smile.

"Do you think I entrusted the entire project to you?" he asked coldly. "I have received a message this morning from our research facility in Lebanon. At my direction, they've been working on incorporating Khattib's linking protein with the vector. As you know, our brothers there live with the enemy at their throats every day. Life is cheap there, and there are many prisoners to purchase. Tests will be conducted on subjects from our first target population, now that we have refined the targeting mechanism using Khattib's linking protein."

The assistant could not hide the pained look on his face. This was *his* project, and he had foolishly thought he'd been involved in every aspect of the research. He was the one who brought the project to the Order, only to be undermined by the man he respected the most.

"Ah, I see your disappointment. Don't be offended. Our goal is far more important than hurt feelings. I was protecting our interests. Call it insurance. The weapon is ready," continued the Architect. "In our own labs, under my direction, we will continue to tweak the targeting mechanism while our colleagues in Lebanon finalize the vector. We are so very close. This jihad will soon come to a decisive end."

13

S O, ARE YOU STILL THINKING dirty bomb?" Emma asked as they sped past Boston Common to Khattib's Beacon Hill apartment.

"I certainly think it's a possibility," Lee replied. "If what the CIA says is true and Khattib had links to terrorists, I still think he was working on some sort of weapon. Like Adams said, he was an Arab scientist with access to a lab who died under questionable circumstances. Maybe from radiation exposure while trying to create a dirty bomb. Maybe something else. What do you know about his work at this Cambridge Institute for Genetic Research?" Lee finally was comfortable enough with Emma's fast driving to allow himself to thumb through Khattib's record.

"It's a private company that conducts contract research for various organizations and agencies in the region. They do a lot of genetic research. I've treated some of their researchers in the past since we maintain their occupational health records."

"What did you treat them for?"

"Many are on medical surveillance programs. Researchers frequently work with animals or harmful chemicals. If any are exposed to hazards, we take care of them. Usually we see needle sticks or bites from a research animal."

"Did Khattib ever come to your clinic?"

"No, not that I know of. I didn't see any clinic notes in his record. Manny didn't mention anything other than his initial employment physical."

"What exactly does genetic research involve?" Lee asked.

"I don't know exactly what projects the researchers at CIGR are working on. In general, though, genetic research involves finding treatments and cures for cancers and genetic disorders by using DNA to come up with drugs to affect or modulate the specific damaged or diseased genes. Gene therapy is often used in treating cancer. A new gene is inserted into a cell, and the gene uses the cell's normal processes to make proteins that help treat the cancer."

"Why wouldn't a company just do its own research instead of paying someone else to do it?"

"Many do," Emma said, swerving to miss two cyclists. "But some don't have the resources or the need for a large-scale specialty lab like CIGR. It's more cost-efficient for them to contract CIGR to conduct the limited amount of research they need. CIGR is one of the biggest lab vendors in the area. Very influential. They have a lot of clients and produce a fair amount of scholarly papers each year."

"After we see Khattib's apartment, we'll head over there to see exactly what projects he was working on," Lee told her.

"Sounds like a plan. Where *is* Khattib's apartment?" Emma asked.

"It should be on the next block," Lee said, glancing down at a map on his smart phone. "Number 217. So, how many speeding tickets do you get a year?"

"Not as many as parking tickets," she answered with a smile.

It was a nice smile, and Lee felt a tinge of recognition. Gina had the same striking smile. Cancer had taken her quickly. Much too quickly. In the end, friends didn't even recognize her. But he did. Until the day she died, the warmth of her smile was still there. It was the hallmark of her short life. In contrast to his brash and abrasive personality, Gina's nature was calm and soothing.

When Lee's sister first introduced him to Gina, a teaching colleague at an elementary school in Lee's hometown of Carmel on the California coast, he fell for her immediately. Gina would later quip that the feeling wasn't mutual. Lee could see why. He had just returned from Iraq and was a mess. But privately Gina had admitted that it was love at first sight. Neither of their respective friends thought the relationship would last. On the surface, they appeared to be polar opposites. But a year later, they were married in the same small church in Carmel where he had been baptized.

Gina filled a deep void in Lee's life. After his father died from a heart attack when he was still in high school, Lee was angry at the world. Indeed, he had enlisted in the Marines for the sole purpose of going to war to vent his pent-up rage and frustration that his father had been taken from him at such an early age. He would either kill or be killed, and it didn't really matter much to him which one came out on top.

Gina had been his one source of light and goodness in the world after he returned from a war that didn't help him get over his father's death, but rather drove him into a deeper darkness. She taught him that life was precious and every moment should be cherished, instead of living a life of revenge and anger. He believed her and, with her by his side, was finally able to enjoy life. But her premature death shattered his world and plunged him into a spiraling abyss that only alcohol could numb.

Lee shook off the wave of depression threatening to overtake him. He forced himself to look up at the row of houses and counted the numbers. "There it is," he said. "Just pull up front and double park. I'll take care of any ticket you get today."

"Does that include speeding tickets?" she asked.

"Don't push it, Doc," he said, allowing a smile.

Emma parked the car along the curb in front of a four-story late-nineteenth-century brownstone. "Which apartment?" she asked as they got out of her car.

"Two C. And stay behind me as we go in, okay?"

Lee reached back into the car and pulled Khattib's house keys from the large folder that Waters had given him.

"I guess that horseshoe didn't help Khattib much," Emma said, seeing the talisman hanging from the dead man's key chain. When Lee didn't respond, she added, "Has anyone been in the apartment yet?"

"The police sealed it off. I called them when I was given the case yesterday and told them not to disturb the apartment in any way. I wanted to go through it myself," he replied. "Which marks the very first time local law enforcement complied with the Feds without any pushback. Funny what possible radiation contamination will do for you in terms of cooperation."

They climbed the four steps to the entrance, and Lee cautiously opened the large arched front door, allowing Emma to enter. They made their way up the staircase to the second floor and found apartment 2C.

With a glance at Emma, he put the key in the lock beneath the yellow police tape. It turned easily. After a final nod to Emma, he opened the door.

The last thing either of them expected to see was Khattib standing in the apartment.

14

THEIR SHOCK gave the young Arab enough time to scramble out of the apartment through the open window beside him.

"Stop!" Lee yelled as he followed the man through the window. "Wait here," he called to Emma before descending the fire escape. He peered over the rail to see the man slide down the lowest length of the ladder to the sidewalk below. In a flash, the man was sprinting across the street.

Lee slid down the old iron rail in pursuit.

"Khattib!" he called after the young man. "Federal agent. Stop. Now!"

But the man kept running, over the crest of Beacon Hill and down the slope that led to the Common. Seeing his target, Lee continued the pursuit down Beacon Street. He was trailing by a good thirty feet but was gaining. Pedestrians grabbed their children and jumped out of the way as the two men ran past. Lee passed beneath the monument to Robert Gould Shaw and his Civil War comrades, now only ten feet from his prey. But his adversary picked up speed and dashed to the right just as Lee was about to grab the back of his collar.

The chase continued up narrow streets. Lee concentrated all of his strength into his legs, muscles throbbing as he urged them to move faster. Getting closer, and knowing he wouldn't hold out much longer, he decided to make his move as they entered the intersection at Mt. Vernon Street.

As Lee reached out to tackle the man, the sound of a horn shattered his focus.

He looked to his right, but it was too late.

Lee saw a momentary flash of light as his head hit the hood of a taxicab. Pain screamed in his forehead. He rolled off the car and landed hard on the asphalt. Screeching brakes finally stopped the taxi just inches from Lee's face.

When the clouds above him stopped spinning, Lee raised his head up. Once his eyes could focus, he scanned the street for the young Arab. The man was nowhere in sight.

By now a small crowd had gathered around Lee and helped him to his feet. He assured everyone, including the nervous taxi driver, that he was fine and limped back to the apartment building, angry with himself for letting the man get away.

Emma was rifling through Khattib's desk as Lee entered the apartment.

"Did you get him?"

"No, but I did manage to hail a cab. The hard way," he answered, holding his head.

"Have a seat," commanded Emma, eyeing the welt on his forehead and trickle of blood running down his cheek. She was surprised that, for a split second, her concern for his injuries went beyond her role as a healer. "Did you lose consciousness?" she asked quickly.

"No, just my pride."

"Any blurry vision?"

"No, Doc. Really, I'm okay," he answered, standing up.

Emma wasn't convinced but gave Lee some space. She would watch him for signs of a concussion.

"All right, but let me know if anything changes. That's a nasty contusion there. You might have a small intracranial bleed."

"I don't see any," he joked.

"In your head, you stubborn cop."

He nodded briefly to show that he knew that. "I can't believe he got away. I was inches away from him."

"Was that Khattib? It looked just like the picture from his ID."

Pulling out the photocopies of Khattib's driver's license and passport from the folder Waters had given him, Lee replied, "It looked like him to me. But then again, I mostly saw the back of his head."

"Don't be so hard on yourself. We'll find him. Here, this might cheer you up. Look what I found." Emma walked over to the cheap pressboard desk in the corner of the room. It was strewn with flyers to join the jihad of the Islamic Brotherhood. A poster taped on the wall showed a gruesome drawing of a head draped by a bloody kaffiyeh. An Arabic word was printed underneath.

Lee studied the flyers.

"Maybe Manny and Adams weren't so far off the mark," Emma said.

"Yeah. My CIA brethren may have called it right for a change. Looks like ol' Jawad really may have had ties to the Islamic Brotherhood."

"But who did we just see? No way the ICU would have mis-identified a patient, especially one who had just died."

Lee scratched his head, sorting through that possibility. "Maybe Khattib wasn't the one in the hospital. Anyone could have had his ID. And as sick as the person was, no one would have been surprised if he didn't look like the picture on the ID. Remember, the patient never regained consciousness in the hospital. It could have been someone else. I've seen stranger things. What would Adams have done to confirm the identity of the body?"

"Not much. He is required to compare the face with the ID. Khattib, or whoever it was, had already been admitted as a patient under the name on the ID, so as long as there was no reason to doubt the identity, that would be enough. Tomorrow we can get fingerprints and do a dental exam on the body for a more positive ID. In the meantime, what now? Now that Khattib's alive."

"*Maybe* he's alive. I just said it was *possible* someone else had his ID."

"But then who else would be in his apartment?"

"Good question." Lee was staring at the desk. "Don't you find something strange?"

"You mean, other than seeing a ghost?"

"Where's his computer? I mean, Khattib had earned his doctorate recently and was working as a researcher. You'd think he would have a computer here somewhere."

The two surveyed the small studio apartment.

"I didn't see one when I was snooping around," Emma said.

"Wouldn't you think a researcher would have a desktop at home?"

"He probably has one at his work. His laptop may be there, too."

"I'll get the Feds to come out here and collect all these pamphlets and dust the place for fingerprints. In the meantime, let's keep the Khattib sighting to ourselves for now, okay?"

"You mean you don't want anyone to know you're seeing ghosts?" she asked, and they both smiled.

"Let's just say I don't want to get locked up in a loony bin until we solve this case. Besides, sometimes keeping some info in your hip pocket helps with an investigation. Agreed?"

"Okay," she replied. "What now?"

"Well," Lee said, grabbing his backpack and throwing it onto the bed. "Let's see what Khattib was up to here."

He pulled out a small hand-held device from the bag.

"Is that what I think it is?" asked Emma, staring at the box.

"This is a genuine government-issued, direct-from-the-lowest-bidder, extremely antiquated Geiger-Müller counter," Lee replied with a grin as he switched it on.

"Does it work?" she asked with a hint of sarcasm.

"Does it *work*? I'm insulted. Government equipment *always* works," he said as he banged the device on the desk until he was rewarded with a digital clicking sound. "Just needs a little help getting started from time to time."

The sound emanating from the Geiger counter reminded Emma of the Cold War era black-and-white movies she used to watch as a child. She was surprised that the monotonous, pulsating tone had not changed at all.

"I thought the Boston police already did a Geiger counter reading."

"They did. But measure twice, cut once, my father the carpenter always told me. Especially when dealing with radiation. That last part was mine."

"I figured that," Emma replied dryly.

The two walked slowly around the studio with the Geiger counter. Lee went to the most obvious place first. He pushed aside the jihad pamphlets and handouts scattered on the desk. But the wand made no sound as he waved it over the top. He looked at Emma and raised an eyebrow. Slowly he moved the wand to the two drawers on the left of the desk. Over the bottom drawer, the device made a familiar squawk, startling Emma.

Lee carefully opened the drawer and pulled out two small yellow canisters. Written across the front, just below the international marking for radiation, was a label that read: YTTRIUM-90.

"Well, maybe our boy was up to something, after all," Lee said, placing the canisters on top of the desk.

"Yttrium-90 is used in medical research. It's a treatment for cancer, among other things. He may have been using it in his research," Emma replied.

"Maybe. But it's also an isotope product of nuclear fission."

"Wait a minute," Emma said, struck by an idea. "Khattib went to the ER late the night before last, right?"

"Yeah," replied Lee.

"Just under forty-eight hours ago. The half-life for yttrium-90 is short—less than three days. You shouldn't be getting such a strong reading with this small quantity if Khattib put it here *before* he went to the hospital, at the most, forty-eight hours ago. Probably longer. It should have almost fully degraded by now."

Lee looked at the containers. Emma was right. Nuclear material, by definition, gives off radioactive particles. If, as she stated, ytrrium released its particles quickly, it would be relatively inert after a few days. Since Khattib hadn't been in the apartment for two days and these containers were still emitting particles, they must have been placed here *after* Khattib had gone to the hospital.

"Was he working with someone else?" Emma asked.

"Could be," Lee said, reaching for an explanation. "We know there's one body in the morgue and another was just here in the apartment. It would be very unlikely he was building a dirty bomb on his own. He would need funding, coordination, and resources."

"Or maybe someone planted it here after Khattib died. Like maybe the guy that just jumped through the window," Emma said.

Lee had to consider that possibility as well. This case was getting more and more bizarre. They were going back and forth between terrorist-related dirty bomb activity and an unrelated natural death. At this point, he wouldn't be surprised if it the answer was none of the above. His head began to hurt.

"Let's see what else we find," he said. He continued to sweep the apartment with the Geiger counter. But five minutes later, finding nothing further, he switched off the device and replaced it in his bag.

"So, some radioactive material—but no handling gloves or equipment or other traces of nuclear material," Lee recapped.

"Can we get fingerprints off the yttrium-90 canisters?" Emma asked.

"Definitely," Lee said. "I'm going to get this entire place dusted. Including the terrorist propaganda. They'll tear apart every inch of this place looking for clues."

"So, what now, Sherlock?" asked Emma, knowing a full-blown investigation would take time.

"Well, like Adams said, this is one more piece of information." Lee tapped his fingers on his thigh as he tried to make all the information fit together. "Believe me, nobody would like for this to be a natural death with no foul play involved more than me," he said. "But it's starting to get complicated. I think it's time to see what Khattib was up to at his work."

"I hope the ghost doesn't show up there, too," answered Emma.

"Actually," Lee replied, rubbing the welt growing on his aching head, "I kinda hope he does."

15

THE MAN STOOD BEHIND a large oak tree in Boston Common and watched as Lee and Emma got into a red Toyota Camry parked on Beacon Street. He was confident that he was far enough away to outrun the big man again if he needed to, although he had almost been caught.

What were they doing in the apartment? Had they discovered anything? He would have to find out what they knew.

If he hurried, he just might be able to make it to his car and tail them. At least he got a good look at the woman and her car. She should be easy to track down.

He walked up one of the many narrow, steep side streets of Beacon Hill and found his car. After getting behind the wheel, he pulled out his phone. There was a call he needed to make.

16

THE CAMBRIDGE INSTITUTE for Genetic Research sat on an impressive stretch of land along the Charles River. The well-manicured grounds and winding path that led to the entrance were evidence that no expense had been spared in the complex's construction.

Emma exhaled in awe. "Maybe I should work here."

Ever since they left Beacon Hill, she had noticed that a dark cloud had fallen over her new companion. She tried to start conversation a few times, but Lee just stared out his window, responding to her attempts with one-word answers and nods. She wondered if she had said something to offend him. Or maybe he was still upset about losing Khattib.

"Lee, are you okay? Is your head still hurting?"

He stirred in the passenger seat. "I just get lost in thought sometimes. It's been a rough year," he added, contemplating the deaths he'd endured over the past several months. "I'm fine. Thanks for asking."

"I can imagine any shoot-out would be traumatic, let alone one involving a child," she replied.

He couldn't argue with her on that point. So many people in his life had died. People he couldn't save. The girl in Iraq. The boy in Lincoln Heights. T-Bone, whose death still weighed heavily upon him. But there was one more, one that trumped them all. Although they'd only known each other for a few hours, he was beginning to feel comfortable with Emma. She was not like the other cold-hearted doctors he'd known. After a pause, he decided to tell her. "My wife died last year."

"I'm so sorry," she replied.

"She had liver cancer. It didn't take long once we knew, which was good, I guess. Wouldn't wish it on my worst enemy."

Emma pulled to the side of the entrance road and waited for him to finish. She could tell that he had never really spoken about it to anyone.

"I met Gina after I came back from Iraq. It was a rough tour. Too many of my friends died," he said quietly. "I had gotten kind of numb to it all by that time. I went home to visit my family in California. My sister Vanessa and I are real close, and she noticed I wasn't the same. I guess she thought Gina would help me find the old Lee. Well, she was right. Gina was an elementary school teacher, just like Vanessa. They taught together in the same school. Sometimes I felt like one of her students," he said with a faint smile.

Emma listened patiently, unwilling to break the spell.

"Gina became my solace. She calmed me down. Soothed me. Through her my old self was able to come alive again. Before my father died. Before the horrors of Iraq. I left my work in explosive ordnance and got out of the Marines. I was done with that life. I went to college and got a job at DHS. I just wanted to spend the rest of my life with her."

Emma glanced over and noticed his face turn sour.

"But it was all a mirage. We'd hardly exchanged vows when she learned the awful news. She suffered for months. Just like my buddies suffered in Iraq. And I was just as helpless here as I was there."

"There's nothing you could have done for her, Lee. We have no real cure for liver cancer, and nothing you or she did caused it."

"They put her in a trial," he said with a bitter laugh. "Some experimental drug. We were told that all the studies showed great results. The only problem was, she never got the drug. She was in the *placebo* group of the study and ended up with no treatment at all."

Emma was shocked. "That's unethical. In cancer trials, you receive either the research drug *or* standard therapy, never a placebo."

"Yeah, well, that's what the lawyers said, too. Nothing came of it, though. Some researcher got slapped on the wrist. Protected by the pharmaceutical company he worked for. A lot of good that did Gina. So you can understand why I'm not a big fan of researchers."

Emma paused. What could she say? She reached out to touch his hand in a gesture of sympathy.

A rapping on the driver's side window startled them both.

Emma rolled it down, and an imposing security guard with a neatly pressed blue uniform bent down to speak to them.

"Good afternoon. What is your business at CIGR, ma'am?"

Lee was in no mood for niceties. Without saying a word, he flashed his badge at the guard.

The guard examined his credentials. The expression on his face made it clear he was unhappy that his authority had been usurped, and he jabbed a finger toward the main building down the street.

"You'll have to move along. There's no stopping or standing on the street. Fire hazard," he said. "The parking lot is in front of Building One."

Lee knew the type all too well. The guard had a chip on his shoulder and felt the need to boss around a federal agent.

"Thank you," Emma replied mildly, and pulled the car back onto the road.

The three-story administration building was an architectural wonder, framed by tall glass panels on all sides. The afternoon sun reflected off the green glass, bathing the two investigators in an eerie glow as they approached. Inside, another security guard greeted them. After checking Lee's DHS identification and Emma's Harvard ID, the two were issued visitors' passes, then told to wait on an ornate but uncomfortable sofa in the reception area.

They sat in silence for ten minutes. Emma was unsure how to continue their previous conversation. She could tell Lee was uneasy in the research facility. She could hardly blame him, knowing that researchers working in one similar to this callously let his wife die.

The chime of Emma's cellphone broke the awkward silence. It was a text message from Sue at the coroner's office.

Phagocytosis assay and chemotaxis tests negative. Normal neutrophil function.

"That's odd," Emma murmured under her breath.

"What is it?" Lee asked as an attractive brunette in an expensive suit walked over to greet them.

"Dr. Hess and Agent Jansen, it's very nice to meet you. I'm Stephanie Reilly, Dr. Singh's executive assistant. Dr. Singh will see you now."

"Thank you," Emma answered.

They followed her to a private elevator that took them directly to the third floor. The elevator opened into an outer office, probably the assistant's, thought Emma. To the right was a large conference room with an extraordinary view of the Charles River.

"This way, please," the woman directed, knowing how visitors often were distracted by the view. But Lee had his eyes on the doors ahead of them. "Dr. Singh is waiting for you."

Next to the conference room was a set of smoked-glass double doors. Stephanie opened them for her guests, revealing a middle-age man with receding black hair standing behind a modern glass desk. He was impeccably dressed in an Armani suit and gold watch, probably a Rolex, Emma thought as it glimmered in the sunlight streaming into his office.

"Good day," Singh said with a tilt of his head. "Very nice to meet you both. I'm Arjun Singh, director of CIGR. The Boston Police were here this morning and told me you would be coming."

"We're here to investigate the death of one of your researchers, Jawad Khattib. You knew him?" said Lee, handing Singh his card.

The doctor gave the card a cursory look. If he was impressed by the federal agent, he didn't show it.

"Of course. We are a large facility, with several offsite labs, but I pride myself on getting to know my employees, especially the scientists." He made an exaggerated gesture toward the chairs across from his desk. "Please, have a seat."

Lee reluctantly accepted, knowing that he was probably sitting in the exact spot where CIGR's million-dollar corporate clients were courted.

"Dr. Khattib was one of our brightest molecular biologists. Very talented, indeed. His death is such a tragedy," Dr. Singh stated, his smile of greeting turning into a frown.

"Yes, of course," Emma said. "Can you tell us what project he was working on?"

"I believe he was on the Gaucher project."

"Gaucher as in Gaucher disease?" Emma asked.

"Yes, the very same. Dr. Khattib was searching for a new approach to the treatment of Gaucher using gene therapy."

"Isn't Gaucher a genetic disease? It causes blood problems in kids, right?" asked Lee, straining his memory to his college biology courses.

"It affects many systems in the body," Emma said. "The circulatory system is one of them. Gaucher is in a class of disease we term 'inborn error of metabolism.' In persons affected with Gaucher disease, there is an ineffective enzyme called glucocerebrosidase. It's found all over the body and helps, among other things, maintain cell membranes in organs. When the enzyme doesn't work, as in Gaucher, you can have damage in these organs. It can be a debilitating and fatal disease."

"Very impressive, Doctor. You have an extraordinary reputation in the academic community, and I can see it's well deserved," Singh said approvingly. "Dr. Khattib's research focused on gene therapy to suppress the expression of the deficient protein and replace it with an effective one. You see, Agent Jansen, if we could inject a new gene into a diseased host, that new gene could, in theory, cure the disease. This technology, in various forms, is currently used in cancer studies, but it is relatively unusual in the study of other diseases."

Emma knew the topic of cancer would be a difficult one for Lee. "How far along in his research was he?" she asked, attempting to steer the discussion back to Khattib's work.

"We're working on hundreds of projects, Dr. Hess. I'm afraid I'm not completely up to speed on all of them. But I do believe he was getting promising preliminary results. I think he had found a way to create a linking protein for the gene coding the disease."

"What do you mean by a linking protein?" asked Lee.

"It's a term that Dr. Khattib himself had developed," Singh explained. "You see, the problem with gene therapy, even in cancer research, is that it's quite difficult to get the synthetic genes to incorporate onto the correct spot on the patient's chromosome, or DNA. We can inject manufactured genetic material into the cell, but, until now, it couldn't incorporate into the host's DNA to make the treatment permanent. Thus, the treatment effects are limited and quickly fade, requiring further treatment. But Dr. Khattib created a protein that allows the manufactured genetic material to find and link to the defective gene on the host's DNA and incorporate itself into the actual chromosome in place of the defective gene." The doctor watched Lee carefully, presumably expecting the agent to be baffled, but Lee looked like he was following fine.

"Not only does this make the therapy more effective and long lasting, but it also ensures that the therapeutic gene affects only individuals with the defective gene. Dr. Khattib called it a linking protein for this reason. It only targets, or links with, the defective gene for which it is designed. If there is no defective gene with which to link, there will be no effect whatsoever."

"You're saying this protein can look for the bad gene, tag it, and replace it with the good one you manufacture and inject into the patient? And people without the bad gene would not be affected at all?"

"That's the idea, Agent Jansen. But not only does it tag the defective gene, as you say, it also renders that gene ineffective. Thus, the new therapeutic gene, once incorporated into the host's DNA, can transcribe the desired protein to permanently correct the disease process."

"So, in essence, Khattib found a way to tag the bad gene and turn it off with his linking protein, allowing the new gene to replace it?" Lee summarized.

His voice had a wistful tinge, and Emma could tell he was really thinking: *Where was this technology when Gina needed it?*

Singh smiled. "Precisely."

"That's incredible, Dr. Singh. This is a major breakthrough in gene therapy. Why isn't his research more widely known?" asked Emma.

"Well, his results were mixed. There's still much work to be done before this technology is available for human trials. For each success he had, there were many failures."

"What about radiation? Did Khattib's work involve using anything radioactive?" asked Lee.

"No, not at all. Any research using radioactive nucleotides, radiation therapy, or imaging is done at our facility in California," Dr. Singh replied, puzzled. "Why do you ask?"

"I don't suppose Khattib traveled to that facility anytime recently?" continued Lee.

"No, Dr. Khattib's research kept him fully occupied here. I can't see how he would have gone out there anytime recently. That facility is highly controlled and regulated. They would have contacted me before allowing him entrance. Besides, I would know if any of my researchers were involved in any other project, especially in California. When we take on a project locally, we work on it here. If we need work involving radioactive material, we have our California lab work on that part of the project and send us their results. But, honestly, we have enough on our plate here."

Although the subject of Khattib's research was fascinating, Emma was beginning to feel that the visit to the lab was a dead end. If Khattib had been involved in terrorist activity, it would likely have been on his own time, and in a more private location than CIGR offered.

"So, Khattib was able to develop a linking protein for Gaucher. What about the new genetic code to cure the disease?" asked Emma, still wondering how they had managed to keep such a medical breakthrough a secret.

"That was not part of our project. We were only contracted to create the linking protein."

"And who is your client for this project?" asked Lee.

"As I mentioned earlier, Agent Jansen, I cannot recall specific clients for every project. I will have to go through our contracts to get you that information."

"Please do that, Doctor. It might be helpful," prompted Lee.

"Can we see his lab?" Emma asked.

"Of course. Stephanie will take you there, and I'll call you as soon as I have the information on who sponsored Jawad's research," Singh answered, holding up Lee's business card.

"Thank you, Doctor. You've been very helpful," Emma replied.

Singh smiled as Stephanie stepped into the office, on cue, and escorted them out.

"How long did Khattib work here?" Lee asked Stephanie as they rode the elevator down to the basement.

"I'd say about a year or so. This was his third project, I believe."

"Did you know him well?"

"Pretty well, I guess."

Lee noticed that a subtle change had come over Stephanie's demeanor. They had been friends, at the very least. Maybe more.

She qualified her statement. "We had lunch in the cafeteria a few times, and I would visit him in his lab from time to time."

"You have a cafeteria here?" Emma asked, surprised the facility had enough employees to support the expense.

"We sure do," Stephanie said, her mood brightening. "We employ over a hundred full-time staff at this facility alone."

"The building doesn't look big enough for that," Lee said.

"Most of the research is done in the basement. You see, many of the projects involve organisms that are sensitive to light and temperature. We can control those variables best underground."

The elevator doors opened when they reached the basement, and they followed Stephanie down a busy corridor. Scientists, lab assistants, and technicians strode between rooms, all wearing white lab coats and eye protection as they wheeled samples from place to place.

"So would you say you and Khattib were friends?" Lee asked.

Stephanie answered smoothly this time. "Yes. We were friends."

"This might sound awkward, but understand that we have to explore every possibility. Do you know who he spent his free time with? Was he a member of any groups or organizations that you know of?"

"I know exactly what you are asking, Agent Jansen, and no, Jawad was not a terrorist," she said, squaring off with him. "He was a good man. He was not a zealot or fundamentalist in any way. I never heard him talk about politics and yes, he drank alcohol and ate pork, in case you were wondering."

Her defense of her colleague was admirable, but if Khattib was in fact a terrorist, the last person to know it would be his coworker. Sleepers, or terrorists working on foreign soil waiting to strike, are trained to blend in and make friends with the locals. The Boston Marathon bombing had made that clear. But it was worth a try, Lee thought.

"Thanks for indulging me," Lee said. "The question had to be asked. Let's check out his lab, and then we'll be out of your hair."

A closed door at the end of the corridor was marked with yellow police tape. Stephanie pointed at it and the three stopped in front of a placard that read J. KHATTIB.

Stephanie shifted the police tape aside and unlocked the door, using a key on her keychain that Lee assumed was a master key.

Then she turned the handle and swung the door open for the visitors.

"What's this?" asked Lee in astonishment, glancing at the bare desk with open, empty drawers.

"What about his research? Where are all the samples?" Emma added, looking at the lab bench where only a few unused test tubes lay.

Stephanie stood dumbfounded in the doorway as the three peered into the empty room.

17

A S A GENERAL RULE, the Architect didn't like to fly. He would tell everyone that his bad back made it difficult for him to take long flights, but that wasn't entirely the truth. The bigger issue was his fear of enclosed places. With the proper medication, his body could tolerate many hours in first class or on a spacious private jet. His psyche, however, was a different matter.

Images of the small closet in a faraway land where he spent years of his childhood were still vivid in his memory, as they were in his nightmares. Few knew of this fear, but then, none knew of his painful past. How could they? He let no one get that close. He lived alone, slept alone, and interacted with as few people as possible.

After obtaining his Ph.D. in chemistry, he was fortunate enough to have patented a few drugs that made him a wealthy man. He used that wealth to sequester himself from the world and everything in it, all except for the Order. It was the one thing that truly mattered to him. The Order was the family he wished he'd had as a child. With such a family, his childhood would have been perfect.

"How was the flight?" his host asked, shaking hands with him. His fellow leaders in the Order knew how uncomfortable flying was for the Architect. The purpose for his visit must be vital indeed, his colleague realized.

"My back is a little stiff, but otherwise it was fine. Thank you for seeing me on such short notice."

"Anytime, brother. How can I be of assistance?" he asked as he closed his office door, assuming this was going to be a private conversation.

The fraternity of the Order was as close as it was secretive. In fact, it was unheard of for anyone associated with the Order, leader or ordinary member, to deny the reasonable request of another. The unified strength and success of the Order relied on its members assisting each other to obtain powerful strategic positions across the globe. Once in power, members in the Order then used their resources and influence to assist each other further and promote the group's initiatives.

"I came to you because this matter is very sensitive. A man in your position, I know, needs to be careful when using telephones and electronic devices. Big Brother, as they say, is always listening," the Architect said with a smile.

"Is there something wrong with the project? I heard about the death of one of the researchers. Does this in any way compromise our goal?"

"Not at all," the Architect replied, assuring his host, a young but influential member of the Order's prestigious inner circle. "But I do need your assistance to ensure there are no further interruptions."

"Of course. What can I do?"

"As you know, the Department of Homeland Security is looking into the researcher's death. There is one investigator who is getting too close for comfort," said the Architect. "I have already tried to misdirect his efforts, but, unfortunately, he is more tenacious than I was initially led to believe."

"I see. And there is still the matter here in DC. From what I understand, the DHS is still vigorously pursuing those who killed the agent's partner, despite my efforts. They have not yet located Ajeel, but they have his family. This could be a problem. We'll have to bump up our timeline and complete the project before DHS finds Ajeel. If he talks, even I won't be able to stop the authorities from finding out about Astrea."

The Architect was current on this matter as well. "I understand. We are close to completing our project. But I will accelerate our work to produce the finished product sooner than initially planned. This should not be a problem, provided you can assist me with the DHS."

"I'll see about getting them off our backs and buying us some more time. But it won't be easy, and I'm not sure how long I can delay the investigation in Boston. I'm having a difficult enough time slowing things down here in DC. You must work on your end to eliminate the threat as well."

The Architect made a noise that sounded halfway between a cough and a snort. "Rest assured, my friend. I will deal with Agent Jansen and Dr. Hess."

"Good. I'll make some calls and see what I can do," his host replied, pressing the intercom on his phone. "Jane?"

The Architect's host glanced at the picture on his desk as he waited for the response. In the picture, a small boy and girl played on the beach with their mother. Their olive skin contrasted sharply with the white sands of Hawaii during last year's vacation.

Everything he did was for them. For his family.

His children were born in America, but, although his father was a naturalized U.S. citizen, both he and his wife had been born overseas. They had met in college and immigrated to America over a decade ago. From an early age, his father, a member of the Order himself, had prepared his son for a life in America, and he had mastered English while a child. By the time he reached American shores, his accent was barely noticeable. Hence, his assimilation into American society was much easier than was that of other ethnic minorities living in Florida.

"Yes, Senator," Jane answered.

"Would you get me Homeland Security on the line? I need to speak with Secretary Roberts right away."

"Of course, sir."

18

THAT IS QUITE ODD," Singh said, a puzzled look on his face as he walked around the small office. After a call from his assistant, the lab director had gone to the basement immediately.

"How about his work station in the lab? Is there anything there?" Emma asked. *How could Khattib's office been emptied without anyone noticing?* she wondered.

"No," Stephanie replied. "Jawad worked in here. He used that bench, and he always worked alone."

"Why would he work alone?" Lee asked. "It looks to me like there's a lot of interaction between scientists here, people milling about in and out of labs and offices."

Emma was thinking the same thing. Perhaps there was more to Khattib's work here than she had thought.

"There may have only been enough work for one researcher or perhaps there was a provision in the contract that he work alone. Many of our clients are very protective about their corporate patents. Again, I would have to refer to the details of the contract," Singh replied.

"I want to see the contract right now," Lee said. "I need to know who was financing his research."

"Do you think this had anything to do with the needle stick?" Stephanie asked.

"What needle stick?" inquired Emma.

"Two days before Jawad died, he told me he stuck himself with a needle he was using to inject one of his mice. He said he didn't report it because he was wearing gloves and didn't think the needle went all the way through."

"I sincerely doubt that had anything to do with this," Singh replied dismissively. "I can't imagine anything related to Gaucher disease could have caused Khattib's death."

Emma wasn't so sure. "What was he injecting? I need the test animal," she told the director.

"They're gone," Stephanie said, pointing to an empty corner of Jawad's research area. "He used mice and always kept them there."

"That's not normal animal research protocol, Doctor," Emma chided, turning to face Singh. "The animals are supposed to be kept in a controlled, monitored location, not in individual offices."

Singh nodded quietly, accepting the rebuke.

"There are a lot of guards here at your facility, Dr. Singh," Lee said. "We were stopped and questioned in the driveway before we even reached your campus. Yet Khattib's notes, computer, research, and test animals are all missing. How do you suppose they were taken from this office without anyone noticing it or reporting it?"

"I really don't have an answer to that. But, trust me, I will get to the bottom of this," Singh said.

Lee and Emma exchanged glances.

With nothing else to investigate in the office until the forensic team arrived to take fingerprints and samples, the two investigators decided to take some readings. For the second time that day, Lee took out his Geiger counter. This time, however, it remained silent as he swept it across every surface in Khattib's office.

"We really need to get as much information on Khattib's research as possible, Dr. Singh," Emma said when they were through.

"And the people who are paying the bills. I need that today," Lee added sternly, deciding not to follow the statement with a threat. Yet.

"As soon as I know something, you will be the first I'll call," Singh said briskly. "Stephanie, we have work to do."

"Dr. Singh, I'll be sending over some federal agents to take prints and samples from this office. They'll also have a warrant to search any room they choose, so be nice to them. Please let your guards know and have them keep anyone from entering this office in the meantime."

"Certainly. Stephanie will show you two out."

"And I'll have a copy of the contract for Khattib's work here by day's end. Correct, Doctor?" Lee said.

"You will. I will make sure of it."

Neither Emma nor Lee spoke until they were in her car and on the road out of the CIGR compound. Yet it was clear they were on the same wavelength.

"I don't believe him," Lee said flatly. "One of his researchers is dead, and Singh had no idea who sponsored the research or what the details of the project were? Come on, that's impossible. I mean, what if it was hazardous material and others were at risk of exposure? Don't you think, as CIGR director, he would have a better idea of the projects going on under his roof?" He glanced over and saw her confirming nod. "I think Singh knew *exactly* what Khattib was working on. And all of his work is gone? His computer? Samples? Even the lab animals? With that much security? I don't think so. Someone doesn't want us to know what he was working on."

"I agree. But who? Singh? His client? The man we saw in Khattib's apartment?"

"I wouldn't be surprised by anything at this point," Lee answered. He began to think out loud through everything they'd learned so far. "So, we know Khattib, or at least the man in the hospital we think was Khattib, died very quickly and violently from some crazy inflammatory response to something. Maybe radiation, maybe something else."

"Right," Emma said, picking up the thread. "It's interesting that he got a needle stick the other day. That could be the route of the exposure if this wasn't radiation poisoning. He may have stuck himself with one of his samples as he was injecting a mouse. It happens all the time. But there are two problems with this theory," Emma went on, debating her own hypothesis. "First, no pathogens have shown up yet in his blood. Second, we have no research samples, test animals, or evidence to identify the agent he was working with." She let out a breath. "It looks like I'll be running even more tests on the corpse tomorrow."

"At least an infectious or biological agent that Khattib may have gotten from a needle stick rather than from a cough or physical contact with another person would limit the risk of spread to the general population," Lee said.

"Generally speaking, that's true. But if it was a biological *weapon* and it was still in the research phase, the delivery methods could be refined at a later time." Emma looked over at Lee to make sure he was following her point. "Depending on the agent used, the vector could just as easily be aerosolized."

The Boston Marathon once again popped into Emma's head. The thought of hundreds, maybe thousands of people ending up like Khattib made her shiver.

"Okay. We know that his day job was to find a cure for Gaucher disease," Lee recapped. "So we have to consider—"

Emma slammed the brakes and swerved onto the shoulder, almost causing a three-car wreck on Memorial Drive.

"What?" Lee exclaimed. "What is it?"

"I can't believe it," Emma said slowly, the color draining from her face. "The linking protein. The needle stick. Genetic research. Could it be possible?"

"Emma, I don't understand. What are you saying? Could *what* be possible?"

This possibility was more terrible than any radiation scare. "Gaucher disease is most prevalent in the Jewish population. As many as one in every fifteen Jewish people has some form of it."

"What's the connection?"

"Look, hear me out. The yttrium-90 we found in his apartment couldn't have been linked to Khattib. Even if he brought it to his apartment the day he died, it would have decayed long before your Geiger counter registered any radiation when we were there. Besides, there was no radiation detected on his body."

"True," interjected Lee, "but both the hospital team that cared for him and the coroner thought that radiation exposure was a possible cause of his death."

"Sure, I would have come to the same conclusions reviewing the initial lab reports if I was working him up as a patient in the hospital. Remember, radiation was on the top of the differential diagnosis, but there were other things on that list as well. Doctors try to consider *all* possibilities in the more difficult cases. But radiation exposure decreases the immune cells by damaging them. I had Sue Chen run special tests that wouldn't have been ordered in the ER or ICU. Khattib was crashing so quickly, the doctors focused on preventing sepsis from killing him. At the time, radiation exposure seemed plausible from his presentation and the lab results."

"Okay, I could see how they may have jumped to that conclusion, especially after they received the call from DHS telling them to be on the lookout for a terrorist connection. But why not radiation?" Lee asked.

"Because even though his immune cells were decreased, there was no damage to their morphology. They had normal shape and function. As I said, radiation damages the shape of the immune cells. This wasn't the case with Khattib. We also can't find any gut bacteria growing in his blood. Usually the cause of death in severe radiation poisoning is sepsis from this bacteria. Both of these facts suggest that radiation was *not* the culprit." Emma explained. "It's not a dirty bomb, Lee. This was something else."

"Something else?" he asked. "Like what?"

"It's an *ethnic* weapon. He's going after their genetic code."

Lee stared at her blankly, waiting for more.

"I think Khattib was part of a plot to wipe out Israel with a bioweapon that targets a unique DNA sequence that's widespread in the Jewish population."

"We need to go see Waters right now," Lee said gravely.

19

IT WAS A SIMPLE TEXT MESSAGE. In fact, anyone reading it would not give the single line a second thought. But the message was crystal clear to the man behind the wheel. He had been trailing the red Camry all day and was eager to do more than just follow his two targets. Now he had the green light he was waiting for. After all, he and his associates had worked too hard to have their plans ruined by some nosy doctor and a down-and-out federal cop.

The text from the Architect was a godsend. He could finish off this distraction and return to his work. There was still so much to do. Mistakes had been made, forcing them to accelerate the timetable for full implementation of the Order's project. With a little luck and no further interruptions from outsiders like Hess and Jansen, their plan could be completed on the Architect's new, more aggressive schedule.

He sat idle a quarter mile back from where his targets had abruptly pulled to the side of the road. Their sudden move had forced him to quickly steer onto the shoulder himself. *What had caused the Camry's driver to act so impulsively?* he wondered.

No matter, he thought. He now had the authority he needed to end this. He put on his gloves, popped open the hidden chamber at the back of the glove box, and withdrew his Glock 42 pistol. He attached an Impuls-380A silencer, never taking his eyes off the car in front of him.

As he reached for the door handle, the Camry's brake lights illuminated. The car was moving again.

He cursed under his breath in his native language, angry that he hadn't been able to take care of the problem back at the apartment. At that time, however, the deaths of the doctor and DHS agent had not been approved. Indeed, the Order's leaders believed that such a move would cause unwanted attention, especially from the American government. They were probably correct, he allowed. They usually were. But now, as Jansen and Hess continued their investigation, the risks were growing. They had to be silenced.

The text left the man no doubt as to the Order's decision. Security had to be tighter. Things had to be stepped up a notch. Emma Hess and Lee Jansen had to die.

The man put his car in drive and pulled onto the highway, maintaining a safe distance behind the red Camry. The only question that remained was when the assassinations would take place.

20

A N *ETHNIC* WEAPON?" Undersecretary Waters asked, running his hand through his thinning hair. This was not the news he was hoping for. "Doc, you've been reading too many novels."

"I wish it was science fiction, but, unfortunately, genetically engineered ethnic cleansing may be closer to reality than previously thought," Emma replied. "Most of the technology involved in creating an ethnic weapon already exists. The biggest problem has been finding a way to target the unique genetic code in a specific population, but it sounds like Khattib solved that."

"But the coroner's report states that he died from radiation exposure," Waters retorted, wishing that he had retired last year as his wife had wanted. "You mentioned you found radioactive material in his apartment. Is that related?"

"Doubtful," Lee chimed in.

"We found traces of yttrium, which is a common isotope used in medicine," added Emma.

"Okay. Did Khattib use this in his research?"

"No," Emma replied, "not that we can tell. But it is widely available, especially if you're a medical researcher."

"The fact of the matter is Khattib wasn't building a dirty bomb," argued Lee.

The undersecretary glared at Lee. "No, that *isn't* a fact. You haven't given me any conclusive evidence that a dirty bomb isn't planted in Boston somewhere. In fact, I'm even more nervous now that you tell me you didn't find much in the way of bomb-making material. The CIA is saying he's a terrorist. The hospital and coroner were worried about radiation, and you found traces of radiation but no bomb in his apartment. That leads me to wonder where the bomb is."

"There *is* no bomb," Lee said, raising his voice. "That's what we're trying to tell you. This weapon can be much more devastating than any bomb you can imagine."

"I understand that, Agent Jansen. I also understand that you recently lost your partner back in DC and that's probably still weighing heavily on you. Maybe clouding your judgment. But I need you to focus on what we know, not what we think. You say that Khattib didn't use yttrium in his research. Enough exposure to yttrium could cause radiation poisoning, right?"

"Well, yes, but—" Emma replied.

"*And*," Waters interrupted, "Khattib, as a medical researcher, could have had access to yttrium. Hell, you found it in his apartment. You see my dilemma here? There're more clues pointing to a dirty bomb than to an 'ethnic weapon.' I can't let another terrorist bomb go off in Boston. I'm sorry, but we've got to focus on the most prominent, real-time threat, and I still see it as a bomb."

"Then you're blind," Lee snapped, and stormed out of the office. The undersecretary's inability to consider alternative threats was one thing; his bringing up T-Bone's death was enough to push Lee over the edge.

Emma and Waters watched Lee slam the door for the second time that day, causing a few agents in the Fusion Cell to turn toward the noise.

"I'm not done with my investigation into Khattib's death," Emma told Waters. "We're still waiting for some tissue sample results to come back, and I won't be able to examine the body until tomorrow morning. What if I had absolute proof that it wasn't radiation poisoning that killed Khattib? He had a needle stick in his lab just a day before—"

"Look," Waters interrupted her again, somewhat exasperated. Emma noticed the dark circles under his eyes. He was obviously under a lot of stress. "I get a call from the governor yesterday to find out anything I can about a terrorist link tied to Khattib's death. The only tangible leads I have are the reports from both the coroner and Mass. General suggesting radiation as a cause of death. Couple that with a heads-up from the CIA to look for a link to terrorism. That's it. No names, nothing else from DC. Believe me, if you have anything solid, I'm all ears. Until then, I have to put together the few clues I do have and assume some terrorist was working on a dirty bomb somewhere in Boston and it's my job to find it. I'm not putting people in the greater Boston area at risk by failing to run down what few leads I do have.

"The governor wants me to scrutinize every known source even remotely associated with terrorist activity in eastern Mass," Waters added, pointing to the monitors on the walls in the busy room. Maps and video surveillance cameras from throughout Boston lit up the screens. All major transportation, government, infrastructure, and population centers were represented. "Every resource I have is working on this. I have a full-blown crisis on my hands that started as a precautionary investigation to rule out any chance of terrorist activity."

"Can you at least put some pressure on the coroner to let me examine Khattib this evening?" Emma pleaded.

"Dr. Hess, you know how prominent Dr. Adams is in the medical community. That means a lot here in a city that has some of the best hospitals in the world. If Adams says to wait until the morning, then we have to wait. Besides, it would take me at least until then to get a court order forcing his hand. Let's play nice and keep him on our side."

Emma watched as a dozen agents surveyed the video net of all of Boston, searching for any signs of radiation using monitors and probes hidden throughout the city.

"Okay," she relented, understanding Waters's predicament. He was right. They had no real evidence, only a hunch based on her medical opinion.

"How about you keep looking into this ethnic weapon thing and keep me updated. Let me know what you find after you examine Khattib's body," the undersecretary said.

"I'll call you tomorrow," she replied. "But if the tests show conclusively that Khattib didn't die from radiation exposure, you agree to at least entertain the possibility of an ethnic weapon."

"Deal," he said, his weary eyes staring at the monitors showing the crowded streets of downtown Boston. "God help us if you're right."

Emma left Waters in the Operations Room and returned to the parking lot. Lee was standing outside her car, talking on his cell phone.

"Erik, I need you to do me another favor."

"Sure, Lee. What is it?"

"Run a name and company for me. The name is Indian: Arjun Singh. He's the director of a company called Cambridge Institute for Genetic Research here in Boston. See what you can dig up on them in our system."

"No problem. Hey, Lee, listen. We searched Ajeel's house. Found a bag with bundles of cash. More than enough money to do some major damage."

Lee knew what that meant. "No way an organized terrorist cell would keep that much cash in one location unless they were ready to make a purchase."

"Exactly. But what were they shopping for?"

"Could be anything: explosives, weapons."

"The amount of cash we found could buy a lot of weapons," Kaiser replied.

"Or maybe…just one weapon."

"A nuke?"

"Maybe…" answered Lee, trailing off. He thought back to the intercepted communications that ultimately led to his and T-Bone's trip to the Arabian Café in Alexandria, Virginia. Someone at the café had been talking to al-Harbi about a new weapon. Was it possible that Khattib was working on that very weapon? Could the two cases be related? That would mean the suspects from the Arabian Café ambush were somehow connected to Lee's latest assignment, too. "Did Daif and Sanabel Ajeel know Jawad Khattib?"

"I don't think so. But they're denying everything at this point. We haven't broken them yet. I'll keep on them."

"Thanks. Good work, Erik. Keep me posted and let me know what you hear about CIGR."

"Sure thing. Out, here."

"Was that about your partner?" Emma asked.

Lee nodded. "Not much yet. We'll see what DHS has on our pal Singh."

Emma beeped the door locks open, and they both got into the car.

"I have another class to teach in an hour," she said. "After that, I'll go see if Dr. Adams is back. Maybe I can convince him to let us see the body tonight. At the very least, I can go over the pathology slides with Sue Chen. Maybe run some DNA tests on the tissue samples she has from the autopsy."

"Good idea. I'll head back to the hospital to see if Manny was able to track down any of those cultures drawn when Khattib was in the ICU."

Emma sped down the block. "I hope the labs shed some insight into the cause of death," she said. "If those cultures are negative and the body's clean, we got nothing."

"I don't think that's going to happen," Lee replied. "We're onto something, I know it."

21

LEE SAT BACK in the passenger seat as he pondered the case. What were the terrorists in DC going to buy? Was he rushing to conclusions in assuming the case in Boston was related? Regardless, if Khattib or CIGR or someone else was making a weapon of mass destruction, where was it?

He rubbed his forehead. Working two cases hundreds of miles apart was tough, especially after just losing his partner. But he had Emma. Lee glanced over at her, catching a flash of her leg as her skirt rode up above her knee as she worked the gas pedal. He was surprised that he'd noticed. He'd been dead to that sort of thing for so long.

Lee refocused his thoughts. "Do you think Khattib figured out a way to tag a bad gene and replace it with a therapeutic one?"

"Well, gene therapy has been around, at least in theory, for decades," answered Emma. "It's a remarkable concept, really.

Basically, it's a matter of inserting a new genetic code into a damaged cell to alleviate symptoms of a disease. This therapeutic gene sits in the cell, producing proteins or other substances that treat the symptoms. But until now, as far as I know, no one's been able to get the new gene to actually insert into the host DNA, to make the changes permanent."

"If what we have now works to alleviate symptoms, why the need to insert the new gene into the DNA?" Lee asked.

"Unless the gene is permanently integrated into a patient's DNA, the effects are limited," Emma explained. "Continuous retreatment is needed for the patient to retain benefit from the therapy. But once inside the DNA, the effects of the new gene become permanent. If Khattib was able to create a linking protein to insert a new gene wherever he wanted in someone's DNA, it's truly a game changer."

"But what about an ethnic-specific weapon?" Lee asked. The discussion was drifting into an area in which Lee had little experience. He appreciated that Emma could fill in the gaps.

A warning note came into her voice. "There's a debate in the medical community about the applications of gene therapy and this technology. I read an article a few months back about gene therapy and ethnic-specific weapons. You see, the Human Genome Project is relatively well known. It's a fantastic project that's responsible for most of today's genetic breakthroughs. It's mapped out the entire human genome, or DNA, and identified many individual genes linked to specific diseases. With this knowledge, we can create therapies to help cure disease."

Her fingers played on the steering wheel, reflecting her excitement. "Another project has been going on as well, called the Human Genome Diversity Project," she continued. "Not as well known. The HGDP has collected DNA samples from different populations throughout the globe. It's published articles looking at anthropologic, migratory, and disease-prevalence data of these populations. This is also important work."

"Sounds like it could be useful." Lee nodded. "But, in the wrong hands, also potentially dangerous."

"Exactly. Some people worry that scientific data that points out genetic differences in specific populations can be misused by extremists or even corrupt governments. Some have even suggested that it may be possible—in theory, at least—to build a weapon to target these particular genetic differences in populations."

"So instead of tagging bad genes and replacing them with good genes, a weapon could do the opposite?" Lee mused. "Maybe insert a gene that can be harmful in a specific population or race where that gene is prevalent?"

"That's one possibility, yes. It's all just theory, really. The science isn't there yet, as far as we know. Like I said, we don't currently have the technology to tag bad genes and permanently replace them on the chromosome with different genes. But if Khattib developed a linking protein that can do just that, the ability to wipe out an entire population by targeting their ethnic DNA becomes a hell of a lot more possible."

"And the Human Genome Diversity Project has already found and published specific genes that are unique to certain populations?" Lee inquired.

"Some of that information is out there, yes. Gaucher is one example. Other genetic sequences for specific populations throughout the world have been documented as well," Emma explained. "It's one way that people are able to track their ancestry to different continents and even down to individual tribes. Ethnic groups can have a single gene that is unique to them, no matter how diluted the group's DNA has become from mixing with other ethnicities. If a destructive protein can be engineered to attach to that ethnic-specific gene and modify or destroy it, it could devastate an entire race of people."

"The ultimate ethnic cleanser," Lee muttered as they approached Harvard Medical School.

"You said it."

Emma pulled into the parking garage, and they walked back to the Harvard T.H. Chan School of Public Health on Huntington Avenue.

"I think I'm going to get my teaching assistant to take over my class this afternoon. I really want to see if I can convince Dr. Adams to let me examine the body before he leaves for the day."

"Okay," Lee said, looking down at his phone at a text he just received. "Manny was able to get copies of all the labs and doctors' notes from Khattib's hospitalization."

"Good. I only received the summary. We still don't know what triggered the inflammation that killed him. If it strikes again, we won't know how to treat it unless we can figure out what the weapon is and how it works. I'll review the notes tonight to see if I can come up with anything."

"If, of course, Khattib is truly is dead, you mean," Lee interjected.

She gave him a look of disbelief. "This is making my head hurt. Let's regroup later to go over what Manny gives you. We can meet in my office. Do you know where it is?"

"Yep. Already staked you out this morning. Nice lecture on ricin, by the way."

"Stop stalking me," she replied with a grin and waggle of her finger.

Just then Lee's phone rang. "Jansen," he said.

"Jansen, it's Jay Kowalski. How's everything going up there in Boston?"

"Fine. We're going over all the medical evidence to see how the scientist died," he said, wondering why the DHS director was calling him.

"Good. Listen, I just got a call from Undersecretary Waters. He was mad as hell. Said you're going rogue on this investigation."

"That SOB," Lee replied, prompting Emma to stop and listen in. "Just because he's set on his conclusions doesn't mean I have to blindly follow. I have my own leads. I shared them with the illustrious undersecretary, but he didn't want to hear anything that deviates from his own misguided conclusions."

"I understand, but everything we're getting from CIA suggests Khattib was a terrorist. Lee, everyone's worried about a dirty bomb going off in downtown Boston. Just work with Waters on this one, okay?"

"But he's wrong."

"If he's wrong, then great. No bomb. But if he's right, he'll need your help. You're our expert on dirty bombs—that's why you're there."

Lee felt like he was banging his head against the same wall. "As the expert, I'm telling you there's no dirty bomb."

"Just work with Undersecretary Waters, okay?"

Lee held back. Jay Kowalski was a friend as well as his boss. Jay, his former Marine commanding officer, was the one who helped him get into DHS. Lee never allowed himself to forget that. "All right, but I'm continuing to investigate my own leads."

"That's fine. Just keep an open mind. Unless you have any evidence to the contrary, we still have to consider a dirty bomb, okay? And stay in touch with Waters. If you run into any trouble with him, let me know and I'll talk to him."

"Fine. But you have to do me a favor. Dr. Hess, the Harvard toxicologist and occ med doc you had me contact when I got up here, wants to have a look at the body. The coroner's stonewalling us. I asked Waters to help, but I doubt he'll lift a finger for me."

"Okay. I'll see what I can do."

"Thanks. And don't worry, I'll play nice with Waters," Lee said. "Out here."

Lee shook his head. He didn't want to be rude to his boss by cutting the call short, but he also didn't want to hear any orders he might later end up disobeying. He had promised to communicate with Waters. Kowalski said nothing about *working* with Waters.

"Who was that?" Emma asked.

"My boss in DC. Apparently, Waters was none too happy with my attitude earlier and went crying to Mommy."

"Well, you *were* kind of hard on him."

"He's a desk jockey. But I'll be a good little soldier for now. It's the least I can do for Kowalski."

"Kowalski? Is that your boss?"

"Yeah. He was my former commander in Iraq. A good guy. He brought me into DHS."

"What did you do in Iraq?" Emma asked, curious.

"Explosive ordnance disposal. I did it before I went to college. The early part of the war. I was a Marine. Served with Kowalski in Karbala. It's a sacred city in Iraq—important to the Shi'ites."

"That must have been stressful."

"I suppose. No more stressful than the duties of every other American over there. But we had our moments, I guess…" Lee trailed off, his mind drifting to a particular day in that sandy city, one that had scarred him for life. He tried to brush away the vivid memory. "I used to picture the devices in my head," he said, laughing weakly. "I could see in my mind the inner workings of the mechanical triggers and electronic detonators. It was almost like a game."

Emma looked concerned. "There's more to the Karbala story, isn't there?" she said quietly.

Lee took a deep breath. He hadn't spoken much about the events of that day. Of course, he had confided in Gina. She had held him tightly those first few weeks upon his return. She was the one who helped him deal with the guilt. The psychologist he was forced to see after the shooting in Lincoln Heights broached the subject of posttraumatic stress disorder, but Lee wouldn't open up. For some reason, though, he opened up to Emma.

"There's a holy time in Islam. The Shi'ites commemorate when one of their early leaders and his family were massacred. It's called Ashura, and they get very emotional. Tensions run high. The Sunni soldiers guarding the streets were on alert for any attacks from Shi'ite militia groups and Muqtada al-Sadr's insurgents. I was there supporting the Iraqi EOD units clearing the streets of IEDs. That's improvised explosive devices," he clarified, and she nodded. "There was a young Shi'ite girl, couldn't have been more than seven or eight, walking in the streets. She approached the group of Iraqi soldiers that I was assigned to. It was obvious to all of us that the girl was wearing a suicide vest. We could see the bulge from the partially hidden explosives and the wires protruding from her jacket. I yelled at her to stay away, but she kept walking toward us. The Sunni soldiers raised their weapons. They were going to shoot her before she could get any closer. I begged them not to shoot. But they told me that she was just a Shi'ite terrorist. That it was okay to kill her."

"That's terrible," Emma said.

"I finally jumped out from behind the barricade and ran up to the girl. There were hundreds of locals all around us, pounding their heads and cutting their chests with knives. It's part of the tradition of Ashura, symbolizing how their leader was murdered centuries ago. Everyone was screaming antigovernment and anti-U.S. slurs. It was complete chaos. I tried to stand between the girl and the soldiers so they couldn't get a clear shot at her. She was staring at me, tears in her eyes, as I tried to disarm the vest as fast as I could."

"Who would do such a thing? Put explosives on a girl..."

"Probably her family," Lee replied. "Or an insurgent threatening her family. Life is cheap in war. I was able to trace the wires that went to the detonator and clipped them. She saw the relief in my eyes and relaxed some. I think I even saw a smile cross her lips. She raised her arms. I don't know why. Maybe to give me a hug. I'll never know."

"They shot her?" Emma said, shocked.

"Two rounds. One in the chest, the other in her head. I screamed as she hit the ground. It was madness after that. The Shi'ites surrounding us were already in an uproar because of Ashura. They ran past me as I checked for a pulse, knowing there was no way I was going to find one. I looked up and saw the villagers storm the checkpoint. AK-47 fire rang out and more people screamed. So many innocent people died that day."

"They left you alone?"

"It wasn't because they loved Americans, I can tell you that. I just sat there in disbelief, unable to take my eyes off the girl. She was so young. Then shadows around me blocked out the sun and I looked up. Dozens of Shi'ites, covered in blood, surrounded me. Suddenly it became eerily quiet. They had killed the Iraqi soldiers. Tore them limb from limb. I was next. But as they closed in, a man shouted at them. They backed away, letting him in. He was probably in his fifties but looked older. He stood there staring at me while two younger men came and picked up the girl's body. The crowd broke up and followed the two men carrying the girl as they walked down one of the side streets. That left me and the old man. I noticed a tear in his eye as he turned and walked away."

"They let you go? Why?"

"They saw that I was trying to help her. Maybe they felt enough people had died that day. I don't know. But not a day goes by when I don't think about. it."

"That's understandable. What you went through, Lee," she said, moved by the story. "No one should have to go through something like that."

"Well, I did. And so did many others. I was a mess when I got back to the States. Then I met Gina. She helped me find myself again. She got me back on my feet. I went to college, got my degree. After Gina heard from one of my Marine buddies that our old commanding officer was with the DHS, she got in touch with him."

"Kowalski?"

"Yep. He believed in me. Gave me a second chance after I got my degree and brought me into the DHS. He knew what I'd been through in Iraq and knew that I was good at my job."

Emma put a hand on his shoulder. "Lee, you can't save everyone. The Iraqi girl. Gina. Your partner back in DC. Even this case. I know you're trying. Maybe to make up for some of the losses you've experienced. Maybe even to gain some control back over your life. But you don't need to do this alone. Let people around you help you. We might need Waters."

She's right, he thought, looking at his watch. "We'll see. I gotta go meet Manny. He finishes his shift in 30 minutes. I'll see you back here in a couple of hours."

"Okay. I'll call you when I leave the coroner's office."

Lee stood on the street corner, watching Emma walk away. Standing there, deep in thought about all that had transpired in his life over the past decade, he failed to notice the young Arab watching him who stepped off the curb and headed across the busy street.

22

THE MIDAFTERNOON DOWNTOWN TRAFFIC was already picking up. Emma decided to take the T rather than drive: She'd shave at least a half hour off her round trip by taking the short walk to the Orange Line followed by a quick bus ride that let her off around the corner from the medical examiner's office.

The sidewalk was crowded as Emma passed the colleges that lined Huntington Avenue on her way to the subway station. Students poured out of the buildings, eager to spend a few hours at local pubs before returning to their dorms to study.

Emma had always been a good student. At times like this, she missed her days as a Columbia undergrad. Harvard Medical School was even more demanding, but it cemented her love for medicine. She had a deep, rewarding feeling every time she was able to help a patient. This more than made up for long hours, the heavy med school debt, and the demanding lifestyle of a physician. While many of her colleagues had abandoned medicine due to declining pay, onerous regulations, and increasing litigation, she remained true to her profession, to her passion.

Fall in Boston was turning to winter, and a chill hung in the air as Emma headed for the entrance to the Orange Line. She couldn't shake the feeling that she was being watched. She looked over her shoulder, searching for seedy characters lurking in the shadows, not that she'd even recognize them. Khattib's case and the talk of terrorism at the Fusion Center made her edgy. Unfortunately, cloak-and-dagger cases weren't covered in medical school.

She entered the station and descended to the subway platform. The crowd swelled as commuters tried to beat rush hour. Emma stood on the edge of the platform, waiting for her train to arrive.

As she stood in the crowd, Emma thought through the details of the case. Khattib's official research was Gaucher disease. As such, he would have had access to samples with the genetic code for the defective gene. If he could create a linking protein for a gene that caused Gaucher and replace it with a gene that destroyed the host, one-tenth of the world's Jewish population could be lost. It might not destroy Israel, she thought, but it would be a devastating blow both strategically and psychologically. Israel's medical infrastructure would be pushed to the brink, with huge numbers of patients admitted to ICUs across the country. And if an ethnic bioweapon preceded a conventional military attack, it might be enough to turn the tide of battle in favor of Arab or Iranian invaders.

But Khattib was not Jewish. Why would a weapon that he constructed against Jews have affected him if he did, in fact, accidentally inject himself with the prototype? It was unlikely that he had the Gaucher gene, given that he was an Egyptian Arab. Surely Khattib would have researched his own background prior to developing a weapon against the disease. At the very least, he would have used a Punnett square to ensure there were no traces of the disease in his immediate family.

The other nagging issue was the man in Khattib's apartment. There was no doubt that someone with Khattib's ID died at MGH and was now lying in the city morgue. In these litigious times, Khattib's identification would have been checked and rechecked upon admission, again at his death, and finally at his body's transfer to the morgue and autopsy. Most likely facial recognition against the ID on his body would have been enough initially, although the likeness may not have been a perfect match due to illness. After what he had been through, Khattib would not have looked much like his ID photo. But he was unconscious throughout his admission, and, at the time, the priority was saving his life. However, Adams would have pursued further confirmation of the identity during the autopsy. She'd have to confirm that with the coroner.

If the deceased was in fact Jawad Khattib, then who was in Khattib's apartment?

"Attention, passengers," the overhead speaker announced. "The next train for Oak Grove is now approaching."

Emma looked to the right and saw the train entering the station. She was holding her spot just behind the yellow line as the crowd behind her pressed forward. When the train was only a few feet away, she felt an open hand press hard on her back. Her ankle turned as it crossed the yellow line, the heel of her shoe breaking and pitching her forward. Emma stumbled toward the track in front of the oncoming train.

She closed her eyes tightly, hoping that it would be enough to shield her from the train's tremendous force. Besides, if she was going to die, she didn't want to see it coming.

Just then a hand reached out from above her and grabbed the shoulder of jacket, pulling her to safety just as the train rushed by with a strong gush of air and the piercing blare of its horn.

Emma spun around to see her rescuer's face. It was the second time she had seen the man today.

"Come," Khattib's ghost whispered. "We must get away from here quickly. It's not safe."

The man could have let her die there on the tracks. Instead, he had saved her from certain death. That earned him enough trust for her to follow him away from the train station. Besides, she had questions that needed answers.

23

LEE AND MANNY sat in the Eat Street Café at Massachusetts General Hospital.

"Good call on your part, teaming up with Emma. She's one smart lady," Manny said between sips of Red Bull.

"She's been a lot of help. And so have you," answered Lee, taking a bite of his glazed doughnut. "So, what are your thoughts on who we saw at the apartment?"

"All I know is that it wasn't Khattib. No way the General would have made a patient ID mistake like that. Besides, the coroner did an autopsy, right?"

"Yeah. I don't doubt someone's dead, but was it Khattib or someone else with his ID?"

Manny didn't buy the theory. "Why would someone that looked like Khattib have his ID and present to the ED?" he asked. "Could have been anyone back at his apartment. I'm sure the Islamic Brotherhood or whatever terrorist group you think he was with would want to sweep the apartment to get rid of any evidence."

"What about Emma's thoughts on an ethnic bioweapon?" Lee asked the former Army Ranger.

"Now, *that's* interesting. I spoke with the ICU team this afternoon, and they weren't convinced it was radiation sickness either, but with a low ANC coupled with the intel they got from your boys, they certainly considered it."

"I'd still like to know who from DHS made that call."

Manny held up his hands in innocence. "No idea, man. Those are your peeps. You'll have to ask them."

The next time Lee saw Waters, he would do just that.

"An ethnic weapon," continued Manny. "An amazing concept, really. You know how famous people trace their ancestry to some indigenous group on a remote island or jungle somewhere? We only have about twenty-five thousand genes in our DNA, but each gene is made up of a specific sequence of pairs of DNA subunits called nucleotides. There are literally billions of these nucleotide base pairs. The average gene is made up of a couple of thousand nucleotides but can be made up of many more. To blow your mind even further, Lee, think about this. All of our genes, everything we see in the human body, come from proteins made by just two percent of our DNA."

"What's the rest of our DNA used for?"

"That, my friend, is the riddle of the Sphinx. We have no clue. We know that some of it, so-called junk DNA, are nucleotide sequences that don't encode for any proteins. They may have been used by our prehistoric ancestors millions of years ago, but as we evolved, these genes became obsolete. Other parts of our DNA have genes that originate from organisms that have been incorporated into our chromosomes. Viruses, et cetera. But there are specific sequences of nucleotides and genes that are unique to certain populations. All of these genetic variations are what makes individuals different but populations similar. If you can identify these unique sequences in populations and create a way to target those genes, it is theoretically possible to destroy an entire race."

Lee absorbed the thought of a lab-designed genocidal weapon. Scientists could literally wipe out everyone on the planet. But, he reminded himself, they couldn't save Gina.

"How could this science be used as a weapon?"

"Easily," Manny replied, finishing his drink and leaning back in the metal chair. "You could replace the ethnic-specific gene with one that encodes for something bad, like a cancer, for instance. Put it right into someone's DNA. Remember, your DNA controls the entire body. What better way to destroy the body than to program its own DNA to do it? But all this is still theory. The good news is that we haven't been able to insert manufactured genetic sequences into specific locations on a person's chromosome. Even in cancer research, that's been problematic."

"What if I told you Khattib did find a way to do just that?" Lee asked.

"I would say that mankind has a serious problem on its hands," replied Manny.

Lee's phone broke the silence.

"What? When? I'll be right there," Lee said into the phone as he rose and grabbed his coat.

"What's up?" Manny asked.

"Someone just tried to kill Emma," Lee said.

"Our phantom?"

"That's what I'm going to find out."

"I'm coming with you," said Manny, and ran after Lee.

24

WITH TRAFFIC, it took them almost twenty minutes to drive the three miles to the Harvard Medical School campus. When they reached the Kresge Building, Lee and Manny skipped the painfully slow elevator and took the stairs to the fourteenth floor. Lee struggled to keep up with Manny as the men reached the top.

As they entered Emma's office, their jaws dropped when they saw the face of the man sitting across from her.

"Gentlemen, meet Mr. Khattib. Mr. *Ashraf* Khattib," she said with a wave of her hand.

The two men stared at the young man sitting with a solemn look on his face. He certainly resembled the picture on Khattib's ID, thought Lee.

"Brother?" Manny asked.

"Jawad was my older brother," Ashraf answered in heavily accented English. "We are one year apart."

"You were in his apartment?" queried Lee.

Another nod.

"Ashraf is a student at Yale. Veterinary studies. When he heard about his brother's death, he came up here to snoop around a little. Tell them what you told me, Ashraf," coaxed Emma.

"My brother was murdered," he said flatly.

"Why do you think he was murdered?" Manny asked.

"Jawad came to see me in New Haven last week. He told me that he feared his research was not what it appeared."

"Well, that's an understatement," Manny retorted.

The young man's face remained impassive. "You don't understand. Let me explain."

"Please do. And while you're at it, explain the radioactive material and Muslim Brotherhood propaganda we found in your brother's apartment," Lee demanded.

"Jawad was not a terrorist. Just because we are Arab and Egyptian does not make us Ikhwan Muslimeen," he replied. "I do not know where it came from, but it did not belong to my brother. He did not work with radioactive material and he was not making a bomb."

"Go on, Ashraf," Emma said gently.

"He was researching a way for gene therapy to cure Gaucher disease. He was trying to create proteins to help identify the defective DNA sequences to allow treatment."

"Yes, we know," Lee said impatiently.

"Let him finish," Emma chided.

"The preliminary steps of his research called for him to create a prototype of the linking protein to test on animals. For this, he designed a protein to target the albino-deletion complex in mice." The man's eyes flickered as he looked around to see if everyone followed him. "If his prototype was successful, he would move on to the human model to modify the linking protein, as Jawad called it, to attach to the defective gene in Gaucher. Throughout every step of his research, he was required to send samples of his work to the principal investigator for further testing and analysis."

"And who was that?" asked Lee.

"Jawad didn't know." Khattib ran his hand over his face. There was no mistaking the grief and frustration in his gesture. "That began to concern him. He noticed that some of the linking protein samples he sent away came back to him altered. The altered prototype he injected into the mice killed the albino mice. When he examined their cells, however, he found only a massive inflammatory response, with nothing suggesting the cause. The linking proteins that he created were harmless," Ashraf Khattib continued more forcibly. "Their only function, as originally designed by Jawad, was to identify and tag the albino-causing gene, not to have any other effect. Treatment for the defective gene was not part of his research."

"Who was supposed to do that research?" Lee prodded.

"Jawad did not even know if such research was being conducted. His project was limited in its scope." The man looked at them earnestly. "But his results were incredible. Never before had a linking protein been designed that would have the ability to seek out a specific genetic sequence and bind to it so treatment could target and replace the damaged gene. It was a remarkable achievement."

Manny and Emma nodded their heads in agreement.

"How do you know all of this?" Lee asked skeptically.

"We are both scientists as well as brothers," Khattib said with a private smile. "Jawad and I were close. We discussed our work all the time, especially since his involved animal models."

"What else did Jawad tell you?" asked Emma.

"He said that the mice should not have died, and he asked me for my insight into what might have killed them. I told him that he should again inject the live mice with the altered prototype he received back from the principal investigator. This time, however, he should analyze their DNA to see what changes the serum caused at the genetic level. That was the last time I spoke with him."

"It had to be the needle stick," Emma informed them. "Whatever changes they made to his prototype that killed the mice must have also killed Jawad."

"And what about the poster and propaganda we found?" pressed Lee.

"I told you, we are not terrorists. I don't know who put those in his room," Khattib protested. "I have visited Jawad in his apartment many times. He has never had posters like the one I saw above his desk. Jawad never spoke of jihad or extremism. He was a scientist. That was his life. He was happy here in America. He had no interest in politics."

"So what were you doing in his apartment?" Lee asked.

"Same as you. I was looking for my brother's killer. I was hoping there might be further clues to his research on his computer. Surely his death was related to this research."

"Where *is* his computer?" Emma asked.

The young man's eyes widened. "I don't know. He had a desktop that he kept in his apartment. It was gone. Perhaps taken by the same people who hung that poster," he said to Lee.

"Ashraf, why did you run when you saw us in the apartment?" Emma asked.

"I didn't know who you were. My first instinct was that you were the ones responsible for his death. I waited outside his apartment and watched you go to your car. I noticed the HSPH Faculty sticker on your windshield and used my phone to look you up on the School of Public Health website. Once I realized who you were, I decided you were also trying to discover what had happened to Jawad."

"He's good, Lee. Any room for him at DHS?" Manny asked.

"Let's get back to the case," Lee said, ignoring Manny. "So, you've been following us?"

"No. I've been waiting near the quad, hoping to see Dr. Hess's car return to the parking lot. I wanted to tell her who I was, to ask if we could work together to find out who is responsible for Jawad's death. But she was with you, and I wasn't yet sure who you were. I waited until she was alone and then I followed her, looking for a safe place where I could approach her."

"And that's when someone tried to push me in front of the train," Emma added. "I was waiting for the T when someone pushed me just as the train pulled in. Thank God Ashraf was nearby. He grabbed my shoulder and pulled me back onto the platform. He saved my life."

"Did you see who pushed you?" Lee asked.

"No. The platform was packed. It could have been anyone. Believe me, we didn't stick around to ask questions."

Manny said, "I think maybe we need a new strategy. The old one doesn't seem to be working very well."

Lee frowned at him again. "This is getting out of hand. Someone tried to kill you, Emma, have I got that right?"

"So it seems," she answered, and a shadow of fear entered her face.

"Don't you see? We're getting close," Manny said excitedly. "They're scared. Scared enough to try to kill you. We can't give up now."

Lee thought grimly that they were in much murkier waters. "I'm going to find out who's responsible."

"No, we are," Emma reminded him.

"Count me in," Manny said.

"I want to help as well," said Khattib. "Jawad was my brother. Whoever killed him is also trying to smear his reputation, labeling him a terrorist. It's too late to save Jawad but not too late to save his legacy. Jawad was a gentle man."

"Okay, okay," Lee said, raising his hands. "We work together on this. But everyone here agrees that they will stand down if and when I say it's too dangerous. We've already had one close call today. Agreed?"

"Agreed," Emma said.

"Okay," replied Khattib.

"No way, man," Manny said. "I didn't spend all that time in Ranger school to back off when things get dangerous. Besides, you might need someone to bail you out of trouble, Jarhead."

"Jarhead?" Emma repeated with a puzzled look.

"Don't ask," replied Lee, shaking his head. "I made the mistake of telling Ranger Rick here that I was in the Marines. Never mind."

"Okay, well, you soldier boys work that out," Emma teased, looking at her watch. "I've had about as much excitement as I can handle for one day. It's too late to go over to the coroner's office now. I called Sue Chen before you guys got here and told her I'd see her in the morning at eight. Now I'm going to go home and have a closer look at these medical files."

"Let's regroup in the morning," suggested Lee. Emma was right, it *had* been a full day. But there was something he still had to do, and he wanted to do it alone.

Manny said, "Lucky for you I have the next three days off. So it looks like y'all are stuck with me. See you at the coroner's office at eight a.m."

"Will you be all right tonight, Ashraf?" Emma asked.

"I'll be okay," he said quietly. "I have friends in Boston. I'll be at the coroner's office at eight o'clock tomorrow."

Lee watched the young man closely as he left the room. He had a pretty good sense about people, and Ashraf Khattib didn't seem to have any ulterior motives.

"Let me give you a ride home," he said to Emma after Manny made his exit.

"I'll be fine, Officer, really."

"Let's just make sure, okay?" Lee pressed. "Someone already tried to get to you once. Who knows what else they'll try?"

Fear again showed in her eyes. "But why me?" she asked. "I'm just a doctor, not a law enforcement agent."

"Because they've researched you. They know your reputation, and that you may be on to them," Lee said, trying to be gentle. "Manny's right, they're getting nervous. And nervous bad guys make *me* nervous."

"But how would they know what we know? That we're putting the pieces together?"

"That's what I'd like to know. I'm not sure who to trust. In fact, we're checking you into a hotel until this blows over," Lee announced, having just thought of it. "I'm not taking any more chances. Cash only, no credit cards."

Emma pursed her lips and stood with her hands on her hips for a moment. Seeing his firm resolve, however, she relented.

"Okay. You win. But I need to go to my house first to pick up a few things."

Lee understood her resistance. She considered herself a strong, independent woman and felt confident enough to take care of herself. But she had to realize that she was out of her element if terrorists were involved. "All right, but then straight to the hotel."

The two walked down the street to Lee's car without saying a word. Lee knew, despite Emma's earlier attempt at levity, that what had happened to her at the train station shook her up. He recalled how he couldn't sleep for two nights after his first firefight in Herat. Some people never got used to it.

"Are you sure you're okay?" Lee asked after driving a few miles toward her home in Brookline.

"I'm fine, really. It's just been a long day," she said with a feigned smile. "I need some rest."

As they pulled up to Emma's home, Lee checked the vehicles up and down the street.

"I'll just be a minute," Emma told him, her hand on the doorknob.

"Wait," he said. "Let me come up with you. Just to make sure it's safe."

This time his protectiveness earned a grateful smile.

"Thanks," she said.

Emma unlocked the door to her apartment. Through the opened doorway he saw the large windows in her living room, flanked by light curtains lined with trailing yellow flowers. The feminine touch startled him, although he should have expected it.

"Let me take a quick look around," he said, stepping inside before Emma had a chance to protest.

Although she was touched by the chivalrous gesture, she felt he was being overcautious. Emma stood in the living room by the front door as Lee walked around the apartment, turning on lights and checking closets. Finally, he returned to the living room.

"Okay, all clear."

"Thanks," she said with a smirk and went into her bedroom to gather some clothes.

A minute later, she was back with a gym bag and laptop. She placed the bag on the sofa and unzipped it.

Lee noticed some lace peeking out from the pile of clothes and instinctively turned away. He felt dormant feelings begin to reawaken within him that both surprised and thrilled him. He'd only known his new "partner" for a short time—but her effect on him was undeniable.

"Okay, all ready," Emma replied, zipping up the bag after stuffing the laptop inside on top of her clothing. As she stood up, she noticed Lee was blushing slightly. She allowed a small smile to cross her lips. Did that mean what she thought it meant?

She hoped so…then again, maybe her apartment's overzealous heater was to blame.

"We'd better go," Lee said abruptly, and the moment was gone. Without saying another word, he led Emma down the stairs and back to the car. Soon they were back on the road again.

Lee used every trick he knew to ensure they weren't being followed to the Westin near Copley Square, where he had her check in under an assumed name after flashing his badge and speaking with the manager.

"You'll be safe here," he told her in the lobby.

"Thanks, Lee," she said, gently touching his hand. "You get some rest yourself. Remember, we're a team. We'll figure this all out together."

Lee smiled. It was a genuine smile. He felt his old self reemerging. It felt good.

He nodded and walked back to his car. Then he pulled out into traffic and pressed on the accelerator.

He still had work to do this evening.

25

"I JUST LEFT LONGWOOD. Hess and Jansen have gone for the evening," the man reported.

"Why did you not kill them?" the Architect asked angrily. Wasn't that why the man was a fellow member of the Order's elite leadership, because of his specific skills?

"Why don't *you* do it?" the man retorted. "I don't work for you, remember? We all have our roles to play. It *must* look like an accident. There has already been enough attention because of your ill-conceived project. You stick to your job and let me do mine. We don't need to make a bigger mess."

The Architect hated to let the insult pass, but he had no choice at this juncture. Time was running out. The man on the other end of the line was nothing more than a hired gun, a soldier in the war. The Architect was one of the generals. But his brethren had decided to send the assassin to help contain the problem. So, for the moment, he would play along.

He took a deep breath and continued the conversation. "So what is your plan, then?"

"It's already arranged. By this time tomorrow, you'll be free to finish your work without interference."

"Tomorrow, then," the Architect replied, and hung up. He stared at the phone and thought about the man with whom he had just spoken. Once the project was complete and his own influence in the Order expanded, he would ensure that the assassin disappeared. There would be no room in *his* organization for such brutes. Perhaps he would even use the new weapon on him. Why not? Sooner or later they would need to expand the application of the weapon to other ethnicities.

"Yes," he said to himself in his darkened office. "Once *I* control the Order."

"Sir" came a voice accompanying a soft knock on his door.

"What is it?" he replied, awakened from his daydream.

His assistant entered, his eyes straining to see the shadow seated at the desk.

The Architect was accustomed to the dark. In fact, he preferred it. After all those years of living in darkness, as terrifying as it was when he was a child, it was now a source of comfort to the old man.

"You have a VTC. From Lebanon."

The Architect reached under his desk and turned on his computer. Always cautious about the watchful eyes of others, soon after the introduction of the internet, he had developed the habit of keeping his electronic devices off to minimize hacking and unauthorized access to personal files.

"Come," he said to his apprentice. "Let us see their progress since your little mishap with Khattib."

The assistant used his hands to guide him around the chairs in front of his boss's desk. Yet it wasn't so dark that the old man couldn't see the hurt look cross the younger man's face. He didn't usually permit any sign of weakness from his subordinates, but he took a perverted pleasure in knowing he controlled the lives of those around him.

The light from the computer monitor cast an eerie glow on the Architect's thin, sharply angled face.

"I advised our colleagues overseas to refine the targeting mechanism using Khattib's research as well as their analysis of the prototype he accidentally injected. Let us hope they have some good news for us."

As the Architect spoke, he logged into his computer and opened the video teleconferencing application. On screen, a number of faces appeared in a room filled with tables and lab equipment.

"Good day, sir," said a heavyset woman with a thick accent, her graying hair pulled back in a bun. Her plump face took up most of the VTC screen.

"Hello, Nora," the Architect replied. "I trust the project is on schedule?"

"Ahead of schedule, actually," the scientist said proudly. "Khattib was brilliant. I analyzed the samples you sent me from his lab. He was much further along than I expected."

"That's good to hear. And the vector?"

Nora's smile broadened further. "See for yourself."

The woman bun turned the video camera to her left. Along the wall were two glass cylinders large enough to hold a person. Nora worked the camera so the image at the bottom of one of the cylinders came into focus. When the assistant saw what was inside, he began to dry heave into the nearby trash can. But the Architect leaned in to the monitor to get a better look at the twitching body lying in a pool of blood, sweat, urine, and vomit.

"It worked much quicker this time," Nora announced proudly.

"Good. Good," replied the Architect. "And the victim's ethnicity?"

Nora's smile drained away. "I'm afraid we're not yet there. He was a prisoner, yes, but not from the targeted group. I am trying to assess what went wrong with Khattib's vector that made it unable to couple with the linking protein for our target's gene. But this test has brought me closer to the answer. Let me work on the vector some more. I hope to have the refined version very soon."

The Architect was glad he had brought Nora onboard. He had hand-picked her to be the principal investigator at the project's testing center in Lebanon after hearing her speak at a conference on genomic vector therapy in Geneva a year earlier. It was rumored that she had ties to terrorist groups in her youth, which made the Architect confident to approach her. The Order had already vetted her through their numerous deep sources, but he wanted to personally gauge her passion for the cause. He was not disappointed. She was an ardent supporter of the movement. Of course, she had personal motives for developing an ethnic weapon: Foreign forces in her own homeland needed cleansing.

"Keep working, then," replied the Architect. Nora bowed her head dutifully.

The old man closed the VTC program. "You've shut down all of research operations in this country and pulled all of the material and samples into our lab here?"

"Yes, as you instructed. The last samples just arrived a few hours ago," his assistant replied.

"Good. I want you to continue to work with Nora by VTC to refine her vector so it's compatible with the weapon and linking protein we have here. She has the genetic mapping of our first target population. You have all of our samples here as well as Khattib's research. The two of you should be able to come up with a working prototype. In the meantime, I will buy you some time."

26

IT SHOULD BE RIGHT around here, Lee thought, checking his map. As he passed police headquarters, he wondered if he should stop and have them run a name for him. Perhaps he should give Roland Waters a second chance, as Emma suggested. If he was still suspicious about the man after this visit, maybe he would ask Waters to run the trace.

Lee pulled alongside a line of stopped buses, put the placard reading "Department of Homeland Security—Official Business" on his rental car's dash, and locked the door.

As was his habit, he scanned the busy building as he walked into the open atrium. Beneath the large "T" sign, he saw what he was looking for and approached the window.

"Excuse me, ma'am," he said, holding his badge up to the window. "Can I speak with you for a moment?"

The forty-something uniformed woman eyed Lee suspiciously but opened the door to her small booth.

"Can I help you?" she asked.

"I hope you can. Several hours ago, a woman was pushed in front of a train here—" he began, still standing at the door.

"Whoa, wait a minute," she said. "I've been here all afternoon and no one was hit by a train."

"Someone pulled her back at the last minute. It wasn't reported."

"Then how do you know about it?" she asked suspiciously.

Lee didn't appreciate being on the wrong end of an interrogation. He decided, however, to play nice. Technically, she could make things difficult and tell him to go to the Massachusetts Bay Transportation Authority central offices or the MBTA Transportation Police.

"The woman is working with me on a case. You have surveillance cameras on all the platforms, right?"

"Yeah," she said. "But nothing happened. I told you, I didn't see nothing."

"Can we just take a quick look? It would have been around four fifteen this afternoon," he answered, estimating the time Emma left him for the coroner's office.

"Come on in, then," she said with a frown, and waved him into her small glass booth. The two barely fit inside so Lee remained in the doorway, looking over the portly woman's shoulder as she fidgeted with some controls beneath the small black-and-white security monitors.

"Four fifteen, you say?" she asked.

"That's right. Should have been around then. Inbound side."

"Uh-huh."

He strained his eyes watching the small figures on the screen coming and going like a swarm of ants.

"Wait, right there," he said, recognizing the woman with blond hair wearing a tan jacket.

"Uh-huh," the attendant muttered again, switching the video from rewind to play. "Pretty, ain't she? You sure you're not just stalking her?"

Lee let the question pass with a feigned smile as the people on the screen came to life. A crowd on the platform began jostling for position. He could only make out the side of her head and shoulder, the rest obscured by the crowd. As the train arrived, he caught a glimpse of Khattib's face next to Emma's. But then the view became obstructed again. As a large man stepped away, however, Lee saw Khattib's hand on Emma's shoulder and her astonished face looking into his eyes.

For a moment Lee was angry with himself. Emma had almost been killed, and he had left her alone. Still, Emma was right about one thing. He couldn't save everyone by himself. He needed help. Apparently more of it.

"I still don't see anything," the attendant said, her patience wearing thin.

"Right there, don't you see it?"

"I see a man making for your woman. That's all I see," she said, eyebrows raised.

No, it was definitely there. The moving crowd concealed the exact moment Emma was pushed, but the setup was in place. It was obvious to him who had pushed Emma.

"Can you print this out,"

"Sorry, sugar, this monitor's for watchin' only."

"Okay, well thanks very much for your help," Lee said, taking a picture of the paused frame on the monitor in front of him with his smartphone.

"If things don't work out with between you and your honey, you know where to find me," she said with a girlish lilt.

As Lee walked back to his car, he took out his phone. He was about to call Erik Kaiser but remembered his latest resolution. He decided he would play nice with Undersecretary Waters. Besides, Waters would be able to get him the information he needed much faster. Lee dug into his pocket for the card that Waters had given him. It had his private number on it—presumably for emergency use only. While this wasn't exactly an emergency, it was definitely urgent.

"Hello, Undersecretary Waters," he said after someone picked up.

"Who is this? Do you know what time it is?"

"It's Agent Lee Jansen from the Washington office. I met with you earlier today. I know it's late and I'm sorry for disturbing you."

"Damn it, Jansen, it's after midnight."

"Sorry, sir. But can you do me a favor and run a check on an Ashraf Khattib for me? It's important. I wouldn't be bothering you if it wasn't."

"Khattib? I thought his name started with a J. Jerald or something."

"Yeah, Jawad. This is his brother."

"This side investigation of yours is starting to become a pain in my rear, you know that, Jansen?"

"I know," Lee said. "Yours and mine both, believe me. Will you do this for me?"

"Fine. But if this is a dead end, you get on board with my investigation. Understood?"

Lee took a deep breath. "Deal."

"I'll have the information for you in the morning." The line went dead.

Lee decided it was time for him to head back to his hotel. There wasn't much more he could do at this late hour. Even though he wasn't tired, he knew he needed some sleep. He had a feeling he was going to need plenty of rest for what lay ahead.

27

I DON'T BELIEVE IT," Emma protested as Lee drove her from Copley Square to the coroner's office the next morning. "Why would he be involved with something that would kill his own brother?"

Lee had picked her up at the hotel at seven thirty. He wanted the time alone to tell her his thoughts about Khattib. He was also aware that he liked time alone with her, even if they spent it discussing the case.

"Emma, I've seen Iraqi parents send their sons and daughters on suicide missions against U.S. troops, so nothing surprises me anymore. They're called extremists for a reason. They'll stop at nothing to further their cause, no matter how disturbing it may seem to us. I called Waters last night and he's running a check on Khattib. I should hear something back soon," replied Lee.

"Did the video show him pushing me in front of the train?"

The answer was technically no, although Lee's gut instinct had filled in the blanks.

"There were too many people between you and the camera," he replied. "But it's clear he was coming at you, and the next thing on the video is you falling toward the tracks."

"But it makes no sense. Why would he push me, just to pull me back to safety?"

"I haven't figured that one out yet," Lee admitted. "Maybe he was trying to earn your trust so he could get close to us. Know what we've found out about the case. That would make it a lot easier for whoever he's in cahoots with."

Emma turned toward him. "That's pretty thin, don't you think?"

"Maybe, but it's all I've got right now. Remember, we keep every possibility on the table, right? Those are your own words." Although Khattib was young and seemed sincere about trying to find the person responsible for his brother's death, Lee wasn't ready to take him off the suspect list just yet. Sleepers lived double lives for a reason, fooling even those closest to them.

"I'm still not one hundred percent convinced," she said.

"Me either. But the risks are too high for us to not play it safe."

"So what now? Do we tell Manny?"

"My guess is that Manny has the same suspicions I do. With his background, he's probably more paranoid than I am. I'll pull him aside when I get the chance and talk with him. In the meantime, let's keep Khattib close and see what he's all about. Just don't talk too freely around him. Okay?"

Emma let out a sigh. "I have to tell you, this case is intriguing, but it's far more draining than anything I've worked on before. Not to mention more dangerous. Getting pushed onto the Metro tracks is the closest I've ever come to dying, and it really shook me up. I haven't cried in years, but after you dropped me off at the hotel last night, I have to admit I broke down."

Lee was sympathetic. "Hey, facing death can be an eye-opener for even the bravest person. You are, after all, human."

Emma nodded. "Lee, something has been puzzling me."

"What is it?"

"How did the DHS find out about Jawad Khattib's death so quickly?"

Lee had asked the same question.

"I mean, I'm just curious," she continued. "It seems like you and I were pulled into this really fast. Sure, the ER would have informed the Mass. Department of Public Health about Khattib's gruesome death. But the health department normally takes a few days before it contacts us to help with an investigation. I'm sure it would have taken the same amount of time for it to contact DHS, if it ever did at all." She twisted around so that she was facing him. "I understand that national security may have been at stake, but still, we were brought in right away and fed a story about Khattib being a terrorist."

"It's a good point," Lee admitted. "Regardless of what the CIA said, I haven't seen that Khattib was on any terrorist watch lists, so it's doubtful his name would have triggered any interest with us. But remember, anything even remotely related to a radioactive device would come to us eventually." He found himself thinking out the most logical threads. "Let's keep a tight circle for now."

"Okay." Emma nodded as they pulled into the parking lot of the Office of the Medical Examiner. "I'm anxious to take a look at Khattib's corpse. So far, the test results I'm seeing would not suggest that the inflammatory response that killed him was from radiation, a bioweapon, or even an organism. I want to run some genetic testing on the body to see if there are any noticeable alterations to Khattib's DNA."

"Looks like the gang's all here. That's Manny's tank over there," Lee said.

She had to laugh. "Why does it not surprise me that Manny drives a Hummer? Do they even make them anymore?"

"You can take the doctor out of the Army…" Lee said, and they shared a smile.

"Still, I'm glad he's on our side. He's a little unorthodox, but I hear he's a great ER doc," Emma said. "I hope he and Sue have had time to go through some more slides and have something more concrete for us."

"One thing I learned from my investigations," Lee told her as he parked next to Manny's Hummer. "When one door shuts, another usually opens. Investigations like these are never clear-cut. But the clues are out there. It's rare for the bad guys not to make mistakes. We just have to be patient and find them." He pulled on his door handle. "You ready? I have a feeling we're in for an interesting day."

28

THE INITIAL SLIDES weren't very helpful," Sue Chen began, fidgeting on her stool as she looked into the microscope. "There was nothing out of the ordinary on microscopy. Nothing that would have caused the devastating immune response that was seen in this patient. The initial cultures were negative, and the final ones should be back later today or tomorrow."

Chen rolled her stool over to another bench, hitting Manny in the shin as she did. "Oops. Sorry."

"It's okay. That's why the good Lord found it fit to give me a spare," he said with a smile as he lifted his other foot in response to the researcher's blush.

"I texted you the results of the neutrophil function tests," Chen continued, composing herself. "They were normal."

"That would rule out radiation poisoning, right?" Lee asked.

"That's right. Radiation damages the function of neutrophils," answered Emma. "And no gram-negative bacteria so far?

That also rules out radiation exposure, since radiation would have destroyed his GI tract and released normal gram-negative flora that grows there into his bloodstream. So, as we suspected, radiation did not kill Jawad Khattib."

By eight fifteen, Adams had not yet arrived. His assistant told them his day usually started between eight and eight thirty, and only he had the keys to the morgue. The bodies were stored directly beneath them. The four investigators huddled in Chen's lab and continued to search for answers.

"So he died from sepsis, but the negative cultures mean no pathogens were growing in his bloodstream to cause it? How can that be?" asked Manny. "Something *had* to cause the immune response."

"Well, since we were talking about inflammation and wanted to rule out infection, I ran an ELISA on his blood," Chen replied, referring to the enzyme-linked immunosorbent assay used to identify smaller viruses undetectable in standard light microscopy.

"What did you find?" Emma asked, picking up on the researcher's excitement.

"Nothing, actually," Chen answered with a smile.

Emma and Manny exchanged confused glances.

"But," she continued, "I then ran a PCR, and that was a coat of a different color."

"Horse," Manny chimed in.

"I'm sorry?" Chen asked.

"Horse of a different color. Not coat. Sorry," Manny said, waving his hand. "Go on."

"Well, the PCR, or polymerase chain reaction," she said, explaining to Lee, "usually isn't great for picking up most viruses. *But* this time, we got lucky."

"What is it?" Emma asked.

"The culprit is nonprimate lentiviruses," Chen said proudly, handing the printout to Emma. "It was barely detectable, but I found trace SRLVs in his blood."

"SRLVs? But that doesn't make sense," Emma replied.

"What's that?" asked Lee.

"Well, one type of small ruminant lentiviruses are basically floating pieces of lentiviruses. But they don't cause sepsis or SIRS," Emma told him.

"That can't be right," said Ashraf Khattib, hearing the conversation as he walked into the lab. "Sure, lentiviruses may cause some mild disease, but not anything as severe as sepsis. Furthermore, *nonprimate* lentiviruses are very unlikely to cause any pathology in primates. Namely, humans. Certainly not enough disease to trigger the deadly immune reaction found in my brother."

"Unless it wasn't meant to cause the disease," Emma said, thinking aloud.

"What else would it have been used for?" asked Lee.

"SRLVs are some of the best viral vectors currently used for delivering gene therapy into a cell," Emma explained. "As relatively benign viruses, SRLVs are great at injecting their own genetic material into human cells. If someone puts manufactured genetic code into an SRLVs vector, and couples it with Khattib's linking protein, the new gene would be able to incorporate itself into a specific location on a host's DNA. Once there, whatever effect the new gene was designed to create would be permanent."

"Viral vectors break apart and dissipate completely once they enter the cell," Manny added, following Emma's train of thought. "Therefore, it would be difficult to find any trace of intact lentiviruses in the body once it delivered its DNA into the host's chromosome."

Chen stared at him, impressed.

"What? So I watch *House* from time to time," Manny joked. "Why would Khattib be messing with vectors and manufactured genes, anyway?" he asked Ashraf Khattib. "I thought you said this stage of your brother's research only dealt with developing a protein that tagged specific segments of DNA, not the delivery vehicle or treatment in humans."

"That's right," Khattib said. "He was focused on the linking proteins and native gene segments in mice. Someone must have tampered with his specimens. A much later stage in his research would have involved using vectors. The goal would have been to insert a therapeutic gene into a patient's defective genome after it was marked by Jawad's linking protein. Once Jawad had tagged the gene of interest with his protein, the next step would be to determine if a vector could link with it and turn on the new gene."

"But in this case," Manny said, "the manufactured gene meant for the mouse killed him?"

"I still don't get it," Lee said. "If all this is true, how could it have affected Khattib? I mean, he's not an albino mouse. I thought the whole purpose was to develop a linking protein for a specific gene—in this case, the *mouse's* gene. He wouldn't have the same albino gene as the mouse. For someone without the target DNA, the manufactured gene wouldn't work because Khattib's linking protein would have nothing to attach to."

"Whoever is paying the bills was probably very excited about Khattib's breakthrough and wanted to see if their weapon could work," Manny said. "I'm sure their intention was for Khattib to inject the altered sample into the albino mice as a test for the weapon. But instead, he accidentally injected himself with the vector."

"If that was the case, then the vector failed," Khattib added. "It should only have worked on the albino mice tagged by Jawad's linking protein. But the weapon, if we can call it that, was deadly despite the absence of the albino gene."

"Obviously, the vector isn't finished," Emma continued. "That's why you were able to find pieces of it, Sue. It probably broke up before delivering the weapon into Jawad's DNA. The weapon made it into his cells but not into his DNA. The vector, in this form and without a targeting protein, is unstable. Put a powerful genetic weapon inside it and unleash it on the public, it would decimate an entire population, without regard to race or genetic makeup. That means if terrorists are behind this, they're running the risk that a global pandemic would reach their land as well—wherever the hell that is. I doubt very much they'd want that. If they can perfect the vector so it doesn't break apart when combining with Khattib's gene-specific linking technology, then someone gets to pick and choose which race they want to wipe off the face of the earth while preserving others."

"How long before they perfect the vector and targeting protein so the bad guys don't have to worry about being killed by their own weapon?" Lee asked.

"That's the million-dollar question," Emma responded. "Vectors, by definition, need two things. A host, in this case Jawad Khattib. And an agent that the vector was carrying, presumably a bioweapon. We don't even know what effect this bioweapon is supposed to have or what genes, if any, it targets. That's why we're here. Hopefully, the answers lie in Khattib's DNA," she concluded.

Lee looked at his watch. After eight thirty.

"Do you have the same idea I have, Marine?" Manny asked.

"Let's do it," Lee answered, and the two men walked over to the stairs leading down to the morgue.

"Where are you going?" Chen asked.

"I'm tired of waiting. Sorry, Sue, your boss is going to be mad at us," Lee said.

"You're going to break into the morgue?" asked Emma.

"You said the answer is right downstairs. You want to know what genes the weapon targets, right? Why are we racking our brains trying to figure this out when you can run some DNA tests on the body?" Lee asked.

Emma leaned back against the wall as the color drained from her face.

"What's wrong?" Lee asked, moving toward her.

"You don't suppose..." she said.

"What?" Manny asked.

"The weapon. I know what it's targeting. They're—"

Just then a deafening explosion rocked the lab, throwing equipment everywhere.

29

THE ARCHITECT'S CELL alerted him of an incoming text. He pulled the device out of his pocket and checked its screen. It was the message he was waiting for: IT'S DONE.

"Finally," he said.

His assistant entered the large office and stood before his boss's antique desk.

"And how is the project coming along?"

"Quite well, actually," the young man replied.

The Architect noted a trace of arrogance in the answer. *Fine,* he thought. *Let the boy have his moment.* He'd had his feelings hurt over the transfer of the project to Nora in Lebanon. His naïve assistant did not understand that secrecy was paramount in this business. His move was an attempt to compartmentalize the project so that no one person had too much knowledge. Except for the project leader, of course. Namely, the Architect himself.

The mission was more important than personal egos. Was that not why Bruno was sent to him, to ensure the project remained secure? Perhaps now his troubles were behind him. He glanced once again at the message on his phone before putting it away.

"I was up all night working with Nora via VTC," answered the assistant. "We believe we've found a way to modify the vector so it'll work with Khattib's linking protein. There should be no more indiscriminate releases of the weapon."

"You believe?"

"Well, Nora needs to perform some further tests. Apparently, she's out of test subjects," he replied, frowning. "But we're fairly certain the new method will be a success."

"Good. We're already behind schedule. Have Nora complete the tests and send the new vector samples here as soon as possible. Arrange a private jet so there are no issues with customs or security. Once you receive the new vector, combine it with the weapon. I want a working vector that can target the selected population's genome by the end of the week."

"Of course, sir," the assistant answered, and quickly left to carry out his master's command.

Things were back on track. The lab results were promising. The authorities were out of the way, for the time being at least. And the new weaponized vector was nearly ready. The prototype vector targeting Khattib's mice failed because it would not interact with his linking protein and disintegrated upon entering the bloodstream. A minor glitch, apparently, as it took his team only one night to fix. He was actually surprised his scientists missed it. Nora and even his assistant, with all of his faults, were both exceptional researchers.

With a working, weaponized vector and Khattib's modified linking protein, he would now be able to tag the ethnic-specific gene. The weapon itself had also been tweaked so that it was activated only in the presence of the linking protein attached to the host DNA.

He leaned back and looked out over his mountains. Project Astrea was finally close to completion. Soon the world would experience his work.

The Architect was proud, indeed.

He thought about his childhood in Beirut many decades ago. His life was about to come full circle. His membership in the Order and his support for Project Astrea all stemmed from his childhood's fateful events in the war-torn Middle East.

Now, a lifetime later, he would have his revenge.

30

INTENSE FLAMES licked Emma's body as she struggled to see through the thick smoke that engulfed her.

She coughed to clear away the acrid taste of carbon that filled her lungs.

Red emergency lights in the lab gleamed, as the main power had gone out with the blast. Behind her, she heard the *whoosh* of the fire continuing to stream out of oxygen lines near the research benches, feeding the blaze.

"Lee?" she called out, her voice scratchy. "Lee?"

There was no answer.

Emma looked around and noticed something was missing. Water. There was no water. She looked up and her worst fears were confirmed. The overhead sprinkler system wasn't working.

Did that mean the alarm was disabled as well? Did anyone even know the fire was burning them alive?

Emma crawled through the rubble searching for survivors. "Sue? Manny? Khattib?" she cried out hoarsely. But there was no response.

Her throat started to burn and her breathing became shallow. Noxious gases had replaced the oxygen as it was consumed by the roaring fire. Emma found it hard to focus her thoughts.

The temperature rose quickly as the fire raged. She began sweating profusely. Her head hurt and she felt faint. Emma knew the signs of carbon monoxide poisoning and realized she had very little time left before she would succumb to its effects.

She could barely make out a silhouette on the ground in front of her, and she crawled to the motionless body. It was Lee.

She shook him hard and screamed his name, but there was no answer. No movement. Just as the fire began to overwhelm her senses, she thought she detected breathing. Lee's pulse was weak but palpable.

Again she tried to rouse him, but his eyes remained closed. Grabbing his thick arm, Emma attempted to lift the former Marine. His large frame wouldn't budge.

She heard a feeble cry coming from her left. Emma crawled as fast as she could toward the sound. Though her vision was blurry, she was able to feel her way toward the young researcher.

"Sue! Are you okay? Are you hurt?"

"My legs. I can't move them" came the weak reply.

Emma looked down at the woman's legs. A large metal shelving unit had fallen on top of the petite microbiologist, pinning her to the ground. Beside them, the wooden bench that Emma had been sitting upon collapsed.

Summoning all of her strength, Emma pushed on the heavy shelves in a frantic attempt to free Sue Chen. Nothing. Chen cried out in pain.

"Hang on, Sue!" Emma pleaded.

She pushed again, this time bracing her feet against the wall behind her. Chen howled as the heavy shelf inched across her damaged legs.

Energized by her limited success, Emma continued to put all of her weight into the shelf. But it would give no more. Exhausted, Emma called out to the woman, telling her to hang on. But there was no response.

By now, Emma had begun to fade. The deadly combination of fire, smoke, and exertion had brought her to the brink of collapse. Her vision tunneled and she felt nauseous. She began to cough uncontrollably, which caused her head to hurt more. She was too weak now to crawl. Her arms gave out on her and she collapsed on top of Sue Chen.

For the second time in as many days, Emma Hess saw her life flash in front of her.

31

EMMA AWOKE to the familiar sounds of emergency room monitors and beeping. Cool air blew on her face. Her eyes slowly focused on the faces of Lee and Manny. They stood over her and looked worried. Lee leaned in close to speak.

"Hey. How you feeling?" he asked with a gentle smile.

Emma nodded her head, too dazed to answer, unsure of how badly she was hurt. Her hand moved to her face as she forced her fingers to remove the oxygen mask.

"How's Sue?" she asked. The voice that came from her mouth was unrecognizable to her —it was an elderly woman's voice, scratchy and weak. Her mind cleared only to fill with pain. There were burns on her hands and arms, and every muscle she moved hurt.

"She'll be fine," Lee reassured her. "Her legs are a little banged up."

Manny leaned in from the other side of the gurney. "Small tib-fib fracture from the shelf that fell on her," he told her. "Nothing a cast and a little rest won't fix."

"Manny's been watching over her like a hawk and lecturing her orthopedist on how to be an orthopedist," Lee said with a grin.

"Dr. Burrows," Manny said, shaking his head. "What a jerk."

Emma noticed bandages on Manny's arms and burns on Lee's neck and face.

"How did we get out of there?" she asked.

"Ranger Rick here saved the day," Lee said, pointing his thumb over to Manny. "A real-life superhero."

"Nah. It was a team effort. Army and Marines, saving the day," replied Manny.

"Manny carried you out of there. I came back to the land of the living in time to help him get the shelf off Sue."

"The blast?" she asked.

Manny winked at Emma. "Now you know why I never went into research. Too dangerous."

Emma tried to sit up and felt a stabbing pain in her back.

"Easy now. You've got some mean muscle spasms going on back there. Maybe even a trap strain. Just lie back and relax. Doctor's orders," Manny told her.

"Where's Khattib?" Emma asked.

Manny looked over at Lee, who hung his head.

"Emma, he didn't make it. He was too close to the blast," Lee said.

"Hit his head on a metal bench. Hard. Never regained consciousness. I'm sorry," added Manny.

"He saved my life on the T," Emma replied. "He wasn't a part of this, Lee. He wasn't with them."

The two men stood quietly, unsure of what to say.

"This has to end. If someone has gone this far to stop us, even willing to kill us…" she said.

"I know," answered Lee. "It has to be something big. And I'd bet it's almost complete or whoever's behind this wouldn't have taken such a drastic step to keep us away."

"Well, we're no closer to finding out who's responsible than we were on day one," Manny said.

"You started to tell us something just before the blast," Lee said to Emma. "Something came to you when you were looking at the slides. Something about the weapon. What was it?"

Emma noticed the pleading look in Lee's eyes and searched her memory for answers, but found none. "I can't remember. The whole thing's a blur."

"That's okay. It'll come back to you. Just rest now," Lee said.

"No, we can't rest. There's no time. "Whoever's behind this will be ramping up the project to get it done," she told him, ignoring the pain as she sat up.

"You're in no condition to go anywhere," Lee told her, putting his hand on her shoulder. "Emma, you brought the investigation this far using that amazing brain of yours. We need it now more than ever. But you need to rest and get your strength back first."

She fell back onto the bed.

"I'll be back, okay?" Lee said, placing the oxygen mask back on her face. "You take care of yourself in the meantime."

Emma saw the warmth and concern in his eyes. It had been a long time since someone had looked at her that way.

Lee turned and walked out, gesturing for Manny to follow.

"Emma's right," Lee said, once they were out of earshot. "Singh will accelerate his schedule now for sure. I need to make my move."

"Singh?" Manny asked. "How can you be so sure he had anything to do with this? We really don't know all that much. It's just speculation at this point."

"Maybe so, but Singh's been holding out on us. There's no way he doesn't know who's funding a project that he himself admitted was cutting edge. And, if what Emma was saying back in the lab was true, who better than Singh to switch the samples and report the results back to whoever's pulling his strings? He's stalling, probably waiting for us to get knocked off. I'm tired of playing defense. Now it's my move, and I'm taking it."

"That might be a little premature, there, cowboy. We should probably have more to go on before we break down some doors."

"Manny, do you think Singh or whoever is behind this is going to let us get more evidence? The longer we wait, the closer they are to deploying whatever it is they're creating."

"Or knocking us off," Manny added, looking at the burns on his arms. "Okay, I'm in. Let's go see Singh."

"No, Manny. Please. I need you to stay here to watch Emma and Sue. Whoever tried to kill us will figure out soon enough that we're still alive. You know they'll be back. If they're bold enough to blow up a medical examiner's office and lab in downtown Boston in broad daylight, they won't hesitate to come into a hospital to finish the job. Can you stay and make sure they're safe?"

As much as Manny wanted to argue with Lee, he knew the agent's assumptions were probably correct. Sue Chen was especially vulnerable. Her fracture would keep her immobilized until the swelling reduced enough for a cast to be placed. She might even need surgery down the line.

"All right. I'll stay here, but you stay in touch. And don't do anything foolish, Marine. You hear me?"

"Deal. Thanks, Manny. I'll call when I get to CIGR."

"Whoever did this is going to pay. They got me mad. Just let them try coming into my hospital," Manny stated.

The two men shook hands, then Lee headed for the staircase, confident that nobody would get past Manny.

As he walked down the corridor, he heard a familiar voice behind him.

"Just a minute," said Roland Waters, coming out of the elevator with Erik Kaiser. "I need to speak with you, Jansen."

32

"UNDERSECRETARY WATERS, I'm glad you're here." said Lee. "Someone tried to kill us at the morgue. Ashraf Khattib is dead. The police were here for a few hours, but someone pulled them off—why? Whoever did this will most likely be back to finish the job."

"I know about Ashraf Khattib. The same guy you told me to check up on last night ends up dead here today. Jansen, how come there are dead bodies wherever you go?" asked the undersecretary. "You were sent up here to *assist* me, not make more work for me."

"We're on to something," Lee replied.

"Don't be so sure. Boston PD and FD along with a dozen of my guys have been combing through what's left of the morgue. Looks like there was a leak in the gas line. It was an old building," Waters told them. "Nothing nefarious. That's why I pulled law enforcement away. I need all the manpower I have on my case."

"Are you saying this was an accident?" Manny asked.

"And you are?" Waters asked.

"Dr. Manny Ortiz. I was in that building this morning and I'm telling you, someone was behind that explosion."

"You can? How? Who was behind it? Where's the proof?"

"It was no accident Ashraf Khattib was killed and my colleagues hospitalized. Don't you see that?" Lee asked, exasperated.

"Agent Jansen, I know you have been through a lot. We'll keep looking into the explosion, but so far it seems that it's nothing more than poor maintenance. Believe me, when I heard about the explosion, the first thing I thought about was terrorism. But that building was over a hundred years old. We've had a number of explosions throughout the area over the past several years, all traced back to gas leaking from old pipes. We found evidence of leaks in the rubble. Nothing else. No devices, no explosives, no timers or triggers. Nothing suspicious," Waters replied, softening his tone.

"Come on, can't you see they're trying to get rid of the evidence?" Manny stated.

"What evidence?" Waters replied. "There *is* no evidence. You have shown me nothing to convince me of this ethnic weapon."

"Undersecretary Waters, don't you think it's at least a little suspicious that the morgue explodes right before we were going to examine Jawad Khattib's body? Like maybe someone was afraid we'd find something? And where was Dr. Adams, anyway? We were supposed to meet him at eight this morning and he never showed up. That's convenient."

"Agent Jansen, I'm sure you wouldn't have found anything different than the doctors at Mass. General or our medical examiner found. If there was something else suspicious with the body, I'm sure it would have been found already. And Dr.

Adams was stuck in traffic. There was an accident in the tunnel this morning. Now, I need you on board with my investigation into terrorist cells in the area. If there is a threat, that's where it's coming from. We need to focus on finding that dirty bomb."

"You're barking up the wrong tree, Undersecretary. Someone's working on a biological weapon that could kill millions of people," Lee said. "And I'm going to stop them. I'd like to have your help."

Waters shook his head. "Really? You were sent up here to help me on *my* investigation, not the other way around. Besides, which terrorist group is behind your *theory*?"

Lee didn't have an answer to those questions yet.

"Exactly. I have the mayor on my back, the president's visit next month, the CIA to answer to, and you with your claim about some science fiction scenario. And still no proof of any of it. Now I've asked you for your help, Agent Jansen. And I haven't gotten it. So, I'm afraid I'm going to have to make a tough decision. But that's my job. You're off this case, Agent," Undersecretary Waters said firmly.

"Fine. If I'm off the case, then I'm taking vacation time. I've always liked Boston. Maybe I'll stick around and see the sights," said Lee.

"Hey, you wanna go see the Pats tonight? They're playing the Giants," Manny asked.

"Nice try," Waters said to Manny. Then he turned his glare to Lee. "I need your badge."

"You have no authority to take my badge."

"Maybe not. But Jay Kowalski does," replied Waters, looking at Kaiser.

"Lee, there was a lot of pressure on Director Kowalski this morning," Erik added. "He took a lot of heat for you. The mayor called the secretary herself and complained that he didn't feel enough was being done to protect the city."

"You never should have been sent up here in the first place, Jansen," Waters replied. "I don't care how impressive your resume was at one point or how much you know about explosives. You've suffered some losses both personally and professionally and they're affecting your judgment."

"The hell they are," Lee snapped, squaring off with the undersecretary.

"Lee, there was no choice," Kaiser said. "Director Kowalski sent me up here to suspend you and help Undersecretary Waters with this case. I'm sorry."

Lee couldn't believe what he was hearing. He took out his badge and dropped it on the floor at Waters's feet.

"And your gun," Waters added. "You're a civilian now, and we have strict gun laws in Boston."

"Bastard," Manny muttered.

"This isn't over," Lee replied, slamming his service pistol into Waters's outstretched hand. He turned to walk away.

"Go back to DC, Jansen. Get some help with whatever's going on in your head."

Lee answered Waters with a raised middle finger just before he pushed through the door leading to the staircase and disappeared.

Waters turned to Manny. "Dr. Ortiz, I need you to tell me everything you know about this case."

"And I need you to go to hell," replied Manny. "I don't work for you. Go get a medical degree and figure it out for yourself."

The senior DHS agent watched the doctor walk away as he and Agent Kaiser stood alone in the hospital corridor.

33

LEE BROUGHT HIS RIGHT FIST hard against the hospital's fire door at the bottom of the stairs. When he reached his car, he sat down in the driver's seat and took a deep breath.

It didn't help.

Waters was right about one thing. Lee's case *was* unfocused. They still hadn't identified any suspects. They had been putting some of the pieces together, but without DHS support, they would get nowhere. Not having a badge wouldn't help his investigation much, either.

Lee was startled by a tap on the window.

He instinctively reached for his gun but touched only an empty holster. Looking up, Lee saw a familiar face and rolled down the window.

"Kaiser, what do you want?"

"Lee, you have to tread lightly. Director Kowalski said the secretary was furious and wanted your head."

"Well, she can have it and my badge. When I'm done up here," replied Lee, turning the ignition.

"What's going on, Lee? I can't help you if you don't tell me what's happening."

Several people knew they'd be in the coroner's office that morning. And Waters was at the top of that list. Adams as well. Was it a coincidence that Adams was late and not in the building at the time of the explosion? He was, after all, the one who issued the preliminary report citing radiation as the likely cause of death. And Lee thought it was more than a bit suspicious that Adams was "stuck in traffic" while he and his friends were roasting in his burning office.

But Kaiser was new at the DHS. Too new to have formed any strong allegiances with the bureaucrats up here. Lee had to trust someone from DHS if he was going to continue his investigation *unofficially.*

"Sorry, Erik. It's been a crazy few days. Everyone is so fixated on the idea of a dirty bomb. But we found evidence that suggests something different, something potentially much worse, if you can believe it."

"Like what?"

"Some new weapon," Lee replied. "A biogenetic weapon, not a radioactive one. Did you find anything out about Singh or CIGR?"

"Not much. Their bookkeeping is a little shady. Been audited by the IRS a few times. Got a few fines, but nothing too serious."

"Listen, I know you're supposed to be helping Waters, but he's wrong about this case." Lee said. "So I need your help. I know it's a lot to ask after what you just saw. But some very good people got hurt, and one is dead."

Kaiser hesitated for a moment. He didn't want to see his career end before it had really begun, but he could tell Jansen was a straight shooter with reason to believe what he said. "Sure, Agent Jansen. What do you need?"

"Keep an eye on my friends in the hospital. Talk to Manny, the doctor I was with. He should be in Emma Hess's or Sue Chen's room. Tell him the Jarhead said you're okay."

"All right," Kaiser replied.

"Keep them safe. Whoever rigged the morgue to explode didn't just want Khattib's body to disappear. They waited until we were all in the building."

"Who?"

"I don't know, but I suspect Singh was involved."

Kaiser was alarmed. "I know what you're thinking, Lee, but it's not a good idea. Undersecretary Waters told you to stay out of this."

"I don't trust Waters, either."

"Why? Don't you think you're being a bit paranoid?"

"Call it a hunch. When a building blows up with you in it, you'll be paranoid as well. Tell me, who's handling T-Bone's case now that you're up here?"

"Director Kowalski said he'd take it on."

"Are the perps talking?"

"The brother, Daif Ajeel, broke during the interrogations. He admitted that his brother Wahab Ajeel was part of Abdullah al-Harbi's terror network and was trying to buy weapons. He said Wahab was shopping around for a new type of weapon to use on U.S. soil. That's what the money was for."

"Did they find any suppliers yet?"

"He didn't give names, but he did say that Wahab found out that one potential supplier was actually one of ours. Wahab backed out of the deal as soon as he suspected a setup."

"Was it? Where there an undercover operations going on?"

"None that I could find. I asked Director Kowalski and he said he'd look into it," Kaiser replied.

"Feds arranging weapon buys for terrorists and no record of it? That would explain why Wahab had an itchy finger the day

T-Bone was killed," said Lee. "It also means that there's a dirty agent in the house. So, the brother didn't give you the name of the agent?"

Kaiser shook his head. "Nope. I guess we'll have to find Wahab Ajeel to answer that one."

Lee didn't see much chance of that happening soon. "Kowalski's smart. He'll run the case down to the ground." Lee looked at the clock on the dashboard. It was already midafternoon, and he had somewhere to be.

"Thanks for your help. I'll be in touch."

"Are you going where I think you're going?" asked Kaiser.

"It's time for this to end," Lee said. "One way or another. Go meet with Dr. Ortiz. Keep an eye on Emma Hess and Sue Chen for me."

"Okay, Lee. But, don't do this. Not alone."

"I don't need backup. But there is one thing I do need. Can I have your gun?"

34

NO, I DON'T HAVE AN APPOINTMENT. Let me show you my card," Lee told the pretty young receptionist. He hoped she wouldn't ask to see his badge.

Fortunately, he had Kaiser's pistol in his holster in his left armpit. As he handed the woman his card, he allowed his jacket to open just enough for her to see the weapon.

"Sorry, sir, it's just that he's in a meeting and can't be disturbed."

"Tell him that he either sees me right now, or he can deal with a team of agents with warrants in an hour," he said with a smile on his face.

The receptionist gave him a sullen look and stepped away from her desk.

"He'll see you now," she said as she returned a minute later with two large uniformed guards in tow.

"I figured he would."

The guards silently escorted Lee to the elevator.

Lee had made some waves at the front desk, but the muscle surprised him. Perhaps his arrival was a threat to Singh, which confirmed his suspicions about the CIGR director.

"Agent Jansen," Singh said, greeting Lee as he entered the office. "Nice to see you again. I have news for you. We've been able to find our records on Khattib's research. My apologies that it took so long."

Singh handed Lee the file.

Lee looked at the first page and laughed. "This is a joke, right?" he said. "The Johnson Company in the Cayman Islands?"

"That is the company sponsoring his research, yes."

"Come on. This is a bogus company and you know it," replied Lee, throwing the file at Singh's chest. In response, one of the guards stepped closer.

"I'm afraid that's all we have about the sponsoring company, Agent Jansen. It's not at all uncommon for benefactors of research to remain anonymous. Overseas corporations provide money to fund the projects all the time. Some organizations do not wish their altruism to be known publicly. At least, not until the appropriate time."

"Is that what you call it, altruism?"

"I call it progress. Our research here makes the world better and mankind healthier."

"Progress? You call ethnic cleansing progress?"

Singh flinched. "I don't know what you're talking about, Agent Jansen."

Lee felt the rage surge inside him. It was time to go old school on Singh and rattle the director's cage. Besides, he was technically a private citizen now, not a DHS agent. Before the guards could react, Lee had Singh pinned to his desk.

"Jawad Khattib's brother is dead, and Dr. Hess and a medical researcher are in the hospital right now because of you and your *altruistic* client. I want to know who's responsible, and you'd better talk fast. I feel a cramp coming on in my hand," Lee said, tightening his grip around Singh's neck.

The guards grabbed Lee's shoulders and managed to pry his hands off the director's throat. They held Lee tightly, his arms pinned behind his back as he stood in front of Singh.

Singh composed himself and stood up to face Lee. His earlier look of fear was replaced now by arrogance.

"You must learn some manners, Agent Jansen," he stated. "But I understand your frustration. It is always disturbing when scientists are injured while performing God's work. Sometimes, however, sacrifices must be made. You must understand this."

"Understand this, Singh: You're finished. You. CIGR. And whoever's financing your operation. I *will* find them."

"Of course you will, Agent Jansen," Singh said in a patronizing tone. "Or should I call you *Mr.* Jansen? How unfortunate that you were relieved of your duties with the Department of Homeland Security. A tragedy of sorts, like the terrible incident at the coroner's office."

Confident that the guards had Lee well secured, Singh approached the agent.

"It's like war, Mr. Jansen," he murmured. "Did you know that medical and scientific advances skyrocket during wartime? Indeed, we have the First and Second World Wars to thank for the incredible array of antibiotics and vaccinations that save so many millions of lives today. Even America's disastrous conflicts in Iraq and Afghanistan have yielded advances in body armor development and traumatic brain injury treatment. Ironic, don't you agree?"

"You're playing with people's lives," Lee said. "You're sick."

"You still don't understand, do you? This isn't about me, or you, or Dr. Hess or Sue Chen. It isn't even about Jawad Khattib. This is so much bigger than any of us. It's about *science*. The advancement of man. You'll see. In fact, it won't be long before the entire world sees. It's a pity that you can't appreciate this. Gentlemen, please escort Mr. Jansen out."

"I'll be back for you, Singh," Lee called over his shoulder as the two guards dragged him out of the office.

"No," Singh said confidently. "You won't."

35

THE ARCHITECT was angry when Singh reported his encounter with Jansen. But the CIGR director claimed that he had revealed nothing of substance. It was enough, however, for the Architect to order him to pack up the remaining files for Project Astrea. The project's research arms had already been shut down. Now the Architect instructed Singh to deliver anything pertaining to the project to him at once.

Singh felt that the Architect was being overly cautious. Lee would not be a problem for long. "I'll take care of the agent, now that you have revealed your involvement," the Architect said during their call.

At the end of the work day, Singh asked the guards to accompany him to his car. An unusual step, perhaps, but Singh had found the earlier confrontation particularly unpleasant. The parking lot was nearly empty, as the lab had closed hours earlier. After the three men entered the parking lot, Singh stopped suddenly when he heard a thud immediately behind him. He turned to see one of the guards fall face-first onto the concrete. Then he saw Jansen squared off with the second guard.

The guard lunged at Jansen, swinging his baton, but Lee avoided the blow and countered with a shot to the guard's abdomen. To Lee's surprise, the guard was unfazed. He slammed his right elbow into Lee's back, sending him to the ground instead.

Then the guard reached down and grabbed the back of Lee's jacket with his left hand and pulled him up to his knees. Gripping his baton tightly, he pulled it back for the final strike. Seeing the baton descend, Lee summoned all of his strength and swung his forearm into the back of the guard's knee. The large man collapsed onto the pavement next to him.

Lee brought his elbow down hard onto the guard's chest and heard ribs crack. The guard sucked wind and gave a short cry. Then Lee wrapped his arm around the guard's thick neck and pressed until the guard passed out. *Fair or not,* Lee thought, *this fight's over.*

Lee stood and turned toward Singh. He was surprised to see the CIGR director still standing there, frozen in fear.

Pain flooded Lee's upper back from the guard's blows as he faced Singh for the second time that day.

"Give me the briefcase," he said.

"But there's nothing of value to you," Singh cried, clutching the case into his chest with both arms.

Lee reached out and grabbed it. The men struggled briefly before the briefcase sprang open, papers falling to the ground between them.

Before Lee could order Singh to pick up the documents, something struck him hard on the back of his head, and everything went black.

36

T HANK GOODNESS you came along when you did,"
Singh said to the barrel-chested man.

"The Architect is very upset with you, Singh," the
assassin replied, towering over the smaller man.

"But I was delivering the documents, as he ordered."

"To whom? The federal agent?"

"No, of course not. He took us by surprise. Look what he did
to my bodyguards."

"Amateurs. Both of them. Pick up the documents and put
them back in the briefcase. The Architect sent me to collect
them personally. He wanted no more mistakes from you. I see
that he made the right decision."

Singh scrambled to pick up the papers and stuffed them into
the briefcase. When he had finished, he handed the briefcase
over to the assassin.

"What are you going to do with Agent Jansen?" he asked.

"I should have killed him earlier. He's become quite the nuisance. It appears his lady friend the doctor has nine lives as well. Don't worry. The Architect has plans for them."

Bruno crouched down and threw Lee over his shoulder with little effort.

"Open the trunk," he commanded. "Agent Jansen and I are going for a ride. I'll be back to deal with you later."

37

THOUGH SHE STILL had a headache from the fire's acrid smoke, Emma had felt strong enough to go to Sue's room on the orthopedic ward, where Manny stood guard. Emma had brushed off Dr. Levine's orders to remain in the observation unit so that she could be by her new friend's side.

"How are you feeling?" asked Manny, seeing Emma at the door.

He had insisted that Sue be admitted to the hospital. Crush injuries could easily turn into compartment syndrome, a potentially life-threatening complication.

"I'm fine. How are you doing, Sue?"

"Better. Although I don't know why I have to stay here overnight," Sue said, pouting.

"Because I said so, that's why," Manny replied.

"Where did Lee go?" asked Emma.

"He went to CIGR this afternoon. Said he was going to get some answers," Manny confessed, knowing the news would not make her happy.

"And you let him go? Alone?"

"There was no way anybody could stop him," Manny said with a wry grin. "He told me that once whoever was behind the explosion realized they had failed, they'd try again. And he's probably right. He wanted me to stay here to make sure you two were safe. Lee's a smart guy, even for a Marine. He'll be fine. Now, let's try to piece together the medical explanation for all of this in the meantime. Lee's going to need our help when he gets back. He'll need answers."

Manny was right, Emma realized. What could she possibly do to help Lee in this kind of situation? Lee could take care of himself if there was any trouble. At least she hoped so.

"Are you *sure* you're okay?" asked Sue.

"No," Emma answered truthfully, sitting down on the edge of the bed. "I'm just not sure about anything. I usually do my best work under pressure, but not today. There's something missing. Something we're not getting. Something *important*."

"Something about this case?" Kaiser asked, entering the room with a couple of cups of coffee.

"Emma, this is Agent Erik Kaiser. He works with Lee. Lee said to trust him," Manny explained.

Emma eyed Kaiser cautiously. She was an inquisitive yet trusting person by nature. Though the events of the past days had made her paranoid, Lee had said to trust the man, so she would.

"Can you remember what you were going to tell us right before the explosion?" Manny continued.

Kaiser handed Manny a cup of coffee and leaned against the wall. Manny had already briefed him after Lee's abrupt departure.

"No," Emma answered with obvious frustration. "Let's go over what we know. Ashraf said that his brother was working on a linking protein and that he knew nothing about the vector, a weapon, or even the true purpose of his research. I believe that, especially since Ashraf was killed after talking to us. I think we all agree that the needle stick injected Jawad with an altered sample that contained the bioweapon as well as an ineffective vector that wasn't able to couple with his linking protein."

"Jawad's linking protein was designed to attach to a mouse gene for mouse albinism," Manny continued.

"Right, which, of course, Jawad did not have," Sue chimed in. "So the only explanation is that the vector failed and released the weapon into Jawad without linking to any gene. That is the only reason why he was killed at random."

"I don't think Jawad knew what was in that fatal sample," Emma said. "At least, not until he started getting sick. From what Ashraf said, his brother was starting to get suspicious. I think Jawad was duped into developing the linking protein for someone who was working on the delivery vector as well as a bioweapon. After he proved the linking protein worked on the mice model, they slipped in the bioweapon to see if it would couple with his linking protein and kill the mice."

"Only the vector didn't get into the mouse, nor did it link up with Jawad's protein. The bioweapon was released indiscriminately in his bloodstream and killed him," concluded Manny.

"But we still don't know what the bioweapon does, thus we can't treat it. What caused Jawad's body to have such an intense response?" Manny continued. "SRLVs don't cause the massive immune reaction we saw. And that was the only organism you found in his blood, Sue."

"The lentiviruses were just the vector. Like you said, that wasn't the gun that smokes," Sue acknowledged. Manny gave her a pass on the failed analogy. "We still don't know what the weapon was."

"He was obviously exposed to something that we can't detect." Emma mused. "The bioweapon itself. That's the missing piece of the puzzle. The genetic code inside the vector. Without that, we can't develop an antidote."

"Khattib's body is nothing more than ashes now," Kaiser added. "I heard the fire chief tell Waters that it'll be days before that building is safe enough to enter."

"Not to mention that everything in my lab was destroyed," Sue said ruefully. "Even if any samples survived, the heat from the fire would have denatured the proteins. They'd be useless to us now."

"Lee seems to think that the director of CIGR, Dr. Singh, is behind this," continued Kaiser.

"*Arjun* Singh?" asked Sue.

"Yes. You know him?" Emma asked.

"I know *of* him. A friend of mine used to work for him. He's not very well thought of in the scientific community," Sue said with a frown.

"Why's that?" Manny asked.

"He's been known to conduct research on human subjects without going through an IRB—an institutional review board," she said, referring to the board that reviews the ethical and moral dimensions of human research projects before issuing approvals.

"Go on," coaxed Emma.

"I don't like speaking ill of people, especially someone I don't know."

"Come on, spill it," said Manny.

"Well, my friend said he was very ambitious," Sue said. "He was searching for the next big breakthrough in genetic research. But he didn't play by the rules. He took shortcuts, totally disregarded standard research protocols. He has a reputation of being motivated by financial rewards and glory rather than advancing science.

"A few years ago, he was working on vector therapy in pancreatic cancer patients. He had all this money, no one knows from where, and paid some of the best scientific minds in the field to come up with a working vector to deliver therapeutic genes into a cancer patient's DNA. The goal was to rejuvenate and replace cancerous pancreatic cells. Some progress was made, but the researchers quit the project after they realized how unscrupulous he was."

"Unscrupulous? How?" Emma asked.

"He was doing everything a researcher's not supposed to. There was no IRB on the project, he was giving placebos to cancer patients, and had questionable funding. It's not uncommon to run double-blind trials," Sue continued, referring to the practice of keeping secret—even from the investigators—which patients receive the placebo or standard treatment and which receive the research drug. "But he wouldn't even share the test results with the researchers themselves."

"How could they analyze the data without the results?" asked Emma.

"That's just it. No one knew the results except for Dr. Singh," Sue replied. "Who knows what samples or results he manipulated? It was just too much for most respectable researchers to put up with. They had no control of their work. Most of the scientists complained that Singh was holding them back and limiting their work. The full scope of the project was never clear to them. If they were given more latitude, they maintained, with the strong financial resources Singh brought to the table, my colleagues felt they could have made some serious progress on cancer treatments and gene therapy. Instead, they felt Singh was more interested in keeping and using the results of their data for his own private purposes. So, the researchers got fed up and left."

"So, after his best brains deserted him, Singh parceled out pieces of the research to other labs," Kaiser surmised.

"Pretty smart," Emma said. "That way only he would be privy to the overall results. The contract lab administrators would welcome the fat paycheck from Singh, and there would be no questions."

Manny pointed out another angle. "I'm sure scientists wouldn't mind putting some of their lab's resources onto Singh's small projects in exchange for the chunk of change they could then use to work on their primary research," he said. "A win-win for everybody."

"But what is his goal and who's financing him?" Sue asked.

"I think that's the question Lee went to get answered," replied Kaiser.

"Speaking of Lee, where do you suppose he is?" Emma asked.

"I don't know," answered Manny, looking at his watch. It was early evening. "He should have been back by now. I tried calling his cell an hour ago, but no answer." He pulled out his phone and hit redial. "No answer."

"I'm worried. Something's not right," Emma said.

"I could make a few calls, maybe get Boston PD to go out there," Kaiser said.

"That'd be great, Erik. Thanks," Emma answered.

"Lee's not going to like that," Manny replied.

"Then he should have called to check in," Emma responded. "Make the call."

Kaiser nodded and left the room.

"What would Singh's motive be?" Sue asked. "He certainly wouldn't get a Nobel Prize for genocide."

"Someone else must be pulling the strings. Most likely Singh's sugar daddy. Whoever's paying the bills is pulling the strings on the research," Manny said.

"Why do you say that?" Sue asked.

"Remember, even Jawad, one of Singh's own scientists, had only a small portion of the research. Ashraf said Jawad sent out his samples. Wouldn't you think that Singh's own lab would put together the final product if he was the project's principal? There could very well be dozens of labs across the country, maybe even the world, that are unwittingly involved, with each researcher, like Jawad, playing a small role in the formation of the final product. In the world of special operations and intelligence, we call that compartmentalization. Keep the big picture closely held at the top, and have the worker bees focus on isolated pieces of the puzzle."

"Terrorists?" Emma asked.

"Maybe," Manny said. "That might explain both the financial resources and the motivation."

"But what can we do about it? The evidence we had—the samples from the lab and Khattib's body—are gone," reiterated Sue.

"And we won't get much help from the DHS without more concrete evidence," Emma added.

The three looked at each other, unsure of their next step. Then Manny's phone rang, breaking the silence.

"Hey, Dr. L., what's up?" he said into his phone after looking at the caller ID.

Emma and Sue watched the blood drain from Manny's face as he listened to the speaker on the other end of the line.

"Thanks. I'm on my way."

"What is it?" Emma asked.

"It's Lee. They found him in the parking lot outside the ER."

197

38

I THINK THEY'LL get the message," Bruno said to the
Architect. As a Sicilian, well versed in the rules of respect,
Bruno had often sent similar warnings to those who interfered in private business. "But we have to keep an eye on
them. Each of the three possesses specific skills that can be a
threat to us. Their combined abilities make them a dangerous
enemy."

"Perhaps. But my guess is that right now they're too busy
licking their wounds to concern themselves with our activities.
Agent Jansen's condition will keep them busy for some time.
At least for a few days, which is all we'll need. The weaponized
vector is close to completion. The target population has been
selected. Soon we'll travel to deploy the weapon. Success is at
hand."

Bruno eyed the Architect cautiously. He was not so sure they
had seen the last of Dr. Hess and her colleagues.

The Architect, however, was confident in the knowledge that the investigators had no evidence or solid leads. Project Astrea was safe. The mission was moving into its final stage, and the Architect could barely contain his excitement.

"You're confident there'll be no more meddling from the outside?" Bruno asked.

"Yes. We are fine, Bruno. Even our problem in DC is under control. You can leave now. I appreciate the Order sending you here to assist with the cleanup after Khattib died. You've done your job well, as always."

"What about the agent? Singh revealed dangerous information to him."

"Jansen? He's finished. By the time they complete his autopsy, we'll have the vector perfected and be long gone. At that point, it'll be too late for anyone to stop us."

Bruno had always prided himself on being a merciless adversary, feared by all who crossed his path. He recognized now that the man standing beside him, however, was far more dangerous.

The Architect was truly a monster.

39

WE HAD TO INTUBATE him about fifteen minutes ago," Dr. Levine reported. "His sats were dropping into the eighties."

"What does his chest X ray look like?" Manny asked, trying to assess why Lee couldn't breathe well enough to keep his blood oxygen saturation above 90 percent.

"Bad. Full of fluid. Acute respiratory distress syndrome."

A security guard had found Lee lying in the parking lot. He was conscious for the first few minutes, but his condition quickly deteriorated.

"He was moaning in pain when I got to him. He mentioned your name. Do you know him, Manny?"

"He's with the Department of Homeland Security. I was helping him with the investigation into Jawad Khattib's death. Remember him from the other night?"

"I do. Puzzling case. From the looks of your friend's blood work, whatever's going on here is just like what happened to

Khattib. I'm sorry," he said, and handed his resident a slip of paper that showed Lee's grossly abnormal lab results.

Manny studied the printout as Emma looked over his shoulder. She saw that it wasn't good. Lee's liver and kidneys were already shutting down.

Manny examined Lee as he lay sedated, clinging to life, on a gurney in the emergency room.

"What are you doing?" Emma asked.

Manny continued inspecting Lee's arms and legs. Then, on his neck, he found what he was looking for. He turned Lee's neck gently, careful not to disrupt the tube forcing vital oxygen into his friend's lungs.

Emma saw it and let out a slight gasp.

At the base of the agent's neck was a small mark. Though it was barely noticeable, the two physicians immediately knew what it was.

A needle's small puncture mark.

"But it's happening too fast," Emma said. "It took a couple of days for Khattib's condition to get this severe."

"They must have modified the weapon, made it deadlier. Probably didn't use the linking protein for this one," Manny concluded.

Sue wheeled herself to Lee's bedside. "Is it…?" she began.

Emma nodded and swallowed. A tear rolled down her cheek as she stared at the man lying in front of her.

"We don't have much time. Sue, can you run Lee's blood? Maybe we can stop this before it's too late."

Manny looked at her soberly. "Emma, we tried with Khattib. There's nothing—"

"No! There's always *something* to do. Something to try. Help me?" she pleaded.

Manny understood. They would do all they could, as fruitless as he feared it might be.

"DePena!" Manny called out.

In a matter of seconds, Millie DePena reached their side, surprised that, for the first time, the resident had used her real name.

"Can you draw me a couple of tubes of this patient's blood? Sue here is going to take it to the lab and run some tests."

"But, Doctor, she doesn't work at MGH," a young nurse standing beside Millie protested.

"Just do it," snapped Millie. Despite her feelings for Dr. Ortiz, she knew he was an extraordinary physician. "Give Dr. Ortiz whatever he needs."

"Where can I run the labs?" Sue asked.

"We have a state-of-the-art facility at my office and lab back at Harvard. Let me make some calls. You'll have everything you need," Emma replied as Millie began drawing blood from the IV in Lee's arm.

"I'll get him admitted to the ICU and stay with him up there," Manny said. "Maybe we can predict the course of disease by reviewing Khattib's case. I just might be able to stay one step ahead and buy us some time. But I'm not a miracle worker. I can't save him, Emma. None of us can unless we find out what we're dealing with."

"I'll do what I can," Sue replied. She had already spent countless hours studying Khattib's slides without finding anything that could have saved him. The cause of the massive inflammatory reaction that took the researcher's life still eluded her. "I don't know if I'll find anything new that'll help, but it can't hurt to try."

Dr. Levine returned to check on his patient. "He's strong," he said to Emma. "That'll help."

"But that won't be enough," she replied, keeping her eyes on Lee. She had encountered many critical patients in her career. But seeing Lee lying on the table broke through her professional defenses. Emma had always been able to maintain compassion while remaining detached—until this moment.

Seth Levine, Emma, and Manny stood quietly at Lee's feet. The three experienced physicians were well aware of the gravity of his condition. Agent Lee Jansen from the Department of Homeland Security was dying a horrible death, and only a miracle could save him.

A shrill alarm from one of Lee's monitors sounded.

"Code blue!" Levine called out as he checked the monitor displaying the electrical activity of Lee's heart. It had gone to flatline. "Get the crash cart in here STAT!"

40

MANNY RIPPED OPEN Lee's shirt and pressed down on his chest with both hands, compressing Lee's heart and forcing it to pump blood. After Millie rushed in with the crash cart, Emma helped her place the defibrillator pads on Lee's chest.

"One milligram IV epi, Millie," Levine ordered. He hoped the epinephrine would be enough to jump-start Lee's heart.

"One milligram epi, got it," Millie cried out as she rushed to the crash cart, leaving Emma to man the defibrillator.

Nurses and residents flooded into the emergency room. The medical professionals took their places around Lee. One of Manny's resident colleagues took charge of Lee's airway to ensure that the chest compressions did not dislodge Lee's endotracheal tube. The ventilator kept oxygen flowing into Lee's lungs as Manny continued cardiopulmonary resuscitation to circulate the oxygenated blood to the agent's brain and kidneys.

Manny's CPR was the only thing preventing Lee's body from completely shutting down.

"Epinephrine is in, Doctor," Millie announced.

Emma looked at Levine. She knew what came next.

"Okay, that's five cycles of CPR, Manny. Let's check for a pulse and rhythm."

Manny instinctively put two fingers on Lee's carotid artery.

"No pulse."

"Analyzing," Emma said to warn Manny not to restart chest compressions until she could determine if Lee's heart was beating on its own.

"V-fib," Emma said as she interpreted the signal on the defibrillator's monitor that displayed the heart's electrical activity. The pulseless rhythm that Emma saw meant Lee's condition was deteriorating.

"Shock him. Two hundred joules," Levine said.

He hoped high voltage would reset Lee's heart after the first round of epinephrine had failed.

"Two hundred joules," repeated Emma, already prepared for the order. "Clear!"

Once everyone's hands were off Lee, Emma sent two hundred joules of electricity into Lee's heart.

His body jumped an inch off the gurney, but his heart didn't start beating.

"Resume compressions and ready another round of epi," Levine ordered.

One of the interns attempted to relieve Manny from delivering the chest compressions.

"Back off!" snapped Manny.

Levine noticed the exchange. "All right, let's focus, people. Remember your jobs in a code. Millie, let's push a three hundred mg bolus of amiodarone."

"Got it, Doctor," she replied. Millie had more experience in codes than anyone in the room and knew the life-saving advanced cardiac life support algorithms by heart. She had the antiarrhythmic medication ready even before the director of emergency medicine had asked for it.

"All right, Emma, after the next round of compressions, let's check that rhythm again."

All eyes went to the small monitor after Manny finished CPR and again confirmed there was no pulse. Everyone held their breath for a moment. But there was no change on the monitor.

"Three hundred joules this time, Emma."

"Three hundred joules. Clear!" Emma announced as she delivered the second shock to Lee.

"Nothing," announced Levine. "Another round of epi, Millie."

Fifteen minutes had passed, and still Lee's heart hadn't resumed beating on its own. Manny continued his chest compressions while Millie drew up the final dose of epinephrine.

Emma knew that Seth Levine would end the code if Lee continued to show no signs of life.

"Come on, Lee, damn it!" she blurted out.

The medical team watched in silence as Manny finished his fifth and final round of compressions. He shook his head as he felt for a pulse.

The team members glanced at one another knowingly.

Manny turned away and pulled off his gloves, anticipating the worst as he let out a quiet expletive.

"Three sixty, Emma," Levine said quietly.

"Clear!" she yelled, even though no one had their hands on Lee.

After the jolt of three hundred sixty joules lifted Lee off the table, all eyes turned toward the monitor.

It was flatline. Lee still had no pulse and no detectable cardiac rhythm.

"Okay, I'm calling it," Levine said.

"No! Live, damn it!" she shouted as she pounded on Lee's chest with her clenched fist.

Manny and Millie both reached for her.

"Get me some Ativan," Levine ordered calmly, anticipating Emma's need for a sedative.

As they pulled Emma off Lee's body, however, a beep from the monitor snapped everyone to attention. A slow rhythm emerged on the tiny screen.

Manny put his hand on Lee's neck. "There's a pulse!" he called.

"Millie, push that dose of epi and make sure that amiodarone drip is going," Levine ordered, seeing a viable rhythm forming on the cardiac monitor.

The pulse was slow, but the epinephrine would take care of that. Lee Jansen was back from the dead...for now.

"Manny," Levine said, motioning him to take Emma out of the emergency department.

"Emma, we've got a heartbeat," Manny said to her softly. "Let Dr. Levine and the team take care of him. He'll be okay now. Come on."

"No, I want to stay," she said, her eyes wet with tears.

"Come on. Both of us are too close to this. You know that. Let's go into the other room and figure out a way to save him. You brought him back. Now we have to find a way to cure him, and we don't have much time."

Emma stared at Manny blankly, lost in the sorrow that had overcome her. She composed herself as his words sank in and allowed him to lead her away from the gurney.

Sue reached out and took Emma's hand as Manny wheeled her to the lounge. Lee was alive. But they knew he would not last long without a definitive treatment against the unknown weapon.

41

EMMA, MANNY, AND SUE sat huddled in a corner of the lounge, racking their brains for a solution. Kaiser entered the ER's break room.

"The nurse up front told me you'd all be in here," the agent said. "How is he?"

"Not out of the woods, but he's still with us," Manny said.

When Seth Levine entered the break room, all eyes turned to him.

"Well, he's tach-ing along," Seth reported, referring to Lee's fast heart rate. "But his BP's holding on two pressures. We're moving him up to the ICU. Critical but stable. For now."

Levine took his glasses off and sat down. It had already been a long evening, and his shift was only half over.

After Lee's heartbeat had returned, Levine started two intravenous medications to help keep his fragile blood pressure in a near-normal range. Then he arranged the transfer to the ICU as quickly as possible.

"Thanks, Seth," Manny told his boss.

"We're good for now. But we all know where this is heading. I hope the ICU can figure out a treatment plan soon," said Levine. "You know how this ended the last time. By the way, before he coded, I was about to tell you what your friend said to me."

"When they found Lee in the parking lot?" Manny asked.

"What did he say?" Emma added.

"He said, 'Astrea.'"

"'Astrea'?" Manny replied. "Are you sure?"

"Positive. I repeated it to him, he nodded and said it again before he lost consciousness. I'm sure. Does that mean anything to you?"

"No," Emma answered, puzzled. She tried to recall if that name had come up at any point during their time together exploring Khattib's death.

"Well, I just wanted you to know," he said before he left the break room and returned to the busy ER.

"Astrea? What could that mean?" asked Kaiser. "Is it a medical term?"

"It doesn't *mean* anything," Sue said. "It's a place. A research facility."

"Where?" Manny asked.

"What kind of research?" Emma wanted to know.

"It's in New Hampshire. Not too far from here. It used to be a big genetics research lab. A lot of scientists worked there, but not anymore. I even had an application in with the lab before they were bought out about a year ago."

"Bought out by who?" Kaiser asked, pulling out his phone again.

"Astrea Laboratories, I guess. That's the new name, anyway. I never heard of them until recently, but they must have some serious money. They bought the old lab, let everyone go, and I haven't heard of anyone else working there since."

"Do you think that's the location of the primary investigator on the research Khattib was working on?" Manny asked her. "Maybe where he sent his samples?"

"Could be. They would have a lot of lab space and equipment up there, just not a lot of scientists anymore," answered Sue. "Pretty remote, too. It's in the mountains."

"Kaiser, hold up a second," Manny said, noticing the agent punching numbers in his phone.

"I was going to have Washington search the database on Astrea. See what pops up," he explained.

Manny shook his head. "Lee was worried about someone being one step ahead of us. I think maybe he was right. After the explosion, I don't know who knows what and who's on whose side. I'm just not in a very trusting mood right about now."

"Manny's right," Emma added. "Lee wanted to keep this between us." She choked on her words as she added, "You can see why, given what's happened."

Kaiser nodded and put his cell phone away.

If Lee had mentioned Astrea, there was a chance that someone at the lab knew how to save him. "I'm going there to pay them a visit," Emma said.

"Are you out of your mind?" exclaimed Manny. "Lee went all lone wolf on us, and look at him now. And he's a trained government agent. You wouldn't last five minutes up there if they really are the people that did this." He paused for a second before adding, "I'll go too."

"Why don't I go instead?" Kaiser offered. "If you think Astrea Labs is responsible in any way for what happened to Lee, I want to take them down."

Emma hesitated. She didn't know Kaiser well but decided she had little choice. She knew it would be foolish to go alone. She replied, "Fine, but just you. No one else from DHS can know. I want to surprise them."

"If Kaiser's going, why do you even have to go, Emma?" Manny asked, concerned.

"I have to go, Manny. Someone with medical knowledge needs to be there to see what's going on. But I have a plan. I'll need both you and Sue for it to work. That's why you need to stay here."

Manny saw the resolve in Emma's eyes. He knew there was no dissuading her.

"Okay, I'm in," he relented.

"You can count on me," added Sue.

"Sue, I need you in the lab. We've got to find a way to stop the inflammatory process before it overtakes Lee. Instead of a cure, let's just focus right now on what we know and slow down his out-of-control immune reaction. Buy us some time, Sue." Emma looked at the clock on the wall. It was almost midnight. "First, we all need to get some rest. We're no use to Lee or anyone if we're exhausted."

"I only need a few hours," Sue said. "I don't usually get much sleep anyway."

"I think all of us in the medical field can function fairly well with little sleep," Manny added.

"Yeah, but I don't want 'fairly well.' We need to be on the top of our game," Emma said.

"Sue technically hasn't been discharged yet. She still has her room on the ortho ward. It's a semiprivate room with two beds," said Manny.

"That's right," Sue chimed in. "But no one's in the other bed."

"Why don't you two go back there and crash for a few hours," Manny told both women. "There's a lounge chair as well. I'll catch some Zs there." Manny still wasn't comfortable with leaving them there alone. He made a mental note to tell the charge nurse on orthopedics to wake him immediately if anyone suspicious entered the ward. Visiting hours were over, so only known medical staff should be coming and going. "One of the security guards here in the ER is a friend of mine. He's working tonight but gets off at midnight. He moonlights as a PI. I'll ask him to hang around for a few hours on the ortho ward to look over us so we can get some sleep. There's a resident call room on the same ward. I'll see if I can use up a few favors and get it for you, Kaiser."

"Thanks. It's been a long day for all of us."

"That's a good idea, Manny," Emma said as she stood up. "In the morning, you can take Sue to my office. I'll call my boss, Rick Caruthers. He'll get you into the building and take you to our labs."

"Okay. I'll talk to Nurse Millie DePena and have her save Lee's blood samples for us to pick up on our way out," Manny replied.

"Sue, you're our last hope," Emma said.

Sue looked uncomfortable with so much riding on her, but she straightened up in her wheelchair and nodded.

"Agent Kaiser, can you make sure Sue gets to her room okay? She knows the way," Emma said. "We'll be there shortly."

"Sure," replied Kaiser. He pushed Sue's wheelchair into the hallway as Emma closed the lounge door behind them.

"What's up?" Manny asked.

"I have something I'd like you to do for me. It's a bit unorthodox and probably breaks more than a few laws," she said. "You say your friend is a private investigator?"

"Who, Darryl? Yeah. Does mostly benign stuff, you know, catching cheating husbands and such. But he'll keep a close eye out for anything suspicious tonight on the ward."

"Good. But I was wondering if he'd do us a little favor."

"I'm sure he will if he can. I've taken care of his daughter a few times when she was sick. He and I are pretty close. What are you thinking?"

"Can you go get him? I want to see if he can give us some help. The *clandestine* kind."

"Sounds like my kind of plan," he said, and cracked his knuckles for emphasis. "The sneakier, the better."

"I figured you'd say that," Emma said, smiling.

42

AS MUCH AS THEY TRIED to rest, sleep eluded Emma, Manny, and Sue. Their minds raced trying to come up with ways to save Lee. Sue wondered what tests she should try on Lee's blood samples while Manny contemplated how he was going to execute Emma's plan. Emma thought about Lee. For some inexplicable reason, she had become attached to him in the short time she had known him. She didn't understand it but felt it. Last week she was just another Harvard physician, researcher, and medical school professor. Now she was thrust into a dark world that she barely understood and had almost died twice. All of her years of schooling had not prepared her for what she had been through.

After a couple of hours of tossing and turning, even under the watchful eye of Darryl Freeman, the three decided that sleep would not come. Besides, the sooner they completed their assigned tasks, the better chance they had at saving Lee, if that were possible. Besides, Emma had a long drive a head of her.

It was still dark when Manny and Sue arrived at Emma's lab at the Harvard T.H. Chan School of Public Health. Against Manny's insistence, Sue opted for crutches instead of a wheelchair to allow her to be more mobile. She was surprised she had been able to win that battle.

The lab, as Emma had promised, was truly state of the art. Sue hadn't had access to such modern equipment since her days as a grad student. She immediately went to work analyzing Lee's blood samples as Manny made them some coffee he found in one of the adjoining offices.

"It's no use, Manny. There's nothing new here," Sue said as she pushed the microscope away from her ten minutes later. "All I see is a slide full of inflammatory cells. No different from what overtook Khattib's system and killed him. There's nothing here that gives me any clue as to what's triggering this response."

"We need to find something, Sue," Manny replied. "What can I do to help?"

"Okay," she said, closing her eyes. "Let me think. Why don't we start by categorizing all the cells we see? Once we know the quantities of each type, we can determine which ones are abnormally elevated. Maybe then we can pinpoint the cause of the increased cell lines."

"Great idea," Manny said, impressed. "Different inflammatory cells respond to different triggers."

"That's right. Each type of cell performs a different function in an inflammatory response. We can better hone our search if we know what cell line is most active. Maybe then we can tone it down or turn it off."

The two worked side by side as the minutes ticked by. It would be dawn soon. They calculated and mapped each microscopic field to quantify the various inflammatory cell lines present.

"That's odd," Sue said.

"What is it?"

"When we isolate each cell line, the largest immunologic contributor is cytosolic nuclear factor-kB. NF-kB."

Manny held his hands up and shrugged. "Okay, help me out here. I haven't had an immunology course since med school."

"NF-kB is a naturally occurring transcription factor in the body," Sue explained. "Once it's activated by the presence of a pathogen or organism, it binds to the genes in our DNA that encode for a whole host of different inflammatory mediators. Basically, it's the master switch of the inflammatory response."

Manny nodded. "We know it's the inflammatory response that's killing Lee, so it's not surprising to see a lot of NF-kB, right? Especially if it's responsible for turning on all the genes involved in the immune response."

"That's true. Something had to turn on the NF-kB gene. We just don't know what that trigger was that did it."

"How about the vector you found in Khattib's blood?"

"I don't see it," she replied, still looking into the microscope. "No elements of SRLVs anywhere."

"If the vector isn't breaking up and leaving traces of its viral shell like it did in Khattib, that means they've perfected it. That's bad," Manny said. "Anything else?"

"Nope. Other than no evidence of SRLVs, everything is looking just like Khattib's samples. Nothing but NF-kB and a lot of inflammation with no indication as to what set it off."

"So, we're back to square one?" asked Manny.

Sue sat back in her chair. "I'm afraid so."

Manny looked at his watch. It was time for him to execute the next phase of Emma's plan.

"Sue, I got to go on a little errand for Emma. Are you all right here by yourself?"

"Sure. The guard's downstairs, no one else really knows we're here. Besides, Emma's staff should be in soon. Where are you going."

"You don't want to know," he said, putting on his jacket.

43

W E'RE CLEAR," the Architect said into the secure telephone. "All external arms of our research in this country have been shut down, and the remaining traces of Project Astrea are on their way back to me. That includes the remaining documents from CIGR. We'll continue to put all three components of the bioweapon together here in my lab and should have a final product this week. Another test subject has been injected. It wasn't a vector test, just a weapon test."

"I thought the weapon had already demonstrated its effectiveness on that Arab researcher," the senator replied.

"Yes," the Architect answered. "This was another last-minute test. And thus far it is exceeding our expectations. The refined weapon had a much quicker response this time."

It had been the Architect's idea to use the weaponized vector without the linking protein on Lee Jansen. Although the vector had been modified to bind with the linking protein, he had no need to target the man's genes. He only wanted to kill the agent and send a message to his colleagues in Boston.

Bruno had wanted to dispose of Jansen the old-fashioned way—with a bullet to the back of the head. But the Architect was wary of more DHS interference. An execution of a federal agent would bring a rapid response from the authorities. Project Astrea had already had enough complications.

Until an autopsy was performed, no one would fully understand the cause of Jansen's death. That would buy them time. The Order might even use their influence to delay—or even manipulate— the autopsy results. By the time it was understood that the agent had been murdered, the weapon and its vector delivery system would be off U.S. soil.

"However," continued the Architect, "we need to advance the timetable of the project's initial deployment. Because of the recent interruptions, I redoubled our efforts in this lab as well as the one in the Levant. Working around the clock, our researchers are just about finished formulating the final product. The linking protein has been modified for use against the first target population, using the data from our test subjects in Lebanon. We've also perfected the vector. It will activate and release the weapon once it successfully attaches to genetic codes specific to the target race. Within the next week or so, we'll have enough of the aerosolized product to begin the next phase."

"So soon?" asked the senator, sounding both pleased and surprised.

The Architect allowed himself a smile. It had been a long, arduous process. Over two years. Money, time, and lives had been sacrificed in the development of the Order's most important legacy. Once news of Project Astrea's success spread, dictators, terrorists, and crime lords across the globe would line up to pay any price for the weapon. And pay more, of course, to ensure their own DNA was not targeted. The additional wealth would lead the Order to even greater international influence. More important, the Architect's enemies would be exterminated.

"Yes, so soon. Please arrange a gathering of the Ten. I will present our research results to our fellow leaders, and we can discuss the weapon's deployment. Agreed?"

"Agreed. I'll confirm a time for you shortly. Excellent work, Philip. I'm happy we brought you on board. You were definitely the man for this job," the senator replied, and hung up.

Philip Peters leaned back in his leather chair and stared out of the window as the morning sun shone its first bright rays on his beloved mountains. Project Astrea was the answer to the world's problems, a way to ensure that world order was maintained by eliminating undesirable populations that threatened security or caused a burden. He was, in essence, only accelerating Darwin's conclusions. The fittest, as determined by the Order, would survive, and flourish.

"Dr. Peters?" his assistant announced at the office door.

"Yes, Richard. What is it?"

"Sir," Richard replied nervously. "It's Dr. Hess. Emma Hess."

Peters saw that his assistant's hands trembled. And this timid child thought he could run Project Astrea. Ridiculous.

"What about her?"

He had almost put Emma and the others out of mind. After all, Agent Jansen was as good as dead.

"She's here, sir. Sitting in her car in the parking lot."

"What?" Peters asked, dumbfounded. *So, Bruno was correct. They are more capable than I gave them credit for.* "Now?"

"Yes, sir."

"Has Bruno returned from Boston?"

"No, sir. Not yet."

Peters pondered his next move.

"Show our guest in, Richard. It would be rude to make her wait."

44

ARJUN SINGH'S 1825 colonial saltbox house stood proudly in one of Boston's most exclusive communities. His lavish lifestyle was necessary to impress his corporate clients. But he also enjoyed the extravagant amenities his association with the Order had brought him.

He had been introduced to the secret organization twenty years earlier as an undergraduate in India. His father, a prominent physicist in Mumbai, was well known and respected. His powerful connections brought Arjun to grad school in the United States. Rajesh Singh often told his son that everyone had to pay a price for a life of wealth and success. That price was responsibility. Like his father, Rajesh was a member of an elite society of overachievers, men and women who had mastered their crafts and were hand-selected to pool their collective talents and resources for a greater good.

The Order reached out to Arjun after he obtained his Ph.D. in organic chemistry. He was honored to join the ranks of his father and grandfather in the prestigious organization, even if he was not allowed tell anyone of his membership. After his acceptance, doors began to open. Faculty positions at well-known academic institutions were offered at every turn, even though he'd barely begun his postgrad work and was still an unproven scientific researcher.

In his high-back armchair before the sitting room's fireplace, Singh contemplated his past. With the shades down, the room was dark, lit only by the embers' glow. Around him, shadows danced on the walls to the music of the crackling fire. Shadows. That's what his life had become.

For all the accolades, the wealth and power his association with the Order had brought him, it did come, as his father had warned, with a price. But for him the price was quite different from what it had been for his father. Because Arjun had not paid his dues by publishing volumes of research, his colleagues in the scientific community shunned him, and he had become an outcast.

His mentors in the Order could do a great deal for him, but even they could not give him the legitimacy he craved. He had tried to conduct his own research, but the Order had interfered. His research, his mind and abilities, now belonged to the Order. To appease his masters, he cut corners and ignored standard protocols, conducting questionable research at their behest. This was necessary, he was told, to keep the Order's anonymity and to develop science that was considered too sensitive or politically incorrect for mainstream researchers. Or, at times, even illegal. Like Project Astrea.

A few years back, after years of frustration with his lack of respect in the scientific community, Singh had tried to go it alone. He shunned the Order's requests and accepted an adjunct teaching position at a small college in upstate New York. He had hoped to start fresh and focus on original research. Finally, he would gain the recognition he craved.

However, not long after he began working at the college, the true reach of the Order became clear to him. Subjects dropped out of his research project, funding was abruptly cut off, and he was let go from his position.

The Order had issued a stern warning. He would not disobey again.

Now, after making amends with the Order, he was again asked to skirt the accepted protocols of his profession for the cause. He pondered this as he sat alone in his million-dollar home. His only companions were paid for with the wealth he accumulated from the Order. Blood money.

He had breached research protocols on behalf of the Order on more than one occasion. Legitimacy still eluded him—

Thud.

Singh snapped his head around and peered into the main hall leading toward the front door.

"Hello? Is anyone there?" he called out.

Silence. His mind was playing tricks on him. He leaned back in his overstuffed armchair and stared deeper into the fire.

His thoughts turned to the recent excitement with the Homeland Security agent and that damned assassin. He wasn't sure whom to fear more, Jansen or the Sicilian. At least Jansen was finally out of the picture. The Sicilian, however—that was another story. The assassin was angry with him for not killing Jansen. But he was not a killer. He was a scientist. Besides, his successes with Project Astrea would ensure his safety for the time being. He hoped.

Again he heard sound.

The Mumbaikar stood and slowly walked into the dark hall.

Could it be the assassin, returning to tie up loose ends? Peters also had been angry with him for revealing too much to Jansen. But he couldn't help it. He'd got carried away in the excitement of the moment. He was so close to the scientific triumph he'd longed for all these years.

Arriving at the front door, he checked the locks. Everything was still secure. The wind picked up outside. He peered out the rectangular glass windows to see the first rays of dawn. He started as the wind blew a tree branch into the window.

As he turned back toward the sitting room, a flash of movement raced toward him.

"Taj! You scared me half to death," he said as the tabby rubbed against his leg. Singh caught his breath and reached down to pick up the fat cat.

Singh was not married. His mother pressed him to wed one of the string of Indian women she had chosen for him. He'd always been too busy to tend to his personal life. Now, perhaps, the time was right. With Astrea, he had accomplished his professional dream. Maybe it was time for an arranged marriage. He could settle down and reap the rewards of his hard work and dedication to the Order.

He flipped through the mental images of the women as he returned to the fireplace. But he stopped cold when he saw a man sitting in his chair.

"Hello, Doctor," the man said, standing up and towering over him.

"What? What are you doing here?"

But the man said nothing.

Singh's heart raced and he started to backpedal. The intruder advanced.

"No!" Singh yelled.

45

EMMA REGARDED her DHS escort. Erik Kaiser was young and resembled a banker rather than a federal agent. Round glasses, a round face with pale skin, and curly brown hair. Emma wished she had Lee or Manny with her. Kaiser looked like he was barely out of college and wasn't nearly as rugged-looking as Lee. She wasn't sure if he could handle whatever was waiting for them in the brick office building at the end of the empty parking lot. For that matter, she wasn't so sure she was prepared either. She put her hand on her jacket pocket for reassurance, then let out a sigh of relief. It was still there.

"Let's go," she said, and opened the car door.

"What's the plan?" Kaiser asked.

"We're going to go into Astrea Labs and demand to see the director."

"What then?" he asked.

"That's why you're here. You have a badge, right?" Emma said.

"Yeah. But I have no warrant. And when Waters finds out, I'll probably have no job either," he said. But Emma was already out of the car and walking toward the building. Kaiser hurried after her. He was beginning to regret his decision to come with her, but remembered that Agent Jansen was clinging to life back in Boston. While he didn't know the man all that well, the thought of a fellow agent injected with a biological weapon infuriated him.

The two continued toward the two-story brick building. As they approached the revolving door, Emma noticed that the few offices she could see through the windows looked empty. No plants, no furniture, or pictures on the walls.

"Can I help you?" a man with a goatee asked as they entered the building. His long white lab coat covered his clothes.

"I'm Agent Erik Kaiser, Homeland Security," the young agent announced, holding out his badge.

"How can I help you, Agent Kaiser?" the man asked.

"I'm Dr. Emma Hess, from Harvard. And you are?"

"Dr. Richard Becker. I'm the lead scientist at Astrea Labs."

"Dr. Becker, we'd like to see the facility's director, please," continued Kaiser.

Becker nodded. He had his orders, although he had no idea why Peters wanted to see them. "Follow me."

The three walked down a long corridor. Emma noticed the bare walls as they approached a door at the end of the hall. The facility was modest and empty, a stark contrast to Singh's extravagant CIGR.

Becker opened an office door at the end of the hall. A lanky elderly man was seated behind a desk.

"Good day," the man said cheerfully without rising.

"I'm Agent Erik Kaiser from the Department of Homeland Security," Kaiser repeated, again flashing his credentials.

"Good to meet you, Agent Kaiser. And this pretty young lady accompanying you. Does she have a name?"

"Dr. Emma Hess, Harvard School of Public Health," she replied coldly.

"Ah, Dr. Hess, your reputation precedes you," he said with a small tip of his head. "Allow me to introduce myself. I am Dr. Philip Peters, director of Astrea Laboratories. Now that the pleasantries are over, how can I be of assistance?"

"Dr. Peters," Emma began before Erik had a chance to speak, "a colleague of mine, another DHS agent, is in critical condition at Mass. General."

"How terrible. I'm so sorry to hear that. Has he been shot?" Peters replied with a concerned look.

"He's been exposed to a biological agent. Before he fell unconscious, he said the name of your lab."

"Astrea Laboratories?" Peters gasped. "Why, I'm afraid that's impossible. I know no DHS agents. In fact, our laboratory is not even functioning yet. After I purchased it last year, we have been rather slow in getting it up and running."

"You mean there's no research going on here?" asked Kaiser.

"That's correct. I barely have enough staff to run the front office. I'm still trying, quite unsuccessfully, to obtain research grants and contracts from the larger pharmaceutical companies. I haven't even purchased lab equipment, let alone hired many researchers."

"Do you mind if I have a look around?" Kaiser asked.

"Although I assume you have no warrant, I have no problem with you touring our facilities, if you wish. Richard, please take Agent Kaiser on a tour."

"Thank you, Doctor," Kaiser said as he turned to follow the doctor.

"Dr. Hess, perhaps you would like to stay here and keep an old man company. I'm quite impressed by your accomplishments in Boston and would love to hear more about them, if you'll indulge me. I don't get many visitors here, especially one as renowned as yourself."

Emma nodded to Kaiser. "It's okay. I'll wait here."

Kaiser seemed unhappy with the arrangement but left.

"So, tell me," Emma began as she sat down in a chair across from Peters. "What research do you plan on conducting at Astrea Laboratories?"

"Oh, the usual kind. Depends on the contracts we obtain, really."

"What about genetic research?" she pressed. "More specifically, ethnic genetics."

Peters leaned forward in his chair. "My, you are bold," he said quietly. "As to your question, I suspect you already know the answer to that, or otherwise you would not be here. How you came to your conclusion, however, is quite a mystery to me."

"I think there are quite a few mysteries going on here as well, Doctor," declared Emma. "So we're even."

Just then the door to Peters's office opened. Emma turned her head just as a man she recognized from the medical library entered.

Peters shook his head slowly, seemingly intrigued by the woman sitting before him. "I hardly think we're even, Dr. Hess, but please explain."

"For starters, I know that you're developing an ethnic bio-weapon to be used against Israel. I don't know which terrorist group paid you to research and develop this weapon, but you are the principal investigator and you have contracted other labs to contribute to your research."

"Bravo, Doctor," Peters replied. "You are not quite there, but close."

Bruno felt an involuntary impulse tug at him. He was, after all, a professional killer. He never toyed with his prey and certainly had never bantered with a foe. His job was to exterminate people in the most efficient manner possible.

Both Peters and Singh, however, took a different approach, one that made him uneasy. They had been careless in speaking with Hess and Jansen. Singh's slip of the tongue probably had led Hess to their lab. These men, these *scientists*, needed to prove their intellectual superiority over their adversaries. It was their weakness, perhaps even their tragic flaw.

Bruno knew that Dr. Hess could not leave Astrea Laboratories alive.

Emma nervously fingered her cell phone as she talked. Three vibrations would mean her plan was in motion. It was the only hope she had of getting the information she needed from Peters *and* leaving the lab on her own two feet.

Nothing.

She realized the text message might not come at all.

She was stalling.

"And you're here to offer your medical and scientific support to these alleged endeavors of mine?" Peters continued with a laugh, as Bruno remained stone-faced. "Or perhaps you think you can put a premature end to this so-called Project Astrea?"

"Actually, I'm here to offer a truce," she told Peters. "You injected Agent Jansen with your weapon. I want the antidote."

"An antidote?" Peters asked.

"I'm sure you didn't develop a weapon without a way to protect yourselves from its effects. Give me the antidote, and my colleagues and I will stop pursuing you."

"Well, that is a generous offer, indeed, don't you think?" replied Peters, looking up at Bruno, who returned a dead-eyed stare.

"There is one problem, though. You see, Dr. Hess, I am a businessman first and foremost. They call me the Architect because I build deals and projects. I happen to have a background in biochemistry, so it was natural for me to lead Project Astrea and coordinate its many research arms. But in business, in order for a bargain to be struck, you must have something with which to trade. And frankly, I do not see that you are in any position to bargain."

Emma willed her phone to buzz. "A life for a life isn't a fair trade?"

Peters analyzed Emma's face. "Interesting. So whose life are we talking about?"

"Yours."

"A valiant attempt, Doctor, but I hardly see how my life is in any danger."

"I assure you that either I get the antidote right now or this twisted little world of yours, tucked away in these quiet mountains, will come crashing down right on your head."

Emma sat calmly. She looked right through Peters.

He narrowed his eyes as he searched her expression. "You're bluffing," he stated.

Emma wondered if the man was guessing or if he knew, from his own sources, that there was no cavalry charging the hill.

As she contemplated her next move, her phone vibrated three times. Emma exhaled and took out the cell phone.

Bruno flexed, drawing his pistol.

"Now, now, Bruno. I don't think our friend here is armed," Peters said.

Emma froze, eyes on the gun's barrel.

Bruno glanced down at Peters, annoyed that the man was careless enough to use his name. He lowered the pistol slightly.

"Slowly," he hissed to Emma.

As she swallowed back the urge to vomit and gathered her strength, she showed the men her phone. Bruno lowered the gun to his waist, but Emma noticed that he did not return it to its holster.

"There, now. See, she's quite harmless. You were saying, Doctor?" Peters prompted.

She stood slowly and approached his desk, looking down at her phone's screen. She hoped the picture was there. If not, this meeting would be coming to a quick and unpleasant conclusion.

Fortunately, the picture she'd instructed Manny to text her was there. She placed the phone on Peters's desk.

"What is this?" he asked, picking up the phone and putting on his reading glasses.

Without waiting for an invitation, Bruno came and looked over his shoulder at the small picture.

"It's Singh, of course."

"And your point is, Doctor?" Peters asked.

"Arjun Singh is now with one of my colleagues in a secure location. He has agreed to testify against you."

Before Bruno could make a move toward Emma, Peters raised a hand. "Just a moment."

Bruno leaned in toward Peters and whispered into his ear. *"You have one minute to fix this before I finish it."*

Peters spoke quickly but deliberately, annoyed at Bruno's interference. "My dear Dr. Hess, Arjun Singh can provide the authorities with no information about me or anything that I may or may not be working on. You'll have to do better than that, I'm afraid."

"You know that's not true, and so do I. Our goal is only to save Agent Jansen. Give me the antidote and we'll release Singh and walk away. I don't care what happens to Singh after that. All you have to do is to provide me the antidote."

Peters leaned back in his chair, gauging his opponent's resolve. Then he threw his hands up in the air theatrically and said, "All right, Doctor. You win."

Peters reached down, opened the bottom left drawer of his desk, and removed a syringe filled with a clear solution.

Bruno looked at him, astonished.

"So, you're saying that you and your cohort will just walk away if I hand you this syringe?"

"That's right."

"And Singh?"

"He'll be released."

"You drive a hard bargain, Doctor," Peters said, leaning across the desk to hand her the syringe. "Now you will keep your word, won't you?"

"I'm not a fool, Peters. I know you can find me and my friends. Would we be any safer if I broke my deal with the devil and went to the authorities?" she asked. She took the syringe from Peters and put it in her coat pocket. "Even if my conscience is compromised, it's a small price to pay in exchange for Agent Jansen's life."

"You're wise, Doctor. You not only saved Agent Jansen's life, but yours and your friends as well."

Emma stood and turned toward the door. She couldn't get out of his office fast enough. She needed to get the antidote to Lee.

"Dr. Hess," Peters called as Emma reached the door.

She turned to see the two men standing by the desk. For a moment, she was sure they were going to kill her.

"I founded Astrea Laboratories for one specific goal. One focus. Do you have any idea who Astrea was?" Peters asked her.

Emma had no time for riddles. She stood at the door, waiting. Bruno's roiling displeasure at the deal she'd struck with Peters was evident on his face, and she worried he would lose his patience.

"Let me tell you a little story before you leave us. Many, many years ago I lived in a monastery. They took me in at a time when

I was very vulnerable. The abbot was a wise man. I stayed with him throughout what you'd call high school, and he taught me much about the world. He used to tell me stories to help me overcome my nightmares after my parents were killed. My favorite was about Astrea, the goddess of the stars. But she was so much more. In Greek mythology, Astrea was associated with purity. The purest of all. She lived among mortal men, until they became too evil for her liking. Astrea became disillusioned with the deterioration of humanity. She abandoned man because of his wicked ways. It was believed that she would return, ushering with her a new golden age. And that time is now, Dr. Hess. The world is ready. Think about it. You will come to understand and possibly even appreciate our actions one day, loathsome as they may seem to you right now."

Emma wondered how someone could be so evil. Then footsteps behind her broke her trancelike state as she glared into Peters's empty black eyes. She turned and looked down the hall. Her heart leapt when she saw Kaiser walking toward her.

"Nothing. The labs are empty," he said.

"We're done here," Emma said. She swallowed her urge to tell Peters to rot in hell. Her only focus was saving Lee.

She hoped it wasn't too late.

46

EMMA DIALED MANNY as soon as she and Kaiser left Astrea's parking lot.

"He bought it," she said on speaker, driving down the winding road away from Peters's mountain. "I have the antidote."

"You're kidding me," Manny replied. He sat in Singh's dining room across the table from the scientist. "I guess the thought of Singh spilling his guts was too much for him."

Kaiser glanced at Emma with a puzzled look as he listened to the conversation.

"Any trouble on your end?" she asked.

"None. He's singing like a canary," Manny said. "He told me about a secret group called 'the Order.' They're the ones who pull the strings on this thing."

Manny stood and stepped into the foyer, out of Singh's earshot.

"Between you and me, I don't think he knows much else."

It hadn't been difficult for Manny to locate Singh's home. It was a risky move, but, one way or another, they needed to find out as much as they could about Project Astrea. Unfortunately, Singh couldn't give them much.

"Singh told me the goal of the Order was to influence the course of world events to their liking."

"How did you get him to talk?"

"They taught us lots of useful things in the Rangers. Interrogation is one of our skill sets. And what I didn't learn from the Army, my Middle Eastern brethren taught me," Manny added. "In other words, you don't want to know."

"Well, we're fine for now. I have the antidote. Once Lee's safe, we can use Singh's testimony to go after Peters and the Order."

"Okay. Drive safely but put the pedal to the metal. I'm not sure how much time Lee has left," Manny replied before signing off.

"What antidote?" Kaiser asked.

"I got it from Peters when you were out of the office," Emma explained.

"How did you get Peters to give it to you?"

"As it turned out, Singh was Peters's man in Boston. Jawad Khattib worked for him. CIGR, Singh's lab, was making part of the weapon. Khattib made it all possible, although he had no idea what he was really working on."

"You know nothing Singh told Manny will hold up in court," Kaiser told her. "He would claim it was all under duress. Not exactly legal, either."

"Maybe not, but it scared him enough to talk. At least we know who we're dealing with. And we have the antidote."

"Are you sure about that?"

"It just *has* to be."

In the past few days, she'd found herself caring about Lee more than she would have thought possible, and the thought of losing him was unsettling.

"I'll talk to Undersecretary Waters," Kaiser said. "He should be able to get a warrant to search Astrea Labs. I didn't see much on my little tour, but I'm sure my guide left out a few locations. We'll go through that building with a fine-tooth comb. If there's anything there, we'll find it," Kaiser stated. "You know, Singh is a dead man now. We have to get him into protective custody as soon as possible."

Emma wasn't worried about Singh at the moment. She looked at the syringe filled with clear fluid and then at her watch. They were hours from Boston. "If you can handle those things once we're back in Boston, we'll all be forever in your debt—and I hope Singh rots in jail when all this is over. Right now, we need to get back to the hospital if we have any chance of saving Lee."

47

LEE LAY COMPLETELY STILL. Tubes, wires, and IVs came from his mouth and nose, and ran under the sheets of his ICU bed. He was as sick as anyone Manny had ever seen.

The ICU's team of physicians, nurses, and technicians had worked miracles throughout the night as they fought to keep Lee alive. Every time Lee's labs returned and showed his organs were shutting down, the team countered to delay the inevitable.

Emma rushed into the ICU. Tears welled in her eyes when she saw how gaunt and pale Lee's once-vibrant face had become.

"Emma," Manny called from the nurses' station, breaking her trance.

"Here, give this to him," she said to Manny, handing him the syringe. "Hurry."

Manny focused on the clear fluid contained in the syringe. "Emma, we have no clue what this is. What if it's a poison? What if it kills him?"

"We have no choice. Look at him." In her head, she knew Manny was right. But she was speaking from her heart.

"Let me get Sue to run some quick tests on the fluid. Let's see—" Manny began.

"No. There's no time for that. He's dying."

"Half an hour. That's all Sue will need for us to be sure. You don't want to kill him," he said softly. "Think about it. As a physician and a scientist. What's the right thing to do?"

If he died while Sue tested what turned out to be the antidote, Emma would never forgive herself. But her anguish would be worse if she poisoned him without running the tests.

"Go. But hurry. He doesn't have long."

Manny hurried out of the ICU with the syringe in hand. He almost knocked Kaiser down as the two passed in the corridor.

"Sorry, Kaiser," Manny said as he continued off the ward in a trot.

Kaiser joined Emma at the door to Lee's ICU room. "I just got off the phone with Waters," he said. "He told me he called the judge after my last phone call. The judge wasn't overly enthusiastic, but said he'd issue a warrant. Maybe as early as this afternoon."

"Okay. By then we should know if the antidote will work," Emma said. She didn't want to talk about the alternatives.

MANNY DROVE to the Harvard T.H. Chan School of Public Health's lab facility where Sue was still trying to find out what was causing Lee's rapid decline. The lunchtime traffic was heavy and he found himself losing patience with the other drivers. Finally he reached his destination. He jumped out of his car and raced up the building's granite steps. A guard stopped him in the lobby. Manny had to swallow his urge to pull the guard up off his feet by his crooked tie and tell him he didn't have time to "show his Harvard ID." Instead, Manny smiled and fumbled through his pocket until he found his hospital ID, then he raced up the stairs to the research floor.

Manny found Sue peering through a microscope in Emma's lab.

"So we have to know what this is before we give it to Lee. It didn't exactly come from a good Samaritan," he finished after relaying what had transpired at Astrea Labs.

"Let's hope it's for real, because I still have no idea what's killing Lee," replied Sue, taking the syringe from Manny. "Let's take a look."

"We don't have much time. I promised Emma I'd be back in an hour."

Sue pulled the plunger out of the syringe and used a pipette to remove a measured amount of the fluid. She placed a drop of the solution onto a glass slide and then put a cover over the sample.

As Sue moved the slide onto the high-powered microscope, its edge caught on the microscope's corner and it fell, shattering at her feet.

"Damn," she cursed.

Manny placed a reassuring hand on her arm and picked up the pipette with his other hand. "It's okay, Sue. We're all on edge. Let me help."

He prepared another slide for her and placed it on the microscope's stage. Sue offered Manny a small smile before she removed her glasses and peered into the binocular lenses.

"Well, it's a crystalline structure. That's about all I can tell from this scope. We'll need to put it through the spectrometer to determine its chemical structure."

"How long will that take?" he asked.

"Fifteen minutes. But we'll have to go to the lab down the hall." Sue started to pick up the syringe and her notebook, but Manny interjected. "Here, let me get that."

Manny was impressed how well Sue was getting around with just one crutch. In truth, though, it wasn't just chivalry that made him carry her things. The last thing Manny wanted to do this afternoon was try to get another antidote from Peters, should anything happen to this syringe.

They walked to the end of the corridor before entering a larger lab that housed a cylinder-shaped nuclear magnetic resonance spectrometer.

"That thing's a monster," Manny said.

"It's actually smaller than most, but larger than some of the newer ones. This will work for us, though."

Sue turned on the machine and placed the sample into the spectrometer.

Knowing that Sue was somewhere between awkward and downright clumsy, Manny stayed close to the petite scientist as she fumbled with her crutch while she worked.

"So, this will give us an image of the chemical compound in the syringe?" asked Manny.

"Yes. The magnet in the spectrometer interacts with the electrical properties of the atoms in the sample. First, it'll give me a printout of the measurements of these chemical shifts, lining each molecule up by atomic structure. I'll then have the computer collate this data and generate a three-D rendering of the sample's molecules," Sue explained. She knew Manny was a clinician, not a bench researcher.

"Sweet!" he replied. "You know, you're pretty smart."

"You're not so bad yourself," she murmured as the large machine processed the sample.

The two sat in front of the computer attached to the spectrometer in awkward silence as they waited for the machine to issue the results.

"Manny, if the technology to create an ethnic weapon is perfected, it would be devastating," Sue said.

"I know. We'll stop them, but we need to save Lee first. What do you think's killing him?"

"I really don't know. Like Khattib, there's nothing in his labs that suggests a cause for the out-of-control inflammation."

"It's the perfect weapon. No trace and no cure."

"Who are these people?"

"From what I can tell, they're a bunch of madmen, but I'm not really sure what to believe at this point. It's hard to imagine a group of people working this hard to annihilate a race of people. But I guess history has had its fair share of crazies with similar goals."

"If they find a way to perfect it—" Sue started.

"I know. Well, we just won't let that happen, will we?" he reassured her.

Sue wasn't sure they could save Lee, let alone understand and stop whatever plot was in motion. "Things aren't looking too good for the good guys," she muttered.

The printer came to life and the analysis took form on paper. Sue leaned over and read the results.

"No, this can't be right," she said. She typed some commands on the keyboard and waited for the molecular shape to appear on the screen.

"What is it?"

"Get Emma on the phone," Sue said.

"What's wrong?" he asked, pulling out his cell phone and hitting redial.

"That injection won't cure Lee."

Manny heard the phone begin to ring. "Why not?"

"It's just Ketorolac," she answered. "An intramuscular anti-inflammatory. Nothing more."

"What? A nonsteroidal? That's all? Are you certain?"

"My research in grad school was on the structure of anti-inflammatories. I know that molecule like the back of my thumb," she said, pointing to the screen.

Manny ignored the jumbled expression. "There's nothing else?"

"The spectrometer analyzed the entire sample. That's it. That's all it is."

"Hello?" Emma asked on the other end of the line. "Manny, what do you have?"

"We got nothing, Emma. Absolutely nothing."

48

PHILIP PETERS AND BRUNO STROZZA stood in Astrea's executive parking lot. Under the watchful eye of Richard, paramilitary guards dressed in black and brandishing Uzi submachine guns loaded boxes and files into the back of a limo.

"I still don't understand why you let her walk out of here alive. Your insistence that they not be killed keeps coming back to haunt us," Bruno said.

"If you recall, I gave you specific instructions to terminate our friends earlier when their 'accidental deaths' would have been less conspicuous. But you failed. You couldn't even kill them after I went to the trouble of having the fire detection system in the coroner's lab disabled. And how difficult was it to push Dr. Hess off a subway platform? My God, man, she's less than half your size."

Peters's words stung, but Bruno held his tongue.

"Killing Hess at this point would only bring further attention, especially since she was accompanied by a DHS agent," Peters stated.

"They'll be back. With a warrant and an army of agents," Bruno told the other man.

"Stop worrying. Dr. Hess is now wasting all of her time and energy trying in vain to save Agent Jansen. That'll give us enough time to relocate before she goes to the authorities. That's why she's still alive. If she and the agent didn't return to the hospital, this place would already be crawling with federal agents. I just bought us some time to leave and prepare to deploy the weapon."

"And Singh?"

"I no longer have any use for him."

"I'll take care of him," Bruno stated quietly, eager to redeem himself.

"Do it quickly. We leave soon," the Architect said, looking at his Rolex.

"I'll head back down to Boston now and fly out from there when the job's finished."

"Good. I'll meet up with you in my overseas lab."

Peters's current focus was to get all of Project Astrea's samples far away from this place. Anyone left behind was on his own.

The two men walked out to the limo as the last of the boxes was loaded.

"I wanted to ask you something, Dr. Peters. Project Astrea has no antidote," Richard began, then stopped midsentence. Perhaps Peters had created an antidote behind his back. It wouldn't be the first time his mentor made changes to his research protocols.

"You're correct. There is no antidote," Peters answered.

"What did you give her?" Bruno asked.

"A harmless anti-inflammatory injection I give myself from time to time when my back is acting up. It's hell getting old, Bruno. It just happened to be in my desk drawer. Dr. Hess will inject it into Agent Jansen and, for several hours anyway, it will appear to reduce the inflammation and slow his downward spiral. She'll waste time sitting at his bedside waiting for a miracle. Have no fear, though: Agent Jansen will be dead by this time tomorrow. And by then we'll be on safer shores."

"Brilliant," Richard said, genuinely impressed by the man's cunning and ruthlessness.

"And then?" Bruno asked.

"Then, my friend, you can take care of our remaining adversaries in Boston. But only after the meeting of the Ten. I received a call from the senator just after Dr. Hess left. It'll be held this Friday at noon in Manhattan. Until then, no loose ends and no more risks. I want no one else snooping around. No police or FBI or DHS. *No one.* After you take care of Singh, there will be no traces of Project Astrea in this country. Any investigation will be spinning its wheels."

"Will they find anything during Jansen's autopsy?" asked Bruno.

"They didn't find anything in Khattib, did they?"

"Enough for Jansen and Hess to start poking around in our business," Bruno pointed out.

Peters sighed. "Thanks to Agent Jansen and Dr. Hess, our misdirection about Egyptian terrorists and a dirty bomb did not have the effect I'd hoped. Not even the propaganda or yttrium samples you planted sold them the story. Granted, we couldn't sell it too hard for fear of shutting down the entire city. We had to find just the right balance. No matter. Everything will quiet down for a day or so while Hess tends to Jansen. And after he dies, the DHS will take some time to investigate. I'll speak to our friend there to make sure they drag their feet. In the meantime, we shouldn't bring any more attention to ourselves. We'll eliminate Hess and Chen *after* the meeting," ordered Peters.

"What about Ortiz?"

Peters smiled. "I have other plans for him. Plans that you'll appreciate, Bruno."

49

"DAMN HIM!" Emma exclaimed over speakerphone. She should have known the cure was a sham. The syringe held nothing more than a glorified intramuscular nonsteroidal anti-inflammatory. Lee was already on IV steroids that were much more effective than whatever Peters had given her.

"I'm sorry, Emma," replied Sue.

"Peters is stalling. We would've lost a day as Lee's inflammation temporarily receded if not for Manny. Wait—" She suddenly had a breakthrough. "That's what I was trying to tell you back in the lab. It's the inflammation!"

"Emma, you're not making sense. We *know* it's inflammation killing Lee, but we don't know the organism or toxin causes the reaction," Sue replied.

"But that's just it. That's because there *is* no organism or toxin. The weapon targets the immune system itself. It initiates a SIRS response without any triggers. Once the inflammatory process kicks into high gear, unable to shut off, it destroys the body. Not only will this weapon select and kill entire populations, it will devastate the medical infrastructure in the process. Hospitals are going to overflow with patients dying from sepsis in their ICUs."

"A manufactured SIRS without an organism? Brilliant. But how can the weapon do that?" Manny asked.

"Lee's immune system isn't turning off, it just keeps attacking itself," Sue said, placing a piece of the puzzle. "That's why we couldn't find any organisms other than the viral vector. There aren't any. It was always the weapon-induced inflammatory cascade working in overdrive."

"Yeah, but now it's killing Lee," Emma said. "I wonder what specific gene the weapon is targeting to keep his immune system running on autopilot."

"NF-kB," Sue said definitively.

"What?" asked Emma.

"That's it, Sue. It must be," replied Manny.

"What are you two talking about?"

"We found huge amounts of NF-kB in Lee's blood. It's one of the first steps in initiating the immune response. That must be the culprit," said Manny.

Emma was struck by this revelation. "The weapon must be a transcription factor for NF-kB. It binds to the genome to start the immune response without any external triggers or organisms. NF-kB just keeps getting produced, stimulating the creation of more and more inflammatory markers, unable to be turned off."

"That's got to be it, Emma," Manny exclaimed.

"Okay, but what can we do to turn it off?"

"That's tough," Sue answered. "I'll have to do a little research to see what inhibits NF-kB. But if the genetic sequence that codes for the NF-kB is already incorporated into Lee's DNA, there's nothing we can do. I can't tell his DNA to stop producing it."

"It hasn't modified his DNA," Emma answered.

"How can you be so sure?"

"Because they don't have Lee's DNA. They don't have his ancestry. Even if they took a DNA sample last night, they wouldn't have been able to process it that fast and create a linking protein to target his DNA. And why would they need to specifically target *his* DNA? The damage that this weapon, in raw form, can cause to Lee is self-limiting if it doesn't incorporate into his DNA. But it will kill him all the same."

"That makes sense," Manny added. "Peters wouldn't risk having us find the linking protein in an autopsy. It would expose too much. I think they just injected the bioweapon with the vector. No targeting protein necessary."

"I hope that's what they did," Sue said.

"Let's do more than hope, Sue. We need a cure," Emma cried. "And fast. Manny, how long before we see if your little toy's working?"

"I tried to call my friend, but he's on surveillance tonight. Can't be reached until tomorrow. I left him a message. I expect he'll get back to me by midday tomorrow with the transcripts."

"Okay. Kaiser's trying to get the DHS to turn up the heat on Peters and Astrea Labs. The police are going to pick up Singh this evening after they get a warrant and bring him in for questioning. I'm sure we'll know a lot more about the Order after that," replied Emma.

Which is more than we can say about Lee's condition, she thought. They had made an important discovery, but they were also running out of time. What no one knew, probably not even Peters, was how long it would be before Lee's body could no longer fight an immune system stuck in overdrive.

50

EMMA STOOD in the empty parking lot under the bright fluorescent lights. The crisp air of the New Hampshire mountains filled her lungs. She was flanked by Manny, Roland Waters, and Erik Kaiser.

"I'm telling you, the place wasn't deserted this morning," Emma said.

"There was certainly someone here recently," Manny answered. He poked at the trash in a garbage can left near Astrea Labs' front doors, now secured by a heavy chain around the handles.

"Well, there's no one here now," said Waters.

Kaiser had arranged for the New Hampshire State Police to meet them at the facility to serve a warrant and conduct a thorough search of the facility.

"There's nothing here, Agent Kaiser," Waters said, hitting the heavy chains with his hand.

"We came all the way up here. Can we at least go inside?" Emma pleaded.

Waters nodded and walked to the back of his car, popped the trunk, and took out a large bolt cutter. "You got ten minutes, then I'm leaving."

After Waters cut the chain, Emma and the three men entered the abandoned research lab. The State Troopers stood guard in the parking lot.

"No one's home," Waters said as they entered the reception room, his voice bouncing off the walls.

"Undersecretary, there were people here earlier," Kaiser replied.

"They had to know we'd be back. I'm sure they took everything with them," Manny added.

"That was a pretty stupid move, coming up here without backup, Kaiser," Waters said.

"Peters's office is this way," Kaiser replied, trying to move the conversation forward. He led them down the long corridor he and Emma had walked the previous day. Waters pushed open the heavy door to Peters's office. Though it contained the furniture that Emma had seen earlier, the desk was bare. Waters walked over to it and opened the drawers.

"Empty," he announced, to no one's surprise.

"I'm sure the labs are cleaned out as well, but we should check," Emma said.

"Sure thing, Doctor. We at the DHS are at your service," Waters remarked sarcastically. "How many people did you say were here?"

"Peters was with another man here in his office," she answered. "His name was Bruno."

"A third man took me to the labs," Kaiser added. "There were a few other cars in the lot."

"And because of your visit, they just packed everything up and left. Is that what you're telling me?"

"They're hiding the evidence," Manny added.

"Uh-huh," Waters muttered. "Evidence about this Project Astrea you were telling me about?"

"That's right," Emma replied.

"And what led you to Astrea Labs and this nefarious Dr. Peters?" the undersecretary continued.

"Lee mentioned the word 'Astrea' before he lost consciousness at the hospital," Emma answered.

"And that prompted you to barge in here demanding answers? Because of a single word uttered by a delirious man."

"That's right," Emma retorted. "And Peters confirmed that he ran a project called Astrea."

"Did you hear this admission, Agent Kaiser?"

"No," answered Kaiser. "But I wasn't in the office. I was checking out the labs."

"Dr. Hess," Waters replied, dropping down into the desk chair. "I really have tried to work with you on this. You've given me very little, yet I put my primary investigation on hold to come all the way up here. I used every last favor I had getting a warrant without probable cause. You still have no evidence that a biological weapon was used on either Khattib *or* Jansen. And you found nothing in the lab, Agent Kaiser. These are very serious accusations you're throwing out, yet none is substantiated. For all you know, this may just be a new strain of a naturally occurring virus we can't identify yet. Surely your field has limitations, Doctor. I do not believe we are so sophisticated that we can detect every organism on the planet."

"That's true, yes, but—"

Waters's cell phone rang and he held up his index finger.

"Undersecretary Waters," he answered. "Is that so?" His gaze drifted to Manny. "Okay. Right. Let me know what else you find."

Waters hung up the phone.

"As I was saying—" Emma began.

"Dr. Ortiz, when was the last time you saw Dr. Arjun Singh?" interrupted Waters.

Manny was surprised by the question. "I went to his house this morning to ask him some questions about Astrea Laboratories. He confirmed that Philip Peters was working on a project called Astrea for a group called 'the Order' and that his own lab, specifically Jawad Khattib, was conducting a part of that research. Everything he told me supports our conclusions that it's some kind of bioweapon that's killing Lee."

"Uh-huh. You guys didn't talk about anything else?"

"No," Manny said, growing irritated, "but you should talk to him. That's what you get paid for, isn't it?"

"Well, you know, I'd love to, but Arjun Singh is dead. He never showed up for work this morning. Boston PD found him dead in his home," Waters reported, standing up and coming face-to-face with Manny. "Execution style. Very professionally done, I might add. Two to the chest, one to the head. You were in the military, weren't you, Dr. Ortiz? Rangers, I believe?"

"What?" Emma asked. "You don't actually think that—"

"You've got to be kidding me. With all that's going on—both Khattib brothers killed, Singh murdered, and Lee in the hospital dying, forget about the possibility of someone making a biological weapon of mass destruction—you think *I'm* the killer here? What Cracker Jack box did you get your badge from, anyway?"

"Agent Kaiser, let's bring Dr. Ortiz in for some questioning," Waters said.

Kaiser was astonished by the turn of events. "But, sir, what about Peters?"

"I don't see anything here that's even remotely incriminating. For all I know they're out at a company picnic."

"You're insane if you think I had anything to do with Singh's death," Manny exclaimed. "You can't even see how dangerous your ignorance is."

"That's it," Waters said, enraged. "Cuff him, Kaiser, and put him in the back of my car."

"This is not helping at all. He's not responsible for any of this," protested Emma.

"Oh, and you were with him at Singh's house this morning?" Waters asked as Kaiser reluctantly handcuffed Manny and started to lead him out of the office.

"No, but what about Ashraf Khattib? Are you telling me Manny was willing to blow himself up at the coroner's office?" protested Emma, following them out of Peters's office and down the hall.

"Good point. Was Ashraf Khattib killed? Yes. Did Ortiz die in the explosion? No. Maybe he knew just where to stand in the room. The bottom line is I have a corpse filled with bullet holes and this man was likely the last to see him alive," Waters replied as they walked out to the parking lot.

Kaiser led Manny to the backseat of Waters's car. Emma couldn't help but notice that Manny seemed completely unfazed. Obviously he'd been through worse.

"Emma, my phone's on the seat of your car," Manny told her. "Wait for the call from Darryl. And keep working with Sue. Find the cure for Lee. Don't worry about me. This jerk can arrest me, but it won't stick."

"Waters, you have to listen to me," Emma said. "You've got to get men out here to go through this place. You've got to track down where Peters went with the samples. He may already have the weapon perfected. It's just a matter of time before it's used to kill countless innocent people. You have to stop him."

"Listen, all you guys have done is complicate things and cause me delays in my own investigation," Waters said, climbing into the driver's seat. "Now on top of all that, I have to deal with a deceased lab director, two dead Arab brothers, and a federal agent in the hospital clinging to life. And you've still given me no tangible leads. The governor is going to go ballistic when he learns that I wasted time on this cockamamie theory of yours."

"Can't you see that this is all related? We've told you who's behind this. What more do you want?" Emma pleaded.

"Proof. Something I can use. Even if your Dr. Peters and Project Astrea exist, what now? Where can I find him? What evidence do I have to arrest him? The only person that may have had any information is dead. And this man was the last to see him," Waters barked, pointing to Manny in the back seat. "What am I supposed to think?" Waters slammed the door and turned the engine over.

Kaiser shrugged and told Emma, "I'll keep an eye on Manny and see if I can reason with the undersecretary."

"Get in the car, Kaiser," Waters called out through the open window. "And, Doctor, if you really want to help someone, you should find your friend here a good lawyer."

The car sped out of the parking lot, followed by the State Trooper car. Emma was left alone to contemplate her next move. It was up to her and Sue now. They were still no closer to saving Lee or finding Project Astrea. People were dying all around her, and many more faced a similar fate if she didn't find a way to stop Peters.

She returned to her car and started the long drive back to Boston, hoping that Sue was having better luck with a cure for Lee than she had had with Peters.

51

I CAN'T BELIEVE they arrested Manny! He didn't kill Dr. Singh," Sue cried when Emma called with the news.

"I know. We'll have to find a way to convince the DHS to let him go. Any progress on a cure for Lee?" Emma said as she hit eighty on the expressway heading back to Boston.

"There's only one possibility that I've been able to find, and it's a long shot. *Yersinia pestis* secretes a group of proteins called Yersinia outer proteins." Emma was familiar with the deadly organism. *Yersinia pestis* was the scientific term for the organism that caused the plague. "There is one specific protein in this group, the YopP, which is a natural inhibitor of NF-kB. If the bioweapon is just a transcription factor for NF-kB, the effects would be limited, and it'll eventually run out. The problem is, the huge amount of NF-kB that this weapon is producing will kill Lee before his body can break it down. If we can block the NF-kB that's being produced, his body will have a chance to clear it. But, again, if the bioweapon linked with his DNA and altered it to *continuously* produce NF-kB, then there's nothing we can do."

"Let's hope that's not the case. I've heard of YopP before, but I didn't know it was a treatment for SIRS," Emma mused.

"It's not. Probably wouldn't work for true SIRS, since there would be organisms present in SIRS that directly cause the body to continually produce the inflammatory cells. But with Lee, if the amount of NF-kB being produced is finite, YopP may block it all," explained Sue.

"So you're saying that to cure Lee, we have to give him the plague?" Emma asked.

"Not quite. If I had access to any *Yersinia* samples, which of course I don't, I might be able to isolate the YopP from the virulent anaerobe and just inject the protein into Lee, not the organism. He wouldn't actually be injected with the plague."

Emma dismissed this qualification. "Okay, I'm going to call a friend of mine at BU. He's the occ med doc for their BSL-3." The Level 3 biosafety containment laboratory housed many dangerous biological agents stored for research. "I'll see what he can get for you. It won't be easy, but I'll call in all the favors I have to get you the samples you need. How much time do you need on your end?"

"If you can get me the *Yersinia* samples or some YopP, it won't take long at all. All I need to do is isolate the microbe's protein, then hope it can inactivate Lee's runaway NF-kB."

"All right. I'll see what I can do. Tell me, and please don't sugarcoat it for me, how's Lee doing?"

"He's not good, Emma. They have him on continuous dialysis. His kidneys have completely shut down. His liver's not doing too well either. The doctors are worried."

"So am I. If you receive the *Yersinia* before I get there, you know what you have to do, right? The ICU team would take days to approve of this approach so we're going to have to go it on our own, Sue. Whatever the consequences. We're running out of time."

"I understand. I'll do what I can. Hurry back."

Once Emma clicked off and started thinking about next steps, she realized that finding a way to save Lee might also be the only way to save them all. Peters would surely come after them, and soon. Singh had been murdered, and clearly the goal was to frame Manny.

She knew that Lee would find a way to stop Peters before they all ended up dead. If, of course, they could find a way to save Lee. She dialed her friend at BU and prayed for a miracle as the phone rang.

EMMA BLEW THROUGH every speed limit and covered the distance from New Hampshire to Boston in record time. After arriving at Mass. General, she ran up to the ICU and Lee's room.

Her heart stopped when she saw the empty bed. Powered-down dialysis equipment stood in the corner. She could barely breathe.

A nurse walked by and Emma grabbed her by the arm.

"What happened to Lee Jansen?"

The nurse looked surprised. "He's gone," she said, and walked away.

Emma felt her knees go weak. She was too late. If only she hadn't wasted time on the trip to New Hampshire. Perhaps she could have done more for Lee there.

"Emma?" Sue said as she hobbled on her crutches through the open door.

"Sue! What happened to Lee?"

"They moved him into the room across from the nurses so they can monitor him more closely. He's in terrible shape, Emma. Full-blown DIC and sepsis. They already transfused two units of blood and ordered two more."

"Show me," Emma said. They walked the hall together.

Sue led her to Lee's new room. For the moment, the agent was alone.

Emma gasped. She had seen many critical patients, but this time she felt something deeper. A life she had begun to explore was fading away.

"It didn't work?" she asked quietly.

"I don't know," Sue replied. "I haven't given it to him yet. Your friend dropped it off about a half hour ago, and I just finished isolating the YopP. I have it with me."

A spark of hope returned.

"Hurry," Emma said quietly, looking out to the busy nurses' station. "Give it to me."

Sue also looked around. She understood Emma's apprehension and discreetly handed her the syringe.

Emma walked over to Lee and put her hand on his sweaty forehead. Her eyes began to swell with tears. He was pale, close to death, she knew. She held up the syringe and examined the fluid inside. She closed her eyes and said a prayer, then reached down for the port on one of Lee's many IVs. It took only a few seconds to inject the contents of the syringe into the IV line.

"What are you doing?" demanded voice from the doorway.

Startled, Emma jumped away from Lee's bed.

"What did you just give him?" asked Dr. Daniel Cody, the ICU's attending physician. Emma had never met Cody but knew his fierce reputation.

Cody strode into the room and grabbed the syringe from Emma's hand. He looked up at the monitor and they both saw Lee's condition was unchanged.

"What the hell is this?" he asked again, holding up the empty syringe. "What did you just give my patient?"

"Hope," Emma replied quietly.

52

A HOSPITAL SECURITY OFFICER stood behind Emma as Dr. Cody continued his interrogation in the ICU's negative-pressure room. Normally used for critically ill patients with communicable lung infections, it happened to be the only empty room available.

Emma decided she had nothing to lose. She told Cody the entire story, from Khattib's needle stick to Manny's arrest earlier that day.

"Let me get this clear," Cody pressed, after almost a half hour sequestered with Emma in the quiet room. "Some secret international group is conspiring to ethnically cleanse Israel, and they infected my patient with this weapon? And you think the plague will cure him," he asked, holding up the empty syringe.

"I told you, the YopP will block the inflammatory response that's killing him," Emma repeated.

"YopP has been tried in the fight against sepsis before," Cody continued, shaking his head. "It won't work as long as the pathogen inside the patient continues to stimulate the immune response."

"Haven't you been listening?" asked Emma. She knew she was in big trouble, but she was frustrated that she hadn't won Cody over to her course of action. "There *is* no pathogen."

"Oh," Cody continued with a hint of sarcasm, "that's right. Your young, deceased scientist found a way to target an ethnic-specific gene and make the body kill itself. It all makes sense to me now."

The security guard grinned, but Cody shot him a stern look.

"Frankly, I'm surprised at you, Dr. Hess. You have an impeccable reputation as a clinician *and* scientist. I would have thought that you, of all people, would have left emotions out of your clinical decision making. Giving a patient an experimental agent without testing it first is a very serious offense," he said, getting close to her face. "I especially don't like people playing God with *my* patients. I'm fighting a losing battle here just trying to keep that man alive, and I don't need you injecting him with some far-fetched treatment that may kill him before I can even find out what's wrong with him."

"I already told you what's wrong with him," Emma said, standing her ground, "but you're not listening."

Cody stood up straight and nodded to the security guard. "Well, now you'll have a chance to tell the authorities about your wild theories."

The hospital guard approached Emma, taking out a set of handcuffs.

"Emma!" Sue shouted. A second later, her face, perspiring from trying to run down the hall with a crutch and cast on her leg, popped into the room. "It's Lee! He's awake!"

The two doctors, followed by the security guard, rushed past Sue and ran to Lee's room. An anesthesiologist was removing the intubation tube as they entered.

"I was in the next room intubating a patient when the nurse called for me," Dr. Alexandra Milos told them. "He said our patient here was fully awake and trying to pull out his tube." Milos tapped the endotracheal tube that was forcing oxygen into Lee's lungs. Lee was looking at Emma, who had come up to his bedside. She smiled and placed a reassuring hand on the agent's forearm.

The anesthesiologist proceeded to pull the tube out of Lee's mouth, eliciting a wince from him.

"There, now," Milos said, providing some suction. "All done. Your throat's going to hurt for a while, and it'll be difficult for you to talk. But you're breathing fine on your own."

"How do you feel?" Cody asked, checking Lee's vitals on the monitor. They were all stable. His heart rate and blood pressure had returned to normal. "Nurse, let's start weaning down the sedation and drips," he ordered, hoping that Lee would not need any more blood pressure support.

Lee gave a thumb's-up sign.

"Maybe I was a little hasty in my assessment of your treatment, Dr. Hess," said Cody. "You still should have come to me first before giving him anything. But he does seem to be improving. I'll draw some labs and see if we can get him off dialysis." He allowed a slight smile of wonder as he left the room, leaving Emma and Sue flanking Lee's bed.

"Sue found a cure, Lee. You're going to be all right," Emma said with a broad smile.

Lee mumbled something inaudible.

She leaned her ear close to his mouth to hear what he was trying to say.

"What about Astrea?" he asked in a scratchy voice.

"That's another story, I'm afraid," Emma replied grimly.

53

I CAN'T BELIEVE how good you look," Kaiser said to Lee. Twenty-four hours had passed since Lee was extubated, and his strength was rapidly returning.

"Since there was never any organism invading your body and damaging tissue, once the inflammatory effects of the bioweapon were blocked, there was no reason you wouldn't recover quickly," Sue explained.

"Thanks to you," Emma said, putting an arm around Sue's shoulders and causing her to blush.

"I'm just glad you surrounded yourself with such a great team, Lee," Erik added.

"There's one missing. What are we going to do about Manny?" Lee asked, sitting up in his hospital bed, his color back to normal.

"Director Kowalski is looking in to it, but it won't be easy," Erik explained. "He's being held on suspicion of murder. The investigation is ongoing, but without any information exonerating him, I'm not sure if anyone can get him released."

"He was clearly set up," stated Emma.

"Yeah, and I know by who," Lee muttered.

"We've been through this, Lee. Do you know how hard it'll be going after Undersecretary Waters? He's got a solid reputation at DHS and has strong support from the governor here in Massachusetts. You can't go around bad-mouthing high-ranking DHS officers."

"The more that I think about it, the more I realize that Waters has been dragging his feet the whole time," replied Lee. "He's done very little to help us but was right there to arrest Manny."

"I never understood why he wouldn't listen to us," Emma chimed in. "The bioweapon theory was certainly more plausible than a dirty bomb, especially in light of everything that was happening to us."

"Yeah. He arrested Manny with far less evidence," Sue added.

"I know why he wouldn't listen," Lee answered flatly.

"Careful, Lee," warned Erik.

"Come on, Erik, you know what I'm saying. Waters *has* to be in on this. It's clear that someone inside the DHS is involved, and that person has to be fairly high up. It may even be the same person that was trying to sell weapons to the terrorists in DC. Maybe *this* weapon. Hell, it might even be a group of people. And what if they're also with this Order group. How else would the DHS have found out about Khattib's death so quickly? Waters probably requested someone from Washington come up here to keep his name clear. Now Khattib's brother Ashraf is dead, Manny's locked up, Peters and the weapon are gone, and it all happened in Waters's backyard. You don't find that the least bit suspicious?"

"I admit, it is strange. When I get back to Washington, I'll talk to Director Kowalski and see if we can get internal affairs involved in both cases. It doesn't help you not letting anyone at DHS know you're doing better."

"You just keep telling them I'm the same. Still in critical condition in the ICU. I don't want anyone knowing that I'm getting my strength back," Lee said. "It was Emma's idea and a good one. Peters may get complacent thinking I'm still out of the game."

"Director Kowalski's going to be mad. He wants to come up but I keep telling him the doctors won't let anyone in to see you. I don't know how much longer I'll be able to hold him off."

"Well, just keep trying. In the meantime, what are we going to do about Peters?"

"We still don't have evidence against Peters or that a bioweapon even exists. Undersecretary Waters is still officially chasing down terrorist cells in Boston looking for a dirty bomb."

"We have evidence of a bioweapon inside me," Lee said, holding up an arm.

"No," Sue replied, shaking her head. "Any trace of what was injected into you is gone. The only thing left are some viral fragments, just like in Khattib."

Lee dropped his arm.

"I'll try to keep tabs on Undersecretary Waters. Remember, I'm still supposed to be working with him on his case."

"Thanks, Erik. We'll stay in touch," Lee replied.

"See you guys later," Erik said, leaving the room.

"What *are* we going to do about Peters?" Sue replied. "He could be anywhere. He may not even be in the country anymore."

"I may have an idea," Emma said, as Darryl Freeman walked in, nodding his head to her. "There's something you all need to hear."

54

THE MEETING OF THE TEN, the sacred leadership of the Order, was held in a private room in the penthouse of a large luxury apartment building in Manhattan. The Order had many members, followers, and supporters but only ten members actually led the organization. These ten served for life or until the other nine deemed them unworthy of leadership, either medically or philosophically.

This group of international overachievers was comprised of businessmen, academicians, politicians, entrepreneurs, scientists, and even a former footballer turned actor from Europe. As diverse as the membership was, all of the leaders had a unified goal. Created over a century ago, the Order originally sought to gather together the most intelligent, powerful, and influential individuals from across the globe to meet quarterly to discuss important international issues and solve them. Over time, however, the Order began to formulate policy and construct a new world order, even determining who should lead nations and which wars should be fought. Once the Ten made a decision, the Order's members throughout the world set out to implement it.

Occasionally, emergency meetings of the Ten were held, usually called by one member to discuss an immediate or emerging threat. Philip Peters had called such a meeting today to discuss Project Astrea, the Order's current focus.

"Thank you all for coming on such short notice," he began.

It had been a week since he'd asked for a meeting to discuss the progress of Astrea and to obtain assistance on keeping the project in the shadows.

"As you are all aware, I am tasked with directing Project Astrea. Let me first say that the project is well ahead of schedule. We have completed the research and manufacture of the three main components of the ethnic bioweapon. These are the targeting mechanism, the delivery vector, and the weapon itself," Peters explained. "The target mechanism is a manufactured linking protein that searches for the desired ethnic-specific DNA sequence in the host and binds to it. If this unique sequence is not found, the target mechanism will have nothing to attach to and the bioweapon will not be released.

"In the targeted population, however, this binding of the target mechanism to the DNA triggers the release of the bioweapon. The viral RNA from the vector will incorporate the weapon-producing genetic sequence into the host DNA. This does two things. First, it prevents an effective treatment, since, in essence, the victim's now-modified DNA will continue to produce the weapon. Second, and most importantly, it will allow us to create vectors with linking proteins specific to ethnic groups with unique DNA sequences that we wish to target. All that is required are small modifications of the current linking protein to fit and target these unique sequences. This way the bioweapon can go after specific groups of people, leaving the rest of the world unaffected.

"The delivery mechanism is the key," Peters continued, looking at the other nine people sitting around the heavy oak conference room table. As most of the leaders of the Order were not scientists, he simplified the details as much as possible without insulting their intelligence or diluting the importance of what he was saying.

"The viral vector we use allows the weapon and linking protein to enter the victim's body at the cellular level. Once inside the cell, the vector uses its RNA to incorporate the gene for the weapon into the victim's own DNA. This way the weapon, which is a DNA sequence that turns on and exaggerates the body's inflammatory cascade, can be incorporated into the victim's genome and will therefore be resistant to treatment. Basically, it will become a permanent part of the genetic makeup of the victim.

"The beauty of the bioweapon structure is that it can produce almost any results we desire, depending on what synthetic genes we insert into the victim. With this breakthrough linking protein and vector technology, we can cause victims to get cancer, shut down their organ systems, or die from sepsis. And with additional research, we can take this project one step further. With the right funding and resources, it wouldn't be a big leap to be able to design the opposite effect: enhancement genes instead of destructive ones. It is theoretically possible to insert an improvement into a host's DNA instead of a weapon. We can, by using the genome-specific linking protein attached to a vector, limit this beneficial gene to ethnicities we wish to enhance. Think about it, gentlemen. We can destroy our enemies on the cellular level and rid the world of undesirable populations that create a drain on our society. At the same time, we can enhance and improve other more desirable populations," he said, looking around and gauging his audience's reaction.

"What about the problem in Europe we discussed earlier?" asked an impeccably dressed man in a very faint French accent. "These foreigners are already ruining our great society. They are overtaking the southern cities along the Mediterranean and poisoning our youth. Soon they will overtake all of us. We will be a minority in our own land."

Peters was frustrated that this man continued to focus on his current regional dilemma rather than the overall worldwide benefits of Project Astrea. But, in truth, Project Astrea was conceived to combat any emerging threat the Order felt was of the most immediate threat to world stability.

"I understand your problems, my friend," he said soothingly. "We here in America have similar concerns. You are not alone in your struggles. That is why Project Astrea was conceived. Now we have a solution. Obviously, there is no gene that encodes for religious preferences, so we designed a vector that will target unique genomes found in the target population to which you refer. The more genes we target, the more specific a population we can destroy. If it is our desire and we have a genetic sample from the target group, we can design a more complex linking protein that can kill or, in the future, enhance a single family or even an individual."

"Does it work? Will it kill the Semites and not affect the rest of us in Europe?" the man continued, referring to the Semitic descendants of biblical Shem in the ancient Levant.

Peters took a deep breath, reminding himself that these men were not scientists.

"Our brethren in Lebanon have been working on this very issue. They have used data obtained from open sources in the scientific community as well as from our own private research to catalog specific genes linked to various races. We have quietly collected samples from thousands of Semites in the Levant. Most races of people have a few genes that are unique to that population. We have identified a number of unique DNA sequences for that particular ethnic group."

"But what about the rest of us?" the Frenchman asked. "How can we be certain that we are all protected from this weapon?"

"My own research lab put the final touches on some work that was done in the field. As I mentioned, we have perfected a linking protein that will couple to these particular ethnic-specific DNA sequences only. Once firmly attached to these and only these sequences, the vector will discharge the viral RNA into the victim's cells and initiate the bioweapon. Anyone without this DNA sequence will be spared. We have tested the bioweapon. Rest assured, it is quite effective, but only in the ethnic populations we select."

"How difficult will it be to modify this vector with its linking protein to attack other DNA sequences outside of the Middle East?" asked another member of the Order. His nation was having difficulties with remote indigenous tribes preventing the government's exploitation of rain forests.

"Very simple. The initial linking protein work was done on a mouse model. Once the technology was perfected in my lab, the necessary modifications were made to allow the vector and linking protein to couple with any specific human DNA sequence we select. Modifying the linking protein to link with a different genetic code is not a difficult task. We have already cataloged many ethnic-unique sequences, even for your rebellious forest tribes, my friend," Peters reassured him.

It had not been too difficult convincing the Ten to select his own mortal enemies as the first group to be cleansed. With all the political unrest associated with the Middle East, the Ten were eager to eliminate one side of the conflict. They had no insight, of course, as to Peters's true motivation for creating the ethnic bioweapon that their influence and money had funded, or his subsequent plans for the region.

"What about all this trouble with the death of your researcher?" the former European superstar footballer asked.

"Don't worry about that," Senator Vasquez put in. "My government colleagues are steering the investigation in other directions, away from Dr. Peters's work."

"I assure you," Peters continued, "the threat of discovery has been eliminated. There is no longer any trace of Astrea in this country. Those with suspicions have been effectively dealt with, thanks to our good friend Bruno Strozza."

Peters gestured to Strozza, and Bruno replied with a slight nod of his head.

"As Senator Vasquez has confirmed, the seeds of deception we planted have grown fruit," Peters continued, "and the trail veers far away from us and Project Astrea."

"Are there any limitations on the effects of the weapon?" a Swiss minister asked. "Is a cure for the Homeland Security agent possible? Surely someone in his position would be a dangerous adversary going forward."

"As I mentioned, once the new DNA sequence for the weapon is incorporated into the genome of the target population, there will be no cure. However, this was not the method we used with Agent Jansen. My goal with him was to demonstrate to you the power of the bioweapon and to focus the efforts of those looking into our business on saving his life and keep them away from Project Astrea while we relocated. There was no need to use a targeting protein on the agent and risk the discovery of our breakthrough linking technology on autopsy. However, Jansen will die nonetheless. Are there any other questions?"

"Just one," Lee announced as he flung open the conference room door. "Are the penalties for ethnic cleansing and mass murder just as severe abroad as they are here in the United States?"

55

HOW IS THIS POSSIBLE?" Peters asked.

"No, I'm not a ghost," continued Lee as he walked around the table toward Peters. "I am alive and quite well. Well enough to make some arrests. Looks like you're not as smart as you've led your colleagues to believe, Doctor. Your bioweapon has a flaw."

Peters scanned the room and saw the startled expressions of the men he had had in the palm of his hand just moments earlier. "This is a private meeting, on private property. You have no right to be here," Peters replied, desperate to reclaim a superior position.

"It's a long story, but I'm pretty sure you're not going to like it. The ending's going to be a real downer for all of you as well," Lee said to the visibly nervous men seated at the table. "Dr. Emma Hess visited your friend Dr. Peters in his lab in New Hampshire recently looking for the antidote for your bioweapon. But Dr.

Hess was multitasking during that visit. She didn't go there just for the cure."

Lee held up a listening device no larger than a dime.

"You see, Dr. Manny Ortiz, who you tried to frame for the murder of Arjun Singh, has many friends. One of them is a private eye that eavesdrops for a living. Dr. Hess planted a listening device she got from him under the chair she sat in during your meeting in your office. Everything you said, including the phone call you made *after* she left, setting up this very meeting, was recorded."

"You fool!" the Frenchman exclaimed to Peters.

"You have nothing on me," Peters said defiantly.

"Don't be so sure. Your office wasn't the only room bugged," Lee replied, looking around the large conference room. He walked over to an oil painting and pulled out another surveillance device from behind the ornate wooden frame. "We had plenty of time over the past week to prepare this room. The next little team meeting you fellows are going to have will be in a maximum security federal prison."

Silence fell over the room as members of the Ten replayed the last hour in their heads, wondering if they'd said anything incriminating.

"But wait, there's more," Lee said, arms spread wide like a television game show host. "I hope you all enjoyed the lunch and beverage service here today. All of the glasses and silverware that were cleared from the table earlier are, as we speak, being fingerprinted and swabbed for DNA samples. I'll have all of your identities by the end of today, and that information will be sent to INTERPOL and to the local authorities where each of you resides. Of course, Senator Vasquez, there's no need for that in your case. I'm well aware of who you are. By the way, I've really enjoyed your speeches on C-SPAN."

The men seated around the table glared at Peters and then began grumbling angrily among themselves.

A lone voice rang out. "You were brave but foolish to come here alone," the assassin said, rising from his chair.

Strozza approached Lee, pulling a large-caliber handgun out from under his jacket and pressing the barrel against Lee's forehead. "You may have survived the bioweapon, Agent Jansen, but I'm certain you are not fully healed. Let's see how you do against old-fashioned lead."

Peters, too, noticed the fatigue on Lee's face. The agent obviously had used every ounce of energy just to enter the room.

"Give me one reason why I shouldn't just end this right now," Strozza said.

Lee feared his bluff was being called. But he did have a backup plan.

"Then you would also stand trial for the actual murder of a federal agent instead of just attempted murder," Kaiser stated as he entered the room with three uniformed police officers, weapons drawn.

At the sight of the authorities, the men seated at the large conference table all rose at once and raced toward side doors leading out of the room. The Ten had escape plans for every contingency. This room had been selected, in part, because of its numerous exits. Personal security guards and vehicles were waiting for the men at each escape route. While some of the Ten would undoubtedly be caught, those who reached freedom would use their influence to get their brethren released.

Peters grabbed his attaché case, pushed open a secret doorway hidden in a wall panel directly behind him, and disappeared as the mass exodus of the other members kept Kaiser and the police officers otherwise occupied.

Lee knew he needed to act fast, before Peters was out of his grasp for good.

He punched Strozza in the stomach as the Sicilian's attention was diverted. Lee then brought his knee up between the hired killer's legs as hard as he could, dropping Strozza to the ground. Then Lee raced across the intervening space through the hidden door after Peters.

On the other side of the door was a small landing above a long spiral staircase. Looking down, Lee saw Peters descending the narrow steps. Taking two rungs at a time, he went after his prey.

Bruno Strozza composed himself and got to his feet to go after the troublesome DHS agent. From the top landing, he saw Jansen and Peters descending the staircase, and he fired a round at the agent. He missed his target by inches, and the bullet ricocheted off the railing right next to Jansen's left hand.

Lee kept his eyes on his prey and continued down the stairs, gaining on the frail Philip Peters with each step, knowing that Strozza's next shot might stop him.

Peters reached another landing halfway down the four-story stairwell, pulled open a heavy door, and went through, the door slamming behind him.

Though Lee was feeling lightheaded from the exertion, he jumped down the last four steps to the landing and pulled open the door.

Another shot rang out, and Lee felt a searing pain on the side of his neck.

He was hit.

But he got through the door, and it closed behind him. He found himself in a small, empty room. He put his hand on the wound and found it was barely bleeding. He'd only been grazed. Lucky. Twice. When would this lucky streak end?

The room had two other doors, one on each side. Peters was nowhere in sight.

Lee wanted to keep after Peters, but knew he needed to get rid of Strozza while he still had enough strength left to fight.

He leaned against the inside of the heavy door and waited.

Lee could hear the man pounding down the stairs. He turned the knob without moving the door, so that it would swing open without catching.

Then he coiled all of his remaining strength into his legs and waited until the footsteps stopped. The assassin was on the other side of the door.

The moment Lee felt the door swing open, he rammed his shoulder hard into it, slamming it into the face of the assassin.

Lee heard the man scream as he toppled backward and then over the railing. He walked out onto the landing and looked down the spiral staircase. Two stories below him lay Strozza's broken body, a pool of blood widening around the dead man's head.

His relief was short-lived, as the delay might have caused him to lose Peters again. He went back into the room and opened the first door. It was a closet.

The second door opened into a narrow hallway with several doors, a single elevator, and a staircase at the far end.

Lee tried each door as he went toward the stairs. All were locked. The display over the elevator indicated that it was on the ground floor.

Peters had made it out of the building and onto the streets of Manhattan.

The madman was gone.

56

WHEN LEE RETURNED to the conference room, he found Kaiser standing next to New York's finest. Beside him was Emma. Four men were in custody, sitting in gloomy silence.

So, five escaped, and one, Bruno Strozza, was lying at the bottom of the staircase, Lee assessed to himself.

"What happened?" Emma asked, pointing to Lee's neck and the drops of blood on his shirt collar. His face was sweaty with the telltale signs of exhaustion.

"Bullet just grazed me. It already stopped bleeding," Lee said. "I'm fine."

Kaiser poured Lee a glass of water from the pitcher on the table.

"Thanks," he said, gulping the water down.

"You look pale," Emma said. "Sit down."

"I'm all right. Getting my strength back. We got half of them, anyway," he said, looking around the room.

"Where's Peters?" Emma asked.

Lee shook his head. "Let's step outside."

Kaiser and Emma followed him out into the hall, while the police officers kept watch over what was left of the Ten.

"Got away. But the big man is through that door, down a few flights of stairs. You'll have to go get him, though. He's in no condition to move on his own."

"It's okay, we'll find Peters," Emma said.

Lee wasn't so sure. A fugitive with Peters's contacts and resources would have little trouble disappearing.

"You and Manny came up with a brilliant plan, putting that bug in Peters's office. Then I lose him," Lee complained, angry with himself.

"Don't be so hard on yourself," Kaiser said. "Maniacs like Peters always resurface. It's power they crave. He won't be content hiding in a spider hole somewhere."

"And we still have those four in the other room," Emma said.

"Probably not for long. It won't be easy making any of this stick in court," Kaiser said. "They'll challenge the legality of the surveillance, especially the bug you put in Peters's office up in New Hampshire."

"Maybe by disrupting their key leadership, we can delay their immediate plans to release the bioweapon in Israel," countered Emma.

"Hopefully. We also have your testimony about their attempt on your life, Lee," Kaiser replied.

"Thanks to Sue, who came up with the idea of swabbing the silverware, we'll soon know who leads the Order," added Emma. "Even the ones who got away."

Lee wasn't satisfied with their limited victories. "That's all fine and good, but Peters still got away and we don't know where the bioweapon is. If we don't stop him, he'll use the weapon to the fullest extent possible, with or without the blessing of the rest of the Ten. I'm talking all-out ethnic weapon of mass destruction."

His gloom quickly spread to the others. "If he can find a way to aerosolize the bioweapon, he'll have widespread, rapid dissemination," Emma said. "And if he uses the linking protein to incorporate the weapon into the target's genome, there's no medicine that would be able to stop the resulting slaughter."

"We can put Peters's name and photo at all of the major airports and transportation centers. Maybe we'll nab him as he's trying to leave the country."

"That won't work, Kaiser. My guess is that he has a private jet hidden at some small rural airport and will be gone soon," replied Lee.

Kaiser brought up a new point, reflecting the need for a strategy looking forward. "Lee, we need help if we want to find him," he said. "I know you're worried about people in the government being behind this—"

"You saw Senator Vasquez sitting in there," Lee replied.

"I know, and I don't doubt it. But the investigation is way past the point of just you and me working on this under the radar. I understand that it was necessary to keep our knowledge of this meeting to ourselves. If Peters found out we knew about the meeting, he surely would have canceled or moved it. Then we'd have nothing. But now we have incriminating recordings from Peters's office *and* from this meeting, *plus* four of the top leaders of the Order. I think it's time to bring in Kowalski."

"I do trust Jay," Lee allowed, knowing that Kaiser was right. Lee had even contemplated bringing Kowalski into their plan to raid this meeting but decided that he and Kaiser could do it alone. In retrospect, perhaps they should have had more help. Maybe fewer of the Ten would have escaped. At least now they finally had enough evidence to bring to his boss, even if it wouldn't stick in court. "You take the tapes from here as well as the ones Emma got from the bug in Peters's office." He jabbed a thumb toward the boardroom. "Make sure these four clowns make it down to DC, including the senator. NYPD will help you."

"No problem," Kaiser said. "My uncle's a captain here. He's the one I went to for all this backup with no questions asked. He'll help me expedite their return to DC without any interference."

"Good. I'll call Kowalski and be in DC right behind you."

"I'm coming too," Emma said.

This offer took Lee by surprise. He didn't like the idea of dragging her further into what was shaping up to be a huge mess. "Emma, why?" he asked. "You know that I'm going to get my butt chewed for this. I may even be fired for arranging this bust without a warrant or informing my superiors about it." He met her intent green eyes head-on. "Jay's a friend, but he's also my boss. He doesn't like being kept in the dark. This is going to be a big deal. A U.S. senator is being detained, for crissakes."

"All the more reason for me to be there," she countered. "I can attest, firsthand, to what happened at Astrea Labs. I was the one who bugged Peters's office, not you. Also, my medical knowledge of the case may help DHS plan how to counter the weapon."

"She has a point, Lee," Kaiser added. "I mean, after all, you were out of it for a few days."

Lee hadn't looked away from Emma. It wasn't like he wanted her to go back to Boston. "So both of you are teaming up on me now?" he asked.

"If that's what it takes," Emma replied with a smile.

Lee gave in to what felt like the inevitable. Emma had already gone way beyond her duties as a research scientist. "Fine. Let's all go."

57

THE SLEEK PRIVATE JET touched down on the tarmac just before midnight. Nora and Richard Becker, who had arrived in Lebanon earlier in the week, watched through a plate glass window as Peters disembarked and walked into the private terminal.

"Sir, what will become of the Order?" Richard asked as his boss sat in a comfortable recliner in the VIP lounge. The arrest of Senator Vasquez was front-page news. Although the reports offered few details about the Order, thanks to friends the Ten had in media outlets, Richard knew it was only a matter of time before the world became aware of their secret organization.

"Relax, Richard. The Order is more than just ten men. Our organization is widespread and more powerful than you are aware. Only four of our members were detained in New York, and they will soon be released. If not, we will select new leaders," Peters said confidently.

Peters, Becker, and Nora, flanked by two bodyguards, waited in the lounge while a facilitator took Peters's passport to immigration. They drank hot tea and ate fresh dates while they waited to begin the long journey into the central Lebanese highlands to their final destination. By early morning Peters would be sleeping in his old home once again. It had surely changed over the half century since he had left, but it would still be home. It would always be his home.

After Project Astrea was fully operational and the deadly weapon was launched for the first time, his mountain homeland would attain the status in the world that it deserved. From there, Philip Peters would oversee the new world order.

The facilitator returned with the passport, rubber-stamped by the immigration official on duty after he was handed an envelope full of Lebanese pounds.

"All clear, sir," he told Peters, handing him back his passport. "The cars are ready outside. We can leave now."

"*Shukran*," replied Peters. He hadn't spoken the language in years. It was not his native tongue but that of his adopted land. His own people rarely used it, but he had learned it as a child to communicate with those around him. That skill would come in handy as he assumed his new role in this old land.

"But why Lebanon?" Richard asked.

"Because this is where it all began. And this is where it will end."

58

"DON'T BE SO NERVOUS," Emma told Lee. It was late in the afternoon and they were still waiting in the outer office of the secretary of the Department of Homeland Security. Lee had never been up to the executive floor of his DC headquarters.

"I'm not nervous. I just wish you hadn't come all the way down here. Bad enough I'm going to get a pink slip. I'd hate for you to get reamed out as well."

She touched the back of his hand briefly, to recognize her appreciation that he was thinking of her welfare. "Have you seen Erik yet?"

"No. I called him just after we landed. He had already arrived on a private flight from New York with the tapes and detainees. He couldn't find Kowalski, so he contacted the secretary's office directly, like I told him to. I haven't heard from him since."

Freeman had brought the recordings and transcripts to the hospital for Emma to listen to as Lee was recuperating. Emma played them for Lee and Sue. From the listening device they left in Peters's office, they learned about the meeting of the Ten in New York and confirmed there was a mole inside the DHS. Lee was glad he kept the fact that he was recuperating a secret. After New York, Lee sent Erik back to DC ahead of him to give the recordings to no one but Secretary Roberts.

"So that's why we're here?"

"Yep. To await our fate," Lee said with a rueful smile.

The doors to the elevator that they had come up in fifteen minutes earlier opened. Manny and Kowalski stepped out and approached them.

"Hey, gang," Manny said. "Back from the dead, Lee? Boy, you Gyrenes are hard to kill."

Emma hugged her friend, and Lee shook his hand.

"Good to see you, Manny."

"Thank your friend Kowalski here. He bailed me out."

"Don't give me all the credit," Kowalski replied. "After Secretary Roberts found out about your lone-wolf escapade in New York, she sent me to get the good doctor and bring him here."

Lee was ready for the implied accusation. "Listen, Jay, sorry I didn't tell you about New York. It's not that I didn't trust you, but I didn't know who else would be listening or might find out. I just couldn't risk a breach."

"Hey, I understand. I would have done the same thing," Kowalski said easily. "Don't worry. Listen, no matter what happens today, know that you did good. I'm telling you that because there's a lot of talk around here about why you went it alone. Senator Vasquez's lawyers are screaming that the raid and bug were illegal and that he should be released. Frankly, it's a mess."

The door to Secretary Roberts's office opened and the secretary herself waved them in.

"Agent Jansen, Drs. Hess and Ortiz. Thank you for coming down to see me on such a short notice," she began, settling back in her chair. She was flanked by Undersecretary Waters and Erik Kaiser.

"As you can imagine," she continued, "I was quite distressed when I heard what was going on in Boston and then in New York."

"I can explain," Lee said. "But first, I want to clarify one point. Dr. Hess and Dr. Ortiz had nothing to do with my actions."

"That's not at all what I hear. In fact, I think they were knee deep in this case, with you all the way."

Lee shifted uncomfortably as he stood in front of the secretary's desk.

"Actually, it's my understanding that the only one that was not involved was Waters here," she continued. "And that's why, effective immediately, he is no longer an undersecretary at the DHS."

"What?" Waters exclaimed. "I don't understand."

"I know you don't, and that's the problem," said the secretary. "I sent Agent Jansen up to assist you in the investigation of Jawad Khattib's death. He needed help and you weren't there for him. These doctors shared vital information with you, and you ignored it. You even arrested one of them."

"That would be me, in case you forgot," Manny said, raising his hand in the air.

"If it wasn't for the raid in New York and those tapes, I don't think we would ever have found out about the Order and their bioweapon, nor would we have any real proof. You're dismissed, Waters. I've discussed this with your governor and he agrees. We'll discuss your new responsibilities with the agency later, after your suspension without pay and a detailed review of your inexcusable lack of involvement in this case. You may leave now."

Waters knew better than to argue with Secretary Carlita Roberts. She was a former prosecutor and a formidable executive within the inner circle of the White House. She was hand-picked by the president to lead the Department of Homeland Security and she would eat him for lunch. At least, he still had his job. For now, anyway.

As he walked out of the office with a stoic expression, Manny gave him wink and a smile.

"Will it be enough—the evidence? Is it admissible?" Emma asked.

"Probably not. But we at least detained half of their leadership and have IDs on the rest, thanks to you all. Drs. Hess and Ortiz, I wanted to thank you personally for all you have done to help us get this far. Agents Jansen and Kaiser, you both have done an outstanding job in what had to be a very difficult situation," the secretary replied.

Lee was standing ramrod straight. "Not that outstanding, unfortunately. Peters got away."

"True. But we've dealt a crippling blow to his organization."

"I'm not so sure, ma'am. I think Peters will quickly repopulate the leadership of the Order, placing him squarely at the helm. He's the key. He developed and still possesses the bioweapon. If he hands it over to whatever terrorist group paid him to create it, Israel and the world is in big trouble."

"You're right, Agent Jansen," she replied soberly. "We've contacted all of our sources throughout the world and gave INTERPOL the identities of the Order's leaders who managed to escape, including Peters. INTERPOL got a hit on Peters's passport early this morning. He's in Lebanon."

"Great," Kaiser said. "Can't the Lebanese authorities pick him up and extradite him back to the U.S.?"

Lee doubted it. "He may very well be making this weapon *for* someone in the Lebanese government," he replied. "Or, at the very least, for some influential terrorist groups operating there. The last thing we want to do is let the Lebanese or some terrorist group get their hands on this bioweapon."

"Exactly," Secretary Roberts answered, rising. "We can't risk getting the Lebanese government involved. Terrorist networks have infiltrated every aspect of Lebanese society, including the government. The spillover from the Arab Spring and civil war in Syria has wreaked havoc on the Lebanese infrastructure. The government there is holding on by a thread. Unfortunately, that limits our options. We were lucky that INTERPOL was tied into Lebanon's airport immigration network and was alerted when Peters's passport was scanned."

"So he's in the belly of the beast with an ethnic bioweapon. That's just great," Manny said wryly. "What the hell are we going to do about that?"

The secretary gave him a curious look. "That's an interesting question, Dr. Ortiz. I've read your service record as a Ranger. A lot of special ops time. It's quite impressive, not to mention your qualifications as a physician. How would you like to take an all-expenses-paid trip with Agent Jansen? I'm sure he'd love to have an expert in emergency medicine and trauma, just in case things heat up over there."

"I've been to a lot of places, but I've never been to Lebanon." Manny grinned.

"How about it, Agent Jansen? I can't offer you much assistance, as our hands are pretty much tied on this one. We can't risk drawing too much attention to the mission. If word gets out, we'll have everyone in Lebanon looking for the bioweapon, and we're the last people they'd hand it over to. Not to mention that the Lebanese government won't like us poking around over there under their noses. As you can imagine, it's a touchy political situation." The secretary's tone darkened as she considered another factor in the planning. "Additionally, I have to find out who in my organization is working with Peters or the terrorists that killed Agent James, if there is a link there. I can't risk sending anyone else outside this room for fear it might get back to this traitor." Her focus turned to Lee, and she rose and moved to stand toe to toe with him. "I've spoken with the director of the CIA. He has an excellent troubleshooter in Lebanon right now monitoring the Syrian situation. He'll be your point of contact and will be there to assist you. Are you up to taking another crack at Peters?"

"When do we leave?" Lee answered eagerly. He still had a score to settle and was thankful for this second chance. "I only ask for one thing in return."

The secretary's eyes flickered, and Lee was reminded that he was still walking on thin ice. "If it's within my power, consider it done," she replied.

"As soon as we clean this up—and we *will* clean it up—I want free rein to bring my former partner's killers to justice here in DC. I want to lead that investigation before the trail goes completely cold."

She had no reservations on that score. "Done. Agent Kaiser, you're back on the Arabian Café case with Director Kowalski until Agent Jansen returns."

"Ma'am, respectfully," Kaiser said, "I was hoping to finish this case first."

"I understand. But, as I said, we have to find that mole. Thanks to the tape from Peters's office, we know that he's working with someone high up in our organization. I can't rule out that, as Agent Jansen suggested in his report on Agent James's death, the mole may, for all we know, have also tipped of the Arabian Café shooters. You two leave no stone unturned until you find the terrorist from the Arabian Café that killed Agent James. Continue to press Daif and Sanabel Ajeel and find out where their brother Wahab is. And when we find him, I want to know the name of the crooked Federal Agent that Wahab was trying to buy weapons from. Don't you worry about Agent Jansen," she said, "He'll have plenty of help in Lebanon. I want to know the person at DHS that the UIC and maybe even Peters was working with."

"Yes, ma'am," Kaiser said, disappointed.

"I'm going as well," Emma added firmly. "The release of this weapon will be a medical Armageddon."

"Emma, no," Lee said, shocked. She had risked her life enough times during this investigation. He didn't want anything to happen to her. He wanted her to be waiting when he returned.

"Manny's a great doc, but his experience is in military and emergency medicine," Emma explained. "My experience in occupational and environmental medicine and toxicology may be vital for securing the weapon."

"She's right, Lee," Manny allowed. "I mean, she's a legend in her field. We never would have gotten this far without her."

Lee was deeply conflicted. The longer she knew him, the more danger he got her into. "I know that, Manny. But, Emma, this is fieldwork. It's going to get messy."

"And what happened in Boston wasn't messy?" she retorted.

"This'll be different. We're talking terrorists with guns in what amounts to the Wild West. I'm not even sure how Manny and I are going to handle it."

"Well then, adding a third person should make it easier," Emma retorted.

"We do have a number of qualified physicians here at DHS that we could send," the secretary interjected. "But, as Dr. Ortiz mentioned, Dr. Hess's reputation is indisputable. All of the medical professionals I consulted with here know of her work." She saw Lee was still very uncomfortable about the suggestion, and she pointed out another issue. "Besides, as I mentioned, I don't know who I can trust in my own organization. And I do agree that, while she's not an operator, she can add the scientific edge you might need to find and contain the bioweapon. I have already spoken with Harvard in anticipation of this meeting. They've agreed to let us borrow you until this is over, Dr. Hess. And MGH will give you some time off as well, Dr. Ortiz."

"Sweet," Manny said, pumping his fist in the air.

Emma looked at the director. She was a strong woman who, no doubt, had to work hard to achieve so much in the male-dominated field of politics and national security. Emma appreciated Lee's concern about her safety, but he was fighting a losing battle trying to convince his director that Emma would be less safe just because she was a woman.

Lee held up his hands in the universal "I surrender" gesture.

"It's settled, then," Secretary Roberts concluded. "My executive assistant will make all of the arrangements. I'd like you on a plane to Lebanon tonight. And I thank you all for your assistance." She returned to her seat to signal the end of the meeting. "And let's keep this between us for now. Please don't tell anyone about your trip. You all know what's at stake here. Let's find this madman and his bioweapon before all hell breaks loose."

59

THEY WERE EXHAUSTED after their six-hour flight to Paris, followed by a long, uncomfortable delay at Charles de Gaulle Airport. They were finally able to board a delayed MEA flight to Beirut, arriving early in the morning. Fortunately, Steve Connors, their contact from the CIA, was there to whisk them through the long lines at the airport and take them to the American embassy.

Connors, their point man in Beirut, was younger than Lee had expected. His short sandy hair framed his clean-shaven face. He was a few inches shy of six feet, medium build, and average-looking enough to easily blend in with any crowd. Perfect for his line of work.

"I have a briefing set up for you all in the regional security officer's conference room," Connors said as they walked into the sprawling embassy complex. "Terry's home in the States on emergency leave, but I think he's going to be called back here early because of this situation."

Terry Saunders was a veteran RSO, and both the DHS secretary and the ambassador felt he should return to Beirut if the bioweapon was launched against Israel. The secretary of state wisely agreed and had called him an hour earlier to find out how quickly he could catch a flight to Beirut. As he was in Alaska attending his father's funeral, he was not expected to be back before the end of the week.

"I know you're all tired," continued Connors, "but the sooner we get started, the better chance we have at finding this mad scientist of yours."

"No problem. We appreciate all the assistance, Connors," Lee said.

"Believe me, we're going to need all the help we can get. This is going to be a team effort," replied the young CIA troubleshooter.

"So, besides us, who here knows about this?" Manny asked.

"Just the ambassador, chief of station, and the DAO."

"Who are they?" asked Emma, unfamiliar with State Department lingo.

"The senior CIA agent in country and the defense attaché," Connors replied as they entered a conference room with maps spread all over the table.

"I thought you were the CIA guy here in Lebanon," asked Emma.

Connors gave a wry grin that Lee knew all too well from overseas experience. There were spooks like Connors assigned all over Iraq. "I have somewhat of a unique mission. I'm not permanently stationed here. I've been in Lebanon for about a month, working on the situation in Syria. My work's complicated. Let's just say I get sent from place to place, working on special projects, putting out fires as needed," he explained.

"He fixes problems," Manny said. "That's why they call him a troubleshooter."

"Something like that," replied Connors.

"Good day," a U.S. Army colonel announced as he strolled into the room with a Marine officer in tow.

At first Manny was glad to see a fellow soldier, but judging by the lost look on the senior officer's face and the exasperated look on Connors's, he realized that this wasn't going to be a productive meeting.

"I'm Colonel Ray Haller. I'm the defense attaché here. This is Captain Nick Shane. He's the leader of the Marine Special Operations Team advising the Lebanese Special Forces. I was told there was a scientist running around Lebanon with some sort of weapon of mass destruction?" asked Haller.

"Why are you involved, Colonel?" Lee asked sharply. "This is a joint DHS–CIA operation. No one told me anything about military involvement."

"Quite frankly, I'm as surprised as you are. I was just told about this meeting an hour ago."

"The ambassador wanted Colonel Haller here," Connors explained. "Especially if there's going to be any need for military intervention down the line. If the bioweapon is launched from Lebanon into Israel, you can bet the Israeli military will be rolling north to crack some heads."

"But the weapon can be deployed any number of ways," Lee said. "The most likely scenario is that it'll be released in aerosolized form on a street in a populated area, not a bombing per se. I doubt Peters will be lobbing canisters across the border. I imagine a lone terrorist with the weapon hidden in a car or bag or something."

"That's right. The heat from a large explosion would denature the proteins in the bioweapon, causing it to misfire or not work at all," Emma added.

"If that happened, how could Israel trace it back to here?" Manny asked.

Connors was the one who responded. "I think that's what Lee was referring to. From what we've seen so far, it's doubtful whoever's paying the Order to develop this weapon will want it traced back to them, hence the lone-wolf scenario. Once Israel finds out or even suspects that there's a weapon with this potential, they'll go on the warpath. Literally. Quite frankly, the world will come after the terrorists. Anonymity is their best friend right now. Besides, Israel won't care who's directly behind it. They'll use this opportunity to go after anyone they suspect is involved. And Lebanon probably won't be their only target, especially if large numbers of Israelis are killed."

"Well, let's not get ahead of ourselves. Hopefully, it won't come to that. So, what exactly are we dealing with here?" Haller asked, taking a seat at the head of the conference table. Shane stood in the corner and listened.

Connors began the briefing.

"Thanks to the great work these three did in Boston, specifically collecting the DNA samples on the Order's leadership, we were able to put together some information on Philip Peters. His real name is Philip Petrosian. He was born in Iowa, where his parents were both professors, but grew up here in Lebanon after his parents got teaching jobs at the American University in Beirut. According to local records, his parents were murdered when Peters was nine years old. The Lebanese authorities shuffled him around to various foster families until he was in high school, as best I can tell. When he finished school, he went back to the States and studied chemistry and microbiology at Princeton. He worked in a number of labs, came up with a few drugs he patented, and did very well for himself. Made a small fortune, actually. Then he fell off the grid. We don't think he ever married. No kids that we know of. No arrest history."

"If he was an American citizen, why did he stay in Lebanon after his parents were killed?" asked Emma.

"Good question. He applied for his first passport while he was in high school. Since he was still a minor, it was cosigned by a man named Davit Petrosian."

"Why was that his first U.S. passport?" Emma asked. "I thought you said his parents brought him to Lebanon after he was born in Iowa."

"Back then, infants didn't have their own passports," Lee answered.

"That's right," continued Connors. "They were added to their mother's passport."

"So we know he was born in the U.S., grew up in Lebanon, then went back to the States for college and to live the American dream," Manny summarized.

"How about an address on the passport application?" Lee asked.

"His high school was a boarding school here in Beirut. That was the address used on the application. The school was destroyed in the eighties during the civil war," Connors continued.

"The man who cosigned for it, what did you say his name was?" asked Shane from the corner, earning a stern glance from Colonel Haller.

Shane shrugged it off.

"Davit Petrosian. Not sure who he was, but, as his name suggests and the fact that he signed for Peters's passport, since he was a minor at the time, he was probably a relative," explained Connors.

"No address on the older Petrosian, I take it?" Shane wondered aloud.

"None that I could find," Connors explained. I've only had a day to research this, though. I have some folks checking the name. Hopefully they'll turn up something soon."

"Okay, well, none of that is earth-shattering," Manny interrupted. "What did you find out about the Order?"

"Believe it or not, we know even less about this Order entity than we do about Peters. It's basically an old fraternity. A group of powerful members from all across the globe, as best as we can tell."

"So, conspiracy theory stuff, right? I mean, like they killed JFK, hid Jimmy Hoffa, and have the Roswell aliens in their basement with Elvis?" Manny asked.

Connors chuckled. "Something like that."

"I don't think this is a laughing matter," Haller interjected.

"It's not," Manny said, turning on him. "But I do think it's funny that you're supposedly here to help us yet you have no idea why or how you can contribute because you have no earthly clue what's going on."

This time it was Nick Shane's turn to snicker.

The colonel pushed his wire-rimmed glasses up on his thin nose and shrugged off the remark. He was not, by nature, a confrontational man. His cautious disposition had served him well during his career as a protocol officer, currently assigned to a political position at the embassy. He was not an infantry officer, which is why he had brought along Captain Shane.

"Let's get back to the case, shall we?" he said, deflecting the comment.

"We know that Peters landed in Beirut yesterday, but we have no idea where he went after that," continued Connors. "From what I can tell from the scattered official records I could dig up, he hasn't been back to Lebanon in the past forty years, but I can't be sure. There's just not a lot out there on Peters. He certainly likes to move around incognito."

"Even if he had been back before, it wouldn't have been hard for him to come in from Syria on the Beirut–Damascus road," Manny added.

"That's right. We were lucky he came through the airport this time, or we probably wouldn't have even picked him up."

"Fighting in Syria?" Lee asked knowledgably.

"Yep. Would have been too risky landing in Damascus these days, then traveling to Beirut over land. Even for a powerful and resourceful man like Peters. He had little choice but to fly directly into Lebanon," Connors said.

"What about his contacts here in Lebanon? Like maybe the ones that are paying him and the Order to build this weapon," Lee asked.

"It's certainly possible that a Lebanese group is behind it, but I sure as hell hope not," Connors replied. "There are a lot of crazies here. Al-Qaeda, Hezbollah, Hamas, ISIS, PLO. You name it, they have a shop on every corner. On top of that, organized crime, both domestic and international, has set up shops here. With the Arab Spring still smoldering here and all the troubles in Syria and Iraq, this is a haven for terrorists and the lowlife profiteers who often accompany them. Lebanon is a powder keg these days. Relations between the Christians and Muslims here haven't been this tense since the civil war. Anything could set off another war, including this bioweapon."

"All the more reason we need to find it," Emma added.

"*We?*" Haller asked, stirring. "You're not suggesting we go out and look for Peters, are you? The Lebanese authorities will be furious. We have no jurisdiction here. It would be a political nightmare. Let them handle it."

"We can't trust the Lebanese government, Colonel," Connors replied. "Each of the groups I mentioned has members in government positions. That's the only reason the government has survived this long, because all the factions have some representation. If they get their hands on the weapon or if they are already working with Peters, they would alert him that we were looking for him before we even leave the embassy. If Peters hears that we're snooping around, he'll be gone in an instant. I bet he has many more resources in this country than we do."

"We need to keep this to ourselves," Lee echoed.

"And find him ourselves," said Manny.

"Obviously, we have to find Peters. This is his baby. We find him, we find the bioweapon," Emma said. "You say you have no idea where he could be?"

"Not a clue," Connors replied. He was used to being thrown into difficult situations. His job as a troubleshooter was to fix problems as they arose. Most agents at embassies were too busy running their own in-country intelligence networks to focus on any one major crisis. If they didn't continually develop and nurture contacts, those sources would dry up. When problems did arise, the CIA would send in a troubleshooter to help coordinate all efforts against it, which allowed the station's agents to contribute but also to continue to focus on their own missions.

But Connors had just received the call about Peters yesterday, and he had absolutely nothing to go on other than that his target had already landed in Beirut. Not being able to use the CIA's contacts in the Lebanese government for fear they would take the bioweapon or were already involved with Peters made the search even more difficult.

"Wait," Emma interrupted. "Peters told me he lived in a monastery as a teenager, but you said he was at boarding school. He mentioned the abbey there. If another Petrosian signed for his passport as his guardian when he was seventeen, maybe this Davit Petrosian was living in the monastery and Peters stayed with him during school breaks. Petrosian may even have been the abbot there. Peters sounded very fond of him."

"Monks do like to keep to themselves, making their wine and all," Manny remarked dryly.

"So?" asked Haller. "How does that help us now?"

"Well, maybe Peters went back to the monastery. They're usually very private and remote. At least it's a place we can start looking. Unless anyone has any better ideas?"

Everyone looked at each other without saying a word.

"Fine," Emma continued. "Can we check the names of monks in the monasteries here?"

"That was so long ago. Even if we had that ability, which we don't without the Lebanese government's assistance, what good would a name do now?" Connors asked. "He could be long dead by now. Many religious sects kept their names and locations hidden from the government to protect them from religious prosecution. Most likely the monastery isn't even still standing due to all the religious wars that took place here over the last century. And even if it still existed, there are so many monasteries from all sects of Christianity hidden in the mountains, I wouldn't even know where to start."

"Wait, you said his real name was *Petrosian*?" Lee asked.

"Armenian! Yes, that's it!" Connors said, catching on to Lee's train of thought. He and Lee began to riffle through the maps on the table.

"Armenian? What does that have to do with anything?" Haller asked.

"Good lord," Shane exclaimed. "*Petrosian* is an Armenian name. If Davit Petrosian was a monk, he probably belonged to an *Armenian* order," he said, walking over to join Lee and Connors at the maps.

"Which narrows our search down considerably," added Connors. "Armenian Christians are a small minority here in Lebanon. Mainly living in the central mountains."

"I'm still not following," Haller said.

"Are there any active Armenian monasteries left here?" Emma asked, ignoring the defense attaché.

"Not anymore, no. Most of the monasteries were destroyed during the many Muslim–Christian wars in the mountains. But I do remember one of my contacts telling me about an old Armenian monastery in the northern highlands, a few hours away from the Beqaa Valley. It was abandoned but still intact, if I recall. There're a lot of drug lords just south of that area and it's a hub for gun running into Syria," Connors said, pointing at a map. His true purpose for being in Lebanon was to track weapons movement into Syria; thus he knew where the majority of illegal arms dealers operated.

"Qadisha Valley?" Manny asked, reading the map.

"Used to be a Roman settlement," Shane added as moved closer to the table. "Then it became a safe haven for early Christians fleeing persecution in the region."

"It's been abandoned, but it's the only Armenian monastery still standing that I know of," Connors continued. "It's very remote, tucked into the Mount Lebanon range running up the middle of the country. A perfect spot for Peters to hide."

"Not so perfect for us," Shane pointed out. "That's some rough terrain in that valley. A difficult approach. That's why the old monks picked it. Steep cliffs, high mountains. Add to that, you have to go through some bad-guy turf just to get close to it. Bad guys that might have set up shop in the monastery, if your boy Peters hasn't. A good spec ops team could infiltrate it, but it won't be easy without being noticed."

"Infiltrate?" Haller repeated. "What are you talking about, Captain? We're here to give our advice. No one said anything about going anywhere. We have no clearance for that."

"It's an old fortress turned monastery," Connors informed the group, ignoring the colonel.

"Secluded, large, hidden away in the mountains, just like the lab in New Hampshire was," added Emma.

"Connors, are you listening to me?" asked Haller.

"I know, Colonel," Connors replied with a sigh. "I know. You don't have permission to go. I understand."

"I have no orders or authority to conduct a military operation on Lebanese soil. And I doubt you have permission either. I doubt the ambassador will approve."

"You're probably right, Colonel. If I were you," Connors said, "I would leave now so you can deny having any knowledge of what we are about to do."

Lee and Manny looked at each other and smiled. They liked the point man right away.

"This entire plan is crazy," Haller scoffed.

Shane glared at the colonel. "No, it's not," he countered. "It'll be tough, yes, but doable. My team can get in there."

"Captain, you and your team are having no part of this *illegal* mission. We were instructed to advise, that is all. We don't know if this Peters character is even there. And if he is, what if he has fifty men holed up there in that fortress with him? You'd never get inside the walls. If you want it done right, call in a drone strike. At least that way they'll be no U.S. personnel directly involved. *That* is my official military advice."

Manny scoffed, "Yeah, that's discreet. The Lebanese government will never notice that."

"Gentlemen," interjected Lee, "I understand the political sensitivities involved with this matter. Connors and I can go to the Qadisha monastery tonight to do a little recon. If we see activity, we can regroup and come up with a plan."

"Actually, Colonel Haller may have a point," Emma replied, not liking Lee's proposal. "Why don't you just send a drone over, at least to see if there's anyone there? It'll be far less risky than going in person, and we'll get the results sooner."

Haller's angry look after Manny's snide comment was replaced with a smug look of validation.

"We could do that, but the monastery is completely covered from the outside," Connors replied, looking more closely at the high-resolution map. "Not even an open courtyard. I don't think we'd see much from the air."

"And," Shane added, picking up the map, "this is a relatively heavily wooded area. It would be difficult making out faces through this heavy forest canopy using a drone. And with all this rain we're having, the drone'll have to fly so low below the clouds, it will probably be noticed and may scare Peters away. To be discreet, this'll have to be a man-packable mission. We need eyes on the ground to get a close-up look at the roads, buildings, doors, to see if there's anyone home. Besides, squatters may have moved in. I'm sure before any operation to go in for a drone strike is approved, the men sitting comfortably on their butts in Washington will want confirmation there are no civilians in the area. Bad enough we take military action on foreign soil without permission from their government; worse still if we take out civilians and have collateral damage while doing so."

"Right. So, like I said, we'll have to go in ourselves. Tonight. Recon the area," Lee said.

"Seems like the only viable option," Shane agreed.

"No, Captain, you're not going on any missions," Haller replied, rising from the table.

"Colonel, my team can go in there much quicker and safer than anyone else," Shane said.

"He's right, Colonel," Connors allowed. "I'm not a special operations guy."

"Speak for yourself," Manny said, eager to go.

"I understand all of that, Agent Connors. But what you're proposing is politically very risky. I am the senior U.S. military representative in Lebanon. I will not allow military involvement unless the Pentagon gives me the green light. I'm sorry, but we're out."

"Can we get that authorization?" Emma asked.

Connors shrugged. "Maybe. But it'll take some big guns."

"I could call Secretary Roberts at the DHS. She's got clout," Lee said.

"Even with that, decisions this sensitive do not move quickly in Washington. It'll still take time—time we don't have. The longer we wait, the more time Peters has to find out we're here and bug out," explained Manny.

"Or worse, release the weapon," Emma added.

"I don't want to risk that, and it'll be dark soon. I hate wasting time sitting here while Peters has that weapon. Besides, we're only taking a look to see if he has a lab there or not," Connors concluded.

"I'm in," Manny emphasized.

"I'm going too," Emma said.

Lee bristled at her suggestion. "I guess it would be no use to tell you what a bad idea that is."

"No, it would not," Emma said with a smile. "Besides, I might come in handy looking for evidence of a lab on the premises."

"She's got a point," Manny said.

"Thanks, pal. You're a big help," Lee said wryly.

"Just saying…" Manny shrugged.

"Okay," Connors said. "It's a two-hour drive from here. We don't have the right gear, and, if I assume correctly, none of us is an expert mountain climber. So scaling the face of the cliffs is out of the question."

"Speak for yourself," Manny repeated.

"Why does that not surprise me?" Emma replied.

"Well, we aren't all Rangers," Connors said. "We'll drive to about a mile from the monastery, then hike the rest of the way alongside the road. We risk being seen, but it's safer and quicker than climbing up the steep ridges in the valley. At least we'll have darkness to conceal us. Besides, we're not storming the castle, just getting a look-see. And scouting out the road will also help us determine how much traffic has been going up there lately."

"Sounds like a plan," Lee said.

"Well, good luck," Haller said coldly, anxious to leave to bolster his plausible deniability. He walked around the table and made his way to the door of the conference room. Before he left, he looked back to see if Captain Shane was following. He wasn't.

"Captain?"

Shane leaned toward Lee. "Get your supervisors to talk to DoD tonight," he whispered to Lee. "If the SecDef orders SOCOM to support you, my general at Marine Forces Special Operations Command would give you my team in a heartbeat. Until then, my hands are tied."

"I understand, Captain. Thanks," Lee replied.

Shane shook Lee's hand and strode out of the room.

"Do you think he'll be able to come with us?" Emma asked Connors hopefully, watching the Marine leave.

"I know he'll try his best. I've got to know him pretty well over this past month hanging out at the Marine House. Nick Shane is a hardcore, seasoned recon Marine. His men tell me stories about his exploits. They worship him. He's about as tough as they come. He knows tactics better than anyone I know, especially in a low-density terrorist environment. He's had some issues—PTSD, drinking—but he's the best there is. That's why I wanted him here, to pick his brain. But he's still a Marine. He won't disobey such a direct order. Especially one that could cause an international incident."

"So it's just us?" Emma said.

Lee fixed a concerned stare on her, hoping she would change her mind. He saw the resolve in her eyes, though, and his heart sank. He didn't want to lose her in what could be a dangerous mission.

"Looks like it," he said sadly.

"Sounds like good odds to me," Manny answered with his usual enthusiasm.

60

DOCTOR, the aerosolized bioweapon is ready," Nora announced proudly. "During our most recent test, the vector remained intact and is actually more virulent as an aerosol. It will deliver the weapon much faster and more effectively in this form."

Peters's two lead scientists stood with him staring at the body lying at the bottom of the large glass shower-like chamber. For the past twenty-four hours, Nora and Richard Becker had been placing prisoners purchased from warlords and terrorist groups into two eight-foot-tall sealed glass tubes to monitor the effects of exposure to various versions of the aerosolized bioweapon.

Nora hit the red plunger-like button on the wall next to the chamber with her chubby fingers, and the rounded glass door of the stall opened for them to take a closer look at the results of their experiment. The former IRA fighter took exceptional pleasure in her work, Peters thought. She was so unlike Richard, his timid assistant, who seemed to not have the stomach for the testing phase of the project.

The test subject, a middle-age man who had the misfortune of breaking down on a desolate road through the mountains near the facility, had been exposed to the gaseous version of the weapon six hours ago. Due to the high volume of smuggling and organized crime activity in the area, coupled with the Order's large cash payments to the local officials and crime lords, the man's disappearance would go unreported and unnoticed. The dead man would never know, thought Peters, that he had made history as the very first victim of the aerosolized ethnic bioweapon.

"Excellent work, Nora. Prepare the seven canisters. *Seven*. Seven plagues for seven sinful cities," he said with a smile. "I want them ready tonight. Our martyrs will leave in the morning for their targets. Then we sit back and let nature take its course."

Peters left the makeshift lab in the dungeon of the old citadel and walked up the spiral stone steps to the main floor. He had come a long way from when he was a child, playing alone in these hallowed halls. The sounds of his tears and laughter still echoed in this great room, as they did in his dreams. His life here with his uncle was much better than the physical and emotional abuse he was subjected to as a foster child in the Arab slums of Beirut and Tripoli. Here he received education and discipline. Here he gained a purpose.

As Peters paused in the hallway, the air, cooled by the thick stone walls, chilled him. In this room, his uncle, the abbot, had told him his favorite stories. Ancient struggles and epic battles between great peoples and religions throughout history rang in his ears and bolstered his imagination. Heroes and villains alike, fighting for total victory for their cause. For their God. For their survival. Would history remember him as the most revered of these heroes? Possibly. To some. To those who mattered, anyway.

But all of his efforts—indeed, the focus of his adult life—was never about glory or fame. His motivation wasn't immortality. Not for himself, anyway. Passion was what drove his actions. In the end, he would earn his just reward.

A small doorway concealed in the shelving unit opened, and Peters's guest stepped into the great room.

"Hello, my friend," said Peters, his back to the man. "What news do you bring from America?"

The man smiled and told Peters everything he knew.

61

THE FOUR AMERICANS in the GMC Suburban drove up the twisting road through the mountains running along the spine of Lebanon. Dusk had come and gone, and Emma was amazed at the surroundings as the setting sun cast a fiery glow over the peaks and valleys leading up to Qadisha. The landscape contrasted greatly with her vision of the Middle East as one vast desert. There was nothing barren here. Lush green trees covered the mountains.

"It's beautiful, isn't it?" asked Lee, leaning over so their shoulders bumped lightly.

"Amazing. I can't believe my eyes."

"There are quite a few skiing resorts farther north in these mountains," Connors told them as he expertly drove the SUV. "Not so many down through here, though. Too many bad guys."

"What kind of bad guys?" Emma asked with a slight tremor in her voice.

"All sorts of lowlifes, holy warriors, terrorists, warlords, organized crime—you name it, and they have a shingle hung out there somewhere. Hezbollah and Hamas have training camps there to the west. ISIS, of course, has a presence, as does al-Qaeda. That's what I was doing out here—trying to find out who was supplying ISIS in Syria with their weapons. That's why I'm somewhat familiar with these mountains."

"Why doesn't the Lebanese government do something about them?" Emma asked.

"Who knows? Corruption. Sympathy. Fear. All these groups have one common enemy. Besides us, of course," Connors replied.

"Israel?" asked Emma.

Connors nodded. "Many in the Lebanese government, despite their public proclamation of peace with Israel, would probably not lose too much sleep if Jerusalem fell into Muslim hands."

"So much pain and suffering, all in the name of religion," she said, shaking her head.

"Make no mistake about it, these are cold-blooded killers. It's not just about religion to them but rather a way of life," Lee added.

"That's right," Connors continued. "You know, when we took down Bin Laden, we found so much contraband in his room. Things forbidden by Islam, including porn on his computer. Children who fight for Islam are often given opioids, despite the official Islamic hard-liners' public stance against the use of drugs. This isn't about Islam. It's an age-old struggle for power, land, and resources. Mainly water. Water's more precious than oil in many parts of the Middle East and Africa. The way these criminals brutally murder civilians and their purported justifications for their jihad aren't found in the Qur'an. It's all a charade."

"Well, they can have it," commented Manny. "I've seen all—"

"Connors, look!" shouted Emma from the backseat, pointing ahead.

Half a dozen men were walking out of the tree line ahead of them, taking positions to block the road. The men were all wearing mismatched military fatigues and civilian clothing, each holding different variations of the AK-47 assault rifle. The muzzles were all pointed toward the Suburban.

"I don't suppose this puppy's armored?" Manny asked from the passenger seat, bracing for the rounds he was sure would be coming through the windshield.

"Afraid not. It's a loaner. Haller has the only other armored GMC, besides the ambassador," said Connors.

"Yet another reason to dislike that guy," replied Manny.

"We gotta stop. They'll mow us down for sure if we don't," Connors said.

"You realize if we stop, there's no way they'll let us continue," Lee stated.

"One step at a time," Connors replied, slowing down the vehicle fifty feet in front of the mob.

"Who are they?" asked Emma.

"Could be any of the groups I mentioned. From the looks of them, though, I say they're just local bandits. Hopefully, they only want our money and vehicle. But, just in case," he said, handing both Lee and Manny pistols, "be ready. This could get messy real fast."

62

I'LL TAKE THE THREE on the right," Lee said. "They're all staring into our headlights, so we have a slight advantage."

"I got the three up front," Manny called.

"That leaves the rest on the left for me." Connors sighed. The last thing he wanted was a gunfight. Not only would it jeopardize their mission, but he had civilians with him. "Emma, when the shooting starts, hit the floor and don't come up until you hear from one of us."

Emma nodded nervously, wishing she'd heeded Lee's advice and stayed in Boston. She had never been so scared.

"It'll be fine," Lee told her with a reassuring smile.

"Keep your pistols concealed and stay calm," said Connors. "Let's see what happens."

"Now's the time, Connors," Manny protested. "We can hit them while they're still blinded by our lights. Then you punch the gas and get us out of here. If we let them close in on us, we're toast. This is our only chance."

"They don't look like terrorists. Trust me on this one," Connors said quietly.

Manny looked back at Lee, who seemed as uncomfortable with the agent's plan as he was.

A man with a black bandana around his forehead, Nike T-shirt, and tan fatigues approached the driver's side and tapped on the window with the muzzle of his rifle. Connors rolled it down as the other men surrounded the car.

Lee and Manny followed the agent's lead and rolled down their windows to get better range of movement for firing their pistols, should that be necessary.

"Wayne bitruh?" the menacing leader asked with a toothless scowl. Connors, who was fluent in Arabic, knew the man was asking where they were going but decided to play ignorant, at least for now. He flashed the man a contractor badge showing he worked with the Lebanese Ministry of National Defense. One of the first things Connors got whenever he operated in country was a government ID associating him with the local authorities. He hoped the bluff would work this time, but it all depended on what group the men were associated with. If they were organized crime, they would probably let the Suburban pass, as they wouldn't want to draw attention to their illegal activities. If they were terrorists, all bets were off.

Toothless scrutinized the ID carefully. Underneath his jacket laying across his lap, Connors switched the safety off the pistol and put his index finger on the trigger. The sound was barely audible, but both Lee and Manny noticed and did the same.

"Afendi!" shouted the man standing next to Lee's door, calling to the leader of the group.

Lee was startled and about to pull his own pistol as the man pointed into the car. *"Shof hun!"* he continued, trying to show the leader something he noticed.

Slowly the leader walked around to Lee's window and reached over him to pick up the map lying between him and Emma. The man's eyes went wide with terror when he noticed the location circled on the map. He threw the map onto Lee's lap like it was on fire and stepped back from the window.

"*Ruhu,*" he said, motioning with his gun to move on.

"Let's go," Connors said, putting the SUV into gear and driving off.

Through the rearview mirror, Connors noticed the men regroup in the middle of the road to watch the SUV.

"What the hell was that all about?" asked Lee.

"Quite frankly, I'm not sure. I've never seen anything like it. It was odd. Almost like they were spooked or something," Connors replied.

"That one guy sure didn't like what he saw circled on the map," Manny added.

"I know. That's what concerns me," the agent said.

"Me too," added Lee. "I wonder what their motive was for letting us go. Was it because they want us to do something about Peters, or because they think we're with him?"

"I guess we'll find out soon enough," Emma said.

As they continued driving, Lee glanced down at the location on the map that he circled with a red Sharpie. They were about a mile from the monastery.

"It's time to hoof it," he said.

Connors nodded and made a U-turn.

"What are we doing?" asked Emma.

Connors pulled the SUV off the road and into the brush. "I just want to be facing the right way if we have to get out of here in a hurry."

They took their backpacks out of the SUV, and Manny led them fifty feet down the side of the mountain so they could hike through the woods just below the road. The thick woods made it difficult to see, despite the full moon, and Manny wouldn't let them use their flashlights. Emma slipped once and almost fell, if not for Lee, who was walking closely behind her.

"Thanks," she said, appreciating his strong hands around her waist. "I don't understand how Manny can see anything out here."

"Me neither. I may have been a Marine, but I'm not a Ranger like him. I'm glad he's here. I'd never be able to make it out of these woods without a GPS," Lee answered.

"Shhh," Manny scolded from the front, even though the two could barely make out his shadow.

"All I can say is, thanks for bringing him," Connors whispered over his shoulder to Lee and Emma. "I'd be wandering around here lost with you, Jansen."

They continued walking for a half hour, Manny circling back a few times to make sure Emma and Lee weren't falling too far behind. Finally a clearing appeared, almost out of nowhere.

"Wow, there it is," Emma exclaimed, emerging from the brush. Just ahead of them along the road loomed a large dark stone structure.

"You did it, Manny," Lee said, putting his hand on his friend's shoulder. "I don't know how in that darkness you got us here, but you did."

"Like I said, Rangers lead the way," he replied with a smile, folding his map and putting it in his back pocket.

Back on the road, the light from the moon illuminated the rest of their walk. In ten minutes they reached the rusty iron gate in front of the monastery.

The former citadel's age was evident in its crumbling walls and old, cracked windows. The structure itself was built into the cliff on the right, while the left side hung over the valley below.

The road that led up to the gate was paved but in bad shape. A thick, heavy chain looped around the gate. From the looks of the corroded lock, this entrance had not been used for a long time, thought Emma.

"No one has come up this way in a while," Lee announced, bending down to look at the road. "The road's covered in leaves and dust. And look at that gate."

The four Americans slowly approached the walls around the fortification. It was quiet. Lee was thankful for the full moon, as he didn't want to risk giving away their presence with flashlights.

They stood at the iron gates for a moment, then walked around the outside of the stone wall until it ended at the side of the main building itself.

There were a few dark windows thirty feet above the wall and one steel door on the side of the building. Manny bent down and touched the ground around the door. "Same thing here. No tracks, nothing disturbed on the ground, rusty hinges. This door hasn't swung open in a long time."

"Maybe we have the wrong monastery?" Emma asked, peering through a crack in the high stone wall. The courtyard inside was deserted.

"Maybe," replied Connors. "But there aren't many monasteries still standing around here, especially isolated and abandoned ones where Peters would be able to complete his work without arousing suspicion. I think we should get back to the embassy before it gets too late and regroup. We'll have to come up with another plan."

"Wait," Emma said, raising her head in the night air. All were quiet, waiting for her to continue. She took her time, letting her senses absorb everything before coming to a conclusion.

"What is it, Emma?" asked Lee, unable to stand the suspense any longer.

"That smell. Don't you smell it?" she asked, leaning into the side of the monastery, eyes closed.

"No, nothing," Connors said.

"Wait. Yes. Something sweet," Lee answered.

"Grapes," Emma replied, opening her eyes and smiling.

"Okay, so there are wild grapes growing in the woods. Are you hungry or something?" asked Manny.

"No, Manny. Not the woods. There's no wind. Not even a breeze. The smell's coming from in here." She pointed at the wall. "It's not a plant. I know that smell. I've spent so much time working in bio labs. That's the smell of *Pseudomonas* cultures growing on plates. Peters's lab is here," Emma stated confidently.

Connors pulled a flashlight out of his jacket and shined the light on the wall. The bright light blinded them all for a moment. When their eyes accommodated, he focused the beam on the wall and worked his way across the side of the monastery. There was nothing but cold stone. Emma put her hand on his and guided the light down to the base of the wall near the ground. There, they saw it. A vent.

Connors put his hand over the vent and nodded.

"Heat," he said with a smile. "How did you know?"

"The weapon is biologic. A viral vector carrying a manufactured gene that produces organic NF-kB resulting in the target's immune system going into fatal overdrive, right?" Emma said.

"Okay, we know all this. So?" answered Lee.

"Don't you see? In order to test his manufactured NF-kB gene, he needs to activate it. The most potent stimulator of the NF-kB gene is LPS, or lipoprotein saccharide. LPS comes from a *bacteria*. That's what we smell. *Pseudomonas*. Gram-negative rods growing in his lab. *Pseudomonas* LPS is the most powerful stimulator of NF-kB genes."

"See," Manny said to Lee. "I told you we needed her."

"Damn, she's smart," Connors said.

Lee wanted to give Emma a hug, but he restrained himself. Mission first. "So, the lab's here. I bet Peters's here as well."

"He sure is," a familiar voice called from the tree line. They all covered their eyes as bright lights turned on from edge of the woods behind them. Men armed with AK-47s emerged from the brush. "And he's not the only one."

"Son of a bitch!" Lee cursed when he saw his boss, Jay Kowalski. "What the hell are you doing here?"

63

ERE WE ARE AGAIN, Dr. Hess," Peters said as Lee, Manny, Emma, and Connors were brought to him by DHS Director Kowalski and three armed guards. After surprising them in front of the monastery, Kowalski led them down a narrow path that traversed the mountain side of the old building to a back door that led into the main hall. From there, they were escorted to the basement lab, where Peters was waiting for them.

"We really have to stop meeting like this," Peters murmured with a grin. "But I assure you, this will be the last time."

"You won't get away with it," Lee said. "DHS, the embassy. Everyone knows your plans and that you're holed up in this place."

"Nice try, Lee," Kowalski replied. "I've been reading the State Department cables. No one at the embassy believes anyone is here."

"Quite right," Peters added. "This monastery was abandoned years ago. We have remained inconspicuous during our time here. I even remembered a secret door that my uncle showed me so we didn't have to disturb the main entrance. You see, the Muslims in this land are not always hospitable to their Christian neighbors. In fact, the secret door was constructed to allow the peaceful monks who lived here to escape when Islamic crusaders and ruffians wished to do them harm."

"So, this *is* where you grew up," Emma stated.

"That's right. And I would have let you all return safely to your car had you not stumbled onto our little ventilation oversight," Peters said, giving Nora a disapproving look.

"I'll take care of them right now," Kowalski said, pointing his pistol at Lee's head.

"Not so fast, my friend. Dr. Hess and I have some matters to discuss. Why don't you show our other guests to the fine living arrangements in the subbasement while I have a chat with my esteemed colleague."

Kowalski didn't even pretend to understand the old man, but he was smart enough not to question him. Lee and Emma had been trouble since the very beginning. Letting them live had been a mistake. A mistake that had come back to haunt them time and time again. He himself had underestimated Lee back in DC. After Khattib died, Peters ordered Kowalski to send an agent up to Boston who would blindly follow the false leads they planted about the researcher being a terrorist working on a dirty bomb. Kowalski had sent Lee, believing he would be distraught and so preoccupied with finding his partner's killer that he wouldn't be able to concentrate on searching for a terrorist ring and weapon. Perhaps, if Kowalski was lucky, Jansen would hit the bottle again, as he did when his wife died and again after the fatal shooting of the teenager in Lincoln Heights.

Instead, Lee and the nosy lady doctor kept getting closer and closer to Astrea, forcing the Order to abandon their bio-weapons research in America literally in the middle of the night. Even Dr. Peters had overlooked the fact that the Public Health Department in Boston would send someone to look into Khattib's mysterious death. Maybe, if the Ten had the foresight to intervene before the all-too-capable Dr. Hess was assigned to the case, things would have ended up differently. Perhaps Jansen, Hess, Ortiz, and the CIA agent would all be home asleep in their beds instead of awaiting their death in the dungeon. After all, without Kowalski's knowledge or permission, Lee had orchestrated the capture of a number of the Order's leaders, and the rest were on the run from their own governments. Why wasn't Peters allowing him to kill these persistent threats right here and now?

"You heard the man. Let's go," said Kowalski, jabbing his pistol into Lee's side.

Emma watched as the four men with guns, with that bastard Kowalski in the lead, led her friends away.

"I have nothing to *chat* with you about, Peters," she hissed.

"Oh, but you do, my dear. You see, I have one last proposition for you. I know you broke your last promise to me, but I'm willing to forgive your transgression."

"You mean when you gave me the *antidote* that was really just an anti-inflammatory?"

"Yes," he said, recalling the ruse with delight. "My apologies. That was very deceitful of me. I had hoped it would buy me some time. Enough for me to leave the country, but not enough for Project Astrea to be deployed before your arrival in Lebanon. Now I need something much more important than the life of one DHS agent. What I want from you now, Dr. Hess, is your *brain*."

"What are you talking about?"

"Look around you," he said, pointing. The room was packed with state-of-the-art laboratory equipment. Obviously, no expense had been spared. It was, Emma had to admit, an impressive facility. On the back wall, near two full-length glass chambers, she noticed seven backpacks on a long table.

"Is that how you're going to murder millions of innocent people?" she asked.

"You're looking at it all wrong, Doctor. The motive isn't murder. It's restitution and rebirth. Let me explain." Peters's voice had taken on a pontifical tone, good for lecturing the masses. "Two thousand years ago, the followers of Jesus Christ preached in this land. During the first century after our Savior's death, Christianity was spread to the Phoenicians and the inhabitants of these very mountains. In fact, before the Islamic invaders conquered this beautiful land, Christianity was widespread. Our ancestors here were butchered by those barbaric invaders. Our holy lands, home to Christians for centuries, were viciously stolen by the Muslims and occupied. My beloved Lebanon finally fell under the dark spell of Islam, and we were persecuted. Look at us today, Doctor. Christians, who only desire peace, are being slaughtered in Egypt, Iraq, Nigeria, and even next door in Syria. Our churches are being desecrated and burned to the ground. There is no place left for us to go, and no one seems to care."

"The persecution of Christians you mention is horrible, but genocide is not the answer. But if you hate Muslims and Arabs so much, then why are you building an ethnic bioweapon for them to use against Israel?" Emma asked, maneuvering toward the door to try to escape.

"My dear, that was your assumption. I never said I was working for terrorists or targeting Israel."

"But Khattib. He was working on a cure for Gaucher disease?" she asked, confused.

"Another deception, I'm afraid. It is so easy to mislead those who do not open their eyes. To protect the project, contingencies were put in place to divert attention from our true cause. Gaucher was one of them. A safeguard, if you will, to mislead anyone who might stumble upon Khattib's work. America is so focused on Muslim extremism, anything suggesting your precious Israel might be threatened is automatically blamed on the Arabs. It was the linking protein technology we sought. It didn't matter if it was initially designed for the Gaucher gene or any other. Once Khattib created the linking protein, we could modify it to go after any ethnicity we desired.

"We allowed the authorities to believe Khattib was a terrorist working on a dirty bomb in order to keep their prying eyes away from my true vision. Bruno, may he rest in peace, planted the yttrium in Khattib's apartment, along with the terrorist literature. But that didn't fool you, did it, Doctor?" he asked with a scowl. "Unfortunately, because you reacted so quickly to Khattib's death, the only radioactive material I could get my hands on was yttrium from a medical source. I was certain, in light of the story we planted about a dirty bomb, that Undersecretary Waters and the local authorities, probably even Agent Jansen, would have believed the material we planted could be used for such a bomb. I should not have presumed you would have fallen for my ruse so easily. Bravo, Doctor."

"And Khattib?"

"I'm afraid poor Dr. Khattib was quite innocent from the very start. Just a tool I was using to create my masterpiece. He never knew, until quite possibly his very end, that he was working on a weapon that was being designed to destroy his own people."

"Arabs?"

"Dr. Hess, did you know that roughly forty percent of Lebanon is Christian? Should the number of Muslims sharply decline, we would be the majority. Project Astrea will help us shift the balance of power in our favor. It is time for us to reclaim our lands. Reclaim Lebanon. Eventually, reclaim all of the Holy Land."

"That was the Order's plan? How were you able to convince them of this?"

"The Order only wanted to reduce the Arab threat to the world order. Europe is under siege from a steady onslaught of Arab immigrants, possibly becoming the majority in some European nations. Eastern Europe is already overrun with Mohammedans. It was easy, of course, to persuade our American allies in the Order to agree to thin out the Arab population in the world. Russia and China are having their own difficulties with Arab-backed Muslim insurgencies in Chechnya and western China. Our way of life is being threatened from all sides by these Islamic incursions. The Ten were all too eager for me to target these animals. I, of course, obliged their demands in exchange for their support and funding and resources. They knew nothing of my own secret plans to reinstate Christianity to its previous glory.

"And this is where you can help, Dr. Hess. You have a brilliant mind and are passionate about your work. I do not think anyone else would have come as close to finding Project Astrea as you did. Champion our cause with the same zeal. Join us, Emma," continued Peters, like a madman creating his monster. "Imagine the peace and stability that would reign in the Middle East once Christianity is again the dominant force in the region."

"You mean once you murder all those who don't believe as you do," Emma said flatly. "I don't think either Jesus or your uncle the abbot had that in mind. That's not Christianity or what it stands for. This is just a perverse twisting of religion to suit your own sick thirst for power. You're no different from the terrorists who took down the World Trade Center or the fundamentalists you say you're fighting against," she said, inching her way toward the door. She was about to make a break for it when Peters pulled a gun from his jacket.

"It disappoints me that you cannot see the wisdom of my vision. I will offer you one last chance. I will even sweeten the pot for you, so to speak. I will let your friends go if you stay and join me. They are all safe in my dungeon, awaiting your decision. The alternative, of course, is for all of you to never leave these walls again. If you refuse, you will become martyrs for the cause," he warned, pointing the gun at her and positioning himself between her and the door.

"I didn't believe you would let us all live when we were in your office in New Hampshire, and I do not believe you now. Besides, I would never be a part of ethnic cleansing and mass murder. You can't succeed, Peters. This is not science. This is madness."

"Oh, I will succeed. And it *is* science. In fact, let me show you the sheer power of Project Astrea so that you may more intimately understand the science firsthand."

"What do you mean?" Emma asked.

"Why, you will become my next experimental subject. I would love to run one final test before we go fully operational in the morning."

64

H OW COULD YOU BETRAY your country like this, Jay?" Lee asked as they were led down a dark stone corridor. He still couldn't believe that his boss and former Marine commander would be a member of the Order.

Connors and Manny each had an armed guard behind them, while Kowalski himself covered Lee. The remaining guard stood outside of the lab in case Peters needed any assistance.

"My allegiance lies much deeper than a flag," replied Kowalski. "I believe in the future, in preserving our way of life. This is a war, and you of all people should understand that. Hell, you were with me in Iraq. You've seen firsthand what the world has become. The savagery unleashed upon the world by Muslims and others. And it's not just in the Middle East. Our cities are infested with crime. It's time for us to do something about it. It's time to bring order."

Lee regarded this justification with contempt. "Many of the world's struggles are due to people like you and Peters, thinking you could kill anyone you chose to just because they were different or didn't fit your vision of what was 'right.' I am nothing like you. I fight to keep men like you from succeeding."

"I'm sorry to hear that, Lee. I really am. I had hoped you would join me. But I was wrong about you."

"Is that why you sent me to Boston? So I would *join* you?"

"No," Kowalski acknowledged. "Peters and I both knew once the DHS got wind of Khattib's death, an investigation would begin. We couldn't stop that, but I could do the next best thing: Send someone who wouldn't have his heart in the investigation. After Agent James's death and all you've been through this past year, I thought you would go up to Boston and fall in line with Undersecretary Waters while working with Kaiser on the Arabian Café investigation. Burning the candle at both ends, maybe throw in some liquor for good measure, would keep you preoccupied and out of our way. I never expected you would become 'super cop' up there. You were a great agent once, Lee, but even you have to admit, your performance over the past several months has been lackluster at best."

"You set me up? You arranged for the shoot-out at the Arabian Café?" Lee asked, clenching his teeth.

"Not quite. You see, Wahab Ajeel and I were going to do business. He'd heard rumblings about our new weapon and wanted to buy it. The Order plans on allowing certain approved groups to acquire the weapon if its use will be against populations approved by us."

"For a fee, of course," Manny added.

"Naturally. Apparently, Wahab Ajeel wanted to inflict heavy damage on the Israeli people. That would be fine with us. Many in the Order dislike the Jews just as much as the Muslims.

Imagine a world where there was no more war in the Middle East. No more Arab–Israeli conflict. Such a world could exist. But, unfortunately, the meeting between Wahab and I never took place. He got cold feet when he realized that my day job was as director in the DHS. I could understand his concern. However, since he discovered my name and position, I became worried that this information might leak out since we weren't going to do business. So an opportunity presented itself to me. While your investigative skills have waned of late, Lee, they had been replaced by aggression. Ever since your wife died, almost every call you went out on ended up in a shoot-out. I thought I would use that to my advantage and kill two birds with one stone, so to speak."

"You tipped them off, didn't you? You son of a bitch. You sent us in there, then told Wahab we were coming, ensuring there'd be shoot-out. T-Bone was killed just so you could silence Ajeel?"

"Damn, you're cold," Manny said.

"But, unfortunately, you weren't able to get rid of Wahab for me," Kowalski continued. "Another failure on your part. Doesn't matter now. I have his brother in custody and will leverage him to find Ajeel. After I finish here."

"So it was you the entire time," Manny said. "Up in Boston. Waters isn't part of the Order, is he?"

Kowalski looked amused. "No. Undersecretary Waters was just doing his job. The job I sent *you* up to do, Lee. Investigating the ruse that I propagated to keep everyone busy chasing their tails and away from Astrea. But you had to be a hero, didn't you, Lee? And now look at the mess you put your friends in. Your final failure."

As they continued to walk down the dark, stone corridor, Lee knew he had to get back to help Emma. Time was running out, and they were being toyed with until Peters decided to have them executed. Lee knew the best time to escape a kidnapping was immediately after being captured. He didn't know if this situation fit, but he understood it was now or never. Any holding area in the subbasement of an old stone fortress like this was not going to be easy to escape.

He glanced over at Manny and Connors, and he saw they were thinking the same thing. He didn't know Steve Connors that well, but he seemed experienced enough and must have had some paramilitary training to be sent to the world's hotspots.

Lee hoped their instincts would take over and that both would take advantage of the opportunity he was about to present them with.

As they made the next turn in the corridor, Lee feigned a stumble and fell to the stone floor. Kowalski and the two guards glanced down at him to see what had happened. That was long enough for Manny to twist on his heels and grab the AK-47 held by his guard. Connors turned on the man behind him. As his companions struggled with their guards, Lee, still on the ground, reared back his right leg and shot it out hard, his foot connecting with Kowalski's knee.

Kowalski howled in pain and went down on his left side. Lee jumped on top of him and struck his former boss hard in the nose with the palm of his hand. A gush of bright red blood blossomed on Kowalski's face. But Kowalski was not yet down for the count. Angry, the DHS director sent a knee into Lee's groin and in a desperate heave threw off Lee off.

After the immediate intense pain in his groin wore off, Lee pushed up from the ground with his hands and sprang to his feet. He froze, however, when he saw the barrel of Kowalski's 9-millimeter pistol staring him down.

A shot rang off to their right, and both men looked over to see Manny on the ground, bleeding from what appeared to be a shoulder wound. Connors was on the ground next to him, held tightly in a headlock by his guard.

"Nice try," Kowalski said, panting. "I know Peters wanted you alive, at least for the moment. But I have come to realize that you are much too dangerous to live. Besides, someone has to pay for this nose." The DHS director wiped the blood under his nose with his free hand as the other held the pistol tightly.

"I don't think he'll mind if I take you out now. You were never going to leave here alive, anyway," Kowalski said, aiming at Lee's head and squeezing the trigger.

The crack of a weapon firing echoed through the stone hall.

65

AH, WELL, I see our little deal is off, anyway. I imagine some of your colleagues tried to escape and were eliminated by one of my associates," Peters said upon hearing the weapons discharge. "Now I want to show you something before we complete our little chat. It's the least I can do for a fellow scientist."

"What I want to see is you behind bars," Emma snapped as Peters led her to one of the glass chambers at gunpoint.

"We both know that will never happen. But, here, let me show you something that will cheer you up. These are the chambers we use to test the aerosolized version of the weapon that you have already seen demonstrated on Agent Jansen and Dr. Khattib. This version works much more quickly than the earlier prototypes. As you are aware, the bioweapon attacks only the gene of interest that is identified by Khattib's linking protein. The first target for Project Astrea will be a unique set of genes found mostly in the Lebanese Arab population. We have identified three specific genes unique to this group and tested many versions on Hamas and Hezbollah prisoners. The bioweapon, complete with Khattib's targeting protein, modified here in our lab to target these Arab-specific genes, has been aerosolized for ease of release and to facilitate rapid dispersion through the population of interest.

"Those backpacks on the table hold the viral vectors that will unleash the ethnic-specific weapon upon an unsuspecting Arab population. Seven of the largest cities in Lebanon will be targeted tomorrow, heralding the coming of Astrea's long-awaited utopian Golden Age. This particular chamber, however, is still loaded with the bioweapon itself, without Khattib's linking protein. The *raw* weapon. Similar to what we used in Agent Jansen, but much more potent in gaseous form. Why don't you take a closer look? From *inside* the chamber," Peters stressed, raising his gun to emphasize his request.

Emma looked around the room for anything to save her. Nothing was within reach. Knowing Peters would shoot her on the spot, she decided to take her chances in the chamber. If Lee, Manny, or Steve Connors could break free in time, maybe they would be able to get her to a hospital and save her. If they were not already dead, that is.

She walked toward the open door of the large glass chamber. Just before entering, she noticed a table with labeled glass bottles and flasks.

As she reached for the glass door of the chamber with her left hand, she swept her right arm across the table, sending the bottles flying, crashing to the ground behind Peters.

A yellow cloud of gas rose from the shattered bottles, surrounding Peters. Emma pulled the heavy glass door of the airtight chamber shut, locking herself inside. Peters, knowing the deadly mixture of hydrochloric and sulfuric acids would produce a highly toxic chlorine gas that could kill him within seconds, struggled through the noxious fumes toward the exit.

But the thick cloud enshrouded him, causing him to fall to his knees and surrender to the effects of the vapor. Though he gasped for air, the chlorine quickly penetrated his lungs and he began to cough uncontrollably.

The chlorine burned his eyes, nose, and throat as the molecules re-formed into acid upon combining with the water on his mucosal surfaces. He scrubbed at his eyes with no relief. A tightness filled his chest, and it became more difficult to breathe.

After only twenty seconds it was all over: Peters lay motionless in the pool of broken glass and chemicals.

Emma watched the chlorine cloud dissipate into the air, becoming less lethal as the ventilation system distributed it throughout the laboratory.

Her relief in knowing that Peters was dead was short-lived, however, when she tried to exit the chamber. The door was locked from the outside.

Then she remembered the purpose of her tomb—to test poison gas on subjects. Of course she couldn't open the door from the inside. While the airtight chamber protected her from the chlorine gas that killed Peters, it also prevented any oxygen from entering.

Emma could feel the air getting thin as she concentrated on taking slow, shallow breaths to conserve oxygen. She banged on the door, hoping someone would hear her. But no one came through the laboratory doors. She was alone, sealed in a locked, airtight chamber waiting for death.

66

L EE OPENED HIS EYES and was surprised to see Kowalski lying beside him, a bullet wound to the back of his head. He looked around trying to figure out what had happened.

The other guards were down as well, and Connors was examining Manny's wound. The answer became clearer to Lee when six heavily armed men in military fatigues surrounded him.

"Agent Jansen, are you all right?" Nick Shane asked. He had left half of his twelve-man team of Marine Raiders on perimeter defense outside the building under the command of his gunny, while he led the other half in storming the monastery and taking down Kowalski and the guards.

"Am I glad to see you!" Lee said as Shane pulled him to his feet.

"Looks like you were about to get whacked," Shane commented.

"Yeah. Listen, we've got to get to Emma. She's in the lab with Peters."

"Lead on," Shane replied. "Klein and Lightfoot, on me. The rest of you help the casualty and secure the rest of the facility."

"Casualty?" Manny asked, standing up and holding his bleeding arm. "It's just a scratch. Hell, I've cut myself worse shaving after a night of drinking you Gyrenes under the table." He picked up one of the AK-47s Kowalski's men had been carrying and followed the others to the lab.

As they turned the last corner, the six men were met with a barrage of automatic weapon fire from the guard outside the lab entrance. In his haste to save Emma, Lee had forgotten that Kowalski had posted a guard. If Shane hadn't tackled him to the ground, he would have been cut in half by the fire. In another moment, however, four quick shots from Klein and Lightfoot silenced the guard.

"Let's go. A bit more carefully this time," warned Shane as they got to their feet.

As the men approached the door to the lab, Shane put his hand on Lee's arm, signaling for him to wait. The Marines would go in first, ensuring the room was clear. Without any commands given, Klein, Lightfoot, and Shane stacked on the door, with Lee and Manny falling in behind them. The door was locked. A single round from Klein's Special Forces Combat Assault Rifle solved that problem, and the men breached the lab entrance.

Immediately upon entering the room, Lee noticed a stench of bleach. He saw a body lying in a pool of broken glass near a tall, clear booth in the corner. He ran over to see who it was.

"Shane," Manny shouted, burying his face in a sleeve. "Cover your nose and hold your breath. That's a strange smell. Not sure if it's poisonous."

While the vapor cloud from the deadly mixture had mostly dissipated, the amount still in the air caused a mild stinging to Lee's eyes. He followed Manny's instructions and held his breath as he closed in on the body. It was Peters, and from the pale blue color of his skin and open, macabre eyes, it was clear that the man was dead. But where was Emma? He looked around and then noticed something lying motionless in in the glass booth to his right.

"Emma!" That monster must have put her in the chamber. Had she been poisoned by the gas too? Lee felt his heart drop at the thought. He had to get to her.

"She's in there!" Lee pointed at Emma, and the rest nodded. He tried to use the handle to open the glass door, but it wouldn't budge. Manny saw the red button on the wall, ran over, and slammed his hand into it. To his relief, the glass door sprang open.

Lee entered the booth and checked Emma's pulse. Her skin was not as pale as Peters's, but her pulse was weak and she wasn't breathing. "Emma, come on," he said softly, "we have to get you out of here."

He scooped her up in both arms and jogged out of the lab, followed by his comrades. Connors closed the door to the lab, locking the deadly vapors inside as Lee lay Emma down on the floor in the hall.

Manny began giving Emma rescue breaths to oxygenate her lungs. Seconds ticked by like hours as he performed CPR.

Color began to return to her face. After a cycle of five minutes of resuscitation, Manny listened to Emma's breathing and watched her chest. There was some movement.

"It's shallow, but at least she's breathing on her own."

"Thank God," said Lee, putting a hand on Manny's shoulder.

Now that the immediate crisis was over, Connors turned to Shane. "How the hell did you guys get here? I though Haller wasn't going to help."

"He may run military affairs in this country, but I don't work for that pansy," Shane replied. "I called my boss at Lejeune and got the general involved. After the SOCOM commander called the SecDef and he had a brief talk with DHS, I got the green light to go. Glad we made it to the party in time."

"We're *all* glad you did," Connors replied.

Emma coughed a few times and then slowly opened her eyes. "What happened?"

Lee brought his face down until she could see him clearly. "It's all right, Emma. We got you out. You were locked in a booth. Peters's dead," he said, helping her to sit up. "What happened in there?"

"He was going to gas me with his bioweapon in that chamber," she said, shuddering at the thought. "But on my way in, I noticed some compounds that would make chlorine gas when mixed. I managed to knock them to the floor before I was trapped inside. The airtight booth was what saved me." She started smiling, seeing how glad Lee was that she was all right. "Except for the lack of oxygen in there."

"I said it before and I'll say it again: Damn, you're smart," Manny said.

"What happened to you?" she asked Manny, noticing the blood on his shoulder.

"Just a scratch," he said.

Emma didn't look convinced, but then something else occurred to her. "The backpacks. They're loaded with the bioweapon. We need to get rid of them," she cried, grabbing Lee's hand to help her stand up.

"Emma, wait. The chlorine gas, remember?" Manny said.

"It's okay. It's only dangerous immediately after the compounds are mixed and release the resulting chlorine gas. That's when it's most concentrated. The lab's a big room with good ventilation. It'll still smell due to the trace amount of chlorine in the air, just like around an indoor pool. But most of it should have dissipated by now. Just leave the door open."

Skeptical, Connors opened the door of the lab. Emma was right. The chlorine smell had already lessened from a few minutes ago. They entered the lab and went to the table in the corner, where Connors and Lee started opening the backpacks. Inside each one were a number of canisters, presumably containing the deadly bioweapon.

"We have to destroy these," Emma said.

"I was told to bring any samples I found back to Washington," Connors replied.

"Connors, you don't know how deadly this weapon is. It's not safe—in *anyone's* hands."

"The U.S. government isn't going to do any ethnic cleansing, Dr. Hess," he stated firmly.

"Maybe not. But remember, Kowalski was pretty high up on the government ladder. Apparently there are traitors everywhere. It's not worth the risk. Please, Connors. We have to destroy everything in here. The computers, the samples, the research. Everything."

"She's right, Connors," Lee replied. "It has to end here."

"I got no problem if this technology never sees the light of day," Shane added.

Connors paused, not sure how to proceed. He had his orders. True, he didn't fully understand the devastating effects, scientific implications, or even moral implications of this weapon. But he was instructed to bring as much of this research and technology back as possible.

"We have to burn it, Connors. We have to burn down this lab and everything in it," Emma pleaded. "It's not safe in *anyone's* hands."

She was the expert, Connors remembered. If she says this stuff was that dangerous to the world, why would any sane government ever want to replicate it? "Okay. We burn it to the ground. I may be knocking on your door for a job when we get back, but let's do this," Connors said. "Is there any risk to the civilians around here if we burn it? I mean, will anything get released in the smoke?"

"No. Just the opposite, actually," Emma replied. "The heat from the fire will completely denature the biological vector and linking proteins. There won't be anything left, and nothing will be released into the air except normal smoke. It's actually the safest way."

"It'll also completely destroy all the computers and any trace of the project," Lee added.

"Sergeant Klein?" barked Shane.

Klein and Lightfoot both came running through the door.

"Sir?" they said in unison.

"Torch it. The whole thing. I want nothing left of this place. Make it big, hot, and burn quick, before the Lebanese government sends in the cavalry."

"Aye, aye, sir," they replied, then hurried to collect the rest of their team and search for gasoline.

67

THREE WEEKS LATER.

Emma was typing furiously on her laptop, making the final edits on her most recent paper. She had written it more quickly than any other article or research paper. But this had been, as she found out over the past several weeks, no ordinary subject.

"I finished running those lead samples you asked for," Sue said, popping her head into her new boss's office.

"Thanks, Sue. I'll get to them in a minute."

Sue watched the intensity on Emma's face as she wrote. It wasn't just her brilliance that made Dr. Emma Hess one of the best in her field. It was also her passion.

"Do you think it'll work?"

"It has to, Sue. I promised Steve Connors, the CIA agent who helped us overseas, that I wouldn't divulge any details of what went on here and in Lebanon. Most of it is still classified. So all I have is my critical analysis of the general technology that can lead to genetic weapons that target ethnicities. There's not much research out there, so this paper has to convince the scientific community to remain vigilant in this field. I'm not sure what impact it'll have, if any. Everyone may just dismiss it as something that won't ever happen."

"But we know it did happen."

"I know, Sue. I know," Emma said, pushing back from the computer and stretching. She hadn't realized how long she'd been sitting in front of the screen. "So, how's Manny doing?"

"His shoulder's much better. He's such a big baby, though, whining about his surgery and Dr. Levine not letting him back to work until his postop recovery is complete. I mean, what did he expect? The bullet tore through most of his deltoid."

"He's lucky it didn't hit bone. I'm sure he'll be up and around, wreaking havoc in the ER, before you know it."

"Thanks for hooking him up with Dr. Barrone. I know he had a waiting list a mile long."

"Rich is one of the best orthopedic surgeons in the field. An expert in repairing shoulders. And we need to take good care of Manny. He's a special guy," Emma said with a smile.

"Yeah, he sure is," Sue murmured. Emma watched with some amusement as Sue turned and limped back to her lab. What, exactly, was going on between Sue and Manny?

Emma went back to typing, putting the final touches on the article. It had to be perfect. So much was riding on it.

"So this is how a Harvard physician spends her day" came a familiar voice from the open doorway.

"Lee!" Emma said, rising and rushing over to give him a hug. "I thought you were in DC."

Lee didn't let her go right away. "Well, we're wrapping things up on the Astrea case, and I decided to make a trip to Boston."

"I'm glad you did," Emma replied, still smiling. "Are they giving you a hard time about destroying the bioweapon?"

"A little. But the secretary stepped in and took most of the heat. How's Manny and Sue?"

"Great. Sue was just in here. Her leg's doing much better, should be out of her cast in another week or so. Manny's recovering well after his surgery. He's trying to return for a couple of shifts in the ER, but Seth Levine won't let him near the hospital."

They shared a smile. "What did Manny say to that?"

"Oh, that he wasn't a Marine so he doesn't need any time off. Rangers don't need to heal, or something along those lines," she said.

Lee laughed outright. "How's the paper coming along?"

"I'm just putting the final touches on it. It's good, I think."

"I'm sure it is, but do you think anyone will listen?"

"I don't know. You know I can't reveal too much because of the secrecy around what really happened, but I'll use all the clout I have to get onto all the speaking circuits and conferences. I'm not sure anyone would believe me even if I tell them straight up just how close we were to another global holocaust."

Lee's voice turned grim. "I hope the scientific community pays attention to it, because I'm getting nowhere in DC. These bureaucrats have no clue. They don't understand how dangerous this technology is. They've already moved past it."

"Well, you keep at it from your end, and I'll do my best up here," Emma told him.

"Sounds like a plan," Lee said lightly. "So, how about lunch to compare notes?"

"Great. How long are you going to be in town?"

"Not long," Lee answered. "I'm flying back to DC late this afternoon. There may be a break in the Arabian Café case. But I have some news. My new best friend has offered me a job up here. That's one reason I came up."

"Waters? He wants you to work for him?"

"Something like that. He's retiring soon, and the secretary offered me my choice of assignments. And Boston is a real nice city."

"You're kidding? So you're really moving up here?" Emma exclaimed, grasping his forearm.

"Looks that way," he replied with a grin.

She leaned in closer. "What's the other reason you came here?"

"Oh, just some non–work-related stuff. Personal, actually." He pulled her in close. "It involves you and me getting to know each other better. How about we talk about it over lunch?"

"I'd like that," she replied.

Emma walked back behind her desk and looked at her computer screen. The document was open to the title page: "Genetic Profiling: Friend or Foe?"

She had never worked so hard on an article. It was by far her best work. It would have to be. She had to convince a tough audience: the world.

But right now she had other important business. Emma turned off the monitor and shut down the computer. She could sense Lee coming up behind her, and she felt herself relax, waiting for what came next.

EPILOGUE

HELLO, BROTHER," Wahab Ajeel said, hugging the younger man and kissing him on each cheek as they stood in the empty warehouse.

Daif returned his brother's embrace, eyeing the Turk standing behind him.

It had been a whirlwind few weeks, and Daif was glad to be in his brother's presence again. After the shooting at the café, the police had shut down the restaurant, searched their home, and even arrested him. Daif was not in the pickup truck the day of the deadly attack on the DHS agents, but he had been working in the café when the authorities arrived. He was, at the time, merely an aspiring member of Abdullah al-Harbi's notorious movement to restore Islam to its rightful prominence in the world. His brother Wahab was one of the caliph's warriors. But after Wahab and his men disappeared in the pickup truck that fateful day, it was up to Daif to carry on.

It had been weeks before Wahab had finally contacted Daif. In his absence, it was up to Daif to take his brother's place in the jihad. But he hadn't the experience or tools to be a clandestine soldier like his brother—a sleeper, as the Americans liked to refer to his brothers and sisters of the faith who lurked in the shadows of the evil empire waiting to strike. Several days ago, however, he had received the long-awaited call from Wahab.

"It's good to see you, brother. Here is the money you had hidden in the closet," Daif said, handing over a gym bag.

"I was worried the agents had found it," Wahab replied, unzipping the bag.

"No. It was there when I was released from the jail, despite the infidels' desecration of our home," Daif explained. "*Alhamdulillah* for the lawyers our brothers arranged for me. I was worried Homeland Security would never let me go. Especially after you found out they were trying to set you up."

"I told you, Daif. Our caliph supports his soldiers," Wahab replied. Abdullah al-Harbi had proclaimed himself caliph in an attempt to unite Muslims across the globe under one Islamic banner. "Were you followed?"

Wahab knew that his family had taken much of the heat since he fled DC after killing the DHS agent. It had been all over the news, and he had been lucky to pass through the airport before the authorities were able to identify him and put him on a no-fly list. He had been out of the country ever since, making the necessary arrangements to return. Today was the first time he had set foot on American soil in over a month.

"No. I drove down from DC, as you instructed," Daif replied. "I had the bag with me the entire time. I paid cash at gas stations and motels. No one knows I'm in Texas."

"And the car?"

"Purchased with cash from an ad in the newspaper," Daif answered. Did Wahab know that he had told DHS about

Wahab's intentions to purchase weapons with the money? Daif had experienced a moment of weakness after days of being interrogated, sleep deprived, and threatened. How he longed to be strong like his older brother. Wahab was a rock. Daif had never seen him anxious—until today.

"This family reunion is touching," the third man said. "But let's get on with it. I don't have all day." At thirty-four years old, Turhan Ozdemir had already outlived most of his peers. Life expectancy for international gun runners and drug smugglers was getting shorter and shorter, it seemed, the longer Turhan worked in the profession. But he was a cautious man, always wary of traps set by law enforcement agencies and ambushes by rival cartels.

Wahab glanced back at the arms dealer. The man cared nothing of their struggle. This was all about the money for him. As much as Wahab hated dealing with mercenaries and sell-outs like this Turk, he had his orders.

After the shooting in DC, Wahab had been instructed to go to Mexico City to meet with Turkish arms dealers to acquire the weapons needed for the movement's big strike on their archenemy. All that Wahab needed was the money he had stashed in his home to complete the purchase.

"The money is all here. Just as I promised you back in Mexico," Wahab replied, turning to face the Turk, throwing the bag at his feet.

Turhan bent down and opened the bag, revealing stacks of hundreds bundled inside.

"It is all there," Wahab said.

"I trust you," Turhan said sarcastically, exposing perfect teeth in a clean-cut, handsome face. "After all, we are *brothers*. Not like these infidels. Right? Isn't that what you jihadists believe?"

Wahab knew the smuggler was mocking him. These criminals had no moral convictions. They may be Muslim in name, but they cared nothing for Islam. Their god was power and wealth.

"When will the next shipment arrive?" Wahab asked.

"Soon. It's in the process of being procured by my contacts in France. You can imagine that such an order is not easy to fill."

"But you *can* deliver?"

"Of course. Nothing is out of our reach," Turhan replied. He zipped up the bag, lifted it off the ground, and motioned towards the ladder. "After you."

Daif looked down into the hole in the ground that his brother and the Turk had used to come across the border. The opening was no more than four feet by four feet and looked to descend into total darkness. There was a ladder sticking up out of the hole.

"Bring it to us," barked Wahab. He had paid good money for the weapons and expected them to be delivered to his feet.

"We waited for two hours. You saw my Mexican laborers leave earlier. You think they wanted to wait for your tardy little brother? Time is money, and I wasn't paying them extra to stand around, wondering if he would even show up. I was about to leave myself."

"It is not my fault I couldn't find your warehouse in the middle of the desert," Daif replied defensively.

"Be that as it may, we are now alone," Turhan stated. "I will not risk getting explosive residue on my hands or clothing handling your merchandise. I have other business here in America and will not be returning to Mexico through the tunnel. There are checkpoints with sophisticated detection devices all along the border and at the crossing points. I will not go to jail for you...*brother*."

Wahab muttered an expletive under his breath. "Come, Daif."

"Here, take my flashlight," Turhan said with a grin.

Wahab snatched it from the smuggler's well-manicured hand.

The two Libyan terrorists descended the creaky wooden ladder. Ten feet down, their shoes landed on packed sand. Wahab was the first off the ladder and turned the light into the tunnel. Three large metal foot lockers sat side by side, taking up most of the room in the tunnel. Turhan's laborers had left them there, in case anyone was waiting for them in the warehouse above.

Wahab walked over to one of the foot lockers. "Here, hold the light."

Daif obeyed and watched his brother open it. Wahab wanted to ensure that the Mexican handlers hadn't taken back the merchandise while he was waiting in the warehouse with Turhan. Inside the locker, secured tightly in cutout foam, were four blocks of Semtex explosives and a large, programmable detonator.

Wahab closed the case. "This will show America the oppression our brothers live under in Iraq and Afghanistan. It will show the world that we are not weak. It will make them fear us," he said with a smile. "After these Turkish criminals secure the rest of our order, the caliph will have his new weapon. And we will assemble it right under their noses, right in the belly of the beast, Daif."

Above them, they heard a thud.

"Turhan?" Wahab called out. "Turhan?"

There was no answer. Wahab turned back toward the ladder just in time to see two canisters hit the rungs then drop to the tunnel floor. Smoke streamed from the canisters in a hiss. The two men panicked. Wahab dropped the flashlight as smoke filled the tunnel. Daif cried out in pain as his eyes began to burn.

"Daif!" Wahab yelled in between fits of coughing. "Ladder!"

They scrambled up the ladder, mucus beginning to stream from their noses. They shut their eyes tightly against the searing pain.

Wahab was about to lose grip on the ladder, but two hands grabbed his shoulder and hoisted him up into the warehouse. The bright lights made his eyes hurt even more as he was thrown onto the cold concrete floor. The smoke was thinner there, and he was able to squint to see. Beside him, Turhan was lying on his stomach, his hands zip-tied behind his back.

"Wahab bin Talal al-Ajeel," Lee said as he took off his mask that protected him from the thick cloud of tear gas around him. He placed a heavy boot on Wahab's shoulder. "You are under arrest for the murder of Agent Tyrone James."

Kaiser and Connors flanked Lee while two black-clad DHS agents zip-tied Wahab and Daif.

"Is that him?" Connors asked.

Lee didn't have to strain his memory to recall the face in the truck that opened fire on him and his partner. "Yeah, that's him. Get this scum out of here."

Kaiser and the other agents pulled Turhan and the Ajeel brothers to their feet and dragged them outside to the waiting SUVs. The area swarmed with agents from the FBI, CIA and DHS, the culmination of weeks of investigating and waiting.

"I never would have found him if it wasn't for you," Lee said, and offered Connors his hand.

"It was your idea. A pretty good one, too," the CIA agent replied, shaking his new friend's hand.

"We were lucky. If Daif had been able to shake us, the DA would have been all over me for letting him go."

After Lee returned from Lebanon and joined Kaiser in the investigation into T-Bone's murder, he arranged to put a tracking device that Connors had given him into the bag of money that Kaiser had found in the closet in Daif's home. Afterward, he arranged to have Daif set free on bail. Then the joint CIA–FBI–DHS task force waited for Daif to move with the money and the tracking device. The call hadn't come for weeks, but when Lee arrived in Boston a few days ago, Shane had called him to tell him that Daif was on the move. The agents were able to track Daif and the money to this abandoned warehouse just outside El Paso.

"So, terrorists are now using drug tunnels from Mexico to smuggle weapons into the U.S.?" Connors asked.

"So it seems," Lee replied, watching a bomb squad bring the foot lockers out of the tunnel. They opened the cases in front of the agents as Kaiser handed Connors Turhan's passport.

"Turkish," Kaiser said.

"Very interesting," Connors replied, thinking aloud. "The Turkish mafia has been supplying opium from Afghanistan to the Mexican cartels for a long time. Al-Harbi must have gotten one of the groups to use their Mexican contacts to smuggle the weapons across using a drug tunnel. But why go through all this trouble for a few pounds of Semtex and detonators?"

Lee looked closely at the devices. "These aren't just regular detonators, Connors. It's not what we usually use for simple plastic explosives like C4 or Semtex. These are sophisticated, complex devices. Maybe for a warhead or something big. My guess is, they were feeling each other out with the small stuff. Making sure each side was serious and taking the necessary precautions to handle a bigger or more sensitive delivery. This was probably a dry run before bringing in whatever was going to be paid for by this large bag of cash," Lee said, kicking the bag full of hundreds.

"Yeah. But what?" asked Connors.

"That, my friend, is why you get paid the big bucks. Our job here is done. Thanks to Kaiser, we got T-Bone's killer. Great job, rookie."

Kaiser smiled at the praise, and the two exchanged high-fives.

"So, what's next for you, Connors?" Lee asked.

"It seems like I'm gonna take a trip to Turkey," he said, looking down at the passport in his hand. "If I can follow the weapons trail, it might lead me to al-Harbi. I have to find out what this 'secret weapon' you said al-Harbi was talking about in the computer chatter from the café. I think you're right. I think this is only the tip of the iceberg."

"Well, if you need anything from me, let me know. I owe you big time."

"I might just take you up on that offer, Jansen," Connors answered. "In the meantime, let's go have a drink. I know a great little place just over the border."

"I'm buying," Lee said. "And the first round is for T-Bone."

ACKNOWLEDGMENTS

I T IS SAID that writing a book is no easy task. While I wholeheartedly agree with this statement, for me, publishing a book was the true challenge. After more than decade of searching for the right team to bring this story to life, I finally found colleagues that believed in my work as much as I do.

Led by the incredible production manager Leigh Camp, this team quickly navigated the complex publishing world to make my dream a reality. A big thanks to eagle-eyed copy editor Debra Manette, to the supremely talented and incredibly speedy interior designer and typesetter John Reinhardt, to the highly detail-oriented proofreader James Fraleigh, and to the masterful cover designer Ty Nowicki, who took my brief description/wish list and transformed it into something impactful and powerful.

Without the contributions of this dedicated team of professionals, this book would have only existed as a file on my hard drive. I thank you all for helping me get it out into the world.

ACKNOWLEDGMENTS

This book is not just a collection of words. Decades of life experiences are wound through the pages. None of it would have been possible without the love and companionship of the most important people in my world: my family. Julie, Alex, Sam and John, thanks for sticking with me through the journey.

ABOUT THE AUTHOR

MICHAEL SHUSKO, MD, MPH, FAAFP, FACOEM, was raised in Long Branch, NJ. He enlisted in the Marine Corps in 1985 after graduating high school.

Dr. Shusko cut his teeth in the military in the mid-1980s and early 1990s. As his first assignment, he attended the Defense Language Institute Foreign Language Center in Monterey, CA, where he studied Arabic. Upon completing his language training, he worked on intelligence missions across the globe. He spent time in Liberia, served as a Marine in the first Gulf War, and worked for several years with the Defense Attaché's office at the US Embassy in Kuwait.

After returning to the States in 1995, Dr. Shusko focused his attention on earning his bachelor's degree in Middle Eastern studies from Rutgers University while studying Persian-Farsi at Princeton. He then transferred to the Navy Medical Corps and enrolled in medical school at Wake Forest University, obtaining his Medical Degree in 2002. He also studied at Harvard University, earning his Master's of Public Health degree in 2013.

Dr. Shusko is a family medicine physician, an occupational medicine physician, and a preventive medicine physician. His Middle Eastern experience and language skills coupled with his background in special operations and intelligence keep him busy deploying around the world. He has traveled extensively throughout the Middle East, Africa, Europe, and Asia, and has been awarded the Bronze Star twice for service in Iraq and Afghanistan.

He currently lives in Japan with his wife and 17-year-old triplet sons.

Vector is the first title in the Tradecraft series. ***Shifting Sands***, book two of the Tradecraft Series, is also available on Amazon. You can sign up to be the first to hear about new releases at MichaelShusko.com.

And, if you enjoyed the book, please take the time to leave a review on Amazon. I read every review and would love to hear your thoughts!

Thanks,

CPSIA information can be obtained
at www.ICGtesting.com
Printed in the USA
LVHW02s0141190318
570301LV00001B/57/P